Copyright © 2022 by Ken Lozito

All rights reserved.

No part of this book may be reproduced in any form or by any electronic or mechanical means, including information storage and retrieval systems, without written permission from the author, except for the use of brief quotations in a book review.

Published by Acoustical Books, LLC

KenLozito.com

Cover design by Jeff Brown

IF YOU WOULD LIKE TO BE NOTIFIED WHEN MY NEXT BOOK IS RELEASED VISIT

WWW.KENLOZITO.COM

ISBN: 978-1-945223-54-9

EXPEDITION EARTH

KEN LOZITO

ACOUSTICAL BOOKS LLC

PROLOGUE

Malcolm Goodwin stepped off the elevator to Z deck. He tried to reassure himself that being banished to the bottom of the alphabet had nothing to do with the less-than-stellar first impression he'd made with Director Berringer of Phoenix Station.

Z deck was reserved for those on monitoring duty. The gray walls were clean, but the stale smell from atmospheric scrubbers that needed to be cycled made him wrinkle his nose. He glanced at the lights along the corridor, expecting them to flicker, but they didn't. He heaved a sigh and walked down the corridor to the rhythmic thumping of bass music coming from an open door a short distance away.

"I love this job!" Robbins shouted from inside the room.

Lights flashed, going through a full spectrum of colors that pulsed in time with the loud music. Goodwin slowed his pace and wondered if he was about to get a headache. He glanced at his chrome wristwatch and focused on the soothing cadence of the second hand as it made its circuit around the dial, inhaling deeply and blowing out a slow, steady breath. He was about to start a twelve-hour shift, and he'd been partnered with Robbins again. The man had more energy than a fusion reactor.

Robbins stuck his head out the door and smiled at him. "Good morning! Howdy, partner. Come right on inside. There's nonstop excitement just over yonder."

Goodwin's shoulders dropped the slightest bit.

Robbins frowned for a second, then tapped his wrist computer. The music volume faded to more acceptable levels, and the lighting inside the room returned to the soft white that wasn't too harsh on their eyes.

"Morning," Goodwin replied.

They walked inside their little cubbyhole tucked into the bowels of Phoenix Station, which was located billions of kilometers away from the nearest planet. The wallscreen to the side showed New Earth, a bright blue planet with luminescent rings that were orbited by a pair of mineral-rich moons. Goodwin stared at the image of home for a few seconds.

"Yeah, that's a good one," Robbins said, nodding approvingly.

"You know why they do this."

Robbins shook his head.

"The bright lighting is so our brains believe it's daylight, which keeps us awake. Default images on the holoscreens showing New Earth is to make us feel more comfortable during our long contracts away."

Robbins pursed his lips. "Geez, you make it sound so clinical. I bet you were the life of the party back in Delphi."

Goodwin snorted a little. "It's oh-six-hundred," he said, raising his wristwatch.

Robbins looked at it and frowned. "Why are you wearing a bracelet? I didn't know you were into jewelry."

Goodwin rolled his eyes. "It's not a bracelet. Haven't you ever seen a wristwatch before? It's a clock. A timepiece." He walked over to his workstation and transmitted his credentials. An amber-colored holoscreen came on with a standard heads-up display.

Robbins sat at the workstation next to Goodwin's and brought up his own console, doing a quick search from the station's info-net. "A timepiece. Came into fashion in the early twentieth century. Whew! Over four hundred years ago." He looked at the watch. "Talk about vintage. How does it even run?"

"It's mechanical. There are gears inside that get stored in a power reserve," Goodwin replied.

"Power reserve... what kind of power source are we talking about here? Early twentieth century would be some kind of chemical battery."

Goodwin shook his head. "Nope, it's purely mechanical. The design predates batteries."

Robbins pressed his lips together appreciatively. "Interesting. So you had the fabricators make you one."

"Yes and no. The parts were created in the fabricator, and I put it together," Goodwin replied. He pulled up the design spec. "Explorer Field Watch. Designed for... It can take a beating."

"Well, yeah. It's made with current composites. That's a lot of small parts. What is this, some kind of hobby or something?"

Goodwin looked away and shook his head. "Assigned therapy."

"Assigned therapy? For what?"

Goodwin eyed Robbins. The man had an insatiable curiosity. He wouldn't pester Goodwin for the entire twelve-hour shift, but he'd be very silent until Goodwin broke down and told him.

"Simmons," Goodwin said.

Robbins blinked. "Simmons?"

"He logged a formal complaint about my... aggressive behavior."

Robbins snickered, and then that became a full-on laugh. "I'm sorry. I really am. Simmons is an idiot."

Goodwin gritted his teeth for a second, nodding at the same time. "Yeah, well he convinced someone at the home office, and they assigned me an enrichment course in watchmaking."

Robbins considered this for a few moments and then looked at Goodwin with his eyebrows raised.

"It's hands-on and it's supposed to help me learn patience."

Robbins leaned back in his chair and spun it around once. "Do you like it?"

Goodwin smiled a little. "Yeah, actually I do. I didn't think I would. The pieces are so damn small, but I like how orderly it is. Everything in it has a purpose and is essential for making it function. It's kinda relaxing."

"Maybe I should try it."

Goodwin snorted. "You'd have to sit still for more than thirty seconds."

"Not a problem."

"Yeah, right," Goodwin replied, sounding unconvinced.

Robbins smiled and leaned toward him. "How are you gonna feel when I prove you wrong? When is your next class?"

"Not until Thursday."

"Fine, I'll be there on Thursday. Wait a second...where did you build it?"

"On the recreation deck."

"Even better. I need to see this. As soon as our shift is done, we're heading there."

"Don't you normally have plans…Marlene?"

Robbins shrugged. "She'll come along. I'll tell her to bring a friend. Girls love watching guys do stuff."

Goodwin shook his head. "Not the girls I've met."

Robbins waved away the comment. "Doesn't matter. As long as it's interesting, they'll be entertained. Oh, oh, I know who Marlene can bring. It'll turn that frown of yours upside down for sure."

Goodwin's gaze flicked to the ceiling. "Fine."

"Fine," Robbins said dejectedly. "Come on, man. You can do better than that."

"You really love it here?"

"Absolutely. We're on the legendary Phoenix Station. It once was the last bastion of hope for the colony. We're in space! Out in the deep dark. How can you not love it out here?"

"Yeah, monitoring our interstellar probe data. Something that an AI can be trained to do."

"Bah," Robbins replied and then raised his hand in a gesture of concession. "AI helps. Of course it helps, but it's not the end-all, be-all solution to every problem."

"How long… Aren't you insulted being assigned to this?"

"Not getting intellectually stimulated by your current posting for the Colonial Research Institute?"

"We pull probe data dumps."

"I know! Isn't it great? We get to see the raw data firsthand before anyone else."

"Yeah, but these probes aren't even from the newer FTL probes they're sending out."

Robbins nodded enthusiastically. "I know. They've been out there for almost three decades," he said, making a wide, sweeping gesture toward the main holoscreen on the center of the far wall.

"FTL exploration probes are all the rage now, but they're not all they're cracked up to be."

"How can you say that? They can cover vast distances quickly and reach neighboring star systems quicker than any of the older probes."

Robbins eyed him for a few moments and sat up. "Sometimes when we move so fast, we miss the important things."

"Space is vast. If we don't move faster, we won't find anything at all."

A message box appeared on the main holoscreen, and then a twin message appeared on both their workstation consoles. The first of the scheduled automated data dumps to be analyzed by them was ready.

"Time for us to get to work," Robbins said.

Goodwin brought up another holoscreen, preferring a multiple-screen workstation. He had a checklist to work through that validated the data they were about to analyze and set about working through it. Over the next several hours they settled into a work routine as they validated the batches of data to be processed.

"I've got a warning box here," Goodwin said.

"Give it," Robbins replied and gestured toward his holoscreen.

Goodwin made a passing gesture and the warning message appeared on Robbins' workstation, as well as the main holoscreen.

"I'll run a diagnostic," Goodwin said.

Robbins leaned forward and opened the message. "This is from the old earth-bound probes—that can't be right. Is the diagnostic finished?"

Goodwin watched various lines of code scrolling through a data window. "It came back fine."

Robbins looked at him and frowned.

"Do you want me to run it again?"

Robbins shook his head. "No," he said and stood up.

Goodwin did the same and they both walked toward the main holoscreen.

A star chart appeared, and Goodwin's eyes widened. "That can't be right. The probes are reporting from the Sol System."

Robbins nodded. "Yeah, the Oort Cloud. The timestamp is from thirty-six hours ago."

"Could the navigation system be broken?" Goodwin asked.

Robbins brought up another data window. "Nope, the log data here shows that the probe swarm is functioning normally."

Goodwin frowned and then brought up his own data window. He queried the probe's automated check-ins, which included navigational data. "Okay, this is strange."

Robbins was focused on his own screen. "What?"

"The logs show regular check-in intervals following a path back to New Earth. Then, between check-ins they reported their location as being in the Oort Cloud near the Sol System. They had thirty percent of their journey done, and then they somehow traveled over forty-two light-years in a little over a day. That's faster than anything I've ever heard of," Goodwin said.

Robbins clapped his hands together once and then rubbed them for a second. "Okay," he said, walking back to his workstation. "Let's follow the protocols. We check everything going step by step."

"But we have to alert Berringer."

Robbins shook his head. "Not yet."

"But this is too important."

"I know that, but we can't go to Berringer with preliminary

findings. We follow the protocols and make sure everything checks out. Then we can howl it through subspace comms."

Goodwin nodded and sat down at his workstation.

"And you thought this assignment was boring."

Goodwin smiled a little and got to work.

1

General Nathan Hayes walked through the colonial Capitol building in Sierra. Over the years, he'd taken every available route to the governor's offices. During his tenure as head of the Colonial Defense Force (CDF), he'd served two different governors and had begun serving a third just a few months ago.

He strode through the outer office past a pair of clerks that called ahead to inform Alexander Preston that the head of the Colonial Defense Force had arrived to debrief him. The office of Governor of the Colony had moved among the various colonial cities to promote a distribution of power so that no one colonial city rose in importance above the rest. It was an effort that seemed necessary, but recently Nathan wondered whether this practice was yet another thing that was going to change. There were no shortages of changes going through the colony on New Earth—a colony that had expanded to include multiple intelligent species and helped establish another colony in a star system three light-years away.

Floor-to-ceiling windows showed a vast courtyard bathed in

sunlight. Aircars flew in the distance, speeding toward their destinations while being guided by automatic flight-control systems. Nathan glanced at the tall city buildings, his eyes straying to the rooftops. There had been a time when those rooftops were home to anti-attack cannons that were critical to Sierra's defenses. Two decades of peace separated two wars that had nearly cost them everything. Nathan still remembered all the preparation, the sleepless nights, and the gnawing doubts that no matter how much they'd accomplished, it would not be enough to save them. Most days these were distant memories, but news of the interstellar probes reporting in on the fringes of Old Earth's star system had brought back a lot of memories, and not all of them pleasant.

"General Hayes," Alexander Preston said, coming to stand next to him.

"Governor Preston, I apologize for the delay. I was just thinking about how much the city has changed over the years."

Alexander Preston was a tall man with broad shoulders and a commanding presence. Nathan had never heard the man raise his voice or show the slightest hint of agitation during his campaign to become the colony's next leader. Nathan's contacts at the Colonial Intelligence Bureau had confirmed that Alexander Preston was a highly intelligent and capable leader. However, a substantial amount of pressure came with the job. Even in peaceful times such as these, being a leader carried a significant weight of responsibility. There was no one else to pass a problem up to, but he felt reassured that the colony had voted in another person who had the hallmarks of a good leader. Some of the other candidates had worried him with their belligerent talk of tactics that would attempt to taint the colony's history, but for the next five years Alexander Preston would take the reins.

"Not a problem. I needed to stretch my legs anyway. Do you mind if we take a walk?"

Nathan shook his head. "Not at all."

They headed toward the nearest stairwell and took it to a rooftop terrace. Nathan looked at Preston for a moment. "You already looking for an excuse to escape your office?"

A deep basso chuckle bubbled up from his chest. "Isn't that why you came here?"

Nathan smiled. "You've only been in office for a few months. It's important that we establish a good working relationship."

Preston nodded. "I can certainly appreciate that, and I agree that it's important that the CDF and the colonial government can see eye to eye." He regarded Nathan for a moment with a thoughtful frown. "I'm the third governor you've had to work with?"

"That's right."

"Maybe I should ask you for advice then."

"I'm always available. That's one thing I can promise you, Governor Preston. I'll give my honest opinion on whatever issue we happen to be discussing, but I reserve the right to be discreet if the situation calls for it."

"I understand the need for a certain amount of formality, but it's just the two of us here."

Nathan looked at the new governor for a moment and nodded once. "One of our interstellar probe swarms has reached the Sol System." Preston blinked several times, and he continued. "They're early—about forty-two years and ninety-three days too early."

"I see," Preston said. "Have the analysts confirmed that the probes aren't malfunctioning?"

"They did, and I also had a team of my own analyze the data."

Preston exhaled a long, slow breath. "Has there been any contact with survivors?"

"Not yet. The drones are still operating under a standard check-in schedule."

"How could this have happened?"

"We don't know. According to the logs, the drones reported in from one location, and then on the next check-in they were forty lightyears farther away without a hint as to how it happened."

Preston folded his arms across his chest, frowning in thought. "News of this is going to get out. I'll need to prepare a brief to address the colony."

"That would be my recommendation. The probes will have more sensor data for us to analyze, so my advice is that people will need to be patient."

Preston nodded. "I don't need to tell you how important this is. We've always wondered whether anyone survived the Vemus Wars back on Old Earth. I thought it would be much longer before we found out."

"Same here. However, the conditions of how this happened concern me from a security standpoint. Outside of some spatial anomaly that we haven't encountered before, we have to consider that some kind of third party moved our probes to their current location. This means they could have decoded our technology. If they could do that, they could also trace where those probes came from. I think it's pertinent that we raise our readiness in case this new third party comes to this star system."

Preston considered it for a few moments. "You're assuming they'd have hostile intent."

"It would be a refreshing change for us if they didn't, but I need to protect the colony."

Preston nodded slowly. "What do you propose?"

"We have defensive measures in place throughout our star system, but I think we can organize a few training exercises strategically positioned that wouldn't cause an alarm. I hope that these precautionary measures won't be necessary, but as my own predecessor would say, it's better to be prepared as best you can for an unknown threat than to let it catch you off guard."

"General Gates. I'd be curious to learn what he thinks about this."

"Me as well. He doesn't know about it yet, but in regard to Old Earth and its various militaries, Connor Gates is our foremost expert."

Preston nodded. "I understand. Regardless of any alien presence, ever since the invention of the I-Drive there have been proposals to send an expedition back to Old Earth."

"The I-Drive has been around for ten years. We weren't ready for a journey so far away from here."

"And now that our probes are at the Sol System, it's going to renew interest in an expedition."

Nathan pursed his lips in thought for a few seconds. "I don't think sending a civilian exploration ship sixty lightyears away is the best way to do this."

"What do you suggest?"

"That depends on a couple of things. I think the CDF will need to be involved. Unlike other star systems, there is a significant potential to encounter hostile forces. Also, we need to reacquaint ourselves with the original mission parameters used with the interstellar probes. These events are a surprise to us all, and we need to do a proper evaluation before I can give you an intelligent recommendation."

Preston smiled. "Intelligent recommendation."

Nathan shrugged. "What can I say? This isn't the first time

I've had to deal with some shocking new development that has the potential to profoundly affect the future of the colony."

Preston sighed. "Thank you, Nathan. I'll make sure my office keeps an open line of communication with the CDF."

"Understood," Nathan replied and paused for a second. "Thank you, Alexander. I will see that the CDF reciprocates in kind."

2

CONNOR WATCHED the small group of academics in the meeting room. "I think we need to accept that the most likely scenario regarding the Bhatdin is that they died sometime during the Ovarrow war with the Krake."

Dash DeWitt's lips lifted. "We haven't exhausted all the options. Nor have we searched the entire planet."

Connor looked at his wife's former student. He'd become an authority on Ovarrow research and diplomatic relations with the native inhabitants of New Earth. "I'm not telling you that you have to stop searching, but sometimes there are no more clues to follow, and we've been at this for a long time."

Lenora cleared her throat. "It's been over ten years since we started this project. We found where the Bhatdin came through a gateway to our world. Dash has excavated the area, but I think Connor is right about this. Unless we find new evidence that can justify keeping this project's activity apart from normal excavation of New Earth ruins, then I agree that the trail has gone cold."

Dash pressed his lips together. "I just think there's more to it than that they simply died."

"I don't like it any more than you, Dash. Sometimes things just don't work out the way we want them to."

"I want to keep the project open. That way, any new discoveries could be routed to the right place. Otherwise, we'll need to rely on archival searches," Dash said.

"Fair enough. You'll head it up then?"

"You bet."

Connor looked away and stopped listening while the others continued speaking. He knew Dash wouldn't give up on finding out what happened to the Bhatdin. They were a mysterious race of Ovarrow from another universe that fled here to help prepare the Ovarrow of this universe for the Krake invaders. He hoped Dash was able to chase the mystery to the final conclusion, but they hadn't found any significant evidence for over ten years. Beyond the facility entombed in an ice cap, there had been nothing. The Bhatdin had helped the Ovarrow increase their technological development, and that had been somewhat successful. The cost was the collapse of the Ovarrow civilization.

The people in the meeting stood up and Connor blinked in surprised. Had he dozed off? He didn't think so. Lenora was gathering a few things into her satchel. Sapphire eyes peered at him intently.

"Did we bore you?"

The room had emptied except for the two of them.

Connor chuckled and shook his head. "Nah. I was just thinking is all."

He gestured for her to exit the room first. "After you, my darling wife."

Lenora smiled sweetly and left the room, after which they walked the hallways of the Colonial Research Institute campus at

Sanctuary. When they exited the building, the sun had already set, but New Earth's rings gleamed in the night sky. Creepers sounded in the night, and the warm glow from the old-style lamps along the pathway seemed to beg to be walked on.

"You've been a little distracted lately," Lenora said.

"Things have been quiet lately."

"I know. It's great, isn't it?"

"The house is empty."

Lenora reached out and gently rubbed his back. "We'll see Lauren and Ethan soon enough. They're busy living their own lives."

Connor glanced up at the night sky. "Yeah, I know."

"What is it then?"

They'd been married for a long time and had developed an instinct about each other.

"The other day, Diaz pointed out that I've had a fifty-year military career."

Lenora pursed her full lips for a second and then smiled. "Has it been that long?"

"He's counting my time with the NA Alliance military along with the CDF."

"Old man," Lenora chided.

"You'd never tell by the look of me," Connor replied.

He didn't look a day over thirty, but in truth he was in his nineties. Prolonging treatments extended the span of human life to more than two hundred and fifty years. He had a long time ahead of him.

Connor arched an eyebrow toward his wife. "We can start talking about your age if you really want to."

"Let's not get mired in the details here," Lenora replied quickly. She took his arm and they continued to walk quietly for a minute. "Does it really bother you?"

"No. Maybe. I don't know."

"I think you're bored."

Connor considered this for a few moments. He'd taken on a variety of roles in the CDF, and each of them had been challenging and rewarding, but lately his heart wasn't in it like it used to be. "Don't *you* get bored?"

Lenora nodded. "Sometimes. It's why I take on new things."

A few years ago, Lenora had become involved with Human and Ovarrow relations as they combined their two societies. She was something of an ambassador, but she also maintained her role as a professor of archeology at the Research Institute.

"I've done that already," Connor said.

"Maybe it's time to retire from the CDF. More of a clean break this time around," she said.

Connor had been forced to retire from the CDF once before after the Vemus Wars but had rejoined for the Krake wars. The CDF was part of him, part of his identity. What would he be without it?

"I don't know if it's the right time for that."

"I'll support you no matter what you do, love, but maybe it's time to move on and let other people shoulder the burden."

Connor smiled a little, and there was a weight to it. Over the years there had been many burdens, many losses, and struggles to overcome. "I don't know, Lenora. What would I even do?"

"What do you want to do?"

"That's just it. What comes next for someone like me? I've been more comfortable with an enemy to fight. I appreciate the peacetime we've had. God knows we needed it, but sometimes I find myself looking for the next enemy to fight. I know it's not healthy, but it's in me. You know what I mean?"

Lenora nodded slowly. "I know," she said. "I think it's

normal, though—this restlessness. Ashley told me how strange it was when Sean grew up."

Connor frowned. "She has two babies now. Are you saying you want to have more kids?"

Lenora shook her head. "No...at least not yet. Not for a while. Ashley waited nearly thirty years before she had the twins."

Connor blew out a breath. "I guess you're right. I *am* restless. So many things have changed, especially in the last ten years with Lauren studying medicine, specializing in infectious diseases in Sierra, and Ethan joining the CDF. Even Noah is traipsing all over the place in the Infinity."

"It's like they've left us behind. Before we know it, Sean and Oriana will start their own family. Life goes on, Connor. We have to move on with it."

The dopplered wail of a CDF combat shuttle sounded overhead as the pilot swung the ship around and landed a short distance away from them. The shuttle's doors opened, and two CDF soldiers hastened over to them.

"General Gates, there's been a situation. General Hayes needs you to return to base," one of the soldiers said.

"I'll be right there," Connor said and turned toward Lenora.

"Go on, I'll be fine," Lenora said.

"Nah, you can come with me."

Lenora frowned. "Are you sure?"

Connor nodded and they started walking toward the shuttle. "You've got the necessary clearances. If this was an emergency, they'd have sent more than just a shuttle."

"It's been a while since I've flown one of these. Do you think they'd let me try?" Lenora asked.

Connor grinned. "Not a chance. These are way different than the C-Cats you're used to."

"I know. They're faster. You used to get so scared when you flew with me."

"That's because you liked to test the limits of inertia dampeners. Come on, let's find out what's happening," Connor said.

3

"WE'LL BE LANDING in about ten minutes, General Quinn," Lieutenant Kendricks said, his voice sounding from the overhead speakers in the transport shuttle.

Their approach to the lunar base showed from a video feed on the nearby holoscreen.

"Thank you," Sean replied and looked at Oriana, eyebrows raised. "What do you think?"

She stared at him for a moment. Her dark, alluring eyes seemed to have a gravitational force all their own. She pursed her lips thoughtfully. "That depends. Are you going to volunteer?"

Sean snorted and arched an eyebrow, his lips lifting into a smirk. "I'm one of the few people who's qualified for it. I can think of a couple others, but this is Earth we're talking about."

Oriana pushed her long dark hair behind her ear. "There might not be a need to send an expedition. The probes could have already made first contact. If they did, they can use subspace comms to speak with us here."

Sean crossed his arms and nodded. "That's true, but I still think we'll send an expedition back to the Sol System."

Oriana frowned. "We never got around to renaming the star system for Old Earth."

Sean shrugged. "Same reason we still refer to ourselves as colonists instead of New Earthers...or is it New Earthlings? I don't know. It doesn't matter."

"We could adopt the Ovarrow name for New Earth," she replied.

Sean winced and shook his head. "Bhaneteranians? Doesn't exactly roll off the tongue. I'll stick with New Earth."

Oriana gave him a sidelong look and smiled with half her mouth. "General Quinn, are you getting set in your ways? Aren't you a little too young for that?"

He chuckled. He was close to fifty years old but still looked to be in his mid-twenties. After thirty years serving in the Colonial Defense Force, he'd risen in rank almost to the top. He was one of two brigadier generals in the CDF and was outranked by only Connor and Nathan.

"If it's not broke, don't fix it," Sean said.

She laughed. "You sound like Harper."

Gerald Harper was an old astrophysicist who lived on the lunar base. Harper was two hundred and ten years old. He was among a small group of colonists who'd lived to such an exalted age.

Sean narrowed his gaze playfully. "Careful or I'll start talking about how great things were back in my younger years." He smiled. "Back in my day, we got things done. We didn't go around renaming things to make us feel like we had somehow made things better... Bah, you don't want to listen to an old coot like me."

Oriana's shoulders shook with laughter. "It still amazes me

that you can make your voice sound like that. Is this what I have to look forward to?"

Sean cleared his throat. "Not for a long time. A very long time."

"I hope I don't get tired of you," she said with mock severity.

Sean grinned. "Never gonna happen. I'm way too charming for my own good."

She leaned over and kissed him on the cheek. Sean wrapped one of his arms around her shoulder and she leaned into him. After a few seconds he cleared his throat. "If I—"

"Yes, of course I'll be going with you. Do you really think I'd let you travel sixty lightyears away from me for the length of a year?"

Sean exhaled through his nose. She'd already calculated how long it would take them to reach Earth and return home. He hadn't done that yet. Sometimes his wife was several steps ahead of him, but the reverse was true for others. "Thanks," he said.

"I wouldn't want you to get lonely, and I've gotten used to having you around."

"So, what you're saying is that you'd be lost without me?"

Oriana sat up and narrowed her gaze playfully. "You," she said and poked his stomach, "can be insufferable at times."

He stared at her with a serious expression. "I'd be lost without you. There, I said it. Are you happy now? Did you get what you wanted?"

She rolled her eyes and then pulled him toward her for another long kiss.

The shuttle flew through the atmospheric shield and into the hangar. After the aircraft was secured, they stood up and walked toward the shuttle doors.

"Time to go to work," Sean said.

Oriana nodded.

They left the shuttle. CDF soldiers in the hangar stopped what they were doing and saluted Sean.

"As you were," Sean said.

Activity in the hangar bay returned to normal.

A female CDF officer stood at attention. "General Quinn, I'm Major Lourenco. The security council meeting has been pushed up. Please, if you'll follow me, I'll take you to the conference room."

"Lead the way, Major Lourenco," Sean said, quickening his pace. "Do you know why the meeting was pushed up?"

"Negative, General," she replied.

"I guess we'll find out at the meeting," Oriana said.

They followed Major Lourenco through the hangar. She led them through a series of corridors and left them in a private conference room. The room was empty except for the two of them. The security council would be meeting in Sierra, but it wasn't feasible to only have in-person meetings.

Sean transmitted his authentication to the meeting, and Oriana was prompted to do the same.

They sat at the conference table and the lights dimmed for a moment. Then the entire room transformed into a holographic replica of the actual Security Council meeting room at the colonial administration building. The hologram was so precise that it actually felt like they were on New Earth instead of the lunar base. The meeting connection even detected small environmental sounds from the meeting room's open windows. Environmental systems duplicated the floral fragrance of blooming lavender bushes and probably a dozen other plants that Sean didn't know the names of.

Around the vast conference table were all the mayors of the colonial cities, including Shetrian, the Mekaal city. Nathan looked at Sean and nodded. Governor Alexander Preston turned toward him.

"We apologize for being late, Governor. We were en route to the lunar base when the meeting time changed," Sean said.

"That's quite all right, General Quinn," Governor Preston replied and looked at Oriana. "Dr. Evans, thank you for joining us as well."

Oriana wasn't a member of the security council. She was a civilian scientist who had a long-standing partnership with the CDF, but she had the security clearances required to be at the meeting.

"I'm at the council's disposal, Governor Preston."

There were two Ovarrow representatives at the meeting. The Mekaal were a group of Ovarrow that had formally joined the colony and had full citizenship. Sean only recognized Stavuris, the political leader of Shetrian, and in colonial terms, he was their mayor. The Warlord was commander of the Mekaal military faction, which was still being merged into the CDF. Sean expected that before another decade passed, the title of "Warlord" would be retired to the Mekaal historical archives. There were many Ovarrow who served in the CDF and had even moved into several leadership positions of senior rank.

"Excellent," Governor Preston said and looked at a short man sitting next to him. "Okay, Ted, I think we can begin the meeting now."

Ted leaned forward and looked around the conference table. "Hello, I'm Dr. Ted Farrell, Senior Professor with the Strategic Scientific Initiative based out of Sierra. As most of you are aware, forty-eight hours ago a swarm of our interstellar probes reported their location as being in the star system known as Sol." He directed his gaze at the Ovarrow. "The Sol System is home to Earth and is where our people come from."

Stavuris gave Farrell an acknowledging nod. "We are familiar with your historical archives about the Sol System, Dr. Farrell."

Farrell nodded and continued. "Investigation is still ongoing as to how the probes traveled over forty-two lightyears in the thirty-six-hour interval between check-ins without a deep-space monitoring relay. Please direct your attention to the star map."

A map of the Sol System appeared over the conference table. Sean noticed that the star map had been updated since he'd last seen it.

"This version of the star map includes data transmitted by the probe swarm," Farrell said.

Sean looked for Connor but didn't see him among the attendants.

"Unfortunately, the data set we have is partial, but it appears that the probe swarm was divided into smaller groups and spread across the star system," Farrell said.

"Excuse me, Dr. Farrell," Oriana said. "This behavior from the probe swarm is not unexpected."

"Ah yes, Dr. Evans. I expected you to chime in about that. Please continue," Farrell replied.

"The probes were controlled by an artificial intelligence that was tasked with exploration protocols."

Governor Preston leaned forward. "So you expected the swarm to divide into smaller groups?"

Oriana nodded. "That's correct, Governor. But," she said and paused for a moment, looking at Farrell, "do the logs show when they divided? That should have been recorded and included in the data dump that was sent back to our monitoring station."

Farrell frowned for a moment. "I'm not sure."

Nathan cleared his throat. "Governor, General Quinn and Dr. Evans were part of the project team that launched the probes from our star system."

"Oh, I see. They're our resident experts," Governor Preston replied.

Sean cleared his throat. "Dr. Evans is the expert. I had input into the security protocols used by the governing artificial intelligence."

Preston nodded. "Understood."

"I've got the log entries," Farrell said, and a semi-translucent, amber-colored data window appeared. "The smaller swarms reported in at the same time as the ones located in the Oort Cloud."

"That means the swarms arrived at these locations at the same time," Governor Preston said. "Look, there appears to be a swarm near Earth. Did we get any data from those probes?"

"No, I'm afraid not," Farrell replied. "A self-destruct protocol was initiated, and we received a partial data burst."

"Self-destruct protocol! Why on Earth would they self-destruct?"

Sean's eyes widened a little and he shared a look with Oriana. He turned toward Governor Preston. "It's part of the security protocols. A self-destruct sequence would have been initiated if the swarms detected the Vemus in the star system. There were also tamper-protection protocols that could have initiated the same thing."

"Dr. Farrell," Oriana said, "do the logs include any information about the cause of the self-destruct sequence?"

Farrell glanced at his personal holoscreen. "I'm sorry for the delay. This data has just come in less than thirty minutes ago. I'm not sure where it would be located."

"Can you give me access to the log data?" Oriana asked. She opened a personal holoscreen.

"Governor?" Farrell asked.

"Absolutely. Give her access." He turned toward Nathan.

"Have any of our patrols along the outer star system detected anomalies?"

Nathan shook his head. "Negative, Governor. We'll maintain our sweep of the system for the time being. Ship commanders are aware of the situation. However, given that we don't know how the probes made it back to Earth, it's fair to assume that if there was another species responsible, they could come here before we'd be able to detect them."

Sean had scouted hundreds of star systems through the space gates. He'd played cat and mouse with a superior enemy force and knew full well how difficult it was to secure a star system. If an alien species intercepted their interstellar probes and shortened their travel time by several factors, they could easily come to New Earth and the CDF could very well be outclassed. This didn't mean they were powerless, but they could be taken by surprise.

"What are your recommendations, General Hayes?" Governor Preston asked.

"That we maintain a heightened state of readiness, Governor. The Colonial Defense Force should move our state of readiness to level two for the next seventy-two hours at the very least. All multiverse patrols through the space gates should be suspended and our battle groups recalled through an emergency recall procedure."

Sean's brows pushed forward. The CDF hadn't been at a level two state of readiness since the Krake wars. They'd maintained several battle groups that patrolled through known Krake universes to scout whether they'd resurface, but it had been over twenty years since the end of the Krake wars, and nothing had ever been detected. The Krake were well and truly gone.

"Excuse me, but are we actually in danger?" Caitlin Moore asked.

"Mayor More," Nathan said, "level two status is what we use when a threat is probable but is not present. To cut to the heart of the matter, I can't be sure whether we're in any danger from an unknown alien species. These are precautionary measures."

"How long do you expect these precautionary measures to be enacted? Is it just seventy-two hours, or will that be extended?" Governor Preston asked.

"Hopefully, we'll know more in the next three days. I won't recommend that the CDF stay at a level two readiness status indefinitely, not without credible evidence to the contrary. However, I will maintain our current protocol deployments in our home system for the foreseeable future," Nathan replied.

Sean had expected Nathan's answer. Managing the security council's expectations was a slippery slope. Nathan had been doing it for a long time, and he made sure his senior officers got their chances to interface with the Security Council and other civilian agencies as the situation demanded. This was to avoid a repeat of the clashing with the colonial government that had occurred during the Vemus Wars.

Could they really have a more advanced alien species traveling here to New Earth? So far, their experience with intelligent alien life forms could never be described as smooth or amicable. The second colony continued to study the Uvai, a planet-spanning fungus that had achieved a heightened sentience the likes of which they'd never encountered before.

"What do we tell the public?" Caitlin Moore asked.

"My office will prepare a briefing based on the information we have, which will be sent to all of you. We'll schedule regular updates, but I think a review of our preparedness plans is in order just to ensure that we're as ready as we can be," Governor Preston said.

Sean approved. He'd become a student of military history

during his time in the CDF. With a situation like this, it was
better to be open with the colony than to generalize or even
downplay the seriousness of these events. He didn't believe for a
second that their probes had somehow traveled to the Sol System
through some kind of naturally occurring phenomena. What he
didn't know was who these aliens were and why'd they'd chosen
to do anything about the probes in the first place. The more he
thought about it, the more unanswered questions continued to
pile up in his mind.

"Sean," Oriana said quietly and gestured toward her
holoscreen.

He looked at the logs entries and nodded grimly.

"Pardon, Governor Preston," Oriana said.

"Yes, Dr. Evans. Please, the floor is yours."

"The self-destruct sequence was triggered because of
significant structural scans associated with the Vemus exoskeletal
material that contained several active power sources. I've
highlighted the areas on the star map," Oriana said.

Several icons flashed red on the star map near Jupiter.

"I'm afraid I don't understand," Governor Preston said. "This
doesn't indicate any Vemus activity near Earth or these other
locations where the probe scanners detected active space stations
or outposts."

Sean raised his hand to get the governor's attention. "That's
because there was enough of a Vemus presence that the AI
followed the protocol to kill the entire probe swarm."

"But they haven't performed a thorough analysis, nor have
they initiated first contact with any human survivors," Governor
Preston replied.

Sean felt everyone's gaze on him, but he remained focused on
Governor Preston. "This was to prevent any Vemus Alpha
Intelligence from learning about our star system and sending

another invasion here. These security protocols were enacted before the invention of subspace communications. We anticipated a sixty-year lag in any data we obtained. Once the probes reached the Sol System, they were to begin exploring it until they reached Earth."

Governor Preston considered this for a few moments and looked at Nathan. "I understand the need for security protocols, but this seems a bit over the top."

"Governor Preston," Oriana said, "I know it appears that way. Believe me, we put a lot of forethought into the design of the probes' AI. The fact of the matter is that the probes never got to explore the Sol System as we intended them to. They simply arrived at these locations," she said and paused for a moment, pursing her lips. "It might be more accurate to say that the probes were released in these locations. Someone placed them there. We can only guess why that is, but the probes were following the standard exploration protocols using the safeguards we had put in place. However, this doesn't change the fact that these other locations contain human survivors. In fact, the probe swarm detected transmissions from an area near Saturn. The swarms were so far out that the communications lag likely delayed the first-contact protocols."

"Which means that they won't have a subspace transceiver to communicate with us," Sean said.

Governor Preston looked at the star map for several seconds. Most of the other attendees were doing the same thing.

"I have a general question I'd like to ask," Dr. Farrell said.

"Go ahead. I'm still trying to sort this out," Governor Preston replied.

Dr. Farrell nodded. "Is there any way to determine whether the Vemus reacted to the probes at all? Could we have triggered something that will impact the survivors?"

Sean blinked several times. He hadn't considered that, but now that the question had been asked, he couldn't help but wonder the same thing. He looked at his wife.

Oriana shook her head. "I'm sorry, but there's no way for us to know that for sure."

"I understand," Dr. Farrell said.

"It's a good question and one I wish we had an answer to," Sean replied.

"I agree," Governor Preston said. "I hope we didn't cause a catastrophe, but the only way to be sure is to send another probe or expedition to find out."

"Another probe isn't going to get the job done, Governor," Sean said.

"He's right," Nathan said. "This requires an actual scouting force."

Governor Preston regarded them for a few moments. "An expeditionary force. With the presence of the Vemus, the CDF will have to be involved."

Nathan nodded. "We'll need time to review that data from the probes and put together a proposal for you to consider."

Governor Preston nodded. "I understand. There are many factors we'll need to account for."

Sean shared a look with Nathan. A text message appeared on Sean's personal holoscreen.

Return to New Earth ASAP: General N. Hayes.

Sean replied to Nathan via text and looked at Oriana. He leaned toward her. "Don't get too comfortable here. We're going back to New Earth."

"I figured as much," she replied.

The meeting continued for a little while longer, and Sean contacted Major Lourenco about getting a shuttle from the lunar base back to New Earth.

4

THE COLONIAL INTELLIGENCE Bureau (CIB) had been born out of a need to balance intelligence reports gathered throughout the colony that included both civilian and military sources. The first iteration of the CIB had been a colossal failure because the director had taken it upon herself to wage a brutal intelligence-gathering and dissemination mission that nearly dismantled the entire colonial government. In the aftermath of the death and destruction that had escalated to include human colonists, there was serious consideration of shuttering the entire CIB, but Natalia Vassar had been nominated by Connor Gates to rebuild the organization from the ground up. Both Connor and the serving governor, Dana Wolf, had agreed that the function the CIB served was essential to the survival of the colony. However, there would be more oversight and a system of checks and balances to ensure that the calamitous events caused by the CIB would never occur again. Natalia had retired from CDF Intelligence to lead the CIB, and her appointment had come with a provision that her deputy director be approved by the governor of the colony. She'd never expected what a valuable asset and friend Deputy Director Jerry Sherman would turn out to be. Not only did they work well together but they supported each other through hardships and trying times.

Natalia's task had been to build an intelligence bureau that people could trust, and after over two decades it was one of the most respected agencies in the colonial government. They had offices in every major colonial city, as well as field offices at the smaller settlements that had begun to be established over the last ten years. Natalia and Jerry shared their duties and had built a diverse list of agents that had expanded beyond human participation. The first Ovarrow field agent had been brought onboard from the Mekaal military almost eight years ago, and this had since expanded to thirty full-time agents.

The mission of the CIB was to ensure the safety and stability of colonial society through investigation and analysis of current and potential threats. Sometimes they'd uncovered an issue that could only be addressed by another government agency. The CIB wasn't meant to solve all the problems that affected the colony but to assist other agencies by keeping them informed of potential and imminent problems.

Natalia walked through the CIB field office in New Haven, one of the four major cities on New Earth. The office was just a section of workstations in the administration building where New Haven's mayor worked. This allowed the CIB to interface with the local mayor, Field Operations and Security, and the CDF here in the city. Natalya ran the CIB with the highest degree of efficiency and had impressed her former mentor and commanding officer, Connor Gates.

Natalya walked to the office at the end of the hall and opened the door. Jerry Sherman stood facing the wall, surrounded by floating holoscreens. He turned toward her.

"Good morning," Jerry said with a companionable smile.

Natalya stepped inside and closed the door. "It's the afternoon."

Jerry frowned. "Already? I guess I lost track of time."

She glanced at the holoscreens. Reports from multiple data sources dominated most of them. Soft classical music played from a nearby speaker.

"I still can't believe there are survivors," Jerry said. He made a swiping motion that minimized all the holoscreens and then brought one back that showed the interstellar probe video feed. Several ships were flying toward an outpost while others could be seen leaving.

"We need to compile a list of assets to include on the expedition," Natalya said.

"What expedition? Has one been announced already?"

Natalya shook her head. "Not officially, but there will be an announcement soon."

Jerry blinked and frowned thoughtfully. "The probes wouldn't have initiated the self-destruct sequence if they hadn't detected significant Vemus presence. But you seem to think the governor will want to move quickly on this."

"All true, and yes, I do. There was never really a question of if we would return to Earth. Ever since the I-Drive was invented, I've known it was only a matter of time."

"What about how the probes traveled the distance to the Sol System?"

"The CDF will have that covered, of that I have very little doubt. They'll be increasing patrols on the outer star system."

"I know better than to question your hunches where the CDF is concerned. What will be the purpose of sending our agents with the expedition going to Earth?"

"They're to assist the expedition by gathering intelligence and evaluating the survivors. They'll need to provide anything they uncover to the leaders of the expedition, so we'll need agents who can work with some autonomy."

Jerry nodded, and she could see him already preparing a mental list of appropriate agents. "That shouldn't take long to put together. When do you need this done by? Did the governor give you a timeframe for when the expedition will leave? I wonder who'll be leading it."

Natalya shook her head and chewed on her bottom lip for a moment. "I haven't received an official request from the governor's office, and I don't expect that we'll get one."

Jerry pursed his lips in thought. "But you still intend to send agents on the expedition."

Natalya nodded. "Yes, so they'll need to be qualified for the mission in some other capacity. That will limit the pool of candidates."

Jerry nodded. "Why don't you make a proposal to the governor? I doubt they'd block the request."

Natalya walked toward the window, turned around, and leaned against the wall nearby. "I'd thought about doing just that. One of the biggest hindrances to our field agents is when someone outside the CIB decides to make use of them. Prior knowledge of our agents to whoever is going to lead the expedition will limit our agents' ability to gather intelligence. They need to be free to work, so their presence must remain a secret."

"I see your point, and I agree with you. Do you have anyone in mind? Someone I should put at the top of the list?"

Natalya smiled. "You know I do."

Jerry grinned.

"I think it's time we bring in Agent Diaz. He has the essential skills that will qualify him to serve an essential function for the mission. Plus, he'll have the necessary contacts for when and if he needs to take action."

"Okay. Without knowing the size of the expedition, I propose we try to get two or three assets who can assist Agent Diaz—perhaps even another agent to back him up as needed."

"The CDF will have their own intelligence team with them, but you're right. We need to know the size of the expedition."

"Who do you think will lead it?"

"I've narrowed it down to two people. There'll be a diplomatic envoy for sure, but from the CDF there are really only two choices, and it'll depend on what one of them decides."

Jerry studied her for a few moments. "Do you want to go on the expedition?"

She thought about it for a second and shook her head. "No. Would you?"

Jerry shrugged. "I've always wondered what happened to Earth, but if there are Vemus there, that's not something I'd want to see. I'm sorry if that appears to make me cowardly, but I'd rather stay here."

"Not wanting to return to Earth doesn't make you a coward, Jerry. New Earth is our home. Regardless, there will be no shortage of volunteers for the expedition once they get the ball rolling."

"Thanks for that," Jerry replied. "I'll get to work on this immediately."

5

THE TACTICAL DISPLAY on Ethan's Talon V space fighter flashed as several icons appeared on the plot. Gigantor, a Jovian class gas giant, was the colossal backdrop, even though it was over twenty-one million kilometers away. He glanced out the side of his ship's canopy at the rest of the Bunny squadron flying in formation.

"No more trainees after today. It's the 7th or nothing. I can't wait to ditch the Bunny squadron once and for all," Massey said over comms.

"Quit whining, Logan. You know you love bunnies," Eva replied and grinned.

Massey laughed. "I could use some comforting, Eva. Maybe after, we could—"

"Not gonna happen," Eva replied tersely.

Ethan grinned and shook his head.

"How many times has Massey crashed and burned now?" Anton asked.

Several chuckles sounded on comms.

"I've lost count, but I'm pretty sure I won the betting pool," Ethan replied.

Another round of laughter.

Sometimes training missions required spending a lot of time in the pilot's seat. They were on a stealth scouting mission, but they were able to use tight-beam comlinks for ship-to-ship comms that were so minuscule they were undetectable.

Massey cleared his throat. "Laugh if you want, but fortune always favors the bold. I'd rather take the shot and fail a thousand times than not take the shot at all. Persistence is one of the foundations of becoming part of the elite 7th."

"You're not lacking in persistence, that's for sure," Eva replied.

"It's just timing the perfect shot that's the issue. Massey's too eager to fire his weapon," Ethan said.

Several people began speaking at once, and Massey began shouting.

Ethan was the team leader for this training exercise, and he used that position to keep the fun going at Massey's expense. "Lieutenant Stone, please mute Lieutenant Massey's comlink. I'm afraid I can't hear with all the noise."

"At once, Lieutenant Gates. I'll take care of this right away," Anton replied.

Massey's comms went silent. Ethan looked to his left and saw Massey's helmet angle toward him. Then he raised his fist and gave him the finger.

Ethan chuckled and gave him a salute, turning his attention back to the HUD. The others continued to talk while occasionally taking a jab at Massey.

Logan Massey was a talker. If he hadn't cut him off, Massey could go on for hours. He'd done it before, and Ethan wasn't

above getting a little payback for similar treatment a few
weeks ago.

One of Gigantor's larger moons had an asteroid field
surrounding it that stretched almost the entire distance to a
neighboring moon. Both were rocky, with high amounts of iron
and nickel. It was the perfect region of space for serving up an
ambush.

The Talon V Stinger class was the most agile fighter in the
CDF. They were highly maneuverable, capable of rotating 180
degrees in 0.3 seconds. With three forward-facing mag cannons,
they could penetrate the point defense systems of outposts and
even some warship defenses.

Ethan opened a comlink to the strike leader. "Captain
Webster, Fighter Wing Charlie has reached the secondary
waypoint. We're about to begin our scouting sweep."

The gruff voice of an Ovarrow replied. "This is Captain
Kujura. Fighter Wing Charlie is late."

Ethan frowned. How could they be late? "Captain, according
to the flight plan, we're right on time."

"The schedule was pushed up. The updated schedule was
broadcast to all acting strike leaders, Lieutenant."

Kujura's smug tone made Ethan grit his teeth for a second.

"My apologies, Captain Kujura, I'll make sure we make up
the time."

Kujura was as by the book as they came. Many of the
Ovarrow serving in the CDF were.

"Negative, Lieutenant. Proceed on your current trajectory.
Begin your sweep. We have intel that there are several enemy
outposts hidden here. You're cleared to engage at your discretion.
Kujura, out."

The comlink severed and Ethan sighed. Damn it. He checked
COMCENT broadcasts and saw that the timetable for the

operation had been moved up. The change had been buried among a flurry of broadcast. He'd missed it, and Kujura wasn't going to let them make up the time. Kujura had had it out for him since training began. It made Ethan want to grab Kujura by his prominent brow ridge and...

He let that line of thought go and rejoined his group's comms session. "All right. I've just checked in with our strike leader and we're running late."

That got the others' attention. The one certainty about the CDF is that you were to be where the brass told you to be at the designated time or you were reassigned.

"I bet you missed the update from COMCENT," Massey said and inhaled forcefully, surprised his comlink had been taken off mute.

"Shut up, Massey. Ethan wouldn't do that," Anton said.

Ethan gritted his teeth for a second. "He's right. I missed the update. It was buried within a bunch of status checks."

Several groans sounded through comms. Being late was going to cost them when their performance was evaluated.

"What did Captain Webster say about this? I think he'd let us make up the time," Eva said.

"Captain Webster isn't our strike leader. Captain Kujura is, and we're not allowed to speed up to make up the time," Ethan replied.

"Oh shit, we're screwed. He hates you," Massey said. "We're not going to make the cut because you had to show off when we first got here. Damn it! I told you not to get on Kujura's bad side."

Ethan pressed his lips together.

"What are you talking about?" Anton asked.

"Ship-to-ship engagement trials. Gates decided that he was going to take out Captain Kujura all by himself."

"Hey, I *did* get him," Ethan said.

Massey laughed bitterly. "Yeah, but you got the rest of us killed because our flank was exposed. Now Kujura's finally getting some payback against yet another cocky pilot."

"You know what you can do, Massey? Just shut the hell up!" Ethan growled.

"No way, man. You fucked up and we're gonna pay the price. Not all of us have the same family connections you do, *Gates.*"

"What family connection?" Vijura asked.

"Oh wow, if it isn't our taciturn resident Mekaal choosing to join the conversation," Massey said. "Didn't you know that Ethan's father is General Connor Gates? He created the entire Colonial Defense Force. There's no way they're gonna ground his son, but the rest of us are pretty much gonna be flushed out the airlock. We'll probably be put on shuttle duty."

"We learned about General Gates. He's among the most honorable military leaders the Mekaal have ever encountered. He wouldn't give special treatment to his offspring," Vijura replied.

"So you say," Massey replied.

Ethan clenched his teeth and gripped the flight controls. He really wanted to shut Massey up. He'd known when he joined the CDF that his famous father would be a factor in everything he did, but he tried not to let it bother him. No matter how much he achieved, there were people who believed his father was the reason Ethan would rise in the CDF rather than basing it on the merit of his own accomplishments. He'd gotten into more than a few fights about it. He had to push harder than everyone else to stand apart and minimize the accusations that he didn't deserve to be there. The 7th Stinger Squadron was the elite A-Wing squadron in the CDF. They expected the best from their recruits, and they didn't care what his family connections were.

Eva sent him a text message. *Massey's an ass. Don't let him get to you.*

He acknowledged the message and didn't reply. Massey *was* an ass, but he was only saying what the others were probably thinking. He shook his head. When would he be past all this crap?

He glared at the tactical plot and then frowned in thought as an idea came to him. "All right, listen up."

"This should be good," Massey said.

Ethan ignored him. "There's a way we can make up the time without increasing our velocity."

"Sounds good," Eva said. "What do you need us to do?"

The others were quiet. Massey started to speak, but Ethan cut him off. "We split up. We can cover the sector faster without increasing our speed and make up the time that way."

"Sure, we can make up the time, but if we find the enemy outposts, we don't have a force strong enough to destroy their defenses," Massey said.

"I disagree."

"You would."

"Look, if you're not capable enough to do this, you might as well just return to base. We'll finish without you," Ethan replied.

Massey muttered something under his breath.

"What? I didn't catch that. Can you repeat yourself?" Ethan asked.

"What are your orders, sir?" Massey asked evenly.

"Anton, you take Massey and Rice with you and begin scouting sector two. I'll take Eva and Vijura with me to scout sector one. Scouting sweep assignments should give us some coverage, but backup is going to be delayed. Watch out for automated defenses," Ethan said.

"Understood, sir. I already know who our sacrificial lamb is going to be," Anton replied.

"Good. You have your assignments," Ethan said and paused for a moment. The edges of his lips lifted. "All right, bunnies, let's kick some ass!"

Rice and Anton howled. Even Vijura joined in the fun as the group of Talon Vs split and raced toward their targets.

Ethan created smaller team comlink channels for Eva and Vijura.

"You enjoyed that, didn't you?" Eva said.

"What? The bunnies thing? Yeah, I figured why not just own it outright," Ethan replied.

He felt like Eva was wanting to respond, but she didn't say anything else.

They staggered their formation. Ethan flew point, with Eva and Vijura covering his six.

"Scan in controlled bursts. Scatter them to reduce the risk of a monitoring post pinpointing our location," Ethan said.

He flew toward a cluster of large asteroids and glanced at the scanner plot. Nothing had been detected.

"You really shouldn't let Massey get to you."

Ethan frowned. "I didn't."

"Yes, you did. I could hear it in your voice."

Ethan engaged his maneuvering thrusters so his forward cannons were pointed toward the craggy asteroid surface.

"You know me so well," Ethan replied.

Eva snorted a little. "I didn't need any biometric scans to show me that your core temperature was probably up, breath quickened, and you had a strong urge to hit something. All the hallmarks of anger. The only thing I don't get is that I thought you and Massey were friends."

"We *are* friends. He's just sounding off."

"Friends," she replied sounding unconvinced. "Really? Didn't sound that way to me."

"Why does it matter to you so much?" Ethan asked.

Another scanning sweep came in, and it hadn't detected anything. He glanced behind him at Eva's ship. He couldn't see the cockpit because she'd angled her ship away from him. Vijura would be doing the same thing on the other side.

"I just thought his comments were inappropriate."

Ethan inhaled a breath and held it for a moment. "They were."

"But you won't do anything about it."

"What do you want me to do? Log a formal complaint?"

"For starters. You're the acting strike leader of this squadron. Massey was insubordinate. I have half a mind to log a complaint myself."

"Don't," Ethan replied. "Just drop it, okay. The last thing I need is to make a big stink about the whole thing, so can you do me a favor and just drop it?"

Eva didn't reply right away.

"Come on, Eva. Please?"

Eva sighed. "Fine, but I don't like it. Maybe the reason you always feel like you have something to prove is because of the things Massey was saying. It's probably happened before, right?"

A new scan report showed up on his HUD. He reviewed and then dismissed it. Eva repeated her question.

"I'm not continuing this conversation. Now drop it. That's an order," Ethan said.

There were a few moments of frosty silence.

"Yes, sir," Eva replied.

They flew mostly in silence for the next hour. Vijura wasn't a talkative person, but sometimes Ethan needed to break up the monotony.

"Even this is taking too long," Ethan said.

"We're following standard scouting procedures. Doing it this way is the safest," Eva replied.

There was less of an edge to her voice now, and he supposed that was a good thing—squadron cohesion and all that.

"I know that, but there has to be a better way. Vijura, didn't you perform a mineral scan a few minutes ago?" Ethan asked.

"Affirmative, nothing has changed since we first entered the region," Vijura replied.

Ethan shifted his helmet to rub an itch at the bottom of his chin. Then he brought up the control interface for the scanner array and changed the filtering priorities that the onboard AI was using.

"What are you doing?" Eva asked.

He inputted a set of coordinates for the updated scanning protocols. "Oh, you know, I'm just going to kick over a few rocks and see what's underneath. Both of you stop scanning for a minute."

"Scanning halted," Vijura replied.

"Sir," Eva began.

"Halt your scans, Lieutenant Eva."

"Scanning halted," Eva replied a second later.

"Thanks, now get ready to resume when I give you the go ahead."

"Would you mind telling the rest of us what you're gonna do?"

Ethan waited for his ship's computer to finish compiling the set of commands he'd loaded into it, which required quite a few sets of complex calculations.

"Scouting for a hidden attack force this way is going to take forever. I have a way to get them to show their hand. They'll give away their position and lead us right to them," Ethan said.

"Sounds impressive. I like this plan," Vijura said.

"How are you going to do this?" Eva asked.

"A trick with the scanner array. I'm increasing the field so that instead of a return scan coming back to me, it'll simply bounce off the mineral deposits on the asteroids, basically making them part of a large array. It'll amplify the signal and hopefully get a response."

"That's like kicking a hornet's nest," Eva said.

"I know, but then we can stop chasing our tails out here and get right to the objective."

Ethan started the scan and felt a wave of anticipation wash over him. A secondary scan showed how the first scan was working.

A comlink opened from Anton.

"Enemy contact!" Anton said. "I don't know what tripped them off, but it looks like a squadron of automated attack drones have launched."

A red flashing icon appeared on his HUD. "Locate and destroy the outpost," Ethan replied.

"Hostile scans detected," Eva said.

"Acknowledged," Ethan replied and opened a comlink to the others. "Anton, we've located the second outpost."

"Understood. We'll try to penetrate the defenses for Outpost Alpha."

"Good luck," Ethan replied.

They flew as close to the asteroids as they could, speeding toward the hostile scans.

An alarm blared. "Enemy turret detected," Ethan said.

Several turrets firing were on them from hidden positions on one of the asteroids. Ethan swung the nose of his ship toward them and fired, rotating his fighter into a role to pepper that area. The turrets stopped firing.

"Got 'em," Ethan said.

They angled their trajectory to cover each other's flanks and cut the engines, allowing their momentum to carry them toward the hot zone.

"Contact," Eva said. "But the turrets are firing nowhere near us."

"Hold your fire. They're trying to get us to give away our location," Ethan replied.

"Roger that," Eva replied.

Ethan peered at the area in front of him. They were heading to an expanse of open space. He swore.

"What is it?" Eva asked.

"There's open space ahead of us," Ethan replied.

He engaged a low-powered scan pulse. "This isn't good. It's over a thousand kilometers wide. Going around it isn't an option."

"We'll get picked off," Eva said.

"Maybe," Ethan replied. The results of his scan were still appearing on his HUD. "I think we can sneak across."

"Sir," Vijura said, "shouldn't we inform COMCENT about the hot zone? They could deploy A-wings to assist."

Ethan considered it. Armored units would definitely help and was a sound tactic right out of the books. "It's a good thought, Vijura…"

"What do you want us to do? Should I open a channel to COMCENT?" Eva asked.

Ethan's eyebrows pushed forward, and he stared hard at the break in the asteroid field. "No," he said.

"But, sir, the reqs state that contacting—"

"Give me a second," Ethan said, cutting Vijura off.

The Ovarrow became silent.

"I have an idea. Don't quote standard combat doctrine. We're never going to stand out from the pack if we always toe the line."

"We'll certainly stand out if we fail to complete the mission," Eva said.

"No risk, no reward. I think they're bluffing," Ethan said.

"What does this 'bluffing' mean? I've seen no detections," Vijura said.

"No, not that. They're trying to fool us. They don't know where we are and they're trying to get us to give away our location. I think we can reach the other side undetected, but I can't do this on my own. I need your help on the other side," Ethan said.

As acting strike leader, he could have ordered the others to follow his lead, but they had time.

Eva sighed. "Go big or go home, I guess."

"I'll follow your lead, Lieutenant Gates," Vijura said.

Ethan smiled. "Okay, let's see if we can pickle the beast."

They cut their engines, putting them in standby, and entered the expanse. They stopped all scans, not daring to risk even a passive scan. If they were spotted, things could get dicey relatively quickly. None of them broke the silence as the Talon V Stingers crossed. Fifteen minutes seemed to go by in the span of a month, and then they reached the other side and brought their engines back online.

"I haven't told you the best part."

Eva snorted. "There's going to be a trap on this side."

"Yup, and there's no way we can sneak past it," Ethan confirmed. "So instead, we use our speed. Keep a tight formation."

The fighters flew in a gunship formation to give them maximum coverage. Their onboard systems detected an active scan pulse.

"Adjust course thirty degrees. Max velocity!" Ethan said.

The three fighters lurched ahead toward a large asteroid with large craggy peaks. With his scanners active, multiple marks began to appear on his HUD.

"Combat drones detected," Ethan said.

The CDF used unmanned combat drones to test a pilot's capabilities outside of the simulators. This was a live-fire test, but the armament was small. Any shot taken by the small fighter would register substantial damage.

"Ten combat drones detected," Eva said.

"I'll give them something to chase. Eva, you take them out. Vijura cover her six," Ethan said.

His orders were acknowledged, and Ethan sped ahead of the others. Flying was something that had just come naturally to him, and training in the CDF had further honed his skills. His father was a good pilot who didn't get nearly as much time in the cockpit as he would have liked.

Ethan fired his cannons at the attack drones in bursts, and they immediately altered course to pursue him. He banked hard to his right and swooped down toward the asteroid's surface. Three of the drones followed him, while the others maintained a defensive perimeter of the outpost.

"You ready, Eva?" Ethan asked.

"Almost into position," she replied.

Flashes of light appeared around his ship as the combat drones fired their weapons. He flew toward a twisty canyon and rounded a corner. Rock spewed into the area in front of him from the drones' weapons. Ethan increased his speed and the fighter's AI assisted his heightened reflexes.

He reached the end of the canyon. "Eva, you better be there!"

The asteroid disappeared behind him, and he barely glimpsed

Eva's fighter as she unleashed a barrage of fire on the unsuspecting drones.

"Ethan! Attack drones above," Eva said.

Ethan engaged his maneuvering thrusters and swung the nose of the ship around. He fired his cannons on full auto, destroying two combat drones. Two more dropped downward to align perfectly with Vijura. The Ovarrow made quick work of them.

"Nice shot," Ethan said.

"Their targeting AIs were too focused on you," Vijura replied.

"See, they're not infallible."

"We still have the outpost to deal with and at least four more attack drones," Eva said.

"We'll start our attack run. Vijura, you get the outpost. Eva and I will get their attention," Ethan said.

He increased power to his thrusters and his ship darted ahead. Eva was barely a second behind. Vijura lagged behind on a different trajectory.

A hail of fire erupted from the outpost's defensive turrets. Both Ethan and Eva swung wide, avoiding the onslaught. He gritted his teeth with a hungry grin. This was what he loved— pushing the limits of his ship to critical levels. He glanced to the upper right corner of his personal HUD. His heart rate was hardly elevated at all. He'd never thought anything of it until one of his flight instructors brought it to his attention. Normally, when pilots, soldiers, or anyone faced harrowing situations, their heart rates skyrocketed. Ethan's remained on an even keel. It wasn't completely unheard of, but it wasn't all that common either. He suspected that his father was the same way. The man had certainly fought enough battles for multiple lifetimes.

The enemy outpost was built into the side of an asteroid mountain near the peak. The gray metallic structure was a hundred meters across. Defensive turrets fired from the roof and several others emerged from the lower decks. The mag cannons stub barrels were in line with heavy shielding.

Ethan changed the ammo configuration for his wing cannons. He lined up his shot, and twin red plasma bolts belched from his fighter, speeding toward the flak cannons. The guard-dog point defense system began targeting the plasma bolts. Ethan fired with his remaining mag cannon. The two top turrets exploded and went offline while plasma bolts slammed into an armored section of the outpost's hull. There was a slight puff of atmospheric gases as the deck collapsed.

Eva fired on the lower turrets.

More turrets emerged and Ethan barely evaded the barrage of their attack. He swung wide.

"You're up, Vijura," Ethan said.

"I have that shot," Vijura replied.

A proximity alarm blared, and Ethan saw the four remaining attack drones flying toward him. The spherical drones had stub wings similar to the Talon Vs.

Ethan fired his mag cannon blindly, hoping that he'd hit at least one of the drones. His other two cannons were cycling their ammo configuration and wouldn't be available for another minute.

"I'm right beside you, Ethan," Eva said.

"Let's plow the fields!"

The two fighters fired their cannons, scattering the attack drones. A bright flash came from behind them.

"Outpost has been destroyed," Vijura said.

"Acknowledged," Ethan said. He looked at the attack drones, but they were offline. "This must have been the main outpost. We took out their control signal."

Eva laughed. "Nice work."

Ethan opened a comlink to the others. "Anton, what's your status?"

"The attack drones just went offline. Massey destroyed the outpost here," Anton said.

Ethan was about to reply when a comlink from COMCENT came to prominence on his HUD. "Lieutenant Gates," Captain Kujura said, "your squadron has been recalled. You're to go to transport alpha."

Kujura sounded angry and Ethan couldn't understand why. "Captain, we destroyed the outposts. The test is complete, right?"

"You have your orders, Lieutenant," Kujura replied.

The comlink severed and Ethan shook his head. He activated the shared comlink to the others. "We're recalled back to the transport. Good job, everyone."

"The test is over!" Massey said.

Eva opened a private comlink to Ethan's ship. "I heard Kujura. What's that all about?"

"I don't know. We achieved the objective. We'll find out when we get back," Ethan said.

A few hours later the bunnies landed in the hangar bay of the transport carrier. Ethan shut down the flight systems and the cockpit lowered through the floor of the ship. It opened and Ethan stepped out.

Captain Kujura was on the flight deck, waiting for them. Ethan and the others hastened over to him. They lined up, saluted a superior officer, and stood at attention.

Kujura walked toward Ethan. Pointy protrusions stemming from his shoulders and elbows pushed against the smart fabric of his uniform. They were hardened like the stubby black claws he had on hands the size of dinner plates. Vertical pupils, almost feline but more like that of a snake, eyed him coldly. "Lieutenant

Gates, you were given specific orders. Did you understand the orders that were given to you?"

"Yes, Captain. We were to scout the sector and destroy any enemy outposts we found."

"Does your vast piloting experience mean you can disregard standard fleet doctrine?"

Ethan felt the heat rise and he stared at Kujura. "I found a better way to achieve the objective."

"By taking unnecessary risks to yourself, your squad mates, and your ships."

"Captain, I don't know what the problem is. You informed me that we were behind schedule, and I came up with a solution that allowed us to make up the time. Our mission was time sensitive and had to be completed."

"Your methods were unorthodox and not in the traditions of the CDF."

"I think you don't like that I found a way to beat your test... sir," Ethan said.

Kujura inhaled sharply, beginning to reply.

"Attention!" Anton shouted.

Ethan stood up straight and looked away from Kujura.

Colonel Jon Walker strode toward them. He stopped and looked at Ethan for a moment and then looked at Kujura.

"What's the problem, Captain?"

"Lieutenant Gates was just demonstrating his propensity toward insubordination."

Colonel Walker looked at Ethan. "Is that true, Lieutenant Gates?"

"Negative, Colonel. I was defending the actions of my team during our test."

"Indeed, the test known as the gauntlet reveals a lot about both pilots and future commanders."

Ethan remained silent. Colonel Walker hadn't asked a question, and he wasn't about to invite a reprimand by speaking out of turn to a superior officer.

Colonel Walker brought up his personal holoscreen. The data from their flight recorders had already been uploaded to the computing core on the transport ship. Walker watched it play out in high speed. When it finished, he pursed his lips in thought.

"Interesting approach. How did you amplify your active scans?" Colonel Walker asked.

"Lieutenant Vijura was tasked with mineral composition scans, which detected deposits of iron, nickel, and palladium. By boosting the signal, I tricked the outpost's defenses into believing that they were under attack. They revealed their locations, and we attacked them."

The edges of Walker's lips twitched, and he turned toward Kujura. "Not the expected outcome, was it?"

Kujura shook his head. "They should have called in the A-wings to achieve the mission objective."

Walker nodded. "That's right, they should have, but there are times when fringe thinking can make the difference between the outcome of the entire engagement."

"Colonel Walker, I think—"

"I know what you think, Captain," Walked said.

"Yes, Colonel."

Walker looked at Ethan for a moment and then looked at the others. "Pilots," he said and frowned.

"Bunnies, Colonel," Ethan said.

Colonel Walker chuckled a little. "Bunnies, you've broken the record for completion of this test by over twelve hours. All of you are to be commended for your outstanding performance and your ability to think outside the box. Your final scores will be tallied, and you will receive your fleet assignments within the next twenty-four hours. Congratulations. Dismissed."

Colonel Walker and Kujura walked away from them.

Ethan looked at the others.

"Twelve hours! We're legends," Massey said.

"Thanks to our fearless leader. It was his idea," Eva said.

The others looked at him. "It was all of us," Ethan said.

Massey eyed him for a few moments. "Sorry for being such an asshole before."

"No problem. I know you can't help it," Ethan replied.

They both laughed.

Anton joined them. "Did you hear? There's going to be an expedition sent to Old Earth."

Ethan frowned.

"That's not news. They've been talking about that for years," Massey said.

Anton shook his head. "No, this is different. Didn't you hear about the probes?"

"Why don't you tell us about it, Anton, and stop playing games," Eva said.

Anton smiled and shrugged. "Just got caught up in the moment. Right, the probes started reporting back from Old Earth, somewhere in the star system. The thing is, they're about forty years too early for that."

"That's crazy. How'd they get there?" Massey said.

"They don't know."

"How'd you find out about it then?" Massey asked.

"It's been all over the news nets. I got an update just now," Anton replied.

Ethan's gaze sank toward the ground.

"So, when is this expedition going to Old Earth?" Massey asked.

"They didn't say, but it has to be soon. They think there are survivors from the Vemus Wars."

"Survivors!" Eva said. "Have they spoken to them?"

"No. You guys really should pay attention to this stuff."

"Geez, enough with the lecture and just tell us already," Massey said.

"Yeah, we wouldn't want to deprive you of the pleasure of informing us of the latest current event to hit the colony," Eva said.

Ethan looked at Anton. "Did they contact anyone?"

Anton shook his head. "That's the rub. The probes self-destructed because they detected a significant Vemus presence."

"The Vemus! That's crazy! How could they have survived?" Massey asked.

"They survived a two-hundred-year journey to come here. Some of them could have stayed behind," Ethan said quietly.

The others looked at him.

Massey frowned. "Hey, what's up, Ethan? What's got you so brooding?"

Ethan looked away from them and saw Colonel Walker speaking with Captain Kujura and Captain Webster.

"Ethan," Massey said.

He ignored them and strode toward the officers.

"What's wrong with him?" Anton asked.

"I don't know. As soon as you mentioned Old Earth, he got weird," Massey replied.

Ethan was out of earshot in a few seconds and walked across the hangar to Colonel Walker.

"Excuse me, Colonel Walker," Ethan said.

The three officers stopped speaking.

"Yes, Lieutenant Gates," Walker said.

"Are you aware of an expedition going to Old Earth, sir?"

"Only just recently. Is there something on your mind?"

"Yes, Colonel. I'd like to volunteer for the expedition, sir."

Captain Kujura stared at him, and Captain Webster frowned. Colonel Walker blinked several times.

"Lieutenant Gates," Captain Webster said, "this isn't something you bother Colonel Walker about."

"I apologize, Captain. Lieutenant Stone was just telling me about the news brief released from the colonial government."

"They're looking for civilian volunteers, Lieutenant," Webster replied.

"I realize that, but the CDF will be going as well. They detected the Vemus. There's no way the CDF isn't going. I want to be on that expedition, sir."

"Even if we were looking for candidates for the expedition, we're not going to bring just anyone on the mission," Webster said.

"But, sir, I just want you to consider—"

"That's enough, Lieutenant," Webster replied.

Ethan clamped his mouth shut.

"Let's go," Colonel Walker said to Webster and Kujura.

The three officers started to walk away.

Ethan gritted his teeth and stared at them.

"Captain Webster!" Ethan nearly shouted.

The three officers stopped and turned around. Stony-cold gazes regarded him.

Ethan inhaled. "My brother was part of the last soldiers to fight on the Battleship Carrier Indianapolis. He died fighting the Vemus, so they could update the *Ark* mission that brought us here. We're here because of him and everyone else who was there. I *need* to be on that expedition. I…"

Colonel Walker walked toward him. "It's all right. I understand."

Ethan stared at the colonel for a few seconds. "Please, Colonel."

Colonel Walker placed his hand on Ethan's shoulder. "I had a brother too, once. He also died fighting the Vemus. I know what you're asking, okay. You hear me?"

Ethan looked him in the eye. "Yes, sir."

"I appreciate the enthusiasm, but that doesn't mean we always get what we want."

"I feel like I owe it to him, and I owe it to my father, sir. I'm not going to give this up."

Colonel Walker looked at him for a moment. "No, I don't expect you will. I can't promise anything, but I'll see what I can do."

"Thank you, Colonel. Thank you so much."

"You're welcome. Now, don't you have some celebrating to do?" Colonel Walker said, pushing his chin up.

Ethan saw that the others were waiting for him. "Thanks again, Colonel."

He walked back to the others.

"What was that all about?" Massey asked.

"You have a brother who fought the Vemus?" Eva asked.

Ethan nodded. "My half-brother, Sean Gates," he said and told them everything he knew about the brother he'd never even met but who'd had the most profound impact on all their lives.

6

THE MAGLEV TRAIN reached the city of Sanctuary at 2 PM. Lauren Gates stood up and retrieved an old rucksack made of vintage canvas with a brown faux-leather bottom and padded straps. She carried it toward the doors and followed the other people out. Once she was clear of the throng, she slipped her hands through the straps and slung the rugged pack over her shoulders.

She walked toward the nearby staircase and left the platform behind.

"Excuse me," a young man said and smiled nervously at her. "I'm sorry to bother you, but could you tell me how to get to the Colonial Research Institute from here?"

Lauren nodded. "Sure, there are aircars that can take you. They're outside the station."

The young man paled. "I hate flying. Do you know if there are ground transports available?"

Lauren smiled. She didn't care for flying much either. "I'm heading there myself."

"Would you mind if I followed you? Oh, that sounded wrong. Hi, my name is Jack, and this is my first time in Sanctuary."

Lauren almost grinned. "I'm Lauren. You can walk with me."

Jack smiled, relieved.

"Are you meeting someone at the institute?" she asked.

"Yeah, I'm supposed to meet with Dr. Isaacson. I'm starting my internship with him tomorrow."

"He's really good at his job. You'll like him. He's great with new interns."

"That's a relief. I really didn't know anything about him. Were you his intern?"

Lauren shook her head. "No, my mother teaches there so I got to know a lot of the people who work there."

Jack's topmost luggage container began to slide off the top, and Lauren pushed it back into place.

"Thanks," he said. "Who's your mother?"

"Dr. Lenora Bishop. She used to head the archeology department there, but now she only works part time. She's on a bit of a sabbatical."

Jack's eyes widened. "*She's* your mother! I've heard of her. She's involved with the Ovarrow. Wow, you're Dr. Bishop's daughter. That's amazing!"

Lauren smiled.

They walked through the doors and waited in line for ground transportation.

"Do you work for the institute?" Jack asked and frowned. "I'm sorry if I'm asking too many questions. I'll leave you alone now. Thanks for getting me here."

Lauren chuckled. Jack reminded her a little bit of Ethan when he was younger but without all the bravado. "That's quite all right. No, I don't work for the institute. I'm a doctor at the Quinn Medical Center in Sierra. I'm just here for a quick visit."

A comlink chimed from her wrist computer.

"I'll leave you to it. Thanks again, Lauren."

Lauren smiled and waved. Then she stepped to the side. A vidcom opened and showed her brother's face.

"Hello, Ethan. I was just thinking about you."

"Did you tell them yet?"

She shook her head. "No, I just arrived at Sanctuary. I'm heading to Mom and Dad's now."

Ethan nodded. "Do they know you're coming?"

"Mom does."

"Look, maybe don't mention that I volunteered for the expedition."

She gave him a long look. "Ethan, I'm not going to lie to them for you. They're going to figure it out. Especially Dad."

"I know, but you know how he gets sometimes. He could block it. At least for me he could," Ethan said.

"No, he won't. I don't think he will. Maybe you should have told them sooner."

"I haven't been assigned yet."

Lauren waved at Jack as he got into a ground transport. The next one came, and she climbed inside. She gave the automated driver the address and then turned back to Ethan.

"So you might not even get selected."

"I wouldn't say that. I've got a good shot. Colonel Walker is volunteering. He fought with Dad in the Vemus Wars."

"Well, I'm going there now to tell them."

"Do you think you'll get selected?"

Lauren stared at her younger brother for a moment.

"Right, medical doctor with a specialization in infectious diseases. I guess you're either a shoo-in or a no-brainer."

Lauren smiled. "I shouldn't have a problem with the selection committee."

Ethan nodded and his expression turned serious—almost vulnerable, which was rare with him. "We're doing this for the right reasons. He was our brother. We owe it to him and everyone else who helped save us."

"It *is* the right reason, Ethan. Both for him and for Dad."

"He's not going to like it. He'll insist we don't owe him anything."

Lauren shrugged. "Yeah, but it feels right to do it."

Ethan stared at her for a moment and then nodded. "I wish I could be there with you, but we're traveling to Phoenix Station."

"Oh, that's right. Congratulations on making it through. You're part of the elite 7th Squadron."

"That's right. The best of the best. You'd be proud. I'll have to tell you about it."

"I *am* proud of you, little brother."

"Same here, big sis," Ethan said and glanced behind him. "I have to go. Let me know how it goes. I should probably call Mom later."

Lauren smiled and the comlink severed. She leaned back and sighed. She'd thought it was best if she told them what she was planning in person. It wasn't going to be easy, but it was necessary. She just hoped that her father understood.

Her childhood home used to be on the outskirts of the settlement, but it appeared that the city was catching up to the Gates family home. The rover came to a stop at the entrance to a paved road that led to her house, but she couldn't see the house through the thick woods.

She climbed out of the rover and closed the door. Two CDF soldiers stepped out of a black rover parked nearby. Her father must be home or the security detail wouldn't be on post.

One of the soldiers nodded a greeting. He had broad shoulders and an athletic build. He smiled. "Can we give you a ride to the house, Dr. Gates?"

"No, thank you. I'll walk," she replied.

"What a shame," he replied.

Lauren grinned. She'd been around soldiers all her life. He was handsome and she was certainly tempted. "I'm sure you'll find a way to recover. I hear the Salty Soldier has a fertile hunting ground."

The second soldier laughed and the first tipped his head to the side.

Lauren walked away. She might have put a little sway to her step but not too much.

"You're killing me!"

Lauren stuck her arm up and waved without looking back. It was spring in Sanctuary, and there was no shortage of blooming plants that filled the air with the familiar scents of her childhood home. The lavender bushes smelled as sweet as she remembered. She found that the older she got, the more difficult it was to find the time to return home, and this was only going to be a short visit.

She walked to the front door and the facial recognition and biochip scan cleared her to enter. She walked into the open entranceway.

"Hello?" she called out.

The door to the right opened and her mother walked out, grinning.

"There's my girl," her mother said and hugged her.

"Hi, Mom."

Her mother had long auburn hair and bright blue eyes. Lauren's brunette hair had a reddish tinge, thanks to her mother, along with her own bright blue eyes.

Her mother sighed. "God, your hair is absolutely gorgeous. So thick and with the perfect wave."

"Is Dad home?"

"Yes, he's in his office in his hobby building."

Lauren arched an eyebrow. "Mom, he has prototype weapons and vehicles in there. It's more than just a hobby."

Her mother smiled at her. "You wouldn't believe what we have here."

She followed her mother into an open kitchen.

"Tea?"

Lauren nodded. "Yes, please. Earl Grey."

A few minutes later Lauren sat with a steaming cup of tea in front of her. She added a little bit of honey and cream, then sipped it.

"I'm sorry things didn't work out with Doug."

"It was best for both of us."

"It's not awkward at the medical center?"

Lauren shook her head. "Not at all. Oh, and Ashley says to tell you hello."

Her mother nodded and eyed her for a moment. "I know why you came."

"You do?"

"Of course I do."

"Does Dad know?"

Her mother pursed her lips for a second. "I don't think so. This is still quite a shock for him."

"Ethan's worried he'll try to interfere."

Her mother shrugged.

"What do you think about it?"

"I don't know what to think, to be honest. Oh, I think we should send an expedition back to Earth. We certainly owe them that."

"I agree, but I feel like you're hesitant about it."

Her mother sipped her tea and set the cup down on the counter. "I'm always going to worry about you. Your father is the same way."

The back door opened and her father walked inside. His eyes widened and a broad smile appeared. Lauren stood up and gave her father a big hug. He grinned as he gave her a bearhug and swung her around the room, reminiscent of when she was a little girl.

"It's so good to see you. When did you get here?" he asked and looked at her mother. "Did you know she was coming?"

"I've only just arrived. I sent Mom a message this morning."

Her father nodded. He towered over most men and had a deep voice. "Is everything okay?"

Lauren grinned. "Of course."

He looked at her for a few moments in that fatherly way of his.

"Dad, I'm fine. I came here to talk to you and Mom about something," she said.

His expression became somber. He sat on one of the stools and crossed his arms in front of his chest. "All right, kid. You're up. What have you got?"

She was twenty-five years old, and her father was the only one she'd let get away with calling her a kid.

She looked at them both for a moment. "I'm volunteering for the expedition going to Earth."

Her father blinked a few times and frowned. "I'm sorry," he said, his arms going to his side as if he were bracing for something. "You're what?"

"Dad, I'm going on the expedition to Earth."

Her parents exchanged looks. He licked his lips and shook his head. "No."

Lauren frowned and glanced at her mother for half a second. "I'm not asking for your permission, Dad. I'm going."

"No, you're not."

"Connor," her mother said.

Her father looked away from her and scratched the side of his head for a second. "You have no idea what that expedition is going to encounter."

"Dad, there are survivors there."

"I know, and we know nothing about them. All we do know is that there are Vemus there. After all this time, they're still there."

Lauren looked away for a moment as her thoughts came together. "I want to help them."

"You can help the people here."

Lauren sighed. He wasn't taking this well. She knew he'd be upset, but it was so much more intense than she'd anticipated. "Dad," she said.

He stood up, and his steely-eyed gaze slammed into her. Her father wasn't like most of the men in her life. He'd done so much in service to the colony, and he carried the weight of that burden with him.

"Dad," she said again, calmer.

He bit the bottom of his lip. "I don't want you to go."

He stared at her and her throat thickened. He was so worried, and she tried to think of something she could say to set his mind at ease. But he'd seen too much, and nothing she said would console him about it.

"I have to go."

"No, you don't. You don't have to go."

"Yes, I do."

"No—"

"Dad, you're not going to stop me," she said and paused for a

moment. "And you're not going to stop Ethan either." As soon as
the words left her lips, she immediately wished she could take
them back. She'd just used Ethan as a way to divert her father's
wrath.

"Your brother, too! Lenora," he said and shook his head.
"Him I can stop."

He stormed past her.

"Don't," Lauren said. "Dad, don't," she said, following him
outside. "We have to go!"

He stopped but didn't turn around.

"Don't you understand? Sean sacrificed himself so the
colonists on the *Ark* would have a chance at surviving the
Vemus."

Her father spun toward her, eyes blazing. Lauren took a step
back.

"How dare you?" he said in a deceptively calm voice. "All he
knew was war. His entire life was fighting the Vemus. He
watched everything he knew be stripped away and continued to
fight because it was all he knew. He hated it, and if he'd had any
other choice, he would have done something else."

Lauren swallowed hard and didn't know what to say. Seeing
the pain in her father's eyes made her go blind for a moment as
tears began to form.

"He didn't have a choice. You do. Don't throw your life
away," her father said. Then he turned around and walked
away.

Lauren inhaled a shaky breath and wiped the tears from her
eyes. Her mother came to her side and wrapped an arm around
her shoulders.

"Easy," she said. "It'll be all right."

"I didn't know he'd be so upset about it. God, Mom, why…"

Her mother rubbed her shoulder soothingly. "It's

complicated. It always was with your father. He's learned to live with it, but he's worried about you and Ethan."

She looked at her mother. "I know he wants to protect us, but you saw him just now."

Her mother shook her head and gave her a stern look. "Lauren, your father loves you more than anything, but you've got to cut him a little slack. He lost a son. He still feels responsible, and no one will ever convince him otherwise. To be honest, it's one of the things I've always loved about him. Your father will hide from nothing."

Lauren considered this and closed her eyes for a moment. "I shouldn't have brought Ethan up. That was stupid."

Her mother smiled at her with half her mouth. "Don't be so hard on yourself. There aren't many people who can stand up to your father the way you just did. You're a lot like him, you know."

"Are you kidding? Ethan is more like him than I'll ever be. I never wanted to be in the CDF."

"There's more to your father than the CDF," she replied. "You're strong like him. You're your own person. We understand that."

Lauren inhaled and sighed. She looked in the direction her father had gone. "Should I go talk to him?"

Her mother patted her arm affectionately. "No, he needs some time to cool off. I'll go talk to him. Are you going to spend the night?"

Lauren had intended to, but now she just wanted to return to Sierra. "I should really get back. I'll come back in a few days."

Her mother looked at her for a few seconds. She wasn't fooled one bit. "I'll walk you out then."

"Thanks, Mom. This wasn't easy, but... well, you haven't said anything about it."

"I understand why you and Ethan feel the way you do. I don't like it any more than your father does, but I understand. You're doing what you feel you have to."

"Will he understand?"

"He does understand. That's part of the problem. If the roles were reversed, he'd probably do the same thing you are."

Lauren smiled a little.

"But it's different when you're a parent."

Lauren hugged her mother. "I love you, Mom."

"I love you, too, dear heart."

7

CONNOR STORMED way past where he'd intended to go. He was almost half a kilometer away from the house before he turned back around. More than a few times he shook his head in frustration.

Joining the expedition. What were they thinking?

The wooded area near his home was quiet. He could remember a time when they'd had to worry about some of the more dangerous creatures of New Earth, but this place had become more of a home to him than anywhere else.

Survivors.

He blew out a breath. They had no idea who had survived. Whoever they were, they were two hundred and fifty years older than anyone he'd left behind.

As he walked the forest path, he spotted Lenora coming toward him in the distance. There was no mistaking her long auburn hair in the bright afternoon sun. The day he got used to that was the day he was no longer a man. The sight of her chased away his anger for a few seconds.

She was coming to talk to him.

Lauren should be smarter than this. Lauren and Ethan probably thought they were honoring a brother they'd never even met. It did make sense, and he hated it.

He looked at Lenora, about fifty meters from him, and sighed heavily. "You never know who you'll run into out here."

She smiled. "Have you seen my husband? He's tall and sometimes has a bit of a temper."

Connor frowned in thought. "I bet it's because people keep giving him good reasons to be upset."

Lenora shrugged and arched an eyebrow toward him. "What's on your mind, love?"

"Oh, you know. Just trying to look after my kids. Keep them from doing something stupid."

"It's not stupid."

"Maybe not, but it's definitely foolish. This expedition is among the most dangerous things the colony has faced in a long time."

"I believe you."

"You're one person, at least," he said. They'd fallen into step as they walked back toward their house. "I've spent a lot of time poring over all the old records we retrieved. The survivors are probably nothing like the people we left behind. There's probably old war tech out there as well."

"You'd know more about that than I would, but Connor, they're still people."

He gazed at his wife and saw something determined in her gaze. "Not all people are the same. If they've survived this long, they don't need our help."

"Would you say the same thing if Lauren and Ethan weren't going?"

"I might not be able to stop Lauren, but Ethan isn't going. I can put a stop to that, at least."

"He'll resent you if you do that."

Connor shrugged. "At least he'll be alive. He can resent me all he wants."

"Connor," Lenora said in a tone that conveyed that he wasn't going to like what she was about to say.

"No, Lenora. I won't do it. I didn't fight in all those wars and watch my friends die so my kids can go off and throw their lives away. I won't stand by and watch them do it."

He couldn't help raising his voice.

Lenora stopped walking and stared at him. He turned back toward her. "You might be able to stop Ethan. It probably wouldn't take much for you to make that happen. You might even be able to prevent Lauren from going. Maybe. But what happens next time they do something you don't like?"

"It's not about what I like. It's about being a father. Watching out for them."

"I know that, Connor. But they're more than old enough to make decisions on their own."

Connor's shoulders slumped a little. They'd raised their children to be independent, capable adults. Now it was biting him in the ass.

Lenora stepped toward him until she was right in front of him. "What about me? Are you going to stop me from going?"

"You," he said, and it sounded halfway between a question and an accusation.

"Yeah, me, Connor. Like you, I'm not ready for them to go off without me. Not like this."

Connor blinked and was at a loss for words. He exhaled a long breath and looked at her. "I was going to walk away from all this. Retire from the CDF."

"Maybe put that off for a little while longer," Lenora said.

Connor just shook his head.

"You may not like their reasons for going, but if you were them, you'd do the same thing. I know you would."

He blew out a breath. "This is all Noah's fault. If he hadn't invented FTL, then none of this would've happened."

Lenora twitched her eyebrows and smiled. "So, you'll tell Nathan you're going to lead the expedition?"

A comlink chimed on his wrist computer. He glanced at it. "Speak of the devil."

"Perfect timing. So, you'll tell him?"

"I don't know. I need to think about it."

"Really?"

"Yeah, really," he said and was surprised by how much he meant it.

They walked the rest of the way back to the house in silence. He knew she wasn't angry with him, and he also knew she was serious about going. That was something he *couldn't* stop.

"I have to meet Nathan at the base," Connor said.

"Okay."

He stared at his wife for a moment. "Am I being crazy about this?"

Lenora shook her head. "No, not in the least. Connor, you've given so much of yourself to the colony."

He closed his eyes for a few seconds and said, "I can't let all of you go without me."

"I know," she said, her voice sounding thick. "I'm sorry."

He held her in his arms for a few seconds and then left for the base. He walked toward an aircar and the two soldiers on guard duty got into their own aircar. He climbed inside and brought up the flight controls. The vehicle went through its pre-flight checks and the status was green. He engaged the flight controls and flew away from his home. He glanced at it and remembered raising his kids there. He'd tried to be around them as much as he could while they were growing up. It had been much easier after the Krake War. Not in a thousand years did he ever think he'd go back to Earth...Old Earth. Old life. The one he'd left behind.

8

THE CDF BASE at Sanctuary had begun as an outpost in the early days of the colony but had become a major operations center for the colonial military. Advanced tactical training included infantry, air and ground combat tactics, and technology development for vehicular, weapons, and defensive initiatives. Connor had built the CDF from the ground up, but the base at Sanctuary had been his home for almost two decades, a feat that would have been unheard of if he'd remained in the NA Alliance Military. The CDF was a much smaller military in terms of sheer size and firepower but had significant technological advantages over the Old Earth militaries he remembered, but that was before the twenty years those militaries had spent fighting the Vemus. If the technological leaps that had occurred on New Earth were any indication of how much change could occur, then trying to anticipate what waited for them in the Sol System was going to be a real challenge.

After setting down on the landing pad near the main building, Connor stepped out of the aircar and walked toward

Nathan's office, his security detail following close behind. As Connor walked through the base, he remembered when the different buildings had been added to the main base or when they'd had to expand its boundaries. He'd seen and done so much that if he stopped to think about it all, he'd be lost in nostalgic revelry for hours. Add a few old friends to that and they'd make a day and a night of it.

Although both Connor and Nathan shared the same rank in the CDF, Nathan was his superior officer. They mostly ran the CDF as a partnership, with the exception that Nathan could overrule Connor. Territorial political entanglements were kept to a minimum, which was much easier in times of peace.

Connor strode toward Nathan's office and saw him speaking with a few officers.

"That's all the time I've got for this," Nathan was saying. "Set up a meeting with Colonel Randall."

The two officers saluted Nathan and left.

"I'm here as requested, General Hayes."

"General Gates, your timing is impeccable, as always."

Connor walked inside his office and Nathan followed him. "Would you like some coffee or tea?"

Nathan eyed him for a moment. "Not necessary, but you look like you could use something stronger."

Connor snorted half-heartedly. "Family."

"Ah yes. They're a blessing most of the time...all the time, but they'll sometimes test you in ways that can make you want to scream."

Connor sighed. "You already know?"

"About both your children volunteering for the expedition? Yes, I know. Saw it on the roster yesterday."

Connor frowned and half a smile tugged one side of his

mouth. "You picked out two names from hundreds of volunteers?"

Nathan chuckled. "God no. There are thousands of volunteers, but let's just say I had a hunch. By the look on your face, it's a hunch I'm sorry to say was correct."

Connor looked away. "It's not just them. Lenora told me she's going to volunteer as well."

"I'm not sure there'll be a need for an archeologist on this mission, not even one as renowned as her."

Connor grinned a little, but his words came out hollow and bitter. "She knows that, so she'll likely apply for the diplomatic envoy."

"Oh, I see," Nathan replied quietly.

"Yeah."

A few moments of silence passed.

"I believe the term to most accurately describe the situation is having your balls in a vice," Nathan said and smiled.

Connor laughed and shook his head. "You got that right. Boy do you ever."

"We'll need to discuss the expedition, but to be honest, before the probes I expected this conversation to be about something else."

Connor nodded. "I was considering retirement or taking on a lesser role in the CDF."

Nathan didn't look surprised. Had Connor really been so transparent, or was it because they'd been friends for so damn long? He preferred to think it was the latter.

"Connor, no one can deny the enormous contribution you've made to not just the colony but humanity. We wouldn't have survived our own war with the Vemus without you, much less the war with the Krake," Nathan said and looked at him for a few moments. "I know you hate it, hate the acknowledgement, but it's the truth and I don't care if you hate it. I still remember, and so do a lot of other people."

The colony had quadrupled in size, which meant that there were generations who had only learned about what the colony had overcome in a classroom. As time went on, the memories would fade. But Connor hadn't been thinking about making history. He'd done what needed to be done because there was no one else.

"Thanks for that, Nathan. You're right, I hate it. The older CDF personnel remember, but the newer generation either looks at me like I'm a legend come to life or they don't believe the legend, and I'm not sure which is worse sometimes," Connor said. He paused for a few moments, gathering his thoughts. "Do you ever feel like the world has outgrown you?"

Nathan chuckled. "Every time I see my children, it seems."

Nathan's children were adults and had their own lives. Some of them were officers in the CDF.

"So what are we supposed to do? Stick around and let people regard us as some legacy artifact?"

Nathan arched an eyebrow. "I know you're not implying that the colony doesn't need the CDF, but like everything else, we'll have to adapt to an ever-changing world, none of which is going to change the fact that we know there are survivors on Earth and that there are Vemus…at least a remnant of them."

Connor nodded. "I'm not going to second-guess the security protocols that were put in place on the drones."

"Neither will I. They were a necessary precaution. We didn't want our grandchildren to have to fight the Vemus."

Connor leaned back on his desk.

"We, and I mean the collective we and not us," Nathan said, making a circular gesture. "We owe a significant debt to everyone who made the ultimate sacrifice for us. It's no wonder that Ethan and Lauren have volunteered to go on the expedition. We're not going to have a shortage of volunteers, not by a long shot, but this next part is off the record."

Connor regarded his friend for a second and then nodded.

"I know you, Connor. This isn't something you can walk away from without regretting it for the rest of your life. It's not fair and it's not right, but that's the way it is. Sean is more than capable of leading the expeditionary force, but the mission will have even better odds of success if you go."

Connor blinked a few times. There it was. The question had been raised and answered all at once. He didn't have to go on the mission. He could walk away from it, and at the same time, how could he live with himself if he did?

"What does the colonial government expect from the mission?" Connor asked.

"They just want to re-establish contact with whoever has survived, assess the status of Earth, and if necessary, offer assistance to the survivors."

Connor looked at Nathan for a moment. "And the Vemus?"

"Eradicate them if possible."

Connor looked away and glanced at the nearby wallscreen. An image of members of the old Ghost Platoon that he'd led for the NA Alliance appeared. They'd been dead for over thirty years. Their lives had been stolen from them because they'd followed him on a mission gone wrong. Their sacrifice was no less than the people who'd fought the Vemus so that the *Ark* could travel to New Earth.

"What do you think?" Nathan asked.

"It's about what I expected."

"I figured as much."

"I'll meet with Sean, and we'll come up with a proposal for the powers that be to consider."

Nathan nodded and then eyed him for a moment. "Things are changing with the colony and the CDF. We'll need to adapt and grow with that. Whether or not you retire after you come back is entirely up to you."

"If I say this is my last mission, then I'll jinx it. But since I don't really hold suspicious practices in high regards, I'm not afraid to say that this will be my last mission in the CDF."

"Just invite all that karma to visit whatever it will on you then."

Connor shrugged.

"The other thing I wanted to say is that with change comes other opportunities."

Connor's eyebrows raised. "Like what?"

Nathan smiled. "A discussion for when you get back. It'll give you something to think about in your copious amounts of spare time."

9

As SHAO FEN waited for the shuttle to dock with the outpost, he saw a comms broadcast from Magnus Station appear on the HUD.

"Ignore it," Shao Fen ordered.

The pilot dismissed the comms request. "We're docked, President Shao."

Shao Fen stood and joined his bodyguard, Cheng Zhi, who was waiting for him at the airlock. Cheng Zhi was just under two meters tall, with a shaved head and dark eyes. He opened the airlock and entered the transit shaft first.

"Clear," Cheng Zhi said.

Shao Fen followed his protector through the transit shaft and into the outpost. He rarely had occasion to leave Magnus Station, but Ivanov Yanovich had been insistent.

The dimly lit corridors were empty but for the two of them. No one suspected that the president of the Sol Coalition would use a maintenance entrance to any minor outpost or station.

Shao Fen had spent his long career preserving the last human survivors of the Venus Wars.

Strange music could be heard farther down the corridor. Shao Fen inhaled a breath and held it for a moment before releasing it in a long, steadying exhale as they entered the outer room of a converted maintenance shop. The ancient Asiatic Alliance outpost had been built over three hundred years ago and should have been decommissioned long before the collapse.

Ivanov Yanovich was in an interior darkened room with six specialized containers used for secure storage. One of the containers was opened, and a metallic square with an ion booster was suspended or held by a mechanical arm.

Cheng Zhi banged a powerful fist on the window and Yanovich turned around. He waved and went through a decontamination trap before joining them. He wore a brown jumpsuit and helmet, which he removed as he entered the room.

Yanovich ignored Cheng Zhi. "President Shao, you're much earlier than I expected."

"You'd be surprised by how much you can learn when you set your own schedule."

Yanovich tipped his head to the side a couple of times in a nervous tick. "I have nothing to hide from you. Thank you for this project."

Shao Fen looked through the window and stepped toward it. "Are they intact?"

Yanovich came to stand by his side. "Yes, they are. Those are isolation containers that block all forms of communications, but we were unable to detect the actual signal that caused the other probes to self-destruct."

"Kill-switch protocol," Cheng Zhi said.

Yanovich pursed his thin lips in thought.

"The signal came from the interior of zeta sector," Cheng Zhi said.

Yanovich frowned. "So you were able to detect it. How? The deep salvage contractors that found these didn't know how they worked."

"How is unimportant," Shao Fen said. "I have it on good authority that these are the last probes. I see you've managed to open one up. What have you learned?"

"It's quite interesting, really. I haven't had a chance to check the others, but this one has a biocontainment system inside. The onboard AI kept throwing up errors about communication being lost, but I've been able to filter that out. These probes came from other humans. They're from something called the Ark Program. Not sure what that refers to, but whoever they are, they sent these probes here."

Shao Fen looked at Cheng Zhi. "See what you can find out about this Ark Program."

"Yes, President Shao." The agent stepped aside and began using one of the nearby consoles.

Yanovich glanced at him and then looked at Shao Fen. "I don't think he's going to find anything on that console. It doesn't have any external connection to the Magnus Station archives."

Shao Fen's lips lifted a little. "You'll find that he is much more resourceful than he appears. What else do you know about the people who sent these probes?"

"I'm still gaining access to the probes' computing cores. It looks like whoever designed the probes is using a layered security protocol to prevent all-out access to its data."

"Will it be a problem?"

The question was seemingly innocent enough, but the implications of an inadequate response carried its own set of actions that Shao Fen would have to take.

Yanovich swallowed hard and shook his head. "It'll just take me some time."

Shao Fen nodded once. "Why would they include a biocontainment system? What's inside?"

"They're samples of something. I'd just gained access to that database when you arrived. If you give me a few moments, I can learn more."

Shao Fen wasn't interested in waiting around to watch Yanovich working.

"I can do it from here," he said and stepped toward a console.

Cheng Zhi turned toward him and gestured toward a holoscreen. "The Ark Program is an interstellar colony ship that left the Sol System before the Vemus were discovered on Earth. There are references in our archives of a mission to override the *Ark* and send it to another star system."

Shao Fen read the data on the holoscreen quickly and nodded. "They drew the Alpha to the edge of the star system. That must be why it disappeared."

Cheng Zhi nodded. "They thought it simply left the star system, but it might have been in pursuit of the *Ark*."

"It was," Yanovich said. "It's right here in the database entries. It looks like this *Ark* traveled over sixty light-years to another star system, and the Vemus followed them. The biocontainment system carries viral samples of an indigenous virus they used to kill the Vemus. I can send you the data I've found so far."

"Cheng Zhi will make a backup of what you've discovered so far," Shao Fen said. He walked toward the window and rested his palms on the frame. Peering at the probes, he let his thoughts arrange themselves in his mind.

"The probes do contain a communications system. Should

we try to contact these colonists?"

Shao Fen narrowed his gaze for a second. Yanovich needed direction if he was to be of any use. "No. What good will it do? Communicating with the colonists isn't a priority. There would be a sixty-year communications lag, and I don't intend to wait that long for a response."

"I wouldn't be alive for a response," Yanovich said.

Prolonging treatments were a historical footnote that hadn't been available since before the Vemus Wars.

"I want you to focus all your efforts on the viral samples. We need to test the claims that it can kill the Vemus. Is it harmful to us? How does it work? How can we create a synthetic version of it? This is to be your priority. You will have as many resources as you need," Shao Fen said.

Yanovich frowned in thought and Shao Fen stared at him.

"I'll need access to Vemus samples."

"You will have them."

"I'll need help."

"You will have it. Convert this outpost into whatever you need. The spacers here will be moved elsewhere. Contact will be limited."

"Limited contact? But how will—"

"All communications will be routed through a secure network on Magnus Station."

Yanovich's mouth opened a little, but then he quickly recovered.

"We'll also need a way to deploy this Vemus weapon, but that can be done in stages."

"President Shao, this isn't something that can be delivered in a week or even a month."

Shao Fen's gaze hardened coldly. "Ivanov Yanovich, if you're not up to the challenge, I will find someone else who is."

Yanovich brought his hands up in a placating gesture. Cheng Zhi stepped toward him, his hand on his sidearm, and Yanovich flinched.

"It's not that," he sputtered. "I, I can do this. I promise you that I can do this, but it will take time."

Shao Fen looked at him dispassionately. "How much time?"

Yanovich winced. "I'm not sure. I need time to review the samples and see if the equipment we have is appropriate for our needs. If I could bring the sample to Magnus Station, then I could—"

"That is out of the question," Shao Fen said evenly. "There will be no testing with Vemus samples on Magnus Station. We cannot risk an outbreak."

"Right, I hadn't thought of that. I just need a week or two to fully analyze what I've got."

"Two weeks," Shao Fen said. "Ordinarily, I'd only give you a few days."

Yanovich began to speak.

"Don't," Shao Fen said, and Yanovich was instantly silent. "I can be reasonable. You'll have your two weeks. Cheng Zhi will be checking on you, and he'll be coordinating the delivery of the supplies you've asked for."

Yanovich inhaled and nodded. "That's fine. That's better than fine. Thank you so much, President Shao. I promise that I won't disappoint you."

"No, I don't expect you will, but if you do...No need to state the obvious," Shao Fen said and looked at Cheng Zhi. "We need to contain the situation. The general public isn't ready for this."

"I can contain the breach," Cheng Zhi said.

"I want no loose ends. We need to control this entirely," Shao Zen replied and looked at Yanovich. "Be at ease, Ivanov. Your work will help us achieve what no one thought possible. If what you've found does bear fruit, we can finally be rid of the Vemus once and for all. And most importantly, we can return to Earth."

Yanovich's eyes widened and then he nodded. "I will do this. I will do anything you ask, President Shao."

"I know you will. I will be in contact with you. Proceed carefully, Ivanov. Your work is of the upmost importance to everyone. And when we do finally go public with this, I promise that everyone will know that Ivanov Yanovich was instrumental in eradicating the Vemus."

Yanovich smiled. There was still a lot of fear in his eyes, which pleased Shao Fen. It would keep Yanovich focused and motivated.

"I will leave you to your very important work," Shao Fen said.

"Thank you, President Shao. Thank you so much for this opportunity to serve," Yanovich said.

Shao Fen left the work area and Cheng Zhi followed him.

He glanced at his protector. "What do you think?"

"He's erratic and impulsive."

"True, but is he wrong?"

Cheng Zhi considered it for a few moments. "Not that I can tell, but I'll make sure the right people work with him—people who can keep him on task and report if he strays. You are aware of Yanovich's wide range of associates."

"Of course. They will need to be watched."

"If you want this contained, I'll need to revisit the salvagers that found the probes. They can't be allowed to share what they found with anyone else. Too much time has passed already," Cheng Zhi said.

Shao Fen walked in silence for a few moments, considering. "Not yet. We can still use them."

"You want me to repurpose them?"

"Yes, it's time we resume the exile program. I think the timing is appropriate. If Yanovich is right, it could take months before our efforts here produce an outcome. During that time, we have quite a bit of work to do."

"Understood, President Shao. Our work will build a better future for us all."

"Yes, it will. No matter the cost."

As they returned to the shuttle, Shao Fen had already begun planning what they needed to accomplish. He couldn't afford to get distracted by colonists who were too far away to be of any use to him. One day perhaps, but for now they might have something that could truly change the future of every surviving human in the Sol System. It was an opportunity that he wasn't going to waste. He would pay any price to see humanity restored to their rightful place and take back what was rightfully theirs. It was time for them to return home. It was time for them to return to Earth.

10

Connor stood alone in the conference room. Given the option, he'd prefer smaller meetings that weren't weighed down by other people's opinions. He'd always started with just a few people and then it would inevitably grow from there.

He glanced at the conference table with the holotank. Not many people knew that the Colonial Defense Force had been conceived in a remote campsite with just himself, Kasey Douglass, Juan Diaz, and Will Reisman. They'd talked all night long. It wasn't planned. They'd just kept going until sunrise, and it had turned into one of the most memorable nights of his life.

The door opened and Sean Quinn walked in.

Sean glanced around the empty room. "Am I late?"

Connor shook his head. "I'm early."

Sean nodded and came to stand next to him. "Isn't anyone else coming?"

"Do we need anyone else here?"

"I can think of a few people."

Connor smiled a little. "I'm sure you could. No, I figured

we'd take a stab at planning the expedition together. Get the skeleton laid out and then go from there."

Sean cocked his head a little while he considered it, then nodded. "Works for me," he said and glanced at the nearby wallscreen. It showed an image of the New Earth landscape. "This place looks familiar," he said, peering at the image. "Foothills over there. There's a campsite here. Look at that. The date is two years after the colony began."

"I know."

Sean looked at him for a moment. "Is that it? The campsite where you, Kasey, Will, and Juan came up with the CDF?"

Connor nodded.

Sean sighed. "That was a long time ago. I wish I'd been there."

"You were on SAR duty with Field Ops as I recall."

Sean nodded. "Yup, that is until Will came to collect me for a special project."

Connor chuckled. "He did have a flare for the dramatic."

They were both quiet for a few seconds. Sean poured them a cup of water each. "So, retirement, huh?"

"News travels fast," Connor replied.

"Not really. Nathan told me you were actually considering it."

"I am."

Sean frowned in surprise.

"Don't look so surprised," Connor said.

Sean almost chuckled. "Can you blame me? What would you do? It's not like you're that old."

Connor arched an eyebrow. "Thanks for that."

Sean grinned. "You know what I mean."

Connor shrugged.

"Honestly, I'm just happy to have someone to pass the buck up to on this expedition," Sean said.

"I guess if the shit really hits the fan, I can always assign blame to my second-in-command," Connor replied dryly.

"Probably for the best."

Connor chuckled. "All right. If you could have anything you wanted for this expedition, what would you bring?"

"That's easy. At least twenty voyager class heavy cruisers and a hundred destroyers to start with."

Connor shook his head. "Somehow I don't think we'll get that many ships for this."

"I was assuming I could have anything I wanted," Sean said and rubbed the back of his head. "Distance aside, this expedition has the hallmarks of a scouting mission. I'd probably frame the core of my ship selections around that."

Connor nodded approvingly. "That's what I was thinking."

"The rub is, how much fighting capability are we willing to bring?"

"If you're dreaming of superior firepower, I can tell you to forget it," Connor said.

"How come? According to Admiral Wilkinson, the Vemus either destroyed or absorbed most of the fleets in the Sol System."

"That's true, but the survivors have also had over two hundred years to rebuild, and the probes detected the Vemus."

"The probe AIs knew how to scan for the Vemus exoskeleton that it grew over other ships. Without the actual scan data, it might have just scanned an old space station or other type of facility."

"The expansion throughout the Sol System occurred for hundreds of years. It dwarfed anything we have here. Even if the survivors only had a fraction of the capabilities of the old alliance militaries, they'd still be significant when compared with the CDF," Connor said.

Sean didn't look convinced. "We're not going there to conquer. We're supposed to establish contact, assess, and give assistance."

"All true, and yet all missions somehow fall short of what we'll encounter."

Sean inhaled a deep breath and exhaled it evenly. "I doubt there'll be open hostilities as soon as we get there."

"Probably not, but the thing is that we don't know anything about the survivors other than that they're human."

Sean frowned. "Okay, what about it?"

"The wars we fought here were against an alien species. We didn't really fight among ourselves. There weren't enough of us for it to become an issue. Old Earth is a different story, and we need to be prepared for what we'll encounter."

"Do you really think after all this time that old grievances will still be around?"

"It's possible, especially if the survivors made it part of their identity. That was at the heart of Old Earth divisions. They were based on old nation-states. If you go back further in history, the divisions are always the same."

Sean considered it for a few moments. "I see your point. I guess I just take it for granted because it seems like the rest of us here outgrew that way of thinking. This is going to be more complicated than I originally thought."

"Now you're starting to understand the gravity of the situation."

"So what do you want to do?"

"We bring a proposal that includes four heavy cruisers with destroyer escorts."

"That's a good-size battle group. I don't know if we'll get approval for that."

Connor nodded. Neither of them were strangers to these kinds of proposals. "They'll likely give us approval for half that..."

"Because it's a scouting mission," Sean agreed.

"So, it comes down to ship capabilities and what we expect we'll encounter on this expedition," Connor said.

"Why does it feel like we're back to square one?"

"The first step is always to agree on the scope. Then we can get into the details."

They spent the next several hours ironing out a force of ships that was agile enough to be able to cope with a variety of hostile scenarios but could also carry enough combat capabilities to ensure the safety of the expeditionary force. Sean knew as much as Connor about fleet tactics and response. They were essentially compiling a general direct-action force that had a wide range of capabilities but was a master of none. They were limited by the number of CDF ships that had an Infinity Drive.

"That's why I insisted on the Voyager Class heavy cruisers. They've been taken to the Second Colony already, so the performance metrics are there," Sean said.

"The I-Drive comes at the cost of four missile tubes," Connor replied.

"The combat drones can make up for it."

The Krake combat drones, which had caused no end of havoc for the CDF fleet during the Krake Wars, had been reverse-engineered and added to the CDF arsenal.

"We can make up for it with a third cruiser," Connor said.

"Yeah, but the security council is concerned with securing this star system. Old Earth isn't as high a priority."

"Then we'll need to make up for it with the destroyers and the smaller attack craft."

Sean snorted. "I wondered when you'd bring up the Talon V wings."

Connor's eyebrow twitched. "I can make a case for all three types."

"And the 7th A-Wing?" Sean pressed.

Connor rolled his eyes. "They'll be assigned to you."

"I've reviewed Ethan's record and that of the rest of the 7th Squadron under Colonel Walker. I wouldn't hesitate to bring them at all. The newbies will have four months to train before we even reach the Sol System. But…" Sean let the rest go unsaid.

"He's my son, and it has the potential to impact my ability to command."

"Actually, I was thinking that having him along would be a great big pain in the ass for you, but Ethan's not like that. It takes a certain amount of stubbornness to forge your own path, especially when your father casts such a large shadow."

Connor snorted and shook his head. "You'd know a thing or two about that."

"A little, but Ethan joined the CDF. Regardless of what he wants, people will weigh who he is when they deal with him."

"I told him that the day he decided to enlist."

"He'll never use it to gain an advantage. I don't think you have to worry about him in that way."

Connor smiled. "Wait until you and Oriana have a family and then talk to me about what I need to worry about."

"Shots fired," Sean snickered, holding up his hands. "I surrender."

Connor waggled his eyebrows once. "In all seriousness, Sean. This will likely be my last mission."

"You'll have to forgive me if I don't believe you."

"You should."

"Well, I don't. That's not a judgement against you, Connor. You could walk away from the CDF, but I don't think you will. Not entirely. Adapt or die. Isn't that what Nathan's always saying?"

"Something like that."

"Oh, and before I forget, I have a recommendation for your XO."

Connor looked at the holotank, which displayed ship names and their current commanding officers. There was also an open group for the civilian contingent they'd be bringing with them.

"Let's hear it."

"You'll like him. His name is Oliver Martinez," Sean said. He brought up Martinez's service record and it hovered in front of Connor.

"He was part of the Trident Battle Group. He's got a long history in the fleet."

"He's solid. Since I can't be your XO, then Martinez is my first choice."

Connor eyed his friend for a moment. Sean had a demeanor that gave the impression he was putting things together at the last minute, which couldn't have been further from the truth.

"Just happened to remember that?"

Sean smiled. "It's just another thing off my long list of priorities."

Sean had always looked after Connor. Even when the CDF had first been created, Sean had watched his back.

"Okay, Martinez it is. It's time to bring our proposal to Nathan. Then we get to go through the whole thing again for the colonial government."

Sean shrugged. "It's all part of the job."

11

CONNOR STOOD on the bridge of the *Douglass*. The holodisplay showed a representation of the ship, along with a list of core system statuses below it. The heavy cruiser had a mass of four hundred and eighty thousand tons, which made it fifty-eight percent larger than the first series of its predecessor. The sheer size of the Voyager class heavy cruiser approached that of an NA Alliance battleship carrier, but not quite. The hull was roughly cigar-shaped, though flattened to provide a narrower profile, but was wider at the top and the bottom to support the superstructure and the mag cannon turrets. Between the turrets were missile tubes. There were fewer missile tubes than on a battleship carrier, but they were larger and capable of handling the new HADES VI missiles, which were a significant upgrade from the HADES Vs both in range and overall destructive power. There were eight heavy-cruiser-sized grazers with three lasers at each end of the ship. The outside of the ship was made of battle-steel gray walls, but the interior corridors were much more pleasing to the eye, especially for nonmilitary personnel. This warship had been designed for a mixed crew of civilian and military personnel, and a certain amount of comfort was to be expected. Improvements of the warship's design reduced the number of crew required to man it and could, in theory, operate without putting it into a spaceport for a year. Even then, they could extend their deployment, taking in supplies found along the way to the Sol System. Contrary to popular belief, water was actually quite plentiful and could easily be extracted from smaller celestial bodies.

Connor looked at the ship statuses of the rest of the expeditionary force. He and Sean had gone through more than a few iterations of the ships assigned to this mission, and he'd come to accept that they simply couldn't bring the size fighting force he wanted. There were increasing concerns that whatever third party had helped the drones reach the Sol System was going to travel to New Earth. Patrols and military exercises hadn't detected anything in the New Earth star system, but Connor understood the precautions that needed to be taken. In just over three weeks, they'd put together the group of ships that were to be part of the Expedition Earth Initiative.

"General Gates," Colonel Oliver Martinez said, "General Quinn has sent his readiness status."

Connor felt the edges of his lips lift. "He's probably getting a bit anxious."

"Agreed, General. He was never one to sit still."

Connor had never worked with Oliver Martinez and only knew of him by reputation. Over the past few weeks, he'd come to know the officer a little bit and found him to be reliable and capable. Sean had left him in good hands.

"All right, Colonel, let's synchronize the mission clocks. Departure in ten minutes," Connor said.

"Yes, General," Martinez said. "Ops, mark the time and sync across the board."

"Initializing, Colonel Martinez," Lieutenant Selina Wilson said.

"Helm, confirm course in nav computer," Martinez said.

"Course confirmed, Colonel. Nav computer is green," Lieutenant Jennifer Simpson said.

A mission countdown timer appeared in the upper right corner of the main holoscreen.

"Comms, give me a broadcast channel," Connor said.

"Comms channel ready, General Gates," Specialist Gabe Marten said.

"Attention Colonial Expeditionary Force, this is your commanding officer Connor Gates. We're about to embark upon an epic journey that will push the limits of our ships and ourselves. You were selected for this mission because you are the most qualified. It's no secret that we had enough volunteers for ten expeditions. Since the invention of the Infinity Drive, we've always known that one day some of us would travel back to the Sol System to search for survivors of the Vemus holocaust. That day is today, and the people embarking on this important mission is all of us. The circumstances of this mission are predicated on the unknown, and our job is to uncover the truth. There are survivors in the Sol System and hopefully back on Earth. It is our mission to establish contact with them. There is irrefutable evidence that there is also a significant Vemus presence in the Sol System. The CDF has fought the Vemus before and survived. Therefore, it is also our mission to give the survivors of Earth the same chance we've had—a life without the threat of the Vemus. Each of us has a job to do. Support each other and uphold the finest traditions of the Colonial Defense Force. General Gates out."

Connor closed the broadcast channel.

"Countdown status update. One minute remaining," Lieutenant Selina Wilson said.

Connor thought about Lenora. She was with the diplomatic envoy on the observation deck. Lauren was likely there as well, but Ethan was aboard the *Odyssey*. He typed a quick message and sent it to his son.

When the countdown timer reached the end, the I-Drive engaged on two heavy cruisers, six destroyers, and one cargo ship. The power levels spiked for a moment as the I-Drive engaged, bending space in front of the ship. The live video feed that showed the ringed, earth-like planet New Earth disappeared from view. More than a few people on the bridge watched it in silence. The journey to the Sol System would take four months, which included a few stops along the way. Depending on what they found in the Sol System, it would be close to a year before any of them saw New Earth again. A majority of the crew had been born on New Earth, and Connor wondered what their reaction would be when they saw the birthplace of humanity. There was a difference between seeing the image of a planet on a clear holoscreen and actually seeing it right outside your window. Connor had been a different man then, and he didn't know what to expect or how he would feel when that time came.

"Colonel Martinez, you have the con," Connor said.

"Acknowledged, I have the con, General Gates."

Connor walked off the bridge with his security detail in tow. His role on this mission was twofold. He was the commanding officer of the CDF, but he was also part of the diplomatic envoy, with an equal vote on the decisions made. This had been Nathan's work. Connor wasn't in support of it at first, believing that the military and civilian roles should be separate. Nathan reminded him that for most officers that standard was appropriate; however, Connor had extensive experience within the diplomatic organization, and the envoy would need his valuable insight. The CDF was under civilian authority, but the appointment gave Connor the influence he might need, depending on what they encountered. He was one of five diplomats. Lenora was also a diplomat. Her experience with the Ovarrow and their unification with the colony had more than qualified her for the mission.

Connor walked onto the observation deck where the envoy and staff had been located during their departure. The entire ceiling was one large holoscreen that showed the waves of transient energy produced by traveling in hyperspace. There were a number of conversations going on.

"General Gates," said a voice with a precise British accent.

Connor turned and saw an Ovarrow walking toward him. The Ovarrow translator automatically assigned accents to Ovarrow at random. Connor never cared for the monotoned computer accent that tried to generalize how all Ovarrow sounded.

"Qenirian, I believe this is your first time aboard one of our warships," Connor said.

The Ovarrow nodded. It was a slow gesture and seemed perfectly natural, but Connor knew it was a habit the Ovarrow had picked up through their interactions with humans.

"Very impressive, General," Qenirian said and glanced up at the ceiling. "Remarkable. They showed us what to expect when the I-Drive was in use, but this view is breathtaking."

"I'm glad you like it."

Qenirian stared at him with his almost feline eyes. "I was honored to be chosen to join the envoy. It is a rather unique opportunity for one of my species to see your home planet."

Connor nodded. Having an Ovarrow diplomat as part of the

envoy was a bit of a surprise, but Connor could appreciate the wisdom in the decision.

"I wish it were under better circumstances. None of us really know what to expect."

"I expect you'll do as you've always done, General Gates. You've led countless missions into alternate universes and created a resistance force strong enough to stop the Krake. Whatever challenges we'll face in your home star system, I'm certain that we are up to the task."

Connor appreciated Qenirian's words, but he wasn't so sure. Dealing with the Ovarrow they'd brought out of stasis seemed a lot more straightforward than what they were likely to encounter in the Sol System.

"You have doubts?" Qenirian asked.

Connor shrugged. "Our mission parameters are simple, but that doesn't mean it'll be easy."

"These things rarely are, but I'm speaking as a member of a species whose association with yours has been hugely beneficial. You've reminded us of what we were before the Krake and inspired us to be greater than what we were. These are important ideals to strive for. However, I get the sense that this journey weighs heavier on you in particular."

In Connor's experience, most Ovarrow were quite perceptive. It was one of the skills that made them effective scouts in the CDF.

"I didn't realize I'd been so transparent."

"I've watched your species for a very long time."

"Do you have any children?"

Qenirian drew himself up. "I have many offspring."

Connor smiled. "I have two, and they're both on the expedition. My daughter is right over there, standing next to my wife."

Qenirian looked. "I see your mate…ah, and your offspring. She seems to favor your mate's appearance with her hair and physical appearance. But her bearing is similar to yours."

Connor watched Lauren for a few moments. She was twenty-five years old, but it seemed like only a short while ago that she was small enough to sleep in his lap. Her hair was darker than Lenora's, but she'd inherited Lenora's bright blue eyes.

"Where is your other offspring?"

"He's on the *Odyssey*."

"Is he a soldier?"

Connor felt the edges of his lips lift in paternal proudness. "Yes, he is."

Qenirian looked at him for a few moments. "I appreciate you taking the time to speak with me. Our work here is only just beginning."

"The pleasure is all mine, and yes, our work is just beginning. We have a long journey ahead of us, and we'll need every bit of that time for preparation," Connor said.

Qenirian walked away from him, and Connor joined his family on the observation deck.

12

LAUREN EXTENDED her hand and grabbed the almost nonexistent ledge. She had barely more than a fingerhold and pulled with enough force to reduce the weight on her other limbs. She then lifted a foot and tested the foothold before continuing to climb.

The *Douglass* was a warship but was part of a new breed of ships designed for long-term deployments. There were a number of recreation areas available to the crew and civilians aboard the ship. More than a week had passed since they departed, and she'd established a routine where most of her time was devoted to mission prep, but she also included daily exercise. Today, she'd chosen rock climbing.

The rock wall had a dynamic face that could change the entire layout to mimic an actual rock wall found on New Earth. Thousands of scans had been uploaded into the computing core and were sorted based on location and difficulty. The wall was sixty meters wide and could accommodate a large number of climbers eager to test their skills. The dynamic rock wall could also shift locations so climbers weren't limited to the height of the recreation area.

Lauren glanced down and found herself staring at the ground with quickened breath. She hadn't realized how high she'd climbed. Her forehead was slick with sweat. She released one of her hands and shook it to loosen the muscles in her arms. Then she grabbed the next handhold above her. Using her back muscles, she hoisted herself up. She was just about to reach into a shallow depression, but there was nowhere for her to get a good grip.

Lauren's brow furrowed while she considered her options. She could move sideways and climb around the depression, but that was going to take time. She was so close to the end, and then it was a free fall down using her ropes to control her descent. The muscles of her mid back were starting to cramp, and she was getting tired. She could try to push herself to the last level with a final spurt of energy, but if she misjudged the distance, she'd fall.

Lauren considered her options again, ignoring her aching muscles. She inhaled several deep breaths, building up her intent. She tensed her muscles and, in an explosion of effort, launched herself up. For a second, she was in the air, and she reached toward the handhold she'd been aiming for. Her palm hit the surface hard, and she snatched at the handhold. Her other hand slipped, and she gasped, trying to hold on with just her fingertips. For half a second, she hung there, and then she simply couldn't hold on anymore. She slid down, her elbow and knees scraping the wall. She gritted her teeth and shoved herself away from it.

The safety-rope harness sensed the increased descent and slowed her down. Lauren shook her head in frustration and lifted her knees toward her chest. She leveraged her feet to absorb the impact with the wall and pushed herself away again. Within seconds she was on the ground, her breath coming in gasps and her hands shaking. She bent over with her hands on her knees while she caught her breath. Eventually, her breathing slowed, and she slipped out of the safety harness.

"That's one way to reach the bottom."

Lauren turned toward the person who'd spoken and stared at him for a moment. She blinked several times in surprise. "What are you doing here, Isaac?"

He gave her a smile that made her blush a little. He had short black hair, a goatee, and a playful glint to his gaze. "Is that any way to greet an old friend?"

Lauren rolled her eyes and smiled.

"Look at you. What's it been? Five years?"

"More like eight."

His gaze widened. "Eight years! Wow, that is a long time," he said and stared at her for a long moment. "You've really grown up." He looked at her as if trying to combine the young girl she'd been and the woman she'd become. His smile widened. "You look amazing."

Lauren almost chuckled and glanced up at the rock wall. "I thought I had it," she said and examined her arm.

Isaac peered at it. "Just a little bruised."

Lauren disconnected the safety harness and hung it on a nearby rack. She removed the lid from her water bottle and drained it. A little water dribbled down her chin.

"I didn't know you were coming on the expedition."

Isaac shrugged. "I was a last-minute addition."

"Really," she said, unconvinced.

"Yeah, really. You can even speak with Dr. Forester if you want. I went to see him before coming here."

Dr. Jake Forester was one of the medical leaders for the expedition and also her direct supervisor.

"I didn't think you were a doctor anymore."

"Oh, I still am. I just haven't been to Sierra for a while. I've been rotating between New Haven and Delphi."

Lauren nodded. She felt like there was something off about the whole conversation, but she couldn't figure out what it was.

"Are you going to take a turn?" she asked, lifting her chin toward the rock wall.

Isaac looked at it for a second and then shook his head. "Not today. Look, I didn't accidentally bump into you here today."

Lauren pulled a towel from a nearby stack and wiped her brow, then proceeded to quickly wipe down her neck and shoulders.

Isaac watched her.

"I need to go take a shower before I return to my research," Lauren said, starting to walk away.

Isaac followed her and she arched an eyebrow toward him. "Are you going to follow me into the showers?"

Isaac smiled. "Yeah," he said wistfully, and then frowned before shaking his head. "Uh, no. I don't know what I'm saying. I'll wait for you."

Lauren crossed her arms under her chest. "Why?"

"It's been a long time and I thought we could catch up."

Lauren's eyebrows raised a little. "I'm busy."

Isaac chuckled and looked at her like he knew a secret. Then he gestured for her to go on without him.

Lauren went into the women's locker room and took a shower. The hot water soothed her muscles and made her feel better. She toweled herself dry, put on her clothes, and left the locker room, almost expecting Isaac to be waiting for her. The whole meeting had felt strange. She stopped in the mess hall and grabbed a small meal to go, heading to her office. She shared a workspace with other medical specialists on the team, so her office afforded her some privacy where she could eat and resume her research at the same time.

As she approached the office, she saw the faint outline of someone inside through the frosted glass. She opened the door.

"Excuse me, I've got the space reserved…"

Isaac looked up at her and smiled. Then he gestured toward the chair next to him.

The office had a table two meters across.

"Isaac, what are you doing? Are you following me?"

"I guess I am following you. I can't help it," he said, eyes gleaming.

She narrowed her gaze, not in the mood to be teased. Her elbows and knees ached from slamming into the rock wall.

"No. No. We're working together. I spoke with Forester, and he agreed to pair us up. Really. Here, take a look," Isaac said and brought up a data window on the holoscreen.

"No one told me about this," she replied.

"Surprise," he said and gestured toward the seat. "You eat and we'll talk."

Lauren set her grab-n-go meal on the table and looked at Isaac. "I don't like surprises. Not when we were kids and not now."

"Oh, come on. We were just having fun."

Their families were close, and she'd spent a lot of time with the Diaz family. Isaac was five years older than she was and had taken a particular amount of pleasure in teasing her.

Isaac leaned back in the chair with a smirk. Lauren really wasn't in the mood for his games. He'd enjoy it too much if she scowled at him. Instead, she turned around and leaned across the desk. She saw his reflection on the blank wallscreen as his gaze slid toward her buttocks.

"Isaac," she said evenly, "why don't you stop the shenanigans and just tell me why you're here? And if you continue to jerk me around, I'm going to make you leave."

Isaac's mouth hung open part way between surprise and a smirk. He lifted his hands in a placating gesture. "Okay, I suppose I had that coming."

Lauren chuckled mirthlessly. "That and a lot more. Three."

Isaac sat up straight and then stood. "You went right to three?"

"Two."

"All right. Fine. Forester told me you were going over the archives on the Vemus studies that were done after the war. I'm interested...I need to understand how it actually works and how we were able to stop it."

Lauren looked at him. He was telling the truth. He was some kind of doctor, but he also consulted with the colonial government.

"You have a background in infectious diseases, right?"

Lauren sighed. "You have a hell of a way of asking for my help."

Isaac licked his lips. "Technically, I was just asking that we..." He shook his head. "I'm sorry. I was attempting another joke. Yes, fine. All right, I'm asking for your help," he said and shrugged. He looked adorable doing it. "I thought it would be fun to work together. I've missed you."

Lauren shook her head. "Jerk. You can be so irritating. I was ready to... You know what, never mind," she said and glanced at the chair beside her. "If you've done something to my chair, I swear—"

"I didn't do anything to your chair. Come on. I wouldn't do

that. I only just got here a minute ago," he said and stepped toward the chair. "See? I'll sit in it."

Isaac plopped down and the chair tipped backward. He yelped as he tumbled to the floor.

Lauren laughed.

Isaac lay on the ground, looking perplexed. "I can't believe you did that."

"Oh, come on. Considering what you've done to me, this was nothing."

He sat up on his elbows. "I'm impressed. I didn't even see you touch the chair. I'm going to keep my eye on you." He stared at her for a second and then raised his hand expectantly. "Aren't you going to help me up?"

Lauren smiled and shook her head, then sat down in the other chair and crossed her legs. "You don't need my help."

Isaac chuckled as he stood up. "I suppose I had that coming, too." He adjusted the chair and sat down. After heaving a dramatic sigh, he looked at her and then grinned. "I heard that you and Ethan volunteered for this."

Lauren nodded. "Yeah."

"Why?"

"You could probably figure it out. It's my father. Everything he did for the colony and my brother, Sean. You know, for years my parents lit a candle on his birthday. At some point I remember asking about it and they eventually told me about him, and how he died fighting the Vemus on the bridge of a warship that my father stood on hundreds of years later. It just felt right to do this. To be part of this."

Isaac watched her for a long moment and nodded. "Hey, I get it."

"But that doesn't explain why you're here."

"I already told you. Similar reasons to you but without the

familial connections. I agree that we owe it to the survivors to go back and help them. I just don't know what we're going to find when we get there."

Lauren nodded. "I know."

"The Vemus War changed the wobble of the Sol System. It's a miracle that anything is left behind."

Lauren opened the lunch container and began picking away at her salad. She took a few bites and looked at Isaac. "There are a lot of people working on this," she said.

"Yeah, but they're not all as reliable as you. You know how stuffy some of these people can be. They go on about how important their research is and get twisted up in knots if someone asks a question that even remotely challenges their theories."

"I've never had that happen to me."

Isaac puffed out a breath. "Yeah, that's because..." his voice trailed off and he stopped talking.

"Because..." she said, dragging out the word.

Isaac rolled his eyes and sighed. "Lauren, come on."

She pursed her lips. "Isaac, come on," she replied in the same tone.

"You're beautiful. I mean look at you. Waves of chestnut hair with hints of red. The spattering of freckles on your nose and face. And those eyes. Geez, I'm sitting here wondering if at any moment they're going to... How many guys watch you when you enter a room? I bet it's a lot. No, don't bother answering. My point is that people, especially men, will never mind speaking to a beautiful woman such as yourself."

Sometime during Isaac's speech, she'd stopped chewing her food. She swallowed and stared at him for a long moment, trying to decide if he was teasing her again. She chewed on her bottom lip for a second and then said. "That's not it. I think the problem is you. Sometimes your mannerisms just rub people the wrong way."

A small grin bubbled up from his chest. He *had* been teasing her. He tipped his head to the side, bobbing it a little. "Yeah, maybe. Sometimes, but I still stand by what I said."

"Oh really. Are you going to sit here and tell me that women don't notice you? That cute little beard and mustache... suave, I think the term is. That grin. So don't even try that lame excuse with me," she said and stared at him for a second. "Maybe you're just a womanizer, and it's something people pick up on."

Isaac's mouth opened a little. "Oh, touché, pussycat. Ay chihuahua! Now I'm really impressed. You didn't get even a little flustered by what I said."

Lauren picked up a black olive from her Greek salad and flung it at him. He swiped it away and laughed. He had quick reflexes.

"All right," she said, "if you're serious, then I'm happy to work with you. But if you irritate me, I want no part of it. That's the deal. Take it or leave it."

Isaac snorted. "I guess I don't have any other choice. Hey, did your mother ever find out about—"

"Hey, we're not going to do that."

Lauren hadn't been the perfect child growing up. She'd had her share of mishaps and was capable of keeping a few secrets. Unfortunately, Isaac knew some of the more colorful ones.

"Okay, as always, your secret is safe with me."

"It better be," she said and brought up a holoscreen. "The Vemus is a viral-bacteria hybrid that afflicts mammalian life on Earth. According to the records retrieved by the CDF, it was first detected in Earth's oceans."

"Huh," Isaac said thoughtfully. "I wonder which ocean?"

Lauren ran a quick search. "First reported sightings came

from the western Pacific Ocean near the Mariana Trench. This says it reached the Asiatic Alliance shores and Australia sector not long after it was first detected."

Isaac brought up a model of Old Earth. Small icons appeared, showing the earliest Vemus detections they had from the archives. He let out a long exhale.

"It spread so fast, and it targeted mammalian life. I wonder why that is?"

"Most of this data was retrieved from old computer systems on Vemus ships. It's not a complete picture, but it's been theorized that it spread among whales and dolphins. They're known to roam quite far. But it wasn't limited to a single species."

Isaac nodded. "It doesn't behave like a disease, does it?"

Lauren shrugged. "There are diseases that spread across multiple species."

"Yeah, but this is one genus type. It didn't just affect the bottlenose dolphin. It also affected all the different species of whales and then spread to land mammals," Isaac said and frowned. "I can't remember the researcher's name, but they thought it was some kind of bioweapon."

"It was weaponized when it was altered to only target humans, but the damage had already been done," Lauren said.

"I mean before that. The thing that makes me go all squirmy is the fact that we have no idea where the Vemus came from. None. Did it occur naturally? You know, evolve on the planet? Or did it arrive on the planet?"

Lauren blinked a few times. "You think aliens did it?"

Isaac considered and then shrugged. "Not when you say it like that."

"Like what?"

"All full of doubt. Judging."

"I wasn't judging. It just sounds a little far-fetched to me."

"Doesn't sound that way now, especially when we consider what happened to our interstellar probes."

Lauren sighed. "You're right. Not when we consider the new piece of evidence. However, let's go less conspiracy theory and something a little more practical."

"Okay, now you have my attention."

"Life did evolve on the Earth, but it also arrived there from comets and asteroids."

"You're referring to Panspermia."

"Yes. And oceans cover a huge portion of the planet, so the idea that the Vemus hitched a ride on an asteroid or something and remained dormant deep beneath the ocean for a long time is definitely conceivable."

Isaac rubbed his beard thoughtfully. "That's a good point, but it doesn't explain the timing. How did it first start to spread? What caused it to spread? What caused it to suddenly become active and decide, hey, here's a niche that I can not only exploit but dominate."

Lauren looked at Isaac for a few seconds. "I like how you simplify things to such a personal level."

"It helps me wrap my mind around something complex."

"I don't know what the catalyst for the Vemus was. It could have been anything from happenstance by some random encounter among sea mammals or an underwater volcano that created the conditions that allowed the Vemus to spread."

Isaac smiled. "You're really good at this."

"We're just speculating. Doesn't mean I'm right about it."

"No, but some people can't stretch their imaginations even a little. But you're right. We can keep going around in circles about this and never know if we're close to having an answer."

"Maybe we'll find the answers when we get there."

Isaac nodded. "Maybe. Hopefully that happens. The other thing that bothers me is whether or not the Vemus have changed."

"You mean changed from the type that came all the way to the New Earth star system?"

"Bingo. Get yourself a piece of chocolate."

Lauren snorted. "I was thinking about that the other day, along with worrying about whether the Vemus we'll encounter are somehow resistant to our countermeasure that destroys it."

Isaac sighed. "It's a wonder you get any sleep at night. Do you stay up just thinking about all these 'what if' scenarios?"

"I sleep perfectly fine, thank you very much."

"Huh, you must be like your father."

"What do you mean?"

"Well, he came up with all the different strategies that the CDF uses to defend the colony. We're here because of him."

"Yeah, and he'll tell you it was a lot of other people who contributed."

Isaac nodded. "Yeah, I get it. We should spend some time speculating on how the Vemus may have changed over the past two hundred fifty years."

Lauren stared at the holoscreens for a few seconds. "All right. You first."

13

CONNOR STOOD in his ready room off the bridge of the ship. The alert had just come through. The forty days it had taken them to reach the probes' last reported location had passed by in the proverbial blink of an eye. He powered off the holoscreens he'd been working on and went to the bridge.

Colonel Oliver Martinez stood as Connor approached the command center.

"General, we're approaching the coordinates of the probes' last reported location. Condition Two has been set for the fleet," Martinez said.

"Understood. As you were, Colonel," Connor replied.

"Yes, General. Helm, stand by to power down the I-Drive," Martinez said.

"Yes, Colonel," Lieutenant Simpson said. She was ready to enter the commands to launch the protocols that would disable the I-Drive and gracefully bring them back into n-space.

"Colonel, I have confirmation of ready status from the fleet," Specialist Marten said.

"Acknowledged," Martinez said.

Connor watched the main holoscreen as the ship transitioned back to n-space. The shifting patterns of hyperspace gave way to flashes as the I-Drive bled transit energy in curtains of azure glow. The flashes of lights cycled downward as their velocity decreased until the ship was once again in n-space. He'd traveled into different universes using a space gate, but they'd just transitioned from going a hundred and seventy-five times the speed of light to the barest fraction of C.

"Sensors are online, Colonel," Lieutenant Tucker said.

"All ships have successfully transitioned back to normal space, Colonel," Lieutenant Wilson said.

"Acknowledged, Ops. Tactical, begin active scans of the area," Martinez said.

The *Douglass* was the flagship of their small fleet of ships, which was really just a battle group. Both heavy cruisers had an extensive scanner array, and the data from them was synced with the computing core of the six destroyers that traveled with them.

The tactical plot window on the main holoscreen was devoid of data. The probe data had indicated that this expanse of space appeared to be empty. It was just an expanse of nothing, and their scans were confirming that.

Connor allowed Martinez to remain in command for this part of the mission. Over the last forty days, he'd found that Martinez was every bit the commander Sean had said he was. Connor had the upmost faith in Sean's ability to command and nearly every recommendation he'd made when it came to CDF personnel had been spot on. Oliver Martinez had the same consistent performance whether Connor was on the bridge or not.

"Ops, you're authorized to deploy the comms buoy," Martinez said.

"Yes, Colonel. Comms buoy is deployed," Lieutenant Selina Wilson said.

"Comms, run a diagnostic on the buoy and ensure a connection to COMCENT has been established."

They waited a few moments for Specialist Marten to complete the diagnostic. "Buoy checks out, and a comlink has been established with COMCENT, Colonel."

Their ships had subspace communications and could maintain a connection with COMCENT, but there had been an ongoing debate as to the range of subspace communications. They hadn't traveled much more than twenty lightyears from New Earth. CDF R&D had designed a deep-space communications buoy that could relay subspace comms signals back to COMCENT. The sparse location wasn't ideal, but the buoy's power core would last for a hundred years. This buoy was just going to be a placeholder until a better location with actual resources available to power a comms relay station was established.

Over the next hour, their scans didn't detect any ships or find any indication that anyone had been to this area.

Martinez looked at Connor. "I think we can stand down from active status."

Connor nodded. "Agreed, set Condition Three."

An automated message was broadcast through the ship announcing the new active status that allowed the crew and passengers to return to normal operations.

"General Gates, I have General Quinn requesting to speak with you, sir," Specialist Marten said.

Connor opened his personal holoscreen and told the comms specialist to send it to him. Sean Quinn's head and shoulders appeared on his holoscreen.

"Things are pretty quiet here."

Connor nodded. "Yeah, they didn't leave a calling card for us to find."

"We're ready to scout ahead."

"Good hunting. We'll meet up in twenty-four hours," Connor said.

"You too, General," Sean said.

The comlink severed, and a few moments later, the *Odyssey* and three destroyers transitioned from n-space.

Martinez looked at Connor and said, "You don't seem surprised by this."

"This is my surprised look, Colonel."

Martinez grinned a little.

"We have to check here, but to answer your question, no I'm not surprised. There isn't anything here. We know the probes were somewhere on this path before they appeared in the Sol System."

Martinez nodded. "Why bother leaving something here when we already know where the probes have gone?"

"Yup, and we still need to do our due diligence."

"Understood, General," Martinez said.

"I'll be back to relieve you in six hours," Connor said.

Martinez frowned. "I thought Major Macmillon was on duty, sir?"

"He was, but I have him inspecting main engineering instead."

"Understood. If you'd like, I can stick around after, General."

Connor shook his head. "Won't be necessary, Colonel."

Connor left the bridge and walked the short distance to a nearby conference room.

Lenora smiled in greeting as he walked into the room.

Samantha Orthon stopped speaking and turned toward him. Qenirian looked at Connor with a stoic expression, and

Fabian Dumont had his fingers bridged in front of his bearded chin.

"Has there been any evidence of the probes?" Samantha Orthon asked.

"Not yet," Connor replied and sat in the open seat next to Lenora. "The *Odyssey* is scouting ahead, and we'll meet up with them in a day. Then, we'll continue on to Earth."

Fabian Dumont leaned forward. "Why is the *Odyssey* scouting ahead of us?"

"So we can build a more accurate picture of what happened here. We haven't detected any alien ships or technology of any kind," Connor said.

"I'm afraid I still don't understand."

"Okay, we've learned how to detect when a ship travels with an I-Drive, bending space in front of the ship and expanding it behind. The evidence appears as a specific form of gravitational waves. For the past hour, the ship's sensors have been trying to detect anything like that. The *Odyssey* is traveling ahead to extend our scanning capabilities. Eventually, they'll overlap."

Fabian Dumont considered this for a few seconds. "I don't mean to question you, but I'm just trying to understand...better understand."

"Go on and ask your question. If I can't answer, that means I don't understand how things work and I should be relieved of command," Connor said.

Dumont smiled. "I appreciate your indulgence with this. If the *Odyssey* is scouting ahead, they're presumably using the I-Drive in some diminished capacity so they don't get too far ahead. However, won't the fact that we're effectively following them mean that they'll distort any evidence left behind?"

Connor shook his head. "I can see why you'd think that. No,

we can filter out any distortion that the *Odyssey* and the rest of the scout force leaves behind while they skip ahead."

"Fascinating," Dumont said.

Lenora cleared her throat. "So we haven't detected anything? No anomalies of any kind?"

Connor shook his head. "If the probes hadn't reported in from this location, we wouldn't have known anything had occurred here."

The meeting went on for another half hour before it ended. The others left the room and Lenora stayed behind.

"One more piece of business I need to discuss with you," she said.

Connor arched an eyebrow. "Not in front of the others?"

Lenora eyed him for a moment. She was serious.

"What is it?"

"It's the training materials we're supposed to check off our lists. You're lagging behind," she said.

Connor had been so focused on the CDF preparedness that he'd neglected the other half of his responsibilities. "I'll get to them."

"Oh, I know you will. That's why we're going to go through some of them right now."

Connor groaned.

"Don't try and weasel your way out of this, Connor. It's important."

"Going over archival data about the alliances of Old Earth might be a waste of time. I'm already familiar with them anyway."

Lenora shook her head. "Only from a militaristic perspective and only if you'd come across it in your former life."

"I think you're underestimating the militaristic perspective, love."

Lenora pursed her full lips. "Oh? Please dazzle me, General Gates."

Connor sat up and leaned toward her. "All right. I had to know more about weapons and combat capabilities. I was hunting a group that operated across alliances."

"So you knew how the average citizen behaved? What they wanted? What their concerns were? You knew how to be a compassionate listener?"

"A compassionate listener? Are you serious?"

Lenora smiled. "Okay, I was just testing you with that. It's important to understand where the survivors may have come from so we can better deal with who they became. It's what we did with the Ovarrow. You did it as well."

"I know I did. I'm more inclined to deal with things like this directly. You know, by speaking to the survivors when we encounter them. Let them and their actions inform me of who they are," Connor said.

Lenora rolled her eyes a little. "You've got an answer for everything."

Connor chuckled. "Not for everything, but when I do have one, it's usually pretty good."

Lenora stared at him for a moment.

"All right, I'll make more of an effort to review the training modules the colonial government has provided. I promise."

"I can accept that. I won't need to report this little infraction to anyone then, as long as you're in compliance," she replied dryly.

Connor frowned in disbelief. "Who *are* you?"

Lenora stood up. "You didn't think you'd get a free pass because you're my husband."

Connor joined her. "No."

"Good. I'm hungry. I've been hearing your stomach growl for most of the meeting."

"I'll have a meal brought up. I need to get caught up on some things."

Lenora smiled sweetly. "Oh good, I'll join you."

Connor gave her a long look. "I really do have to work."

She nodded. "I know."

They stepped out into the corridor.

"It's just that when you're alone with me in a room, you can't control yourself," he said, teasingly.

"Must be all that masculinity. My heart simply can't take it even after all these years."

They grinned and headed to his office.

14

"You're still here?" Eva Trace asked. She sounded more than a little surprised.

Ethan looked up at her and blinked. Her long blonde hair hung loosely to her shoulders. She normally had it tied back so it better fit into their helmets.

"What?"

She snorted, eyes gleaming. "Come in, Lieutenant Gates. This is COMCENT. Are you there?"

Ethan grinned. "Yeah, I'm here. Acknowledged, COMCENT."

Eva shook her head. "Yes, I know. Did you ever leave?"

They were in the tactical training classroom. It was empty and he'd come here after their latest simulation exercise to research combat capabilities of Old Earth militaries.

"No. I mean yes, I did for a little while."

She leaned a little closer to him and sniffed the air. "You need a shower."

Ethan frowned and resisted the urge to lift up his arm to

appraise the situation. "No, I don't. Your nose is just extraordinarily sensitive. I don't know how you live with it."

Eva arched an eyebrow. Then she stuck her head out of the classroom. "Yvonne, could you come in here for a second? Settle something for me."

Lieutenant Yvonne Kazinski walked in. She glanced at both of them and frowned, then threw an accusatory look at Ethan.

Eva smiled proudly. "There, you see? Case in point. Go shower, Ethan."

Ethan looked at Kazinski. "You can't be serious. I did shower."

"No, you didn't. You couldn't have. Or else you need better soap."

"I showered right after the zed ops simulation."

Eva and Yvonne shared another glance and then grinned.

"That was yesterday, stinky. You've been here all night," Eva said and went over to the climate controls for the room. Soon, the fan kicked in.

Ethan frowned and went through the time in his head.

"What are you doing in here anyway?" Yvonne asked.

He'd done it. He'd been in here all night. He hadn't slept or eaten. "I was just reviewing the Old Earth archives to see how they expanded throughout the Sol System."

Eva's eyes widened a little. "All night?"

Ethan sighed. "Evidently. I lost track of time."

"No kidding," Yvonne said and glanced at Eva. "I gotta run."

"Thanks, Yvonne," Eva said and turned back toward Ethan. "You've been pushing yourself ever since we joined the 7th."

Ethan shrugged. "Yeah, well I just want to be prepared."

"Prepared." She pressed her full lips together for a second. "I can understand putting in some extra effort, but you're becoming obsessed with this," she said and gestured toward the holoscreen. "The Expanse Historical Records into the Solar System," she read aloud. "What...why would you need to study this?"

"It's actually really interesting. I thought we had a lot stuff deployed back home, but that's nothing compared to there," he said gesturing toward the holoscreen.

"Why though? What are you looking for?"

"I think it'll help us make sense of what's left if we know what was there before."

Eva pressed her lips together while she thought about it. "You're serious, aren't you?"

Ethan frowned. "Yeah, I'm serious. Why wouldn't I be?"

"I don't know. You just never struck me as a person who does a lot of research. I mean you know a lot about the ships we fly. We all do, but this is something else. This is more strategic, like what officers on the bridge would choose to study."

Ethan heaved a sigh and looked away from her. Then he closed the holoscreen. "It's how I spend my free time."

"No, it's how you're burying yourself under a mountain of data. I just don't understand why you're doing it. I'd hate to see you burn yourself out."

He arched an eyebrow and smiled a little. "You're concerned."

Eva shook her head, dismissing the implication, and said, "Yeah, we're on the same team. It's what friends do."

Ethan's eyebrows twitched. "I've been thinking about my brother. His whole life he fought the Vemus until they killed him. Now we find out the Vemus are still there. I just want to be ready for them."

Eva's gaze hardened in determination. "We will be ready for them."

"He died before I was born. I just feel like he had to sacrifice so much, and now I have this chance to make it worth something."

Eva pursed her lips softly and stared at him for a few seconds. "You already do. We all do."

Ethan shrugged. Then shook his head. "He recorded a message for my father right before he died. He hated his life, and he resented my father for leaving him. Now I have a chance to repay that debt. You must think I'm crazy."

"No, of course not," she said and patted his arm. He felt her warm touch through his shirt. "I get it. Just pace yourself, all right?"

Ethan smiled with half his mouth. "I will."

"And for the love of God, go get cleaned up. I'm not pairing up with you in the simulator if you smell this bad."

Ethan laughed but then he eyed her for a second. "I could use someone to wash my—"

"Nope, not even for those adorable little dimples I see you flashing to the other girls."

"Oh, come on, Lieutenant Trace. You're not like those other girls."

Eva grinned. He wasn't the only one with adorable dimples. "Lieutenant Gates, are you flirting with me?"

"That depends. Is it working?"

"You first."

Ethan chuckled and raked his fingers over his short hair. "You know, flirting is one of those things that's difficult to explain, but you know it when you see it."

Eva laughed and then shook her head. "Get out of here. I'll see you at preflight."

Ethan shrugged and walked out of the classroom. He checked the time and swore. He only had time to eat or shower, but not both.

"Hey," Eva said, tossing him a protein bar.

Ethan snatched it out of the air and smiled. "You complete me," he said and then ran out of the classroom and down the corridor.

He wolfed down the near tasteless bar and ran into the showers. After a quick wash, he dried himself and slipped into a fresh uniform. He left the showers and ran toward the preflight chambers where the rest of the squadron was meeting.

He burst through the door to find that most of the seats were already occupied. He quickly navigated to an open seat and threw a nod toward Eva as he sat down. Massey pretended to check his wrist computer. Ethan made a small flipping-the-bird gesture and settled down into his seat. He looked toward the front of the room. Captain Kujura watched him with that almost permanent Ovarrow scowl.

Captain Mike Webster stood at the podium at the front of the room. He looked up, giving the room a quick scan. "All right, looks like we're all here. I hope you're well rested because we've changed things up for this exercise."

Ethan's stomach sank. The rush of activity from showering and running here were seeping away from him. Fatigue was hovering, and it felt like he was wearing a heavy helmet.

Please don't be a long deployment. Please don't be a long deployment. Not another long deployment, he said to himself.

Captain Webster's gaze settled onto Ethan. "This deployment exercise is going to be fifteen hours."

Shit.

"You'll maintain alert readiness status for the duration."

Fifteen hours in the saddle. No chance to stretch his legs.

"The exercise will involve the use of the armored transport carrier units heading to a hot zone. The mission briefing is being sent to you now. Take a moment to read it."

Small holoscreens became active in front of them and Ethan scanned the briefing.

"There will be no time to waste. Get to your assigned simulators. Single occupants only for this," Captain Webster continued.

"Excuse me, Captain," Massey asked. "Is there time for Gates to grab a quick stim. He looks a little tired."

Several of the others chuckled.

"Dismissed," Captain Webster said.

Ethan stood and they left preflight. As they walked toward the combat simulators, Massey caught up to him.

"Geez, man, you look like crap."

"Looked in the mirror lately?" Ethan replied.

Massey grinned. "First thing in the morning. It's a beautiful sight. Damn, it's a beautiful sight. I love it."

Ethan grinned and shook his head. Massey had an ego the size of a cruiser. Sometimes it rubbed people the wrong way, but they were all a little cocky. Stinger pilots weren't the bashful type.

"Didn't see you at breakfast," Massey said.

"I was busy," Ethan replied, quickening his pace. He had to wake up as much as he could before getting into the cockpit.

The combat simulation area for pilots was the designated and multifunctional training room. It was designed to accommodate many types of training configurations beyond that of a Talon V Stinger. The small, domed-shaped simulators looked like very large eggs, but they could be joined together to mimic the bridge of a ship or that of a combat shuttle and anything in between. The CDF regulated simulation times closely so that all soldiers serving on the ship could maintain their training, as well as develop new skills. This was especially useful during long deployments.

Captain Kujura sent their simulator assignments to their

wrist computers. Ethan slipped into his flight suit and put on his helmet, which sealed to his suit. He saw Eva's blonde hair disappear into her helmet as she climbed into her simulator.

He'd hoped they could have been paired together. They could still talk through comms, but there were worse ways to spend hours in a dark simulator than alone with one Eva Trace. She waved the whole friendship thing like a shield, but she also flirted as if she were interested in something a little more intimate. He hadn't pursued it…much.

He climbed into the simulator and strapped himself into the seat. The door closed and sealed, and the flight controls came online as a perfect rendition of the Stinger's cockpit surrounded him, giving him a view of the flight deck on a Raven Class armored transport ship.

The onboard AI put the ship's systems through its preflight checks. Occasionally, the training module would throw up failed system errors to challenge the trainees, but not this time. His ship was green across the board. He transmitted his status to COMCENT.

He had fifteen hours of this, but it could still be worse, depending on what obstacles were planned. The briefing had them patrolling a potential hot zone where reported pirate activity was taking place. Their transport ship could bring the 7th most of the distance, allowing the fighters to conserve their fuel for combat operations.

The first few hours went by rather quickly. They'd scrambled to intercept pirate forces hidden among a small moon near a lifeless, planet-sized rock. One thing the multiverse had given them was thousands of star systems configurations to base their training exercises on. The training simulations they'd been using since they left the New Earth star system had been different configurations of the Sol System. The analysts had used archived data that was representative of the star system when the *Ark* departed. There were plenty of variations that changed things, like the locations of space stations and colonial settlements throughout the Sol System. Everything else was guesswork regarding what might have happened. They almost always used the Vemus in their training modules but not this one. It was a standard patrol operation, which was part of the reason Ethan's eyelids felt so damn heavy. Every time he blinked he kept his eyes closed a little bit longer, no matter how hard he tried to stay awake.

Klaxon alarms blared and Anton was screaming at him over comlink. Ethan snapped back to consciousness and scanned the data on his holoscreen.

"...hostiles inbound," Anton said.

Ethan's gaze darted toward the tactical plot.

"I can't believe it! Gates is asleep," Massey said.

"No, I'm not," Ethan said quickly, trying to stifle the yawn that was threatening to overtake him. "Copy that. Hostile fighters inbound. I'll cover you."

He slammed the throttle forward, the Stinger's power output burst to life, and the space fighter darted forward.

"Damn it, Gates, that's the wrong group," Anton said.

Another set of klaxon alarms sounded, and his HUD flashed red. Then the readouts on the holoscreens blanked out. He'd died. Outside comms was cut off. Ethan shook his head and swore.

The door to the simulator opened and bright lights came in. Captain Kujura stood outside.

"Report to the CAG immediately, Lieutenant Gates," Kujura said.

The Ovarrow stomped away without another word.

Ethan unbuckled his harness and climbed out of the

simulator. As he stepped outside, he saw Anton, Massey, and Eva exit their simulators.

Massey scowled toward him. "What the hell, Ethan?"

Ethan gritted his teeth. He'd fucked up. There was no use denying it, but he couldn't deal with Massey right then.

He walked away.

"Hey, I'm talking to you," Massey said.

"Leave it, Massey," Anton said. "The CAG will deal with it."

"So what? He falls asleep and we all get reprimanded. That's bullshit. I'm not taking the fall for this. You hear that!"

Ethan gritted his teeth and kept walking. If he stopped or did anything else, he was likely to lose it. Massey's scathing tone sent waves of anger through him. He wanted to tell Massey off, but damn it, he had messed up. They could kick him out of the 7th for this.

Captain Kujura waited outside Colonel Walker's office. "Lieutenant Gates, you wait outside. The rest of you go on in."

Massey glared at him as he walked by. Anton had a stone face wreathed in disappointment, and Eva didn't even look at him at all. The door shut and Ethan waited outside.

He couldn't hear much. He thought he heard Anton speaking. He almost hoped that Massey would do what he always did and sound off at the wrong time, but that was petty and he knew it. He inhaled deeply and sighed, then shook his head and stared at the gray corridor bulkhead.

Ten long, grating minutes later the door to the CAG's office opened and the others came out, walking away from him. Anton paused just outside the doorway and looked at him for a few seconds. Ethan stared back at his friend. With a slight shake of his head, Anton walked away from him.

Captain Kujura leaned out of the room. "Come inside, Lieutenant Gates."

Things were always worse when officers adhered to strict formal address. Ethan walked in and mentally braced himself to have his ass chewed out.

Colonel Walker watched him for a few moments. A readout of a report from Ethan's biochip was displayed on a nearby holoscreen. There was no denying he'd fallen asleep. It was a huge dereliction of duty.

Colonel Walker's gaze glinted like the battle-steel hull of a warship. "I have to say that I'm extremely disappointed in your performance today, Lieutenant Gates. Your actions not only cost you your own life but that of your team."

Ethan focused on a spot on the wall. Colonel Walker hadn't asked him a direct question and he knew better than to offer an excuse.

"What do you have to say for yourself?" Colonel Walker said.

"Colonel, I never thought this would happen. Sometime during our patrol, I just couldn't stay awake anymore, sir."

Colonel Walker gestured toward the nearby holoscreen. "According to this, you slept for nearly fifty minutes. Fifty minutes! How would you like to explain to the families of the teammates you killed that you just didn't think this would happen? That answer is beneath you, Lieutenant Gates."

Ethan started to lower his gaze but stopped. He wouldn't do it.

Colonel Walker stepped toward him. "But you wouldn't even have the option because you're dead. Lieutenant Stone, Massey, and Trace's families are all back on New Earth. They'd get a visit from the CDF to report that their loved ones were killed in the line of the duty. They'd wonder why and go through every stage of the grieving process. What they wouldn't be told is that they died because their own teammate wasn't there to back them up when they needed it. That makes you worse than the enemy."

Ethan clenched his teeth and wanted to sink through the floor.

Colonel Walker stared at him. "That hit home, didn't it? Maintaining your readiness status is just as important as that of any spacecraft. You've failed in this." He shook his head and stepped away from him.

"Captain Kujura," Colonel Walker said, "what's your evaluation of Lieutenant Gates?"

The breath caught in Ethan's throat. This was it. Kujura was going to get what he'd wanted ever since Ethan had been assigned to the 7th.

"Colonel Walker, the 7th is an elite fighting force. We're the tip of the spear. We fly where others can't. Lieutenant Gates's performance has demonstrated a serious dereliction of duty. However, as you've pointed out to me multiple times, Lieutenant Gates has demonstrated the ability to employ clever tactics while achieving mission parameters. It is my estimation that his performance is a reflection of pushing himself beyond his limits."

Colonel Walker considered this for a moment. "Beyond his limits. Do you concur with Captain Kujura's assessment, Lieutenant Gates?"

Ethan swallowed something bitter in the back of his throat. "Yes, Colonel Walker. I should have informed my team leader that I was having a problem that affected my ability to carry out the mission."

"That's the most sensible thing you've said since you walked in here," Colonel Walker replied.

"Colonel Walker, I'd like to add something else," Captain Kujura said. Colonel Walker nodded. "Lieutenant Gates should be stripped of his team leader status."

"Agreed. Anything else?"

"That will depend on Lieutenant Gates's performance, Colonel," Captain Kujura replied.

Colonel Walker nodded and looked at Ethan. "The margin for error is small. There will be no more incidents like this, or your flight status will be revoked. Is that understood, Lieutenant?"

"Yes, Colonel."

"Dismissed."

Ethan saluted the officers and left. He walked a few paces down the corridor and exhaled a blast of air, leaning back against the bulkhead.

Captain Kujura left the office and spotted him. Ethan stood up straight. Kujura didn't say anything and turned to walk the opposite way.

His stomach growled. The protein bar Eva had given him wasn't nearly enough to sustain him. What he needed was a big meal and some serious rack time. As he walked down the corridor, he felt an icy chill on his neck. Losing his flight status was tantamount to being dishonorably discharged from the CDF. He'd be an embarrassment to both himself and his father. Ethan gritted his teeth, promising himself he'd never do anything that stupid again. He was better than his pitiful performance had been in the simulator. Somewhere among the many hours preparing for what he expected to happen when they reached the Sol System, he'd lost sight of the little things that needed to occur so that he could perform at peak performance both for himself and for his squad mates who depended on him. He owed them that. He also knew that there would be no end to the abuse he was going to get from them in the near future. He'd have to take it. Sometimes you just had to roll with it, especially when you deserved what was coming to you.

After scarfing down a meal in the mess hall, he headed back

to observe the rest of the training exercise. Anton gestured for him to join them. Massey and Eva ignored him.

Anton gave Ethan a once-over. "Looks like they chewed you up pretty good."

Ethan exhaled forcefully. "Yeah," he replied quietly.

"Good."

Ethan nodded. "Yeah."

15

THE COLONIAL EXPEDITIONARY force entered the fringes of the Sol System four months after its departure from the home system.

"I-Drive has disengaged, General Gates," Lieutenant Selina Wilson said.

"Acknowledged," Connor replied.

"All ships reporting in, General," she said.

Connor nodded. "Excellent. Tactical, begin a scanning sweep of the area."

"Yes, General," Lieutenant Jim Tucker said.

Their ship deployments were such as to maximize their scanning range. Connor had decided against passive scans. Before they'd returned to n-space, he'd set the fleet to Condition Two.

The tactical plot on the main holoscreen showed a star system he'd never expected to see again. Astrogation had done an accurate job at predicting where the planets of the Sol System were located. Active scans would take some time to detect the remains of the solar infrastructure throughout the star system. They were well within the orbit of the dwarf planet known as Pluto. The video feed from the ship's sensors showed the star was still so far away that while it was the brightest thing in their peripheral, it was still small from their vantage point. It hung there in view like some wayward lamppost in the deep dark. The crew of the *Douglass* stared at the video feed.

A comlink to the conference room with the senior diplomats appeared to Connor's right.

"Congratulations, General Gates, to you and the CDF for getting us this far," Fabian Dumont said. "I never thought to see our sun again."

"Neither did I," Connor replied. His gaze slid toward Lenora and they shared a look. Her lips lifted a little and she gave him a small nod.

The crew on the bridge watched the main holoscreen. None of them had ever seen the star of humanity's birthplace, and the moment wasn't lost on them. They all shared a moment of reverie that Connor was sure was being felt on all the ships they'd brought with them.

"What should we expect?" Dumont asked.

"We've already begun scanning the system. However, it will take more than twenty-four hours to get an accurate picture. We will also begin broadcasting communications on previously known Alliance protocols used at the time the *Ark* departed the Sol System. I expect we'll get a reply from the survivors soon enough," Connor said.

"Thank you, General Gates. Please allow me to congratulate you once again. We'll be preparing a mission update to be sent back to New Earth."

The comlink severed.

Colonel Oliver Martinez came to stand next to Connor.

"Our trajectory should put us on an intercept course with the outpost that was detected by the probes, General."

Connor nodded and peered at the main holoscreen. "Even at this range we have real-time communication with New Earth, thanks to the relays we left behind on the way here, but we can't use that tech to make scanning the star system occur any quicker."

Martinez chuckled. "If we knew what was out there, this would be too easy."

"We know what's out there," Connor replied. "The Vemus are waiting for us, but so are the survivors."

"Our best guess is that the Vemus have a presence closer to Earth. I don't want to invite bad karma, but we should be relatively safe out here. At least we'll see anyone who comes looking for us long before they actually get within firing range," Martinez said.

Connor gave him a long look. "Assuming whatever is out there can't evade our scanning capabilities."

Martinez nodded. "General Quinn warned me you'd do this."

Connor grinned. "He did, did he?"

"Oh yes, he did."

"Is that why you're not surprised by my comments?"

"Not at all, sir. I trust your instincts more than other people's facts. You could say I've been a student of CDF history for a long time."

"Good to know. Definitely good to know," Connor replied.

Over the next nine hours their sensors scanned the star system, and the returns showing up on the tactical plot tugged at memories from another life. Connor hadn't seen the names of the planets of the solar system on a tactical plot since before he'd been smuggled aboard the *Ark*. Memories of his time in the NA

Alliance military stirred within him. It had been such a very long
time that with each blink, long-forgotten memories flashed to
the forefront of his mind—long-lost friends he'd served with and
others who'd only been in the background but had somehow
survived in his memories. All of them were gone, and yet here he
was. This was where it had all begun, and he would see it
through. It was the least he could do.

The sensor data populated the main holoscreen, which
showed significant metallic masses throughout the star system, at
least until Jupiter's orbit. He'd expected those detections.
Humanity had expanded to the middle of the solar system for
hundreds of years. They didn't know if any of those metallic
masses were havens for the survivors of the Vemus Wars or
perhaps vast wreckages of a war fought two hundred years in the
past. Connor pressed his lips together. Not two hundred years in
the past, not for anyone still alive. This was something the people
here had to live with and had somehow struck a balance with the
Vemus presence detected by the colonial interstellar probes. Why
had the aliens deposited the probes throughout the star system?
Had they simply figured out the probes' destination and helped
them along? Again, why would they do that, and what did they
expect to happen because of it?

His latest update from COMCENT was that the New Earth
star system was as quiet as ever, which it had been since the end
of the Krake Wars twenty years ago. Connor and a lot of other
people, both with the expedition and at home on New Earth,
grappled with trying to figure out who or what alien race had
seen fit to help their probes along their journey. He couldn't
afford to allow it to distract him, though. The Vemus, or some
variant of them, were still here in the Sol System somewhere, and
he'd have to find a way to deal with them if he could.

"General Gates," Specialist Gabe Marten said from the

comms workstation, "I've gotten several automated acknowledgements in response to our broadcasts. There is at least a two-point-five-hour lag time in communications. Computer analysis suggests it's a small comms relay station within the orbit of Saturn, sir."

"Acknowledged, Specialist Marten. Helm, plot a course to the relay station, main engine output fifty percent."

"Aye, General Gates. Plotting course to relay station," Helmswoman Jennifer Simpson replied.

"Tactical, set scanning priority for the relay station and the surrounding area of two million kilometers."

"Understood, General," Lieutenant Jim Tucker said.

A comlink from Sean appeared on Connor's personal holoscreen and he opened it.

"We just received the status update, General. I suggest we tighten our formation until we know exactly what we're dealing with," Sean said.

"We have adequate coverage from the destroyers. I don't want our sensor range impacted by the closer formation. We need to know what's out there."

Sean nodded. "Understood, sir."

"How's the crew over there?"

"Ready and able, sir. Also a bit awestruck being here, myself included."

Connor nodded. "Same here."

"I'll leave you to it, unless you have something else for me?"

There were plenty of things racing through Connor's mind at the moment, but he also knew that Sean was among the most capable fleet commanders in the CDF. Connor shook his head. "Not right now."

The comlink disconnected, and he frowned for a few moments. Ethan was aboard the *Odyssey*. Connor hadn't checked his service record in a long time, not since he'd qualified for the 7th A-Wing squadron. It wasn't because he wasn't curious. He was, but if he made a habit of checking his son's military record, he might be inclined to take some kind of action. The CDF was a small military, and old alliance traditions of not having family serve in the same command structure weren't always feasible, especially for the more senior officers. They did their best to avoid it, which was why Ethan was under Sean Quinn's command rather than his own. But still, as a father, he wondered. Lauren was on his ship, and he and Lenora saw her about once a week.

He watched the main holoscreen for a moment. He hadn't quite forgotten times of lengthy communications lag with pre-subspace comms, but it was something he'd come to take for granted. It wouldn't take much for him and the rest of the crew to adjust, but it was definitely different from what they were used to.

16

Magnus Station was located among a cluster of large asteroids a certain distance from Saturn. Shao Fen looked out the wide window of his office atop the main spire of the station. During his long tenure as president, he'd overseen an expansion of the station's capacity and resources. Food-processing plants and metal refineries gave the station and whoever led it the most influence over the people in the solar system.

Shao Fen saw a new priority report enter his specialized monitoring queue and opened it. Ivanov Yanovich had made significant progress with his highly classified project. They were ready with the next phase of field testing for the new weapon against Vemus-controlled locations.

A message came to his personal account from Shao Guo. Shao Fen followed the established security protocols and opened the message.

President Shao,

Exile program has resumed. Five travelers are en route to Earth.

They have the augmented kit, which should allow them to re-establish contact if they survive.

I'm traveling to Yanovich's outpost to check the progress being made there.

The Faithful,

Shao Guo.

Shao Fen deleted the message from Magnus Station's computer core. He was pleased that the exile program was once again in full swing and that progress was being made. Years ago, he'd killed the exile program because it hadn't yielded any results. Earth was still off-limits to them.

The door to his office opened and Nagini Shree walked in with a purposeful stride. Her long dark hair was hidden away in a head wrap. She was a middle-aged woman beyond childbearing years. Nagini had done her duty toward ensuring human survival, but her greatest contribution was from the way she helped him govern.

"President Shao, we've received a broadcast signal using the open diplomatic protocols used by the alliances that pre-date the Vemus," she said.

Shao Fen licked his lips and allowed the saliva to moisten his mouth before he spoke. He noted a small rise in his heart rate.

"Who are they?" he asked.

"They claim to be from a colony sixty lightyears from here. Most of them are descendants from the *Ark* program, which was led by—"

"The NA Alliance colonization program," Shao Fen finished.

Nagini nodded once and said, "Led by, but the participants were selected from among all Earth alliances, including our own ancestral alliance."

Shao Fen was quiet for a few moments considering. "Where are they?"

"They are on their way to Magnus Station."

"Who authorized this?" he asked waspishly.

"They had already discovered our location and were on an intercept course," Nagini answered evenly.

She'd never been overly prone to becoming rattled by his stern tone. She was cool and logical, perfect qualities in a leader.

"I understand."

"They are on their way here now. I could order our station-wide defenses to be spun up, but I would advise against it," she said.

Shao Fen shook his head. "No, you're right to be cautious. No one else would dare come here without being given clearance. We'll need to handle these colonists another way. We will need to assess them, prevent them from destabilizing what we've built here."

"Their initial message indicated they were here to establish contact through diplomatic channels and offer assistance."

"Is that so," Shao Fen replied, rubbing the fingertips of his right hand together. "What will the cost of their…assistance be, I wonder."

"As do I. They've requested that we allow a delegation to come to the station."

Shao Fen nodded. This was all to set them at ease. Very like the old NA Alliance. It seemed that the colonial descendants hadn't strayed far beyond their historical ties.

"I think it's time to assemble the advisory committee and a reception for our visitors. I also want our own tactical assessment of their ships begun. What is the size of the expedition?"

"They claim to have eight ships," Nagini replied.

"Not a very large fleet."

Nagini shook her head. "No, but they did travel sixty

lightyears to come here. I wouldn't underestimate them out of turn."

Shao Fen snorted. "It's not the number of ships..."

"Exactly," she replied and stepped closer to him. "This must be in response to the interstellar probes. It's their probes that came here. What doesn't make sense to me is how they could have communicated back to their colony so quickly."

"They must have a way to communicate that's beyond FTL. A remarkable achievement and something I wish we had. The fact, that they've received an update and then traveled here so quickly means they've unlocked even more of the secrets of the universe that have been out of reach for us."

Nagini glanced out the window, gazing at Saturn in the distance. The distinct rings were visible even at this distance without the aid of magnification. "If they're coming here, we'll need to prepare the patrons of Magnus Station for their arrival."

"Agreed," Shao Fen said.

"You are in an agreeable mood today." Nagini smirked.

"When the situation calls for it. News of our visitors will lift the spirits of everyone here at Magnus Station and beyond. A briefing will need to be broadcast through local channels."

Nagini nodded. She had a distinct way of blinking sometimes when she committed certain things to memory. It was a skill she'd learned while training for her role as his advisor. She had almost perfect recall of events in the past no matter how minute. It was one of the things he'd come to rely on from her. Her recollection didn't come with any events logged from the station's computing core. Sometimes he didn't want anyone knowing what he was searching for in the archives.

"I've sent out the meeting invites, as well as alerting our internal communications team to get the message out there."

"Make sure they keep the messaging simple and easy for people to understand."

"Of course, President Shao."

Nagini left him, and he turned back toward the window. He had much to think about. How would the arrival of these colonists impact the plans he already had in motion? He'd been mistaken to dismiss their capabilities of coming here, and he wouldn't do such a thing again. There was a way he could use them to achieve his goals, but he had to be vigilant in the protection of his people from outside influences. These meetings would test them all down to the lowliest spacer. Shao Fen must remind them of the importance of their sacrifices and not to lose sight of what they've been working toward for all these years.

He brought up a holoscreen and began recording a message to be broadcast throughout the station.

17

Connor watched as Fabian Dumont gestured toward the holotank in the middle of the conference room table. "That's Magnus Station? Why would they be located well away from any planet?"

Magnus Station had multiple large spires and spiral nexuses that attached to several large asteroids. It looked to have been patched together from other space stations and outposts and then refined to form what was depicted in a three-dimensional rendering hovering above the holotank. Connor could easily pick out the defensive platforms that were part of it.

"It's strategic. Not maintaining close proximity to any planets or significant celestial bodies like the asteroid belt of small moons allows them to control the approach of any ships in the area," Connor said.

Qenirian had feline-shaped eyes and light brown skin with high ridges on both sides of his head. The Ovarrow had been quiet for most of the meeting, but now he spoke, peering at the holotank. "This signal structure is larger than even the lunar shipyards. How does it compare with what was known to be in this star system when the *Ark* departed?"

"I'd say it was a bit on the smaller side, to be honest," Connor replied. "According to the data sent from the station, Magnus Station is home to a population of about ten million people. We had many more infrastructures farther in system that were home to a much higher population."

"Remarkable," Qenirian said. "Truly remarkable that your species has achieved so much."

Samantha Orthon cleared her throat. "That depends on how much of it is still around. We don't know if any of that infrastructure is intact. The dossier they sent is light in terms of data in that regard."

"I agree," Lenora said. "What they sent over to us was more of a light briefing than tangible data for us to review."

Connor smiled a little and almost grinned.

"What is it, Connor?" Fabian Dumont asked.

"I believe a majority of the survivors are descendants of the Asiatic Alliance, at least where Magnus Station is concerned. They only provide the minimal amount of information in their communications."

Dumont's eyebrows raised. "I forget that you were something of an intelligence asset for the NA Alliance."

Connor smiled. "Something like that. Remember, we just showed up on their doorstep. A certain amount of caution is to be expected."

"That's reasonable," Lenora replied, "but they didn't address any of our questions about the Vemus."

Dumont shrugged. "It's a discussion point for when we meet in person. Clearance has been given for us to go there."

Connor nodded. "Yes, three transport shuttles, which is

enough for the diplomatic envoy, a platoon of soldiers, and the designated supply caches that have been set aside."

Samantha Orthon frowned and looked at the others. "How many soldiers are coming with us?"

"Fifty," Connor replied.

"Do we really need that many?"

"I'd bring more if I could. There will be protective details assigned to all of you, but they'll be disguised as aides. It's just a precaution."

"Believe me, it's better that we have some protection with us," Lenora said and then leveled her gaze at Connor. "And just one minor point."

Connor raised his eyebrows.

"Protective details will be assigned to all of us."

Connor chuckled and nodded once. "Yes."

"I don't see an issue with this," Dumont said. "I recall having protective details with us in the early days of our relations with the Mekaal," he said, nodding toward Qenirian.

"How will they react to seeing me? By your own accounts, none of these people have ever seen an alien before. Are you going to warn them?" Qenirian asked, looking at Connor.

He glanced at the others and shook his head. "I don't see why we should. It'll be our little surprise."

Samantha Orthon steepled her fingers in front of her chest as she leaned forward. "I don't have any issues with that, but one of the earliest items to discuss with them is in regard to the medical supplies we've brought. Lenora is right, they didn't give us much information so we don't know what assistance to offer them." She paused for a moment. "Who are we meeting with when we get there?"

"It just says we'll be meeting with governing leadership upon our arrival. This means we'll have to learn as we go. Keeps us on equal footing, I imagine," Lenora said.

Connor nodded. "The rest of our ships will be relatively close to the station. General Quinn will continue surveying the area, building up a map of the system. I'd much rather rely on our own sensor data than anything provided by Magnus Station until some amount of credibility is established."

The others nodded. Connor could remember a time when the CDF would get a lot more pushback from the colonial government. That was partially his own fault for pushing so hard to create the CDF, but in the time since then the relationship between the colonial military and the government had improved dramatically. Mutual trust was at the foundation, as well as respect.

Connor regarded the others for a few seconds. "Our envoy has a leader. It's important, at least in the beginning, that the officials at Magnus Station recognize that, but my role here is dual. I could be called away for an unforeseen reason. Therefore, my second point of contact, at least as far as this envoy is concerned, is going to be Fabian."

Lenora had advised him against making her his second for the envoy. They were married, and it would appear to be too much like an old-world monarchy, with which Connor agreed.

Fabian Dumont heaved a sigh. "I don't like a single point of contact. We tried something different when negotiating with the Mekaal, and it just led to a lot of confusion."

"I remember," Connor said.

"Yes, I imagine you would."

"We all have our assigned specialties, so the officials will have points of contact for different types of inquiries. Also, we've had reports of smaller outposts responding to our initial broadcasts. I think it's safe to say that word is spreading about our arrival," Connor said.

"I'll be headlining the distribution of medical supplies, and our doctors are eager to meet these people, assuming they're in need," Lenora said.

Samantha Orthon nodded. "I think they will be. My engineering team has looked over the sensor scans of the station and it shows that significant portions are quite old. I expect the fringe outposts to be in even worse condition, but we'll have to assess as we go."

"I think that about wraps it up for us. We'll head down to the shuttles and be on our way. Before we do, does anyone have something else they'd like to raise?" Connor asked.

No one did.

Connor thought about the Magnus Station defenses they'd detected—mag cannons and energy weapons, nothing to indicate anything like high-yield fusion missiles. But missile tubes were easy to hide, and he'd ordered Colonel Martinez to keep searching for them.

He wanted to meet these people in person. It was important so he could get a feel for just what kinds of people had survived the Vemus Wars and whether they were someone the colony should establish ongoing diplomatic relations with. It was a steppingstone toward their real goal, which was to return to Earth. No mention of Earth had been made in the dossier they'd received. He didn't want to hazard a guess as to what that meant and was experienced enough not to allow his imagination to run away in wild speculation. However, it didn't fill him with a lot of confidence that the officials from Magnus Station hadn't been more forthcoming. They *had* traveled sixty lightyears to get here, after all.

18

THE THREE TRANSPORT shuttles flew toward Magnus Station, which was a massive body of cobbled-together outposts and smaller space stations attached to a hollowed-out asteroid. The *Douglass* maintained a position a hundred thousand kilometers from the station. Analysis of the weapons systems on Magnus Station appeared to be some point defense systems, and Connor recognized larger mag cannons designed specifically for ship-busting. Station defense was something they took very seriously, given the upkeep and probable reliability of the weapons they'd detected. Connor had no plans to get into a shooting match with Magnus Station, but their weapons capabilities were something he'd need to keep in mind.

Magnus Station was a hub that received smaller salvage ships. There were entire sections of the station devoted to processing metals mined from elsewhere.

Connor studied the facility on the nearby holoscreen.

"Looks like they have some manufacturing capabilities," Lenora said.

"There's a lot of ship traffic. They must devote a significant amount of resources to keeping things running smoothly," Connor replied.

"You'd know more about that than I would. I'd guess that if they control food processing, that would give them a lot of influence over the smaller outposts."

Connor glanced at his wife. "Magnus Station is definitely a power base, but is it the only one? We haven't been contacted by anyone else that had anything as big as this place. Is this all that's left?"

"The setup makes sense to me," Samantha Orthon said. "If they were dealing with limited resources, it's better to consolidate them in one location they could protect."

"Their weapons systems appear as if they're well maintained. But there are other areas that look run down and on the verge of failure. They have some amount of refinery capabilities, but it's limited. They're in a patching-up cycle rather than a building-something-new cycle, and they might not have the ability to build anything new," Connor said.

"The tech platforms we brought with us can certainly help with that," Lenora said.

Connor nodded.

Every bit of space aboard the Mariner shuttles was taken up by the supplies they'd brought with them, which included a couple of Levingston Tech Platforms used for building and refining raw materials. Levingston Tech Platforms were large-scale printers that could also produce larger versions of themselves to build up to a truly industrial production facility. They'd also brought additional supplies and equipment aboard the heavy cruisers, but the destroyers didn't have much to offer in terms of cargo capacity. They were warships through and through, but the heavy cruisers had external cargo containers attached to the hulls. They wouldn't help them if they had to fight, but they could be quickly cut loose, and they could always retrieve them if needed. Since the colony didn't have an overabundance of ships, they'd had to find ways to make the ships they did have capable of multiple duties.

Magnus Station Traffic Control (MSTC) guided them to a central hangar hub.

"To the belly of the beast," Connor said quietly.

They flew through the massive hangar bay doors and toward the designated landing pads. There was the slight shimmer of an atmospheric shield beneath them. The CDF shuttles landed, the pilots putting them down with the utmost precision. The video feed from outside the shuttle showed a large delegation waiting to greet them.

CDF soldiers exited the shuttles first and formed three rows off to the side. Then Connor and Lenora walked down the small ramp, followed by the rest of the diplomatic envoy. Together, they walked toward the delegation.

There were six long lines of Magnus Station security personnel dressed in brown uniforms. Each was adorned with a replica of the station in front of a star. As the CDF soldiers approached, the envoy functioned as a barrier between themselves and station security.

People gathered just beyond the line of security personnel and watched them. Connor looked at them and Lenora waved. Some of the spacers waved back at her, but more than a few were reserved, as if they weren't sure what to expect. More than a few gestured toward Qenirian and other Ovarrow that were with them. They'd never seen an alien before.

They continued toward a platform where the Magnus Station delegation waited to receive them.

An olive-skinned woman greeted them. "Diplomatic Envoy

from the New Earth Colony, it is with great pleasure that I'm here to meet you today. I am Nagini Shree, Chief Advisor to President Shao Fen. Be welcome here at Magnus Station."

She smiled warmly and gestured toward an older Asian man who stood behind her. He had short gray hair, and the skin of his hands had liver spots on them. Shao Fen regarded Connor, each taking the other's measure.

Connor introduced himself. "I'm General Connor Gates of the Colonial Defense Force," he said and proceeded to introduce the rest of the envoy.

Shao Fen and Nagini acknowledged the others in turn.

"General Gates, I too am pleased to make your acquaintance," he said and offered his hand.

Connor shook the proffered hand.

Shao Fen had a firm handshake and the gaze of a seasoned leader. "Thank you, President Shao," he replied, recalling the proper way to address a leader from the Asiatic Alliance.

"General Gates," Nagini said, "Honored Envoy, we invite you on a tour of Magnus Station before we attend a celebration to honor such a momentous occasion."

"We look forward to it," Connor replied.

Nagini gestured for them to follow, and the colonial envoy began moving away from the platform.

Connor didn't follow. "Will you be joining us, President Shao?"

Shao Fen had been speaking quietly with one of his aids. His eyes tightened ever so slightly. "I'm afraid I cannot join you for the tour. However, I look forward to speaking with you more at our afternoon meal."

"As do I," Connor replied.

Shao Fen gave him a single slight nod and Connor walked away.

Over the next several hours, Nagini Shree and several other Magnus Station personnel joined them as they were guided on a cursory tour of the station. Connor noticed that station security had a presence wherever they went, and there was always someone available to answer their questions. Connor spent most of the tour listening to the others while he watched and observed.

They traveled through many atriums where people came out to watch them. Wallscreens were active and cycled through images of the station, along with motivational messages that had a central theme:

Sacrifice for tomorrow.

Building a new world for future generations.

Unity.

Lenora walked over to him. "It's different, isn't it?"

Connor shrugged a little. "It is, but I do understand it. They've built a society here where the community has more value than the individual. Reminds me of some of the things the Ovarrow did."

Lenora nodded and glanced at one of the nearby wallscreens. "It kept them motivated, but it changed them. I understand about making sacrifices, but the Ovarrow became militaristic. I don't see that here."

"This is the five-star tour. We're not seeing anything they don't want us to see."

Lenora exhaled a little. "Yeah, I get it. I tried to speak with some of the people and it seemed as if they were reluctant to speak openly with me."

"We don't know what they were told about us before we arrived," Connor said.

Nagini Shree walked over to them. "General Gates, Dr. Bishop, how are you enjoying the tour so far?"

"It's quite interesting," Connor said. "You've had to survive for such a long time on your own. I can't imagine that it's been easy at all."

Nagini nodded. "No, it hasn't. We've made many sacrifices to achieve what we have here."

"We've noticed that some of the people are a little reluctant to converse with us," Connor said.

Nagini's mouth opened a little and then she nodded once. "We announced the arrival of your envoy just a short while ago. They're still surprised that you're here. That you were able to make the journey from so far away."

"I understand. I look forward to getting to know the people here and hope this can be the start of something beneficial for everyone involved," Connor said.

"As do I, General Gates. As do I," Nagini replied.

The tour continued. They were brought to a marketplace displaying both shops and temporary stalls, with patrons who were eager to actually speak with them. Connor wondered if Nagini had somehow signaled ahead for people to be more inviting.

Connor walked toward one of the shops off to the side. It was tucked away in a corner. Two CDF soldiers followed him but gave him enough space to limit their presence. Strings of plastic buttons hung in the doorway. Connor brushed them aside and walked in. A young, dark-haired man stared at a holoscreen and then tapped the holo-interface controls with increasing vigor. A double chirp sounded on the speakers and the young man scowled.

An older woman came through the door from the back. "Pandu! Where are your manners? We have guests," she said and looked at Connor. "Please come in. Come in."

Pandu raised his gaze and his eyes widened. He looked at Connor and then back at the holoscreen.

Connor greeted the older woman and Pandu.

"Mom, they're the colonists from the broadcast today."

"Yes, they are. Something you would've noticed had you stopped starring at that holoscreen," she said.

"It hasn't been that long," Pandu muttered.

There were small plants on rows of shelves behind the counter. The small shop had a rich aroma of different herbs and spices. Connor looked at the woman. "It's fine. I have a son who's a few years older than he is, and I remember going through something similar."

The older woman smiled. "You're very kind."

Connor introduced himself. "What do you sell here?"

"I'm Raya. We have a hydroponics lab behind here that we operate for Magnus Station. In return, they allow us to grow some of our own herbs, spices, and vegetables. Every little bit helps."

Connor smiled. "It smells wonderful in here."

Raya's eyes crinkled along the sides as she smiled. "Thank you so much. May I offer you a cup of tea? It's a cinnamon blend of my own making."

"That's my favorite flavor of tea. I'm afraid I cannot stay for very long, Raya, but I'd like to ask you a few questions if you don't mind."

Raya nodded. "Of course. I'd be happy to answer anything you'd like."

"Do you like living here on the station?"

Raya smiled. "Absolutely. It's safe here, and my work is valued. So is that of my husband. He'll be sorry to have missed you."

"Where is he?"

"He's recycling the water reclaimer filters for the sector. It's a very important position," she said.

Connor noticed Pandu watching him. "Indeed it is," he replied and looked at Pandu. "What about you. Do you like living here?"

"Yes, I have an apprenticeship with the Waste Management Authority."

Connor frowned a little. "Where is that?"

"We're in Sector 74, but the Waste Management Authority has processing plants located throughout the entire station."

Connor nodded. "Is that what you wanted to do?"

Pandu glanced at his mother. "Yes, I'll be working with fungi and other renewable recycling protocols that benefit the entire station."

"I see. What game were you just playing when I walked in?" Connor asked.

Pandu glanced at the holoscreen. "Oh, it's just an exploration-type game. It's asteroid mining, but my salvagers were attacked and I lost my ship."

Connor smiled. "Who attacked you?"

"Just pirates who live on fringe outposts. They like to sabotage the automated drilling machines I had deployed."

"Does that happen a lot?"

Pandu shrugged. "That's what…it's just a game. I'm allotted sixty entertainment minutes before I must return to work."

Connor wondered what Pandu had been about to say, but he probably could've guessed.

Raya walked over to him with a small parcel in her hands and handed it to him. "It's my blend of cinnamon tea."

Connor held up his hand. "Oh, you didn't have to do that."

"You are a guest here. I would be honored to know that you've sampled some of our wares here," Raya replied.

Connor took the parcel. "Thank you. Would it be all right if I had something sent to you later on? I'm afraid I don't have anything to give you, and it's right for me to reciprocate your generous hospitality."

Raya's eyes widened a little and her gaze darted toward the side for a moment. "Thank you, but that's really not necessary."

"You're too kind, but I'm afraid I must insist. It was nice to meet you and your son," Connor said.

He walked out of the shop and made his way to Lenora.

"Where did you go?" she asked.

"Just met a very nice woman and her son."

Lenora glanced at the small parcel he carried.

"She gave me a sample of the tea she makes. I was hoping you could have someone analyze it."

Lenora took the parcel and peered at it for a second. "I can do that," she said and began to access her wrist computer.

"Not right now," Connor said. Lenora frowned and lowered her arm. "Too many people watching. I already did a preliminary analysis, but it's just surface level. Looks like the plant material has been cloned a lot. There isn't much diversity."

Lenora nodded and slipped the parcel into her bag for safekeeping. "I see. If it's been cloned a lot, it'll have less nutritional yield."

Connor's lips lifted. "I did pay attention when you taught me about the need for genetic diversity among florae. Give me a little credit here."

Lenora snorted. "I know you did. Just like I did with all those security protocols. Have you noticed the level of surveillance they have here?"

Connor nodded. "They had a camera in the shop, and I'm

guessing they have them in all the shops. I also saw them in the corridors and atriums we've walked through."

Lenora shook her head. "Privacy must be a thing of the past here."

"Probably for most people," Connor replied.

As the tour concluded, they were led to the ministry deck where a small reception area held tables to accommodate all of them, but the CDF soldiers didn't participate. Instead, they kept a watchful eye. Nagini seemed surprised at that, and Connor assured her that it wouldn't be a problem.

Shao Fen joined them, with Connor sitting across from him. There was a formal dining table located near wide windows that overlooked a veritable garden with small ponds throughout.

Shao Fen noticed Connor watching and said, "Everything on Magnus Station serves a purpose. We squeeze every bit of efficiency from every system at our disposal. What you're seeing is part of our recycling program for water and plants, which are then used elsewhere."

Connor looked at the workers moving throughout the gardens. "I've noticed throughout the tour that you rely on a lot of manual labor. I saw metrics posted at nearly every facility we've visited."

Shao Fen nodded. "Transparency is key for all community efforts. It puts performance right there in front for all to see."

"And the manual labor?"

Shao Fen sipped his wine and then stabbed a soy-based protein cube from his plate. "Much of our machine labor force had to be stripped to maintain critical systems. There is simply not enough to go around, and the people who live here are happy to fill in the void they left behind."

Connor bit into his own protein cube. It had a slightly tangy but salty taste.

"Samantha Orthon is our engineering lead. She'd be able to help address any labor shortages you have," Fabian Dumont said.

Shao Fen didn't answer right away, and Connor was beginning to suspect that he was a little offended.

"President Shao, we're not here to judge how your station is run or how your people have survived," Connor said.

Shao Fen eyed him for a moment. "Aren't we judging each other even now at this very moment?"

Connor saw Fabian go still next to him, but he kept his gaze on Shao Fen. "I thought we were getting to know each other."

Shao Fen smiled. "Indeed, we are, General Gates."

"So help me out here. You must have encountered our interstellar probes."

"Indeed, we have. Right up until they destroyed themselves."

Connor nodded. "That was part of our security protocols that were engaged when a significant Vemus presence was detected."

"We pieced that together. How did your probes come to be here? They evaded our scanning capabilities until a few of our deep salvagers happened across some of them."

Connor considered his response for a few moments. "It's a little complicated."

"Is it? You've said that your journey here took you four months. Wouldn't it be the same for the probes you sent?"

"I'm afraid not," Connor replied. "The probes you encountered were launched over twenty years ago. We didn't expect to hear from them for another forty years."

Shao Fen frowned a little. "You must have developed some kind of FTL communications capability."

"We did. We call it subspace. That's why we were able to receive updates from the probes."

"But that doesn't explain how the probes arrived here."

"We're not exactly sure how the probes arrived here so quickly. Have you or anyone else here that's involved with deep space scans detected any anomalous activity? Something that couldn't be easily explained?"

Shao Fen looked as if he wasn't expecting such a forthright question from Connor. "You'll have to forgive my hesitation. Am I right in my assumption that before you left for the colony you were a citizen of the NA Alliance?"

Connor nodded. "I was. I served in the NA Alliance Military."

Shao Fen nodded as if he'd expected as much. "You've probably already guessed that most of the people here have descended from the Asiatic Alliance," he said and paused for a moment. "The old alliances are gone, General Gates. They were the first to collapse during our war with the Vemus."

Connor looked at President Shao for a few seconds. "The alliances may be gone, but I can see their influence all around us. Let me assure you that neither myself nor anyone else here is interested in dredging up former conflicts between the old alliances of Earth. There aren't enough of us left to continue as we were."

"I'm glad to hear you say that, and I agree with you that the old…struggles should not have the influence they once did. To answer your question, no we haven't detected anything anomalous beyond that of the probes, but I must caution you that our sensors' capabilities are somewhat limited."

"Because of the Vemus?" Connor asked.

"Partially. There are remnant structures that we suspect are home to dormant Vemus hives. Some might not be so dormant if your probes encountered them. We stay clear of them, even though they could be a valuable resource for us. The fringe outposts do as well, but there are some groups that venture on salvage runs to rare materials."

"How long has Magnus Station been near Saturn?"

"Thirty-five years. The station under my predecessor had it located much closer to Saturn and its abundant number of moons. However, we have had our share of difficulties holding onto what little is left."

"So being located here is strategic?"

Shao Fen smirked. "You already know the answer to that question, General Gates."

"You're right, I do."

"Our archives know of a monumental effort in protecting the *Ark* from the Vemus."

Connor nodded. "Yes, an effort led by Admiral Mitch Wilkinson and Dr. Katherine Stone."

"One could surmise that your colony has greatly benefited by the sacrifices of the people here at that time, as well as us, their descendants."

Shao Fen was trying to dictate the terms of the negotiations that they'd been talking around. He was trying to make it seem as if the colony owed them a debt, and Connor did agree with that to a certain extent, but outright demanding it was a bit too bullheaded.

"That's part of the reason we came back here. We also want to know the status of Earth. Is there anyone living on the planet?"

"We haven't been able to go back to Earth. There have been spacers who've tried to return, but none have been heard from again. There are obstacles that need to be overcome to determine whether living on Earth is still viable. But I'd like to get back to your colony. You'll no doubt seek to explore the star system. It's changed quite a bit since you were here last. What you will discover is that Magnus Station is all that's left of the solar system colonies. There are small outposts, but everything sooner or later comes back or depends upon trade with us."

"We will be exploring the star system and we will eventually go to Earth. What kind of obstacles are in our way?"

"We are prepared to share our current intelligence on the subject with you. Your initial communication indicated that you intend to offer your help to us. I'd like to know in what way you intend to offer said help?"

Some of the others stopped speaking and were listening to the exchange between Connor and Shao Fen.

"We will need to do our own assessment of Magnus Station and elsewhere. Those fringe outposts that you mentioned as well. Then we can come up with a plan that will assist and probably lift the living standards of everyone here on the station."

"Nagini has informed me that you have medical supplies with you. We can see that they're distributed to the people who need them most."

"I'm sure you would. We also brought with us a number of medical doctors and specific equipment that can help. We'd like to set up several clinics or even have our doctors participate at your own medical facilities. From the little we've seen here, it appears that you don't use prolonging treatments to extend your lifespans."

Shao Fen nodded and looked away for a moment. "That technology has been lost to us since the Vemus Wars," he replied with a bit of an edge in his voice. "Something else your colony has benefited from because of us. I believe I would be well within my rights to ask for reparations from your colony for the sacrifices that were made for them."

More people became quiet, and Connor knew that they were

being watched. How he replied to Shao Fen could very well set the tone for their entire stay at Magnus Station.

"The colonial government agrees that some degree of reparations is in order. However, it will be predicated on my own discretion to determine how best those reparations are processed."

Shao Fen's gaze became cold. "I see."

Connor leaned forward and felt a spike of irritation of his own begin to rise. "We didn't travel all the way here just to offload a freighter and then head to Earth. Is that what you were expecting?"

"You leave me with very little choice then, since there is a price for your help," Shao Fen said.

Connor chuckled, and the sound of it sent a wave squirming through most of the others nearby. "How hard are you going to make us work in order to help you?"

Fabian Dumont cleared his throat. "Perhaps it's best if we table this discussion for now and revisit it later on."

Connor stared at Shao Fen. He'd be damned if he was going to play into that man's hands. If he wanted to pretend to be a victim, he could go right ahead, but that wasn't going to change the fact that he intended to retain control of how colonial help was given.

The edges of Shao Fen's lips lifted, and he tipped his head to the side. "That would be agreeable."

"President Shao, it's better if we're up front about our stance on these things to avoid frustration and disappointment in the future."

"I think your stance is very clear to me, General Gates."

Connor tilted his head to the side slightly in acknowledgement. This was the first encounter where the two of them probed for the other's strengths and weaknesses. Shao Fen was trying to learn as much about them as he could. The president of Magnus Station knew that the colonials weren't simply going to comply with their every request because of a preconceived notion that reparations were owed. Connor intended to help the survivors of the Vemus Wars, but that didn't necessarily mean pleasing the leaders of Magnus Station. He expected that Shao Fen and others from the delegation would try to negotiate with a bit more tact in the future.

19

LAUREN GATES LOOKED at her father's face on the video comlink.

"When are you coming to the station?" he asked.

"Should be in a few hours. Dr. Forester is already there with a group, and I'm with the third group. We're supposed to meet up with a station rep that's going to bring us to one of their clinics."

Her father nodded. He had a seriousness about him that she'd come to recognize when he was trying to keep track of a lot of things. "Good, just make sure you have a security detail with you."

"Dad—"

"Lauren, I'm serious. I know you're your own woman and can take care of yourself, but this is important."

Lauren tilted her head to the side and smiled. "Dad, I'll be fine. We'll be with a group and there are soldiers traveling with us." She paused for a moment with a thoughtful frown. "Should I be concerned about something?"

Her father blinked a few times before answering. "It's just that…the colony is different. These people are different."

"They're still people, right?" she asked with a small teasing note to her voice.

Her father grinned. "Yes, they are. Most of the people I met are fine, but we're still getting a feel for the place. It's just different from what you might be used to." He arched an eyebrow and peered at the camera. "Look, I'm your father, and being concerned about you is what I do."

Lauren smiled. "That's sweet, Dad. I love you, too."

Her father's eyes went skyward for a second. Someone spoke to him off camera and he threw a nod over his shoulder. "I've got to go. Be careful."

"I will. I promise. I'll stay with the group," she replied, still amused and a little reassured by her father's protective instinct.

The video comlink flickered off. She stood up and glanced around her room on the *Douglass*. The accommodations weren't large, and the apartment was small, with a workspace not far from her bed. She had her own bathroom, though, which was more than her brother had, although she doubted that Ethan cared about sharing showers with other people.

A chime came from the door and she answered it.

Isaac smiled. "Oh good, I caught you before you left."

"I was just about to leave. Let me just grab my satchel and bag," she said.

Isaac stood in the doorway and glanced around her quarters. "Lauren, Lauren. Do you really leave your clothes all over the place?"

Lauren picked up her supply duffle bag. Isaac jutted his chin toward the small couch that held a pile of laundry she needed to fold. She turned back toward him. "What's the matter? Does the sight of my lacy underwear get you all hot under the collar?" she asked, stepping toward him.

Isaac's gaze darted toward the couch.

"Gotcha! Now come on. I have to go." She grinned and ushered him out of her room.

The door shut and Isaac looked at her with a small, guilty grin. "All right, you got me. You knew just what to say."

"Oh please, it's not that complicated. You guys are so predictable sometimes."

Isaac frowned. "Guys? Other men or just me?"

Lauren smiled. "Yes," she replied.

An alert buzzed on her wrist computer. She was running late for the shuttle heading to Magnus Station. She quickened her pace.

"What's the rush?" Isaac asked.

Lauren heaved the duffel bag on her shoulder. It was a little heavy. "I'm going to be late."

Isaac had to speed up to catch up to her. "Oh, don't worry about that."

Lauren stopped at the elevator and pressed the button to summon it. She looked at Isaac. "I don't have time for games, Isaac. I'm heading to Magnus Station to work at one of their clinics. Didn't you see the preliminary reports? Their medical facilities are severely lacking."

The elevator doors opened and they stepped aboard.

"I saw them, but I need your help again." Isaac nodded and bounced up on the balls of his feet with a smile. "I already cleared it with Forester."

Lauren frowned, her suspicions rising. "What did you clear with Forester?"

"You don't have to go to the station."

She exhaled sharply. "Yes, I do," she replied and pressed the button for the hangar bay level.

"No, you don't. Look, there are tons of other doctors already heading to the station. I thought you said you wanted to help the people here."

She rolled her eyes. "I do, and that's why I'm going to the station. Did you really contact Forester? You did, didn't you?"

She raised her wrist computer and looked at the travel appointment. "You cancelled my group assignment. Isaac, what the heck? You can't just show up and turn everything upside down."

Isaac's eyes widened at the vehemence of her reaction. He made a show of looking around behind him. "Have you seen my ass because I think you just knocked it off. Oh, there it is," he said and pretended to scoop it up and slap his behind.

She grinned a little and shook her head. "You *are* an ass."

The elevator doors opened. "You shouldn't have done that," she said.

She walked out of the elevator, and he followed.

"Hey, she-dragon, don't you want to know why I contacted Forester?"

Lauren shook her head. She was still irritated and resisted the urge to swing her duffel bag around. If it slammed into his chest, so be it. "You know what? I think I'll just skip it this time and get on the next shuttle. I'll tell Forester that there was some kind of mix-up. Goodbye, Isaac."

She walked away from him. He didn't follow right away, but just when she thought he'd given up, she felt him following her. As she entered the hangar bay and headed left toward the comms terminal, she spotted Isaac hovering nearby. She glared at him. "Enough, Isaac. What do you want from me?"

Isaac's gaze sank to the floor, and she felt a little guilty for a second. But why should she feel guilty? He was the one who just showed up like some out-of-control comet.

"Go to the station if you want. You'll probably help some people out. God knows they need it, but there are also a hundred other doctors that will be going there over the next few days."

There weren't a hundred doctors, but something in the tone of his voice made her not want to point out that fact. She unslung her duffel bag and let it drop to the floor. Then she rested her hands on her hips. "What is it? What do you think is so important?"

Isaac stepped closer to her, his eyes serious. "Part of the mission parameters is to learn what we can about the survivors— who they are, evaluate their living conditions, figure out the best way to help if we can or if we even should."

She nodded impatiently. "I know that. That's why we're going to the station."

He started to shake his head and then it turned into a nod, as if he were getting his thoughts in order. "Yeah, that's part of it, but getting the real picture of who these people are means we need to travel farther afield."

Lauren frowned. "What do you mean?"

Isaac licked his lips and glanced around for a second before stepping closer to her. "What I mean is that Magnus Station isn't the only place people are. There are outposts and smaller stations, people who need our help and attention. Magnus Station is getting the berwolf's share of attention, which makes sense since there are millions of people here, but they're not the only ones. To get a more accurate picture of how things really are here, we need to meet the people who don't live here."

Lauren considered it for a few seconds and said, "They can just come to Magnus Station."

Isaac shrugged. "You're right, they could, but what if they don't?"

"Why wouldn't they want to?"

"I don't know, but it's possible. The Ovarrow were reluctant to live among their own kind in some areas. We can't just depend on them coming to the station. You know it used to be standard practice for medical professionals to make house calls. This is the same thing, except…"

"We'll be traveling far from the station and the fleet," she said.

"I have a long-range shuttle with supplies waiting. Want to take a ride with me?"

Lauren raised her eyebrows. "Just you?"

Isaac chuckled. "No, there're two soldiers waiting there already. We've got room for one more. I'm a good doctor, but I could use another pair of hands."

Lauren snorted and shook her head, amused. Then she looked away with a thoughtful frown.

"What's that look for?"

Long-range shuttle. They'd be traveling away from the station where most of the expeditionary force was located. She heaved a sigh and looked at Isaac. "It's nothing. All right, I'll come with you."

"Great!"

Lauren narrowed her gaze. "I'm only agreeing to come because you're right about some people not coming here."

Isaac nodded and picked up her duffel bag. "It's the least I can do."

"Maybe you can explain to my father why I broke my promise to him."

They started walking, Isaac guiding them toward the far side of the hangar. "What promise?"

"I told him I'd stay with the group of doctors going to the station. He wanted to make sure I had a protective detail with me."

Isaac pursed his lips. "Well, you will. Burk and Nance are as good as they come. They'll be able to deal with most problems." He gave her a sidelong glance and smiled. "Then there's me."

Lauren rolled her eyes. "Did you forget who my parents are? *I'll* protect *you*, Diaz."

Isaac chuckled and Lauren's lips lifted a little.

20

CONNOR OPENED a secure subspace comlink session to the *Odyssey*. It was answered immediately.

"Connor," Sean said. Connor recognized Sean's ready room near the bridge. "Right on time."

He smiled. "You weren't having doubts, were you?"

Sean shook his head. "Not really," he said and shrugged. "What is it you used to say about being suspicious when there isn't anything to be suspicious about? Yeah, it's something like that."

Connor nodded, knowing just what Sean meant. "Still getting a feel for these people. Also trying not to make snap judgements."

"I've had my team evaluating the data from Magnus Station, which has been compiled along with our own scan data. It sheds some light on a few places farther in system, but they're too far away for even our sensors to get a more accurate picture."

The colonial expeditionary force had more or less maintained its location near Magnus Station.

"It's a slow sweep of the outer system."

"How long do you want us to stay nearby?"

"I think we can start expanding our search capabilities. Start to visit some of the nearby outposts. Just sweep the area to see what's around."

Sean nodded, looking a bit anxious to be doing something. "What about Earth?"

"Not yet. According to Shao Fen, Earth was quarantined early in the Vemus War. They refer to it as an uprising. They used defense platforms to prevent ships from going to and leaving the planet. The platforms are still operational, but they didn't have much recent data on what capabilities they had available," Connor said.

Sean pressed his lips together. "It's a weapons system that hasn't been serviced for over two hundred years. Do you really think it's something we couldn't contend with?"

"Only if we do it the right way. I want to go there just as bad as anyone, but we based our own defense platforms that protect New Earth on what was available here. It's easier to create a ship-busting platform than it is to field a warship. Even if the defense platforms here are functioning at a diminished efficiency, it's still a significant danger to us without a proper assessment."

"Understood."

Connor heaved a sigh. "I know you know this."

Sean smiled a little. "I'm not suggesting we go blindly to Earth and bypass the rest of the star system. But we do have weapons capabilities that they just didn't have here. Remember how long it took us to find a way to beat the Krake attack drones?"

"You know that better than I do."

Sean nodded. "Yeah, and now we've reverse-engineered

them." He shook his head and stared at him for a moment. "What?"

Connor inhaled deeply and sighed. "It's only been a few days, and I just came from a session with an archivist. The problem is that the survivors have lived with the star system and they're familiar with how it is now. We're not, so if going a little bit slower will save colonial lives, that's how it's going to be."

Sean swallowed. "I understand, Connor."

He held up his hand. "It's not you, Sean. I just learned about some of the tactics they used during the Vemus uprising. They'd taken to slinging asteroids at solar colonies to try to prevent the spread of the enemy. They even tried to do the same to Earth, but they couldn't get past the defense platforms. They caused so much disruption among the asteroid belt that it changed the wobble we observed from New Earth."

Sean's mouth hung open. Neither of them were unfamiliar with the destructive power at their disposal. The survivors had fought a war on an almost unimaginable scale. The more he learned about it, the more it stirred the old pangs of guilt that he'd left a son here to face it alone. Mitch Wilkinson might have looked after his son, but he wasn't his father. It had been Connor's job and he'd failed. No matter how much time passed, it didn't change what had happened.

"The Krake did worse to the Ovarrow," Sean said.

Connor closed his eyes for a second. He remembered when Sean had been a fresh-faced recruit defying his own father to join the CDF. Over the years they'd become friends, but Connor regarded Sean as a son—the son that he'd lost. It wasn't fair to put that on someone else, but it had happened.

He nodded. "Shao Fen says there are locations where there are dormant Vemus."

"They confirmed it?" Sean asked.

"They learned not to go to certain places. He also said there were some outposts and salvagers that ventured into some of those places, and they'd bring back things to trade. He's reluctant to trust the reports from the salvagers."

Sean rubbed his beard thoughtfully. "We'll need to investigate those places."

"Yeah, if we can make it safe enough for spacers to go retrieve useful material, that would be good for everyone."

Sean smiled. "I was almost concerned you were going to volunteer us for salvage duty."

Connor shook his head. "Not yet. It depends on what's left. You never know what was left behind. Some of it could be dangerous in the wrong hands."

"Is there friction among the locals?"

"They're people, Sean. It's not one big happy family. There have been skirmishes in the past, and there have been a couple of incidents since we've been here. Strange messages appear at some of the community's gathering places." He shared an image captured by one of engineers on an inspection tour.

"They're among us?" Sean asked. "Doesn't tell you much. Who's among them? What's with that symbol?"

"I'm not sure. I'm going to bring it up later this afternoon."

Sean smiled. "I see you're going to kick over a few rocks."

Connor shrugged. "Yeah, something like that. It might be nothing. Resources have been scarce here, so they've had to manage what's available. Not the easiest position to be in."

Sean nodded. "What about President Shao? What's he like?"

"He's older. He plays his cards close to the chest. You know what I mean?"

"Yeah, I know the type. So that means you're using those diplomatic skills I keep hearing about."

Connor laughed. "Absolutely. They're different here, and I think some of them resent us a little bit."

"They've had to struggle to survive. So did we, but we're thriving. Meanwhile, they're still surviving."

Connor nodded. "You hit the nail right on the head. I've authorized some scouting missions. There will also be some long-range transport shuttles going out to the smaller outposts."

"Okay, good. I'd like to authorize some training missions with our fighter squadrons. They've been practicing in simulators for the past four months, and they need time in the pilot's seat again."

"That's a good idea. Coordinate with Martinez," Connor said and thought about Ethan. He imagined that his son was very anxious to get out of the simulator. "How's Ethan doing?"

Sean smiled. "He's fine. Had a few hiccups a few weeks ago, but that's been worked out. I was almost wondering if you were going to ask."

Connor rolled his eyes. "I wasn't sure if I was going to. I don't want to give preferential treatment, but I'd like to know how my son is doing."

"Oh, I understand. He's a good kid. Hell of a pilot. His aptitude scores are off the charts."

Connor grinned. "He doesn't get that from his mother."

Lenora liked to forgo some of the safety regulations in favor of creating a few of her own. She'd gotten much better, but flying with her had been a white-knuckle affair in the beginning.

"Ethan definitely pushes the boundaries. He's been more serious than his previous psych evals indicate he used to be," Sean said.

Connor nodded soberly. "That's not surprising. Both he and Lauren had very specific reasons for wanting to come on the expedition."

Sean eyed him for a second. "They're not the only ones, Connor."

Connor met Sean's gaze for a moment in silent acknowledgement. "I've got to get going. Maybe one of these times we'll actually get to do it in person."

Sean laughed. "Whenever you need rescuing from diplomatic madness, let me know. I have a team of very highly trained soldiers that are just chomping at the bit for an extraction mission."

Connor laughed. "Get out of here."

21

THE LONG-RANGE SHUTTLE flew away from the ship with Lauren in the copilot's seat. Isaac entered the coordinates into the shuttle's nav system, and once they were far enough away from the ship, he engaged the autopilot. The power output from the shuttle's main engines increased, and they sped away from the expeditionary force.

Lauren looked at the video feed on the holoscreen. There were groups of smaller ships flying away from the colonial ships.

"See, I told you we're not the only ones scouting the area," Isaac said.

Lauren spotted a group of ships flying in a tight formation. "Those look like space fighters, Stinger class. I wonder where they're going."

Isaac peered at her holoscreen. "You think Ethan is out there?"

She nodded. "Probably."

Isaac looked back at his workstation and checked a few subwindows. "Looks good so far."

"Where are we going first?"

"There are a couple of mining outposts a bit far away. I thought we'd go there first, then decide from there."

Lauren frowned and swung her chair toward him. "Decide from there? I thought you registered a flight plan with COMCENT?"

"I did." He arched an eyebrow at her. "Plans can change, Lauren."

"Do they?"

Isaac shrugged. "Sometimes. A list of outposts and stations was provided by Magnus Station, but there are others that we've detected with our long-range scanners. I'd like to check those out."

Lauren narrowed her gaze. "Since when do you have access to long-range scan data?"

Isaac chuckled a little. "It's all in how you ask."

She shook her head a little.

He rolled his eyes. "I requested it. This is all legit." He stood. "Come on, I'll introduce you to Burk and Nance."

Lauren pursed her lips and glanced at the main holoscreen. The long-range plot showed their flight path, and they had more than five hours to their destination. Suspecting that Isaac hadn't told her everything, she stood and followed him out of the cockpit. As they headed toward the shuttle's cargo area, she heard two people talking.

"You've got to be kidding me, Burk. I brought the field kit."

Lauren heard a deep voice chuckle.

"Steady, Corporal Linette."

"You do this after the morning I've had? I swear I'm going to —" Corporal Linette stopped speaking, noticing that they weren't alone.

"Good morning, everyone. Got one more addition to our team here," Isaac said.

Nance Linette was the same height as Lauren. She had short curly hair, pale skin, and an athletic build. Her dark eyes were confident, but she looked a little irritated.

"Hello, I'm Lauren," she said.

Nance smiled. "This is Sergeant Carl Burk," she said, gesturing to a tall, dark-skinned man.

"Ma'am," Burk said. He peered at her with a thoughtful frown. "Dr. Lauren Gates?"

Lauren nodded, knowing what was coming next.

Burk glanced at Nance for a second. The other frowned. "Are you General Gates's daughter?"

When people—particularly soldiers—learned who her father was, they seemed to adopt an air of formality with her. She wished they wouldn't, but sometimes it was unavoidable. "I am," she replied.

Burk's gaze darted toward Isaac. "You didn't tell me *she* was your second passenger."

Isaac pursed his lips. "She was a last-minute addition. Why? What's the problem?"

Burk scratched his eyebrow. "We have to go back to the ship."

Isaac shook his head. "Yeah, we're not going back."

Burk stood taller and his muscled chest pressed against his uniform. "She's a VIP. Protective details for them must have a minimum of six soldiers."

Lauren glanced at Isaac for a second before looking back at the soldier. "Six? Standard protocol for protection details is two soldiers."

Burk shook his head. "They've been updated. It came down from the top."

Anything that came down from the "top" meant it came from her father. There wasn't anything she could say. Orders were orders, and she'd be wrong to put Burk in a position where he'd be disobeying orders.

Burk looked at Isaac. "Are you unwilling to return to the ship?"

Lauren glanced at Nance. The other soldier became still. What had been friendly banter had become much more serious.

Lauren looked at Isaac, who stared at Burk with a slight smirk at the edges of his lips. "Let's take it down a notch, guys."

Isaac glanced at her and nodded. He brought up his wrist computer and began keying something into the holoscreen. Burk and Nance's wrist computers chimed. "Have a look at that, Sergeant Burk."

Burk narrowed his gaze for a few seconds and then looked at his holoscreen.

"That should get us the clearance we need. We can always rendezvous with a CDF patrol and take on more protection if it becomes necessary," Isaac said.

Lauren frowned. Nance seemed to relax, and Burk closed his holoscreen, looking resigned. "Understood, sir. Thanks for clearing that up," he said and looked at Lauren. "Apologies, Dr. Gates. We're good."

"Are you sure, Sergeant? I don't want you to get into trouble," she said.

Burk shook his head. "It's fine. Dr. Diaz cleared it up."

"I think we can let the formalities lapse a little bit," Isaac said. "We're going to be traveling together for a while." He stuck out his hand, and Burk shook it. Something unspoken seemed to pass between the two of them.

Burk turned toward Lauren. "I'm Carl."

Lauren smiled. "A pleasure to meet you, Carl. I assure you that as far as VIPs go, I'm not like some of the others."

Carl smiled. "No, I imagine you're not."

"Doesn't matter," Nance said and grinned. "If anyone even looks at you the wrong way, there will be hell to pay. I'll make sure of it."

"Well, let's hope it doesn't come to that," Lauren replied.

Things became much more relaxed after that. They spent some time inventorying their supplies. The transport shuttle had quite a bit of storage space—more than what Lauren had expected.

"I'm not sure what kind of docking mechanism is available at these outposts, so we might have to do a quick EVA to gain access to some of these places," Isaac said.

Lauren had only been partially paying attention. She looked up from the holoscreen. "What?"

Isaac repeated himself, and Lauren's mouth went a little dry. He frowned a little. "What's the problem? You're cleared for EVAs, right?"

Lauren crossed her arms. "I am, but it's been a while."

Isaac shrugged. "You'll be fine. Might not even be an issue."

Lauren stood. "I'm going to stretch my legs."

They'd been traveling for a couple of hours. She made her way toward the back of the shuttle where the EVA suits hung in their compartments and suppressed a shiver as she stared at them.

"Hey," Nance called out. She must have followed her.

"Hey."

Nance looked at her for a second. "Those two probably didn't notice, but I did. How long has it been since you've done an EVA?"

Lauren swallowed hard, and her eyes darted back toward the suits. She sighed. "Geez, it's probably been over five years."

Nance nodded with a smile. Then she walked over toward the compartment. "No problem. Let's just go over it. Take a bit of a refresher. Is that okay?"

Lauren heaved a sigh and smiled a little. "Yeah, I think that would be a good idea."

Nance gestured for her to come to her side where she went over the basics of the standard EVA suit, how they worked and what the different systems were and their function. It wasn't anything Lauren didn't know, but she was glad Nance was going through it with her.

"I've always loved clicking my heels together to activate the magnetic boots, don't you?" Nance asked.

Lauren chuckled. "I think you've had more experience with this than I have."

She shrugged. "I spent a lot of time at Lunar Base and Phoenix Station growing up. EVAs were par for the course in order to get outside. I'm sure you'll do fine."

Lauren hoped she would. She had never been eager to leave a perfectly good spacecraft for any reason but to disembark onto a landing pad. They practiced getting into the EVA suits a few times and she began to get a little more comfortable with it.

"Thanks for this, Nance. However, I hope we don't have to use them."

She grinned. "I'll be right there with you. We girls need to stick together. You know what I mean?"

Lauren chuckled. She liked the young soldier. She had such an agreeable personality.

"Attention," Isaac's voice came over comms. "We're coming toward our first destination. Does anyone want to join me in the cockpit for first-contact protocols?" he asked and paused for a moment. "Not you, Carl. Nance, not you either, but it's not what you think. Lauren, I need you. Sometimes people just like talking to you more than they do to me."

Nance shook her head and grinned. "He's so funny. Has he always been like that?"

Lauren rolled her eyes and smiled. "Ever since we were kids."

They started heading toward the front of the shuttle. "Oh, you've had to put up with him for a while now."

Lauren chuckled. "Something like that."

"He's a cutie."

She smiled. "And he knows it."

Nance shrugged. "They usually do."

Nance sat in the passenger area with Burk.

Lauren walked toward the cockpit. The sliding door was open.

Isaac glanced at her as she sat down. "Good, you're here."

"How could I ignore such a heartfelt plea?"

He chuckled a little. "I'd be lost without you."

A broadcast comlink became active. "Unidentified ship. You're not authorized to approach. Best be on your way."

Isaac pressed the stud to activate the comlink. "Hey there. We've come such a long way to see you, though."

There were a few moments of silence.

"Piss off or we'll open fire."

"Now, don't be like that. I'm Isaac Diaz on the shuttle Tilderon. Magnus Station should have sent out a broadcast about some new visitors. Both myself and Dr. Gates are medical doctors. We've brought some supplies with us. We just happened to be in the neighborhood and were told you wouldn't mind if we stopped by. What do you say?"

A burst of mag cannon fire was detected by the shuttle's

sensors. Isaac activated maneuvering thrusts and the shuttle altered its trajectory.

Isaac looked at her. "Just a warning shot."

"That's right, wanker. The next one won't be," the man said.

Isaac winced. He hadn't muted the comlink. He grinned a little. "Hey, come on."

"Sir," Lauren said, "please hold your fire. I'll send you the credentials provided to us by Magnus Station."

"Fuck Magnus Station. We don't need 'em. Now get out of here before I actually target your ship," the man said. He seemed as if he was going to say something else, but someone interrupted him.

"We'll go," Lauren said.

"I guess we'll mark Outpost 884 as hostile then," Isaac said.

They waited a few moments more, and Lauren said. "Let's get out of here."

Isaac stared at the holoscreen and pressed his lips together.

A new voice came on the comlink. "Hold on. Shuttle Tilderon, is it?"

"That's right. Who's this?" Isaac asked.

"I'm Sekino. Did you say you have doctors onboard?"

"Yes, both Lauren and I are doctors. We're here to help."

"Come on, Sekino. This is bullshit. Magnus Station wouldn't send any of their doctors out here. Send them on their way."

"Braun, calm down."

Lauren activated the camera to the comlink. "There's a video feed available. It would be great if we could see who we're speaking with."

"Don't do it, Sek. They'll take control of our computer systems," Braun said.

Isaac glanced at her.

"Check the comlink signal. It's just a simple protocol," Lauren said.

"She's right," Isaac said. "Check the layer protocol. Nothing is hidden."

"I'm going to check," Sekino said, and they heard Braun grumble.

About a minute later she saw two men on the shuttle's main holoscreen.

Sekino was of Asian descent. He was older, with short black hair. He waved and made quick introductions. Braun was huge, with thick muscles that bulged against his tight shirt.

"Easy there, Braun. We've got some high-density protein packs for you if you let us dock," Isaac said.

Braun narrowed his blue-eyed gaze.

"You don't look like anyone from Magnus Station," Braun said and looked at Sekino. "The uniforms are different."

Lauren looked down at her blue flight suit. "I can explain who we are. We did just travel here from Magnus Station, but you're right, we're not from there."

Braun leaned toward the camera. "What outpost are you from then? Where'd you get these supplies you say you have?"

"That requires more of an explanation. Probably better in person, but we're not from any outpost you've heard about," Isaac said.

Braun turned to the side and Lauren spotted reddish patches on his neck and arms. Lauren recognized the hallmarks of a problem with his immune system, something that with proper treatment, she could cure.

"Braun," Lauren said, "I can help those patches on your neck and arms. They're from a problem with your immune system, probably psoriasis. I have medicine that can treat it. Are you the only one with it? It can be hereditary."

Braun's mouth slackened and he blinked.

"See," Sekino said. "They're here to help. There are only two of them."

"Actually," Isaac said. "There are four of us." Sekino and Braun looked at them. Isaac shrugged. "I thought it best to be up front about how many people are on the ship."

"I'm clearing them to land," Sekino said and looked at them. "I've disabled our defense systems. You're cleared to dock. Sending coordinates now."

"Thanks, we'll see you in a few minutes," Isaac said and closed the comlink. He looked at Lauren with raised eyebrows. "See, people like you."

"It's called a bedside manner."

Isaac shrugged. "We got it done. I'm just giving credit where it's due."

"Why thank you very much. Maybe you can answer something for me."

"Sure."

"What did you send to Carl that made him change his mind about the protective detail protocols?"

"Oh that," Isaac said and looked at the coordinates sent over from the outpost. He engaged the shuttle's thrusters. "It's nothing."

Lauren gave him a sidelong look. "No, it's not."

He shrugged but wouldn't look at her. He actually made a point of not looking at her by pretending to fly the shuttle, as if it needed all of his attention. He was a good pilot. He could dock the shuttle in his sleep.

"Isaac," she said.

"I…" he began to say and stopped. "I have elevated privileges that get me a certain amount of cooperation."

Lauren frowned. "What kind of privileges?"

"Look, it's nothing. Carl won't get into any trouble, and we can take care of ourselves."

Lauren considered pressing him for more of an answer but decided not to. She could take care of herself, but her father hadn't just elevated the protection details for her; it was for all VIPs. She didn't know why but wondered if they might be getting in over their heads. Isaac didn't look worried at all. She'd have to trust him.

"All right, fine," she said, finally.

Isaac guided the shuttle to the port airlock, which was compatible with the shuttle. No EVA required, thank God.

They carried a couple of storage containers with medical supplies to the airlock.

"We can bring more than this," Lauren said.

Isaac nodded. "I know, but let's see what they need first before we unload what we've got." He scratched the side of his head and looked at the soldiers. "Do you have any training on standard life-support systems?"

Burk nodded. "Yeah, a little bit."

"Same," Nance said. "And food-processing systems."

"Good, we'll see if they'll let you check those systems. Lauren and I will set up shop wherever they give us space," Isaac said.

"They shot at us," Burk said. "At least one of us will stay with you at all times. If you want to check other systems—if they let you—we'll do it together. Are we on the same page here?"

Lauren looked at Isaac. "He's right. We need to stick together. Let's not get ahead of ourselves here."

Isaac bit his lower lip and nodded. "Okay." He smiled. "I'm glad we got that out of the way." He leaned down to grab the end of a storage crate.

Nance grinned and helped him.

The airlock doors opened, and a blast of cooler air greeted them.

Sekino waved enthusiastically at them. "Welcome. Welcome. Come aboard. We're lucky to have you."

Braun towered next to him. He raised one of his hands. "Just a second. I need to scan them for contagions."

"We've followed decom protocols," Isaac said.

Braun's face might as well have been carved from battle steel.

Lauren held up her hands. "Go ahead. Scan away."

Braun looked at her and then stepped closer, raising a handheld scanner. His gazed flicked toward the small screen. "She's clean. Next," he said.

Braun scanned the rest of them, and they were all negative.

"What does the scanner look for?" Lauren asked.

"Various contagions we've encountered, including the Vemus," Sekino said.

Lauren glanced at Isaac for a second and frowned. "Where can we set up?" she asked.

Sekino guided them to an elevator a short distance away that would take them to a small commons area. The elevator doors opened to a roomful of people waiting to see them. Lauren hadn't seen such an age range of people before. Back home, the colonists mostly appeared younger, but here there were quite a few older people mixed with the younger. Some of the children looked a bit on the thin side.

Sekino smiled a little. "We don't get many doctors here. We've had to rely on an old autodoc that hasn't received an update in over a century. We're actually lucky to have it. Some outposts don't even have that."

"Really. Not even an autodoc? How do they get treatment?" Lauren asked.

"Most people have basic first aid skills, but for anything

serious… if they don't have an autodoc, their chances of survival aren't very high," Sekino said.

Lauren looked up at Braun. He'd been listening.

"You said you could cure these," Braun said, gesturing toward the patches of skin near his elbow.

"I should be able to. I'll need to examine you before I do anything."

Braun shook his head. "Not me," he said and looked away. "Amelia, come over here. Come see the doctor."

A woman walked a little girl toward them. She had a significant red, flaky skin growth that nearly shut one of her eyes. The right side of her head was a patchwork of hair and irritated skin. One of her shoulders was lower than the other, and Lauren noted the severe curvature of the little girl's spine. She suffered from more than just psoriasis.

The little girl looked to be about seven years old. She peered up at Lauren with one blue eye that was a mirror image of Braun's. Lauren quickly squatted down so she was at eye level. "Hi there. Are you Amelia?"

The little girl glanced at her father and then back at Lauren. She nodded.

"That's such a pretty name. My name is Lauren. Why don't you come over here and sit down," Lauren said, gesturing toward a small chair next to a folding table. She looked at Nance. "Can you set up a curtain for us, please?"

Nance nodded and looked away from the little girl. "Yes, of course."

Lauren looked at Braun. "Are you her father?"

Braun nodded.

"Okay, please come over here with us," Lauren said.

Braun stepped closer, coming to stand near his daughter. Amelia leaned closer to him.

"Is her mom nearby?" Lauren asked.

Braun shook his head. "She's on a salvage run."

"Oh, okay," Lauren said and looked at Amelia. "Is that right? Does your mom fly the ship?"

Amelia shook her head. "She keeps the engines running and commands the crew."

Lauren nodded, impressed. "That's one of the most important jobs on a ship," she said.

She opened her medical field kit. Amelia watched her carefully. Lauren had worked with kids during her training at Sierra Medical Center, but she'd never seen such a severe case of scoliosis and psoriasis. She picked up a small chrome-colored scanner.

"This will help me get a good look at you. Do you mind if I bring it toward your head? Then I'll run it down to your toes. You won't feel a thing. Is that okay?" Lauren asked.

She often got the best cooperation from kids when she asked their permission.

Amelia swallowed and glanced at her father.

"It's all right, peanut. Let the doctor look at you," Braun said.

Amelia looked at Lauren and nodded shyly. "Okay."

Lauren smiled. She brought the scanner near Amelia's head. "Just relax. I'll even give you a turn."

The Agrius scanner was the latest in bioscan tech, capable of performing a wide cadre of tests. Lauren activated it and the tip began to glow a soft green color. It sampled a patient's skin and could penetrate to the internal organs. It also sampled Amelia's blood. The data was uploaded into the portable console, which her wrist computer had a data connection to. A long list of ailments began to appear on Lauren's HUD, and she felt a pang twist deep in her chest. Amelia suffered from rudimentary things like malnutrition and radiation exposure, likely from faulty shields in the old outpost, to severe cases of autoimmune diseases that had been extinct since before the *Ark* left the Sol System.

A worried frown pinched Braun's expression.

"Is it done? Are you going to give me medicine now?" Amelia asked. "Will this help my eye? It hurts and itches sometimes."

Lauren smiled a little, even though emotions were rising inside her. Amelia had suffered so much. How many more kids and adults here were suffering like this?

"Yes, honey. I'm going to help your eye and your back and everything, I promise. Just sit tight for me," Lauren said and looked at Braun. She wanted to ask him why they hadn't gone to Magnus Station for help. Were things so bad that they'd refuse to help them? She tried to keep the accusation from her eyes, but Braun wasn't fooled.

Lauren closed her eyes for a moment. She shook her head, clearing away distracting thoughts. Amelia needed her and so did a lot of other people. She'd figure out why these people lived like this later.

"I can help her," Lauren said to Braun. "I have medical nanites that will purge the illnesses that have been detected. The curvature of her spine can be corrected too, but it'll require multiple treatments. I can go over everything with you."

Moisture gathered in Braun's eyes. "If you can help my daughter, I'll do anything you ask of me. Anything!"

Lauren saw the utter desperation in Braun's eyes—the fierce protectiveness of a father, along with what must have been a constant strain from watching his daughter suffer and wither away. She knew the hardened glint in someone's eyes who'd seen many tragedies in their lives. They reminded her of her father, and it made her more determined to help Amelia and everyone else here all the more for it. "Okay, I'll get started, but you'll need to be part of her treatment plan. You'll need to monitor for certain things. I'll have a list for you, as well as ongoing applications that I'll leave you with," Lauren said.

She began programing the medical nanites with healing directives so they could prioritize certain ailments over others. An alert appeared on her personal HUD. The scanner had detected Vemus mutations within Amelia's DNA. Lauren frowned and checked the test results. Amelia hadn't been turned into a Vemus, that much was obvious, but mutations had been detected.

"I need a moment, please. I'll be right back," Lauren said.

She walked over to Isaac. He was speaking to Sekino but stopped. She gestured for him to come over to her.

"What is it?"

"Bioscans have detected trace mutations associated with the Vemus."

Isaac eyes widened. "Are we…" he began to say and then stopped.

"I don't think so. She's not actually a Vemus, but there are markers there. They all might have the same. We'll need to scan for it," Lauren said.

Isaac nodded. "Okay, I'll add that to my scan protocols."

"Should we tell them?"

He shook his head. "Not yet. Let's gather some data and then make a decision."

Lauren nodded. "Isaac, they're in worse shape than I ever imagined."

He nodded grimly. "This is why we're here."

Lauren nodded once and returned to Amelia. She was determined to heal that little girl and everyone else on this outpost.

22

LENORA SIPPED her coffee and sighed, giving Connor an approving nod. "We've only been here a week, but I'm so happy you got this brought over from the ship."

Connor lifted his mug in salute, then drank. "Not as tangy as what they've been giving us here."

"Samantha has engineering teams helping to service parts for their water purification systems. It's already improving."

Connor nodded. They'd been making steady progress to help improve critical systems on Magnus Station. Even Shao Fen had become more forthcoming after their initial frosty reception. He still didn't trust him, but they had to work together. Lenora had also found reliable people to work with through her own efforts.

"They need resources," Connor said.

Lenora finished her coffee and set her mug down on the small table. They'd been given temporary living quarters on the station. The entire envoy had a section set aside for them. The rooms appeared to be converted workspaces, but it wasn't anything they hadn't lived in before. Three of the open apartment walls had streaks of gray that could be seen underneath old paint. The rear-most wall was a dark rock that had been smoothed over from when the asteroid had been hollowed out. They had a small bathroom and living space, but that was about it.

"Did Shao Fen make the request?" Lenora asked.

"The formal request just came through," he replied. He activated a portable holoscreen and showed it to Lenora, watching as she quickly scanned the document. She was one of the fastest readers he'd ever seen. "They want us to help their salvagers retrieve material, so it's more like an escort-type mission."

She nodded, still reading the document. Then she looked at him. "At least it's not that far away. Saturn has enough moons to make it a mini star system all by itself."

"It's one of the reasons there was so much infrastructure here. It pales in comparison to what was built near Jupiter and the asteroid belt, though."

"Yeah, but if they can finally get access to the places that were off-limits before, that would help them a lot and open the door for the smaller outposts to get the resources they need as well. What's the downside here?" Lenora asked. She propped her knee up on her seat and rested her chin on it.

"It's a lot to cover," Connor said. He brought up a regional map of Saturn. "They've been focusing their salvage efforts in these sectors, but they're fringe. They've encountered automated defenses in what was previously more populated areas."

Lenora eyed him for a few moments. "And."

"I'll be returning to the *Douglass* for this. I need to be on the bridge," Connor said.

Lenora nodded slowly. "Okay. What about the rest of us?"

"You'll continue on as you've been doing. The cargo ship is staying with at least one destroyer escort."

"You don't think Martinez can handle this?"

Connor tipped his head to the side once. "It's not that. Colonel Martinez is every bit as good as Sean said he was. But I need to be there."

"How long will you be away?"

"Probably a few weeks, depending on what we encounter. We'll make a sweep and take out the automated defenses, then allow the salvagers to go pick the area clean."

"Will it be enough?"

"It's going to be a start."

"A step in the right direction then. I wonder if they'll move the station closer to Saturn after that."

Connor shrugged. "Hopefully they will once we get things stable out here. Then we can work our way toward Earth."

Lenora pursed her lips and nodded. "Any idea what kind of weapons systems they had at these places?"

Connor shook his head. "Not anymore. A lot changed after the *Ark* left. They definitely specialized in ship-busting defensive measures."

Lenora nodded soberly. "I'd be lying if I said I'm not going to worry about you."

Connor smiled a little. "I'd be concerned if you weren't worried. It would mean you're happy to be rid of me."

Lenora grinned. Then she leaned across the table to kiss him. "Never."

They stood up.

Connor stared at her for a moment. "Just make sure you keep your security detail with you wherever you go."

"Of course. You, too," she replied.

"They still don't know how to react to the Ovarrow."

"It took us a while to get used to them."

"I've noticed some of the wallscreens that cycle images and messages have an emphasis on pure human," Connor said.

"I've seen some of those, too. I've asked about that, and it seems to be motivational propaganda-type things."

"That's the answer I got, too, but it's still...just a little off-putting. Who are they targeting? Were there really groups of people who sympathized with the Vemus?"

Lenora frowned. "God, Connor, when you...I hadn't even thought about that. That can't be what it means. The Vemus were monsters. They never wanted to communicate with us. They just wanted...us."

Connor scratched his cheek for a second. "The Vemus were altered. What if there were different kinds?" He shook his head. "It's over two hundred years ago."

"Not for them it hasn't been. It's something they've had to live with. There are places here where there are dormant Vemus."

He nodded. "Not for long if I have anything to say about it."

"Just be careful."

Connor smiled. "Aren't I always?"

She rolled her eyes a little and gave him a small shove. Connor pulled her into his arms and swung her around. He set her down and she stared up at him.

"Don't start something you can't finish, soldier."

Connor growled and Lenora grinned wickedly. He had to leave. "It'll make the homecoming that much sweeter."

Lenora smiled back at him. "I promise."

He kissed her and then headed back to the ship.

23

THE SHUTTLE ENTERED the main hangar bay on the *Douglass*. Connor stood and walked down the ramp to the flight deck. The air was cool and carried a spicy freshness. The atmospheric scrubbers on the *Douglass* were far superior and in much better condition than what was used on Magnus Station. He inhaled deeply and sighed.

Colonel Oliver Martinez stood at the end of the ramp and snapped a salute, followed by the CDF soldiers nearby.

Connor walked down the ramp and returned the salute. "Good morning, Colonel Martinez."

Passengers waited to board the shuttle. There were several stacks of storage crates nearby on grav pallets, and deck personnel began loading them onto the shuttle.

"Good morning, General Gates. If I were a betting man, I'd say you look happy to be back aboard the *Douglass*, sir."

Connor chuckled a little and smiled with half his mouth. "The air is a bit fresher here."

Martinez fell into step beside him. "Nothing but the best accommodations here on the *Douglass*, General."

They walked out of the hangar bay.

"When can we be underway?" Connor asked.

"We can be underway any time you choose, General. However, since this is an escort duty, we have to coordinate with salvagers from Magnus Station, as well as from the smaller outposts, so it's taking a little bit of time."

They walked down the well-lit corridor and stopped at nearby elevators. "Fleet deployment meeting is scheduled at the top of the hour. We have a few minutes to stop in the mess hall if you'd like some real food, sir?"

Connor considered it for a few moments and then shook his head. "That won't be necessary."

They climbed onto the elevator along with a few other people who'd been waiting.

"If you're sure. I can also have them bring you something in your ready room," Martinez offered.

Connor was tempted but just shook his head. "No, I'd rather get underway as soon as possible. We'll just head to the meeting first."

"Understood," Martinez replied.

He proceeded to give Connor the current status report for the *Douglass* and the rest of the ships in the fleet. It was high level, but nothing that would prevent them from leaving. A ship that didn't require ongoing maintenance had a temporary commander. Either the ship would experience a critical failure that ended up costing lives, or they were dismissed from duty. CDF ships had an excellent track record, and the status of the expeditionary force was no different. Not that Connor expected anything less, given the senior officers who served. The CDF hadn't grown so large that it had to foster lackluster officers like the Old Earth alliance militaries.

They left the elevators and walked down a series of corridors to a conference room between CIC and the bridge. Connor entered the room and the soldiers stood up.

"As you were," Connor said.

There were several active wallscreens and Sean Quinn was on one of them. He smiled knowingly. Connor glanced at him and then back at Martinez.

"You were right, General Quinn. He came straight here," Martinez said.

Connor looked at Sean. "How many of these betting pools do you have going?"

"I'm not at liberty to disclose that information, sir," Sean replied with a wry grin.

Connor sat down. Most of the senior officers had already arrived—Sean's prodding, no doubt. "All right, Colonel Martinez, you've got the floor."

"Thank you, General Gates," Martinez replied. "Our mission priorities are to detect and disable any remnant automated defense turrets and installations built near the infrastructure among the moons of Saturn. Keep in mind that there are eighty-six moons or astral bodies that orbit the planet. At least a dozen have high metallicity counts and significant mining installations located there. That's the high-level intro to the mission. Before I go any further, does anyone have any questions?"

Colonel Brad Sutton, XO of the *Odyssey*, indicated he'd like to speak. "Yeah, I do. How do we know there isn't anyone living there? I wouldn't want us to fire on someone's home."

"We'll be taking every precaution. According to Magnus Station Director Pandu Mukhtar, there isn't anyone living there because it's a known hot zone. There are some salvagers who use mobile stations to set up temporary locations along certain fringe locations. We'll be contacting them before we deploy toward the target sectors," Martinez said. He paused for a moment to see whether anyone else raised any questions. "Destroyer commands listen up because you'll be the tip of the spear, while the *Douglass* and the *Odyssey* are in reserve. You'll be broken up into three patrols. First sweep will be for detection and removal."

Sean cleared his throat. "It's important to keep in mind that, based on recent intelligence provided by Magnus Station and our own active scans of the area, automated defense systems will probably be well hidden, so we'll need to take our time. This won't be a quick in-and-out mission."

Major Jane Russo from the Destroyer *Wolf* indicated she'd like to speak. "What about the installations that are well protected? If our objective is to keep those installations intact for salvage, will there be support to root out the defenses that are dug in?"

Russo had been one of Sean's senior tactical officers for years. Connor only knew her by reputation.

"I'll take this," Connor said. "Yes, there will be several Talon V A-Wings on standby to lend support. Look, there's no way to get around the fact that for as much intel as we've been given, we're still blind to what's really out there. The equipment available to Magnus Station and the other outpost is extremely outdated and has been coddled into service far beyond their intended life cycles. That's why we'll rely primarily on our own sensor capabilities. As we go on and gain more experience with what we'll be facing, the quicker we'll be able to go."

"Thank you, General Gates," Major Russo said.

Martinez spent the next hour going through the planned deployments, beginning with the sectors closest to the salvager bases, which would allow them to immediately begin working. Then they'd move their way into the known hot zones.

The meeting ended and Connor went to his office near the bridge. The higher he'd gone in rank the more meetings had come with it, and being part of the diplomatic envoy simply doubled the time he'd spent in meetings. A soldier brought him a tray of food and set it down on his desk. He spent the next six hours going over reports and approving requests that required his attention.

He stood up and stretched. Glancing at the clock, he decided it was time to get in some PT. Never one to sit around, Connor sought out physical activity as often as he could cram it into his busy schedule. He headed to the officer's recreation area, and for the next ninety minutes, pushed his body through various workouts. By the time he was done, his mind and his body felt as if he'd gotten the gunk out. He put on a fresh uniform and made it in time for dinner with the other senior officers.

Martinez nodded in greeting when Connor entered the dining hall. "You're looking bright-eyed this evening, sir."

"I managed to blow off some steam. Worked up an appetite, to be honest."

Martinez nodded. Then his eyebrows raised. "I heard you used to track ryklars on New Earth before they were relocated and even before the space gates. Is that true?"

Connor nodded. "I did."

Martinez pursed his lips impressed. "Not to ask the obvious, but why?"

"They were one of New Earth's most lethal predators. They were also the most sentient, demonstrating more intelligence than Old Earth dolphins."

"I know they were lethal hunters and could coordinate

attacks, but I've been a fleet man my entire career in the CDF. I've never done much in the way of field work or exploration."

A plate with a healthy piece of ribeye was set in front of him. Sautéed mushrooms, onions, peppers, and green beans dripped with juices from the cook's pan. Connor pressed the steak with the tip of his fork and its supple springiness indicated it was prepared just as he liked it. He sliced into the steak and cut away a juicy piece, then stuck it in his mouth and chewed. Buttery saltiness caused a taste explosion in his mouth, and he sighed with contentment.

"We encountered the ryklars on my first day on New Earth."

"You're kidding me."

"Nope. It was during a tour with Field Ops. The ryklars were luring away field workers and then ambushing them. Some even attacked the Field Ops rovers we were using at the time."

Martinez drank from his cup and continued to eat. "I've heard a lot of stories like that from early colonial days. It must have been something to see."

Connor smiled a little, remembering meeting Juan and first seeing Lenora on the shuttle down to the planet. "It was something. Given your rank in the CDF, I expect more expeditionary forces will be assembled for more exploratory missions. Is that something you'd be interested in?"

Martinez considered it for a few moments. Then nodded. "Yeah, I think so."

"Good to know," Connor replied and continued eating his dinner. "After the Vemus Wars, for my brief retirement from the CDF, I started tracking ryklar packs, learning where they traveled and getting a feel for their hierarchy. It was interesting. I think they'll do well on their own."

Martinez nodded. "I don't miss them. I know a few people who work in Field Ops. They don't miss the ryklars either. Too clever, and it could easily escalate a situation when they're involved."

Connor smiled a little. If he'd thought about how many times he'd been surrounded by or had his life threatened by ryklars, he'd probably lose count after a while. "Trust me. That's an understatement."

The next morning Connor walked onto the bridge. Martinez stood up from the command chair.

"General," Martinez said, "destroyers *Wolf* and *Saber* have begun their first sweep of Sector Two."

Connor looked at the tactical plot. The *Douglass*'s powerful scanner array had detected a significant installation built into a partial moon. It was too big to be considered an asteroid, but some recent calamity had caused several significant chunks to separate, exposing rich metallic ores inside.

"Defensive turrets detected by the *Saber*," Lieutenant Tucker said suddenly. Less than a minute later. "Multiple turrets detected."

Connor watched the tactical plot. The destroyers were identifying the active defense turrets. Several new icons appeared on the main holoscreen.

"Hornet missiles are en route to the defense turrets. Thirty percent mass yield for the warhead. Fifteen minutes to target," Lieutenant Tucker said.

The other destroyer patrols also triggered various defensive measures. In sector Four, the *Python* reported several hundred mines had been deployed. They'd even detected several ancient Alliance ships that had been destroyed a long time ago.

"Have Major Burrows mark the area, and deploy demolition teams to disable the mines," Connor said.

"Sending your orders, General," Specialist Gabe Marten said.

Martinez looked at Connor. "That's going to take time."

"Yes, it is," Connor replied.

Destroying the mine field would have been quickest, but the potential for damage to the surrounding areas they sought to preserve was too significant a risk.

"Let's start deploying the Stinger A-Wings. They can help expand the patrol and report any active defenses they encounter," Connor said.

"I'm sure they'll enjoy the target practice, General," Martinez replied.

Connor thought about Ethan for a second. He had no doubt that his son and the other pilots were eager to notch a few targets under their proverbial belts. Making a slow sweep of the area was definitely the way to go. It would give the fleet some experience while building up the confidence of the younger soldiers. He watched the tactical plot and wondered just how militarized the Vemus Wars had left the Sol System. If they were already encountering automated defenses way out at Saturn, what about the rest of the Sol System?

24

THE ALARM CHIMED SOFTLY but insistently from Lauren's wrist computer, pulling her away from sleep. She opened her eyes to a brightly painted room lit by a steadily brightening, soft yellow light on the same spectrum as the sun, and it helped wake her up. She sat up on the bed and stretched her arms over her head, yawning deeply and lengthening her stretch before letting out a long exhale. She blinked a few times and noted the time. She'd slept for seven hours.

Lauren stood up and walked over to the sink, splashing water onto her face and rubbing the last vestiges of sleep away. This was the fifth day they'd been on the outpost. She tried to remember the name or the alpha numerical reference but couldn't. A little under two thousand people lived here, and between her and Isaac, they'd seen most of them. They'd even had Nance and Carl helping them with treatments, in addition to watching their backs—not that they needed it here. Once news had spread about the arrival of not only two doctors but medical tech that had been unavailable for two hundred years, even the most reluctant spacers had been enticed to come to them.

She looked at herself in the mirror. Weary blue eyes stared back at her, and she stifled another yawn. She went over to her duffel bag and pulled out some fresh clothing. She felt rested but also fatigued deep within her muscles and joints. She'd used stims to put off sleep for as long as she could. There were so many serious illnesses to be treated that she'd lost herself in her patients, each with stories of their own. The quality of life was so much less here than what they had on New Earth, but she also witnessed their grit and determination to not only survive but to thrive with minimal resources. Some of the stories she'd heard had broken her heart, but she rarely encountered cynicism, which surprised her. She thought there would be more of it. The people who lived in the outpost were reserved with outsiders, but they'd begun opening up to them, especially when they learned that they weren't from Magnus Station.

Lauren opened the door to find Amelia waiting for her. The patches of excess skin had all but disappeared. Eventually, all remnants of them would be gone as the medical nanites helped regulate the hormonal imbalance in Amelia's nervous system. They'd also performed gene therapy to prevent the autoimmune disease from coming back after the nanites expired.

"Good morning, Dr. Gates!" Amelia said and smiled widely, a pair of large brown eyes gleaming.

"Good morning, Amelia."

Amelia preened and then did a pirouette, spinning once. She was taller now that the curvature of her spin was so much less than it had been.

Lauren grinned. "Very nice. Are you going to help me today?"

Amelia nodded. "I wanted to bring you some breakfast, but

Dr. Diaz told me that you normally don't have breakfast. Is that true?"

They walked down the corridor.

"I'm not usually hungry when I first wake up."

Amelia frowned thoughtfully. "Maybe I should skip breakfast then."

"You're still growing, peanut, so probably not. Are you hungry in the morning?"

"I am. My father says I eat enough to stuff a horse! Have you ever seen a horse?"

Lauren shook her head. "There aren't any horses where I live. Have you?"

Amelia shook her head. "Only pictures from the archives. Wild horses that live on the coast. I like how they run through the water, making it splash. I want to go to the beach someday. Would you go with me?"

Lauren's eyes teared up for a moment, and then she smiled. Amelia's recovery had taken a remarkable turn. She was full of energy and curiosity the way a child should be.

She quickly wiped her eyes. "I'd love to."

"Oh really! When?"

"I don't know exactly when, but hopefully soon. There are still a lot of people for us to help first," Lauren said.

They walked into a common area. It might have been used for storage at some point, but there were tables and seating areas there now. People gathered near the windows, lining up in rows for a group activity. An older Asian woman waved them over.

As they walked toward the group, Lauren noticed that most of them had a lot of grey in their hair, and quite a few men had not much hair at all.

Madam Ko smiled. "Dr. Gates, good morning. Won't you please join us for morning practice?"

Lauren didn't know Madam Ko's entire name. She wasn't sure if anyone did. Braun had told her she'd been exiled from Magnus Station over a decade ago.

Lauren had started to decline the invitation when Madam Ko said, "Doctors need to take time to center themselves, too. Tai Chi can help you do that."

"I've never done it before," Lauren said.

Madam Ko waved away the comment. "Doesn't matter. Morning practice isn't that complicated. It's just movement. Come. You and Amelia can stand at the front."

Amelia's eyes widened and she looked up at Lauren. There was no chance of her declining now. A reminder chimed on her wrist computer, and she muted it so as not to disturb the others.

"All right, but only for a little while," she said.

Madam Ko clapped softly. "You'll be reinvigorated by the time we're done. I promise you. Now watch me."

Madam Ko led the group through various breathing exercises in conjunction with moving their arms, legs, and entire bodies. Stretching her arms wide while breathing and twisting unraveled the tension in her back. She hadn't realized how tight her muscles were. Until now, she'd preferred more active forms of exercise like rock climbing or running obstacle courses, but by the time they were done she felt more relaxed and alert than she had been for days. Madam Ko gave her a knowing smile.

"Please join us tomorrow morning," she said.

"I will try. Thank you for including us," Lauren replied.

Madam Ko smiled at Amelia. "I'll see you later."

Amelia waved and they walked away. "She visits us at our school almost every day. I used to only be able to do some of the poses that the other kids could do, but now I can do more."

The little girl reached up and held Lauren's hand. She gave it a gentle squeeze. "You'll be able to do more and more."

She wondered how many people here were exiles from Magnus Station. She hadn't considered it until it was mentioned a few times while she was recording patients' medical histories.

They entered another open common area. There were large rooms connected to it, and Amelia headed to a classroom nearby. Children's education was something the spacers took very seriously. The kids had classroom lessons in the mornings and other activities in the afternoons that involved physical activity, lab experiments, and helping to maintain the outpost's redundant systems. Lauren thought the organizers struck a good balance between instruction and practical application. It gave people a sense of responsibility, which she felt good about.

Lauren walked over to their temporary exam space that was walled off by a curtain, and for the first time in five days it wasn't packed full of people waiting to be seen. Maybe she and Isaac were finally getting in front of all the ailments.

Isaac emerged from behind one of the curtained areas. He smiled and jutted his chin up once in greeting and then spoke to the person he'd been treating.

Lauren walked over to him. "Where is everyone?"

He raised his hands up. "That's it. We're done."

"I thought there were more people traveling here from other outposts."

"They were, but I told Sekino that we were going to travel to them instead," he said. He keyed in a few notes on a holoscreen and closed the session. "Space travel is dangerous enough as it is. Some of the ships they fly shouldn't be used for scrap, much less still be in service. There have been a couple of incidences of ships losing power in transit here. They were rescued, but still, it's only a matter of time before something worse happens."

"And it gives us a chance to see the other outposts."

Isaac tipped his head to the side. "See, you're learning."

"Heh. I'm sorry. I would have been here sooner."

He smiled a little. "You needed to sleep."

"So do you."

He shrugged. "Not as much as you."

Lauren gazed at him for a few seconds. "You've got them, don't you?"

Isaac frowned and looked away from her. "Got what?"

He began cleaning up the examination area for a few seconds and then turned back toward her. "Oh, I meant to tell you that I've updated their autodoc. I also restocked their medical supplies. Their computer system almost couldn't handle the updated medical protocols, but Braun, of all people, helped me get the system to accept the update."

"That's good," Lauren said and arched an eyebrow. "Stop deflecting."

He stared at her with the look of someone trying too hard. She knew he was keeping something from her. "How do you do that? How do you know?"

She smiled. "I'm a keen observer. Plus, we've been working closely for the past few months, and I've noticed a few things. So which implants do you have? Please tell me it's not the same ones the CDF was using."

Isaac shook his head and his cheeks reddened a little. "No, not those. I need more than two hours of sleep."

Lauren crossed her arms and raised her eyebrows.

"Fine," he said. "They're newer and use a delayed sleep function protocol. I can get by with four hours of sleep."

"Isaac," she said, "physiologically, we're not designed for that. We have a circadian rhythm for a reason."

"I know. Believe me, I know. I only use it sparingly, and you needed the extra rest," he replied.

Lauren stepped closer to him. "That's very sweet, but we share the workload."

He heaved a sigh and nodded, looking quite adorable as he did it.

Lauren gazed at him for a moment, then leaned forward and kissed him. His eyes widened for barely a second, and then he wrapped his arms around her and returned the kiss in full. She'd thought of doing it for a while but kept dismissing the urge as holdover feelings from when they were younger. But the longer they worked together, the more difficult he was to resist. They'd been sharing small intimate moments where they'd stare just a little bit longer, but he hadn't acted on it. Lauren thought she knew why and wasn't about to let it stand in her way.

They pulled away. She liked the way his lips felt on hers, the smell of his skin, and the soft, dark hair of his beard and mustache.

"I got tired of waiting for you to kiss me," she said.

Isaac grinned a little. "I was worried you'd knock me on my ass if I tried."

He'd witnessed one of her judo practice sessions and developed a healthy respect for her martial arts capabilities.

Lauren hitched her hip to the side. "What's a girl gotta do to get you to notice her, Isaac?"

He shook his head and laughed. His cheeks reddened.

"Aww," she said.

He rolled his eyes and then pulled her in for another long kiss. It felt good. It felt really good—so much better than she'd imagined.

Someone called out to them from behind the curtain. It was Braun. Lauren pulled away from Isaac and stepped out.

"Dr. Gates. Dr. Diaz. I need your help," Braun said.

"Of course. What can we do?" Isaac said.

"Sekino told me you intend to visit the other outposts."

"That's right."

"We've received a distress call from one of our deep salvage teams. Your shuttle can get us there the quickest. They said there have been injuries," Braun said.

"Are they on comms now?" Lauren asked.

Braun shook his head. "No, it was just a broadcast. We don't have anyone in the vicinity, otherwise I would've asked them."

"Of course we'll help. Just send us the coordinates. We can depart right away," Isaac said.

They started to walk away from the commons area.

"Can I come with you?" he asked, his eyes tight with worry.

Lauren and Isaac exchanged glances.

"Sure, we can take you with us," Isaac said.

"Braun, who's on the salvage team?" Lauren asked.

Braun's eyes sank to the ground for a second. "It's Wakiya, my wife. I'm so sorry to ask this of you after you've done so much for me already—for me and everyone else here on the outpost. I know you'd intended to go to another outpost today. They need your help too, but..."

"It's your wife," Isaac said with a determined tone in his voice.

"Don't be sorry, Braun. We'll get to them. What about Amelia? Don't you need to tell her?" Lauren asked.

Braun shook his head. "Sekino will take care of her. We're salvagers. We look after our own here on the outpost."

Isaac opened a comlink to the shuttle and told Nance to begin the preflight checks.

Lauren ran back to her room to retrieve her bag of personal belongings and met the others at the shuttle.

She heard a barrage of loud voices as the elevator doors opened to the outpost's docking area. A group of people was gathered outside the airlock. Isaac and Sergeant Burk were outside. Burk wore his sidearm.

"We can't take all of you with us," Isaac said.

Lauren walked toward them.

"Let Dr. Gates get through," Isaac said.

She noticed Burk's hand on his belt near his weapon.

"Excuse me," Lauren said.

Several people turned toward her and gave her room.

Someone shouted, demanding that they be allowed to come on the shuttle. Braun wasn't the only one with family in danger.

Lauren squeezed through to the airlock doors, and Burk gave her a small nod.

Isaac held up his hands. "Time isn't on our side if we're going to get there in time to help."

Lauren leaned toward Isaac. "How about we bring one more person with us," she said. Isaac nodded, and she turned to address the crowd. "We can bring another person with us, but they must be able to help."

"She's right," Isaac said, and looked at Braun. "Who's been on rescue ops and done salvage-type work before?"

Braun looked at the crowd of people, then jutted his chin toward another man. "Jacob."

He was a lean man of average height and looked to be in his early thirties.

Isaac gave him a once-over. "All right, Jacob, you're with us." Then to the rest of the crowd, he said, "We'll send an update as soon as we can."

Burk palmed the airlock and the doors opened.

"I should get my kit," Jacob said.

"That won't be necessary. We have tools you can use onboard," Isaac said.

They walked down the short tunnel to the airlock of the

shuttle. Nance must have been monitoring their approach because the shuttle's airlock doors unlocked. They walked inside.

Burk turned toward Braun and Jacob. "Let's get one thing out of the way. You're guests aboard this ship. Don't go poking around. Stay in the passenger areas unless instructed to do otherwise. Do that and we'll get along just fine. Is that understood?"

They both nodded.

"All right," Isaac said, "the passenger section is through here. Seating is to the left. Burk will show you the rest. Lauren, please join me in the cockpit."

"I've sent the coordinates to you," Braun said.

"Thanks. I'll get them into the nav system, and we'll get out of here."

Lauren followed Isaac to the front of the ship. Nance passed them.

"I hear we have a couple of guests aboard," Nance said.

"Yes, Burk is giving them a tour," Lauren said.

"Groovy. I'll go see if he needs backup," Nance said.

They walked to the cockpit and sat down. Preflight checks were done. Lauren initiated the decoupling of the docking clamps, and they were free of the outpost.

As Isaac flew the shuttle, he brought up a plot on the main holoscreen, and an icon flashed with the coordinates Braun had given them. He stared at it, considering.

"What's the matter?" Lauren asked.

Isaac frowned thoughtfully. "I was just checking to see if we'd detected anything in those coordinates."

"Doesn't look like it."

He nodded. "No, it doesn't. Not sure what's there."

"Maybe Braun knows. We should talk to him." She looked at

him for a second. "What's the matter? Are you concerned about
something?"

"I'm not sure," he said and glanced behind them. "Look, I
like giving people the benefit of the doubt, but we're already on
the fringe away from any help from the CDF. There have been
more than a few questions about our ship."

Lauren's eyebrows pulled together. "You think this is staged
so they can steal our ship?"

He sighed. "I hope not. I don't think so, but I can't rule it
out either."

"Braun wouldn't do that."

"I don't think he would either, but the timing of all this
makes me a little suspicious."

"Burk and Nance will keep an eye on them. Anyway, I don't
think we're being lured away somewhere. Amelia has talked
about her mother going on salvaging runs, and Braun is
definitely worried about his wife."

Isaac nodded and gave her a sidelong glance. "It's probably
nothing. Come on, let's go back and talk to the others."

25

THE SHUTTLE FLEW toward the waypoint, a lone icon well away from the other outposts. Lauren sat in the copilot's seat next to Isaac. There was an open comlink channel to the passenger section where the others watched a duplicate of the holoscreen they had in the cockpit.

"A bit far for salvage runs, isn't it?" Lauren said. She watched a sub-window that showed a video feed of the others.

"Wakiya likes to bring her team on runs that take weeks at a time," Braun said. "The chances increase for more valuable finds that way."

"And they're not registered with Magnus Station," Jacob said.

"Why would anything be registered with Magnus Station? I didn't think you were answerable to them," Lauren asked.

"We are and we're not. Registering a salvage claim lessens the chance of multiple claims on the same salvage," Braun said.

Isaac chuckled a little. "Keeps the officials at Magnus Station from having to settle disputes between competing parties. But it also creates conditions where people are encouraged to share valuable site locations or else risk losing rights to sell to the station."

"Do you always have to go through Magnus Station? Can't you trade among yourselves?" Lauren asked.

"We do as much as we can, but Magnus Station is able to refine raw materials and has the best food-processing capabilities," Braun said.

Lauren shared a glance with Isaac. Magnus Station had the most powerful position in terms of available resources but also to be able to transform scrap into something usable. It must have been a bitter pill to swallow for the people who'd been exiled from the station. They could never completely escape it, even if they weren't allowed to return.

The shuttle closed the distance toward their destination and their scanners began to get a more detailed readout. An image began to appear on the main holoscreen. Lauren stared at it with a thoughtful frown. Something about the shape tugged at her memory. Then the ship's computer system flashed an alert.

Vemus exoskeletal form detected!

Isaac stared at the message. "Holy shit!"

"We've got to get out of here!" Burk bellowed.

The others all started speaking at the same time. Lauren peered at the screen and looked at the scan data.

"Wait," she said. "There aren't any power signatures detected."

"It could just be dormant," Isaac said.

Lauren pursed her lips in thought. "Maybe. Can you change our approach and get a better scan of the other side?"

"I can do that," Isaac replied.

"Why are we still on approach?" Burk asked.

"We're going to circle around it and get a better look before we decide anything," Lauren said.

"Like hell we are," Burk said. "Isaac, you need to get us out of here."

"We can't do that. Our people are there. We can't leave them," Braun said.

"They knew the risks of going there. I won't risk the people on this shuttle if the Vemus are involved," Burk replied.

Isaac shook his head and glanced at Lauren. "I can't take you in there."

"We don't know what's there. We need to do a proper assessment and *then* make a decision," she replied. "Carl." Burk and Braun continued to argue, their voices raising as they did. "Sergeant Burk!"

No response.

Lauren stood. "I'm going back there."

"Lauren, wait. Burk's right. We can't go in there without CDF support."

"Just keep scanning it," she said and left the cockpit.

Braun and Burk stood glaring at each other. Both men were tall and heavily muscled. Lauren stormed over to them.

Nance held up her hand toward Jacob. "Don't do anything stupid."

"Hey!" Lauren said, glaring up at them. "Both of you stop it right now." They turned toward her. "Braun, we don't know if they're alive. Why don't you use the comms systems over there and try to establish contact," Lauren said.

Braun nodded stiffly and walked toward the nearby workstation.

"I'm not going to allow you to be put in danger, Dr. Gates," Burk scowled. The way he said her last name carried all the weighty implications with it, and that was starting to irritate her.

"I understand the position you're in," Lauren said, and Burk shook his head, looking mulish. "No, listen to me, Sergeant

Burk. You're here to protect me. That's your assignment. But that doesn't mean you can tell me where I can and can't go. Look at me. I know you think you're doing the right thing, what you think you need to, but I'm not in the CDF. You're not going to be held responsible for anything that I do of my own volition. You're not responsible for me. I am."

Burk shook his head. "Do you think I'm worried about the consequences? To me? I'm not," he said and stepped closer. She had to crane her neck to look him in the eyes. "You are General Gates's daughter. The entire colony owes him. Generations of colonists owe him. I'm not going to let anything happen to you. Not on my watch."

Lauren stared into Burk's eyes, trying to think of a way to get him to listen to her. "My father doesn't expect or want that. He didn't do all the things he's done so people like you and Nance, or anyone else for that matter, would spend their lives believing he was owed something. That's not who he is. That's not who I am. Do you really think that someone like my father would want us to turn away from people who are in danger from the Vemus? Is that his legacy? Is that who you think he is? Is that who you are?"

The others became quiet, but she kept looking at Burk. Nance joined them. Burk blinked several times and shook his head.

Lauren reached up and placed her hand on his broad shoulder. She leaned toward him and spoke quietly. "Now, let's keep with the finest traditions of the CDF and find a way to help these people. Are you with me?"

Burk inhaled deeply and nodded. "Yeah."

Lauren looked at Nance. She held up her hands. "I was already with you."

Lauren smiled and walked over to Braun.

"She's the general's daughter all right, and she's definitely cut from the same cloth," Nance said.

Burk grumbled a reply.

Lauren tapped Braun on the shoulder. "Any luck?"

He shook his head. "Not yet."

"What about a data comlink? Would the ships computer systems respond to a general query?" she asked.

Braun considered it and then looked at Jacob. "What do you think?"

Jacob shook his head. "I don't think so, especially if they're trying to remain unnoticed."

Lauren looked at them both for a few seconds. "You both need to level with me here. Do you normally go salvaging on dormant Vemus outposts?"

The two of them didn't look at each other, but both seemed to go very still. Braun heaved a sigh. "We take every precaution. Something must have gone wrong."

"Have there been actual Vemus on any of those outposts?" Burk asked.

"Sometimes. They've been dormant for so long that they're usually weakened, but we can detect them if we get closer," Braun said.

"We know how to detect them, too," Isaac said. His voice coming from the nearby speaker. "The protocols are in the shuttle's computer systems."

"How can we detect them?" Lauren asked.

"We've been scanning for the alpha signal that the Vemus used in their invasion and haven't detected anything like it here. But according to the protocol write-up, if there's an atmosphere maintained on a Vemus ship, they communicate using a higher frequency that sounds like clicking and high-pitched squeals. It's akin to that of the mammals of Earth's oceans—dolphins, whales, etc," Isaac said.

Lauren looked at Braun and Jacob. "Do you do the same?"

They both nodded. "Yes."

Nance clucked her tongue. "I never understood how they were able to go dormant like that."

"It's like the whole ship becomes a stasis pod but not exactly. Researchers thought they had a way to efficiently recycle the atmosphere to make it last longer," Lauren said.

Jacob glanced at Braun for a second and Lauren arched an eyebrow expectantly.

"They're more resistant to radiation too, so shielding wasn't as much an issue for them as it is for us," he said.

Lauren thought about the trace mutations she'd detected in the people who lived on the outpost. These mutations could be traced back to Vemus exposure, but they were different and played a role in how fast Amelia was able to heal from her disease. It was like her system needed to be taught what to do and took over from there. Medical nanites did the same thing in colonists, but they didn't have any trace Vemus mutations.

"I'm going back to help Isaac. Keep trying to contact them."

Lauren headed back to the cockpit and saw that Isaac had muted the comlink to the back. There were multiple data windows open on the holoscreen.

"Nice job back there," he said.

Lauren sat down. "It needed to be said."

He nodded. "Yeah. You must get that a lot."

She shrugged. "Not as much as Ethan does. I don't normally work with the CDF."

"Yeah, but Burk isn't the only one who thinks that way."

Lauren stared at him for a long moment.

Isaac cleared his throat. "Look, I love your father. I don't want to give him a reason to hate me."

Lauren smiled teasingly. "I kissed you, Isaac. He's already going to give you the father glare."

Isaac shook his head. "What do you think he'll say when I tell him we're getting married?"

Lauren cocked her head to the side, then punched him in the arm. "Jerk."

"Ow." Isaac grinned. "Ouch. I was kidding."

"Let's not get ahead of ourselves here. It was just a kiss. I don't even know if I want to do it again."

Isaac stared at her, shocked. "Are you…" he shook his head. "You want to do it again. I can tell."

Lauren stared at him with a deadpanned expression. "Can you, now?"

Isaac started to stand up but stopped when Nance stuck her head through the door. "Hey guys. The comlink is muted. Come join the fun, all right?"

Lauren unmuted the comlink. "Sorry about that. Didn't realize we couldn't hear you."

Isaac's mouth hung open and he muted the comlink again. "It's like I don't even know you sometimes," he said quietly. Then, he said to the others, "Okay, the computer believes this was a monitoring or research station."

"Which one is it?" Burk asked.

"I'm not sure."

"Well, you should get sure," Burk snapped.

"I'll tell you what, if they open fire on us, then it's some kind of military monitoring station, otherwise I'll put my money on research. Sound good to you?" Isaac asked.

Lauren looked at the scan data. There wasn't any indication of weapons systems. "Let's engage the point defense systems just in case."

Isaac nodded and keyed in the holo-interface. "Point defense cannons online."

The structure looked to be a smaller version of the outpost they'd come from. Even with the Vemus exoskeleton, it was wider on one end and narrower at the other. Lauren couldn't tell if it was a ship or not. She wasn't as familiar with them as her brother was. Right about then she wished she knew more about it.

Isaac swung the shuttle around, circling the small outpost. As they came around, a magnified view of the station showed several large holes. At some point the station had been shot at, but there was no way for them to determine when it had happened.

"This could have been like this for hundreds of years. There isn't any debris detected near the impact site, so it must have happened a long time ago," Lauren said.

Isaac nodded. "Look at that. The exoskeleton doesn't cover the entire station."

Lauren peered at the video feed. About seventy percent of the station was covered by the Vemus exoskeleton. "Maybe they found a way to stop it."

"Can you zoom in on the open areas? There might be a docking port near there," Braun said.

Isaac flew them closer to the station. No weapons system had been detected. The station seemed dormant.

"There! I see it!" Braun said.

An older, bronze-colored ship was attached to the outside. The ship was all angles and planes, clearly not designed for atmospheric flight at all. One end was attached to the station.

"I can't tell if there's a docking port there," Isaac said.

"Still no response from the ship," Burk replied.

"Braun," Lauren said, "we're close enough for personal comms. Try that. Maybe that'll work better."

Braun entered the comms frequencies they used. "Wakiya, are you there? Do you read me? Is anyone there?"

"Braun!" a woman's voice replied. "Oh my God, is that you?"

"Yes, it's me. We're outside the station, heading toward the ship. What happened? We received a distress call," Braun said.

"How did you get here so fast? We thought it would take you days to reach us," Wakiya said.

"We had some help from some new friends. They're not from around here."

"Please tell me you didn't go to Magnus Station for help. You know how they—"

"It's not them. I'll tell you all about it, but you need to tell us your situation."

Wakiya was quiet for a few seconds. "Torren and Moteki are trapped. We all are. We can't reach our ship."

"Excuse me, Wakiya. I'm Lauren. I'm a doctor. Is anyone hurt?"

"Yes, Moteki is injured. He's going in and out of consciousness."

"What happened?"

"Is Braun still here?"

"It's all right. They're not interested in the claim. This is Dr. Gates, and she helped Amelia. Didn't you get my messages?"

"Must be in the ship's queue. Amelia, is she...is she all right?"

"She's fine. Dr. Gates healed her. You won't believe it until you see it. Now, tell us what happened so we can work on getting you out of there."

"Oh, thank God," Wakiya sighed. "We tried to bring the station online to gain access to main engineering. The artificial gravity generator was malfunctioning and caused instability. I think some of the regulators failed. I'm not sure. But all six of us are trapped and no one can get back to the ship."

"Just give us a second to figure out the best way to get to you," Braun said.

He muted the comlink session.

"A blown regulator shouldn't have caused the destruction she described," Burk said.

Lauren looked at Isaac and he shrugged.

"The exoskeleton could have shifted things around. We've seen that before," Braun said.

"Should we be concerned about their individual life-support systems?" Lauren asked.

"I'll ask," he replied. "Wakiya, how's your life support? Are your reserves doing okay?"

"Yeah, they're fine."

"I don't see any docking ports," Isaac said.

Lauren frowned and peered at the image on the holoscreen. She didn't see anything either, and if the exoskeleton covered the other ports, they'd have to cut through the exposed hull.

"We had to cut through the hull to get access," Wakiya said.

"Braun, tell her to stand by. We'll have to do the same," Isaac said.

He flew the shuttle toward the research station. "We'll have to do an EVA to get inside."

Lauren's stomach sank to her feet. "Wait. Can't we just dock with their ship and use it to get to the station?"

Isaac pressed his lips together for a second and then shook his head. "No... we could, but they said they couldn't get to their ship, so it's probably blocked off somewhere." He looked at her for a second and his eyes widened. "Oh, I forgot. You don't like EVAs."

Lauren gritted her teeth a little. "They're not my favorite

activity."

"Then you can stay here."

Lauren shook her head. "No!" she said in a harsh whisper. "Someone is hurt. I'm not going to let you deal with it by yourself."

Isaac smiled a little. "You're concern for me is noted, but I'm not going alone. The others will be with me."

"Yeah, that's just great. I stay behind because I'm too afraid to do a simple EVA. No, I'm coming with you."

Isaac looked at her. "It's nothing to be ashamed of."

"I can do it. Nance and I went over it on our way to the outpost. It's been a while. I'll be fine. When was the last time you did an EVA anyway?"

Isaac looked away from her. "Not that long."

"It wasn't in the last four months."

Isaac eyed her guiltily.

Lauren narrowed her gaze. "When?"

"I did some training with the CDF on the way here."

Lauren's mouth opened for a second before she spoke. "When did you have time for that? We worked on all the research together and attended all the meetings." She paused for a moment. "Your implants! You've been going on limited sleep for an extended period of time. Isaac, you know that's not safe."

Isaac glanced behind them at the door and leaned over, putting a hand on her arm. "I did use my implants, but not for the entire trip from New Earth. Just here and there. If you want, I'll show you my biochip records. You can see for yourself."

Biochip records were extremely personal. She didn't have any right to look at that data unless there was a medical reason for her to do so.

"Here," Isaac said, lifting his wrist computer and showing her his personal holoscreen.

She held his gaze for a few seconds and then her eyes slid to the data on the holoscreen. She'd always been a quick reader, and she quickly absorbed the data on the screen. Isaac was telling the truth. He had been monitoring his use of the implants.

"They don't let just anyone train with the CDF," Lauren said.

"I have clearance. It's a special circumstance. I can't say any more than that," he replied.

"Why are you so determined to get on that station? Beyond helping the salvagers, that is," Lauren said.

"Just to be clear, I do want to help the salvagers. However, there could also be data on the computing system that the CDF could use."

She narrowed her gaze. "Are you working for my father?"

Isaac shook his head. "No…Well, not directly. If I found something that would help the CDF, I'd bring it to your father's attention, but he hasn't asked me to do anything."

Lauren just looked him, and he turned back toward the main holoscreen. There was something Isaac wasn't telling her. She thought about coming right out and asking him, but they were almost to the station. She wasn't going to let this go.

"You and I are going to have a long talk when this is over," she said.

Isaac kept his gaze on the holoscreen and his hands on the flight-control systems. "Sounds good to me."

Lauren stood and stepped toward the door, looking back at him. She saw the boy she'd grown up with in Sanctuary, but there was more to him. He had secrets that he felt he couldn't share with her. Should she press? It'd been only one kiss, not a commitment. Isaac was entitled to his privacy just as she was to her own. She needed to think about it more, but first she had to put on her EVA suit, get tethered to Nance, and hope she wasn't making one of the biggest mistakes of her life.

26

Lauren put on the helmet of her EVA suit. The smart fabric of the interior suit adjusted to her size and signaled to the outer layer to adjust its fitting. Her neural implants and suit computer established a connection, and the HUD came online. Life-support systems were green. Her mag boots were disabled. She did a visual inspection of her gloves and hands.

"Is everyone suited up?" Isaac asked.

They all checked in.

"All right. I'm going to vent the atmosphere," Isaac said.

The shuttle's computer system began a countdown, and warning messages appeared on a nearby holoscreen.

They'd gathered near the portside airlock.

"The ramp is down. We're ready for egress," Burk said.

Braun and Jacob stood in their borrowed EVA suits.

"These are amazing," Jacob said. He extended his arms and squatted a little, testing his range of motion. "We still use fitted suits. When the smart fabric adjusted to fit me, I thought I'd done something wrong."

Braun grinned. "He started to panic."

"Well, yeah. You would, too, if something started to cinch up your balls without you doing anything," Jacob said.

"You can never be too careful," Isaac agreed.

Nance stood in front of Lauren and passed a tether toward her. "Connect that to the port on your belt."

Lauren did as instructed. None of the others were using a tether, but she knew that shouldn't bother her. She needed it, and it was just a precaution, but it did annoy her just a little bit. She felt like she was unprepared.

"Got it," Lauren said.

Nance smiled knowingly and gave her a small nod, then turned toward the airlock.

Burk looked at them all one more time and opened the airlock. He stepped out of the shuttle onto the ramp, looking around.

"It's clear," he said and walked down the ramp.

Braun and Jacob went next. Then Nance followed.

Lauren stepped onto the ramp and activated her mag boots. She couldn't feel them engage.

"It's because we're still near the shuttle's artificial gravity field. It'll feel different at the bottom of the ramp," Nance said.

Lauren nodded and walked down the ramp. Nance was right. Gravity shifted from exerting a force all around her to only coming from her boots. Though she was fit snugly into her EVA suit, she felt as if she were lifting away from the ramp. The research station spun slowly, and she felt the centrifugal force from it. The inside of her body seemed to lift, which felt odd and familiar at the same time.

"I'm fine," Lauren said.

She walked down the ramp, taking each step with increased

confidence. The EVA suit assisted her movements. She stepped onto the gray hull and Nance watched her.

Isaac came down last and walked toward Burk. He moved as if he'd been doing EVAs for years.

"Excuse me," Braun said. "Jacob is going to check on the ship."

He gestured toward the bronze-colored ship with faded chrome accents about a hundred meters from their location.

"We can't spare anyone to go with you," Isaac said.

"Not a problem. I'll update you through comms," Jacob replied.

The young spacer began walking toward the other ship.

"He can fly it if he has to," Braun said.

"Good to know," Isaac said. He looked around the area and then walked a short distance away. "We can cut away here and enter the station."

They were hundreds of meters from the exoskeleton. It was a lighter gray but with streaks of yellow in it.

"How do you know we can cut through here?" Burk asked.

"Station mechanics. If you look closely, you can see where the panels were fit together. We'll need to cut through the outer hull and then the bulkhead, but it should work," Isaac replied.

Burk nodded. "Sounds like you've done this before."

Isaac smiled. "Once or twice. Hand me the plasma cutters."

Burk handed him a metallic container and Isaac opened it. He powered on the cutters and knelt down, bringing the end of the cutters near the hull and igniting them.

Nance turned toward her. "He's got some skills I hadn't expected," she said over a private comms channel.

"Yeah, he surprised me, too."

"Keeps you on your toes."

They watched as Isaac cut a wide hole through the hull. Burk helped him remove the panel and pushed it away from them. The panel floated away into space.

Braun stepped to the side and checked in on Wakiya. "They're doing okay," he said to Lauren.

Isaac finished cutting through the hull and checked inside. "We can fit through one at a time. I'll go first. Burk you follow after me. Then Braun. Nance you bring up the rear."

Isaac made the hole big enough for them to easily slip through. Lauren disengaged her mag boots and went through the hole. Isaac helped guide her in and then helped her orient her feet so they touched the ground. The angle they'd come in on had them going feet first to the wall.

Her feet touched the ground, and she was face-to-face with Isaac.

"There you go," he said with a smile. "Easy as pie, right?"

Lauren nodded. She engaged her mag boots and stepped out of the way. Burk waved her over and asked how she was doing.

She glanced down the corridor. Ancient debris floated in the distance and reflected off the light of her helmet. Beams of light came from all their helmets. Lauren turned to the right and peered down the corridor. A thick tangle of metal blocked their path seventy meters from their location.

She watched as Nance came through the hole and Isaac helped her get oriented. Lauren detached the tether and it retracted into the small box on Nance's utility belt.

Isaac walked over to her and looked at Burk. "I kinda wish we had some recon drones to help map out the place. Braun, do you have any idea of the layout of this place?"

"Wakiya said they went to the upper levels toward the central station," Braun said.

"That makes sense. It's where they control all the critical systems," Isaac replied.

"We also need to stay away from the exoskeletal material. Especially if it appears to be active," Lauren said.

Nance nodded. "We've been hearing the same throughout our training on the way to the star system."

"It's something that hits close to home," Lauren said.

Burk frowned. "How so?"

"My father lost one of his best friends to it. He was absorbed by the Vemus exoskeletal material while extracting a data dump from a ship's computer system. He said it happened so fast that he didn't have time to react. We need to be careful," Lauren replied.

Braun glanced at them all for a second. "I think we can go this way. There's a stairwell over there," he said while gesturing toward a sign nearby.

Lauren followed the others to the stairwell. It was so dark that their lights only pierced the darkness a little bit. She would hate to be trapped in here without a light.

"Were they trying to restore power?" she asked.

"They were," Braun replied.

"Wouldn't that wake up the Vemus? They can be dormant for a long time," Nance said.

"They only do it temporarily. It takes time for the Vemus to leave a dormant state, and it takes even longer without an atmosphere. Also requires heat," Braun replied.

They climbed up the staircase, going up eight levels. There was an open door with deep gouges on the side.

"Looks like they forced their way inside," Isaac said.

They walked through the door and into the corridor beyond. There were several thick cables running along the walls.

Isaac peered at the cables and turned toward the others. "That's not right. They'd never run heavy power cables along a corridor like this."

"Maybe they didn't have a choice," Lauren replied.

"Okay. Okay, we're almost to you," Braun said. He'd been speaking with his wife on a separate comlink. "We have to hurry."

They kept going. Lauren noticed several dark spots on the power cables. There must have been an overload here when they tried to restore the power.

"This place is really unsettling," Nance said.

"I'm glad someone finally said it," Isaac replied. He looked at Braun. "No offense, but doing this all the time must take a toll on you after a while."

Braun strode ahead. "You get used to it."

Nance looked at Lauren. "I wouldn't want to get used to it."

The farther they went into the station, the more Lauren thought about how unprepared they were for this. They only had basic equipment with them, but there were injured people. She couldn't feel the weight of the medical pack on her back, but she knew it was there.

They walked through a series of corridors and had to backtrack a few times because the area had been blocked off.

"This looks new," Burk said, gesturing toward scorching near a door.

Lauren peered inside. There was Vemus exoskeletal material on the walls that looked as if it were liquid that had frozen like a waterfall. It was gray, but with some kind of icy buildup on the edges. She swallowed hard. She'd read too many records about it to not be afraid. Her father only spoke about it reluctantly.

A sign nearby had directions to the power core and computing core. Dull red bulkhead doors blocked the way.

Isaac looked at Braun. "They didn't restore power, right?"

Braun shook his head. "We bring portable generators to

restore specific systems. Something must have tripped the door-control systems."

Lauren walked toward the bulkhead door, checking along the walls. "Shouldn't there be a manual override?"

"She's right," Burk said and went to check the other side.

"Wakiya, we're on the other side of the bulkhead doors. Are you able to open them from your side?" Braun asked.

Lauren searched for a compartment or control interface, but there wasn't anything. She looked at Isaac and shook her head.

"We can pry them open," he said.

Burk exhaled forcefully. "Nothing on this side."

"I can't reach the door," Wakiya said. "I'm pinned."

Braun stepped toward the doors and felt along the almost nonexistent crease where the two sides met in the middle.

Isaac hastened over to him. "Can you remote access the generator? Do they know which one caused the door to shut?"

Braun asked his wife. "She's asking Torren."

"Good, have her ask him if the generator is still online. That might be what's holding the door shut," Isaac said.

Lauren frowned. She'd accompanied her parents on some of their excursions into Ovarrow ruins, which included bunkers and stasis vaults. "How will that help? Aren't the bulkhead doors designed to fail in a closed state to protect the rest of the station?"

"It depends," Isaac said, and he glanced at Braun. "If the computer systems registered a failure with the power core, then yes, it would remain shut regardless of power. But if it wasn't a failure, then it might open."

The bulkhead doors began to retract but stopped with only a small gap of space. Braun shouted. He grabbed onto the door and pulled. Lauren went to the other side and helped Isaac pull. The heavy doors slowly retracted. Burk stepped between them and pushed. The doors retracted for about two meters and then stopped.

Braun ran through the doors. The inside was some kind of computing core. Rows of the small towers denoting central processing units stretched out in front of them. A short distance from them, several CPUs were overturned. Metallic catwalks overhead were piled onto the middle.

"I see someone," Lauren said.

"Go slow," Isaac said, following behind her.

Lauren squatted down. The gloved hand of someone's arm stuck out from underneath. She reached down and grasped the hand, gasping. It was frozen solid.

"They're dead," she said. She leaned forward, trying to peer through the wreckage. She could see part of the body but couldn't see the head.

Braun came to her side. "That's not one of ours. That suit looks much older...pre-war. They might have lived here during the wars."

Lauren's eyes widened for a second and then she nodded. With no atmosphere, there was no reason the body would decompose. It could remain here for thousands of years, and if it wasn't disturbed, it would remain for longer still.

They continued to search the area and found the salvage team nearby. They were trapped.

Braun rushed to where his wife was. She was lying on her side, facing away from them. The EVA suit was faded blue and looked well past its use-by date. Lauren expected that the others were similarly equipped.

Lauren came around so that she was in front of Wakiya. She was wedged underneath a couple of layers of catwalk.

"Wait. Don't move her yet. Check to see if her suit is punctured."

"It's not," Wakiya said. "You must be the Dr. Gates that Braun has told me so much about."

She had pale skin and dark hair. Lauren could see where Amelia had gotten her green eyes.

"It's not heavy. I just can't get the angle to pull myself out," Wakiya said.

Braun looked at Lauren expectantly.

"Just be careful when you lift it off of her," Lauren said.

There wasn't any blood in the area, so her suit might not have been punctured.

Lauren moved on to a man nearby.

"That's Torren. He's been going in and out of consciousness," Wakiya said.

Torren was wrapped in a tangle of cables. There were long gashes on his helmet. She tried to wake him, but he wouldn't respond.

"Isaac," Lauren said. "Torren has a contusion on his forehead. He probably has a concussion." She opened the panel for his suit computer. "I can't get a biometric reading from his suit."

"It might be damaged," Isaac said. He was a short distance away, peering underneath a metallic slab. "No biometrics registering in this suit. Lips are blue. They're not breathing." He rattled off the list of symptoms, building a final picture, and it wasn't good.

Nance came to Lauren's side. They pulled Torren out, and she leaned over him. "Torren, can you hear me? You need to wake up," she said. She banged a gloved fist on his shoulder, calling out his name, trying to startle him to wakefulness. There was darkened skin on his cheeks down to his neck in streaks. It might have been some kind of body art, but Lauren had never seen anything like it.

Torren started to wake up and slowly opened his eyes. His pupils were fully dilated. Lauren shined a light on his face and moved it away. She repeated it twice, trying to get a reaction. Then he shuttered and blinked. His eyes returned to normal.

"I'm Dr. Gates. We've just pulled you out from where you were trapped. Can you tell me your name?"

He swallowed, blinked slowly, and looked at her for a moment. "Torren," he said, his voice sounding strained.

"Good, Torren. Do you know where you are?" she asked.

He blinked and tried to turn his head. He winced.

"Does your neck hurt?"

"Yeah," Torren replied with a slight nod.

"Okay, try not to move it. Do you know where you are?"

He closed his eyes for a moment concentrating. "Research station."

He inhaled deeply, and as he breathed out, the contusion on his forehead began to fade. The dark reds had changed to a pale pink color. Lauren leaned toward him, believing it to be a trick of the light.

"Did you see that?" Nance asked.

Torren swallowed again. "I'm all right. Just give me a minute."

Lauren examined his forehead, and the large bruise was almost completely healed.

"Is he all right?" Isaac asked, calling out from nearby.

Torren began to sit up, and Lauren helped him.

"Take it easy," she said. "You can sit up but lean back here for a few minutes while I go check on the others."

"I will," Torren replied, his voice sounding stronger. He sucked on a straw from inside his helmet, and an amber-colored liquid flowed through it.

She walked away from him, and Nance followed her. "I'm not crazy, right? His bruise just disappeared."

"You're not crazy. I saw it, too."

They went to where Isaac was waiting. Frozen blood floated in the air like thick, dark globules. Lauren retrieved a sample container from her kit and captured several of them for analysis.

Of the six salvagers, two of them were dead, and the rest had various injuries. Despite being appreciative of being rescued, the salvagers were a little reserved when speaking with Lauren and Isaac. She'd tried to put them at ease, but they became even more taciturn upon learning that they were doctors. She thought Wakiya and a salvager named Moteki had broken bones, but she'd have to wait until they returned to the shuttle to be sure.

Nance looked around. "I don't understand how any of this happened. Did any of them say?"

Lauren glanced up. It looked as if something had shoved the catwalks above to the side.

Isaac followed her gaze and then nodded. "I think I know."

Burk and Nance looked at him expectantly. Lauren arched an eyebrow. "Well, don't leave us in suspense," she said.

"I think when they tried restoring power to certain systems…see the scorch marks over there? Above us to the left. It's a little hard to see. They're small, but they're there. Anyway, there used to be power cables there. I think there was an overload, which was near the life-support systems. It's kept in liquid form until it's needed, but it becomes volatile when it hasn't been recycled. You can see the blast radius a little farther down. See the impression about two meters away?"

Lauren looked where Isaac gestured. "That seems to make sense."

"Yeah," Nance agreed. "How did you figure that out?"

Isaac shrugged. "It wasn't that hard—"

A bright light flashed nearby, and he stopped speaking. "What is that?"

They walked toward where the salvagers had gathered. Braun stood next to his wife.

"We need to get access to the storage areas. The only way to override the security settings is to temporarily restore power. Otherwise, we'll cause too much damage if we cut it out."

Torren, who looked as if he'd never been injured despite the tears on the outer layer of his EVA suit, leaned over the power generator and was connecting it to one of the CPU towers.

"What are you doing?" Lauren asked.

Torren looked at her and bit his lower lip, considering. "Restoring power to the computing core's essential systems."

"Isn't that what caused the explosion in the first place?" she asked

Torren frowned and looked at Wakiya for a second. The other salvagers exchanged glances.

"Isaac figured out what happened. What's wrong?"

Braun looked at her. "Thank you so much for your help."

Wakiya nodded. "Yes, thank you. We'll be all right now. We can isolate the life-support systems to avoid another explosion."

Lauren looked at Isaac for a second and then back at the salvagers. "Aren't you going to leave? We really need to check your injuries with the equipment we have on our ship."

Wakiya shook her head. "Not until we've got what we came for."

Torren opened a holoscreen and began keying in commands for the generator. The lights nearby began to flicker. Several CPU towers started to glow as power was restored to them.

Isaac walked over to one and opened his wrist computer. He pulled out a connector from his EVA suit and plugged it into the data port on the tower. Burk walked over to his side.

Lauren looked at Torren and walked over to him. "You had a pretty bad bruise on your forehead."

Torren glanced at her for a second and shrugged. "Must not have been that bad. I feel fine now."

Lauren stared at him for a moment. Then she brought up her wrist computer and activated her personal holoscreen. "Didn't look that way to me," she said, showing him an image recorded by the camera on her helmet.

Torren peered at the image.

"And this is what it looks like now," Lauren said and put up a second image. The wound was completely healed.

He shrugged again. "What can I say? I'm a quick healer." He turned back to the portable power generator and ignored her.

Lauren saw Wakiya speaking softly to Braun. She felt like the salvagers were worried about something that had more to do with them being there than the fact that they were aboard a decrepit research station with a dormant Vemus presence. She didn't want to make assumptions about their rapid healing. Their EVA suits could have dispensed medical nanites for emergency healing, but given how old those suits looked, she doubted they had access to medical nanites. The outpost only had limited medical supplies, so she could rule out medical nanites altogether.

Lauren walked away from the others and gestured for Nance to join her.

"What's up?" Nance asked.

"I just want you to stand between me and the others for a minute."

Lauren pulled out her mobile lab kit and then the samples of blood she'd found.

"Should I be concerned?" Nance asked, her hand moving toward her sidearm.

"I'm not sure yet," she replied.

She loaded the sample into the mobile lab and began analyzing it. A report appeared on her holoscreen. Multiple small windows opened, showing different analyses that had been performed. One of them caught her attention, and she peered intently at it.

"What is it?" Nance asked her softly.

Lauren exhaled softly. "This just got a little more complicated."

She walked toward Isaac and Burk. Isaac had several holoscreens active with multiple data windows. "Isaac, check this out. Look at these readings."

He stopped what he was doing and looked at her holoscreen. Burk did as well, and his hand jerked toward his sidearm. He didn't yank it out, but he looked as if he was about to at any moment.

"Where did the sample come from?" Isaac asked.

"They were near the two dead salvagers we found. They're not from anyone else," Lauren said.

Isaac looked at her holoscreen and then at the salvagers.

"There's a lot more than trace amounts of Vemus in their DNA," she said.

Burk muttered a curse and pulled out his weapon. Nance did the same.

"Stop what you're doing!" Burk shouted toward the others. "Step away from that console," he said, gesturing toward Torren with his weapon.

Three of the salvagers pulled out their own weapons.

"Hold it," Isaac said while stepping in front of Lauren. "Everyone take it easy."

A salvager called Moteki pointed his weapon at Burk. "Lower your weapon."

"Not gonna happen," Burk replied harshly.

One of the salvagers came around a CPU tower and Nance pointed her weapon at them. "Not smart."

"Come any closer and we'll see how good those weapons really are," Burk said.

"We can talk, or we start shooting. I, for one, would much rather talk," Isaac said.

27

LAUREN MOVED to the side a little so she could see Braun. "Did you know about this?"

Braun shook his head. "You don't understand. It's not what you think."

Wakiya looked at her husband. "You brought them here. You say they're not from Magnus Station, but I'm not going to just sit by and let them shoot us."

Burk scowled. "They could change at any moment. They're infected!"

The salvagers kept their weapons trained on them, not at all startled by the news.

Lauren held up her hands in front of her chest, then moved out from behind Isaac. Wakiya was the leader, so she spoke to her. "This is what I detected in the samples of blood I collected. There are indicators that show an exposure to the Vemus. We detected trace amounts on some of the people on the outpost, but not like this. And it doesn't match up with what we encountered in our own star system."

Wakiya narrowed her gaze for a second. She looked conflicted, and Lauren didn't think she wanted to hurt them, but if they were infected by the Vemus, then they were up against the clock before the infection took over.

"We're not infected," Wakiya said.

"Don't!" Moteki said.

Wakiya shook her head. "They helped Amelia, Mot. Braun said she can stand up straight. Her face looks normal."

"I don't trust them," Moteki said, and the others agreed, except for Torren.

Isaac holstered his weapon. "I'm going out on a limb here and admit that I don't understand what's going on. Lauren detected a Vemus infection in the blood of one of the other salvagers."

"And Torren healed from his wounds without any medical treatment. All of you have," Lauren said.

Isaac turned toward Burk and the soldier glared at him. "Lower your weapon, Sergeant."

Burk gritted his teeth and lowered his weapon a little so that it wasn't pointed at anyone. Nance did the same.

Isaac tilted his head toward Wakiya and the others. "Now it's your turn."

"Do it," Wakiya said. "Mot, do it now."

Moteki lowered his weapon.

Wakiya looked at Lauren and shook her head. "I knew we couldn't keep it from you," she said and pressed her lips together. "You detected trace amounts of the Vemus infection on the people at the outpost, and more than that here, but we're not infected."

Lauren glanced at Isaac for a second and then looked at Wakiya.

"Your EVA suits look a little worse for wear," Isaac said pointedly.

Wakiya's lips lifted a little. "We're different than you. We're not what you'd referred to as infected by the Vemus. We represent an adaptation that occurred over time."

Lauren's eyes widened and she inhaled softly. "You're hybrids."

"Hybrids? What do you mean hybrids?" Burk asked.

Lauren kept her gaze on Wakiya. "It means that some of them had been exposed to the Vemus but weren't assimilated like the ones that served the Alpha. They weren't part of the hive." She paused for a few seconds to get her thoughts in order. "That's why Amelia has autoimmune symptoms. Her body was having trouble coping with hybridization. Was she ever exposed to a Vemus?"

Wakiya shook her head. "No, and neither were any of us. Amelia has been that way since birth. We're lucky she survived as long as she did, but you managed to help her. There are others like her."

"Let's not get ahead of ourselves here," Isaac said. "None of you were exposed to the Vemus? You were born this way?"

"Yes and no," Wakiya replied. "We were born this way, but we have been exposed to the Vemus. They don't—"

A klaxon alarm bellowed nearby. Lauren flinched back at the sound and saw an orange flashing light nearby.

She saw Isaac look at the holoscreens near one of the towers. "Power core is coming online."

"Torren, what's happening?" Wakiya said.

Torren stared intently at his own holoscreen and keyed through the interface. "Damn it. A subroutine is bringing main power back online."

The ground began to shudder. Several flashes happened from farther away.

"Shut it down!" Isaac said.

"I'm trying," Torren replied. "Priority is being routed to the communications systems."

Lauren felt like someone was pushing her to the side. She tried to compensate and had to lean to the side to stay upright.

"The station is starting to spin," Burk said. "We have to get out of here before it flies apart."

"It's not going to come apart," Moteki said.

"Fine, you stay here on a two-hundred-year-old decrepit research station whose support structures have been destabilized by a dormant Vemus exoskeleton."

"He's right. It's not safe," Lauren said.

Braun looked at his wife.

"We can't," Wakiya said. "Not without retrieving what we came for. The payload alone can prop up the outpost's resources for months. We can finally get ahead of them."

"The way to your ship is blocked. The only way off is for you to come with us," Lauren said.

"Listen to her," Braun urged. "Please, just listen to her."

Burk walked toward the door. "Isaac, come on. You too, Lauren."

Isaac detached a small comlink from his suit and attached it to the tower. "Coming," he said.

Lauren backed away from Braun and Wakiya. "Your daughter needs you."

Wakiya glared at Lauren. "I'm doing this for her."

Isaac came to Lauren's side. "We can't make them come with us."

Lauren shook her head. "You can always come back here to get what you found."

Braun looked at Lauren and then back at his wife, his expression tense. "None of you can survive without a ship."

"I can't shut it down. It's not responding to my commands," Torren said. He detached the portable power supply.

They left the computing core. Lauren saw the others following them. Braun was speaking urgently to his wife and the rest of the salvagers.

Lauren glanced at Isaac, who was focused on his holoscreen.

"What were you doing here?" Isaac said quietly to no one in particular while peering at the holoscreen. He glanced at Lauren and smiled a little. "They said it was a research station. I'm trying to figure out what they were doing."

Lauren pressed her lips together for a few seconds, thinking about it as they returned to the darkened staircase. The centrifugal force of the station's spin was pushing them toward the wall. Isaac stumbled and Lauren grabbed his arm.

"Pay attention," she said.

She'd grabbed the railing and Isaac did the same.

He looked at her. "Thanks."

They climbed up the stairs, and Lauren felt like something was pressing down on her. She glanced behind her and saw that the salvagers were struggling with the climb just as much as they were.

They're Vemus Hybrids. She needed to put it out of her mind until they reached the shuttle, but she couldn't help herself. They didn't look like the Vemus her father had fought in the Vemus Wars. Those had been tall, brutish creatures that were more primal than a true sentient being. They were controlled by the Alpha. Were the hybrids vulnerable to an Alpha? Was there another Alpha nearby?

They finally reached the deck level where the shuttle was, but they still had a long way to go. She saw something flash on Isaac's holoscreen. He lifted it up and stared at it for a moment. Then he quickened his pace.

"Come on, we've got to get moving," he said.

Lauren matched his pace. They couldn't run, not with mag boots. It was more like a slow trot. They caught up to Burk.

The soldier looked at them. "Sure, now you start moving."

"Just needed the right motivation," Isaac replied. Then he shouted over his shoulder. "Did you guys even know what this station was used for?"

Lauren heard Braun repeat what Isaac had said to the others.

"Doesn't matter. We just needed the supplies that were left here," Wakiya said.

They navigated down several corridors.

"It's a research station. We've been on them before," Torren replied.

"Yeah, but were any of those researching the Vemus Alpha signal? You know, the one used to communicate and control the other Vemus," Isaac said.

Burk growled. "This just gets better and better. We've got no backup. It's just us here."

Isaac nodded. "I know."

"Well, I hope you've got a plan."

"Still coming up with one."

"So what if they were researching the Alpha signal?" Nance said.

"You don't understand," Isaac replied. "This station has been powered down for hundreds of years and we have no idea why. But when they started to restore the power, the very first thing the computer system does is devote resources to the station's communications systems. What did they want to communicate?"

The floor seemed to shift to the side as if she were standing on a rug and someone had pulled it out from under her. The

EVA suit's computer systems sensed the loss of balance and tried to help. This all occurred in milliseconds. She felt like she was about to stumble but this feeling turned into several long steps until she regained her balance. She kept looking around, trying to hear what was happening inside the research station, and she had to remind herself that without an atmosphere there was no way she could hear anything.

They reached the outer corridor and several chunks of the large hull plating had broken away. Lauren looked out of one of them and saw an expanse of stars racing past her view as the station spun. Nausea made her stomach flip-flop and she squeezed her eyes shut.

"Come on, you've got to keep moving," Braun said.

She felt someone squeeze her arm and pull her forward. Lauren opened her eyes and saw that the salvagers had caught up to them. She glimpsed inside Torren's helmet and saw more darkened streaks on his face. His eyes looked different—almost alien but not quite.

Torren turned away from her. She moved forward.

"Jacob," Braun said. "No, it's all right. We found them. Repeat the last."

Jacob was heading to the CDF shuttle.

"What is it?" Wakiya asked.

"The ship is gone. Jacob barely escaped," Braun said.

"Gone, how?"

"He said debris collided with the ship, and he's trying to reach their ship," Braun replied.

"What happened to our ship?" Moteki asked.

"Jacob said it's been destroyed," Braun replied.

"Not possible."

Lauren had to focus on moving forward. She'd step where she thought she could find stable footing, but the EVA suit seemed to be working against her. She gritted her teeth and stopped trying to fight what the suit wanted to do. After a few awkward steps, she began to trust the suit computers and started to move faster.

Lauren saw Burk hoist Nance toward the opening they'd used to get inside the station.

Isaac turned and waved her over. "You're next." He reached out and held Lauren to him, then jumped into the air. Lauren inhaled sharply.

Isaac's suit jets swung them around and they landed on the station's hull. Lauren got her footing and they headed toward the shuttle. The salvagers' ship was gone, as if eighty percent of it had been sheared off.

"Is it broadcasting?" Lauren asked.

Isaac looked at her, surprised for a second. Then he nodded. "It has to be. But we won't know for sure until we get back on the shuttle."

"Go on ahead. I'll make it to the shuttle."

Isaac shook his head. "No, I'm not going to leave you."

"Don't be so dramatic. The ship is only sixty meters away. You can get there faster than I can."

He clenched his teeth and focused on the area in front of them. His jawline looked to have been carved from stone. "Doesn't matter. I'm not leaving you behind."

"Isaac..."

"Stop it. Just don't. A few more seconds isn't going to make any difference, all right?" he said. He held her arm, guiding her along. "And I'm not being dramatic."

In almost any other circumstance, she probably would've laughed at his tone of voice. He seemed to take certain things personally, while others didn't bother him in the least.

"You're not just a doctor," Lauren said.

Isaac exhaled forcefully. "You want to talk about this now?"

They trotted along. She was breathing faster from the exertion, but she was in excellent cardiovascular shape. So was Isaac.

"Yeah, there's no way for you to deflect. Unless of course you're going to leave me behind."

"You're something else," he muttered.

She saw him shaking his head in annoyance.

"I'm waiting, Isaac."

"No, I'm not just a doctor."

He stopped for a second, and Lauren saw the comlink channel switch to private. "It's only the two of us now."

He was quiet for a few seconds.

"I'm still waiting, Isaac. It's time for you to be honest with me."

"God, I know. I know," he said. "I knew this was coming. All right, fine. I'm an agent with the Colonial Intelligence Bureau. I'm here to help your father assess the political climate of the survivors and advise him and the rest of the diplomatic envoy of anything I discover."

Lauren was so surprised that she was at a loss for words. Her brain seemed to grind to a halt before a deluge of thoughts swept into the abyss. So many things made much more sense to her, but could it be true? No, Isaac couldn't be an agent for the CIB.

"I'm not lying to you, Lauren."

Lauren blinked and pressed her lips together in a tight frown. This was exactly something he would do to trick her. She laughed. It began as a giggle and then unleashed. "You've got unbelievable timing."

Isaac stared at her for a few seconds while they kept moving toward their ship. His mouth hung open. "I'm not playing with you. It's the truth. Look, here are my credentials."

A sub window opened on her HUD. It was an image of Isaac with his name, rank, and some kind of identification number.

"You even had the credentials ready. I can't believe you're doing this now, of all times," Lauren replied.

"I thought about telling you a few times."

"I bet you did. Does my father know?"

Isaac frowned. "I thought you didn't believe me."

"I don't, but now I'm wondering how far you want to take this charade."

"Lauren, it's not an act. I really am a CIB agent. They recruited me almost nine years ago."

Lauren rolled her eyes. "You're a doctor. That license and credentials are real."

"I know. I am. They wanted me to complete my education and become a real doctor. Then I had more training for the CIB. I've been on…"

Lauren arched an eyebrow toward him with a smirk. She knew if she pretended not to believe him he'd either let it go if it wasn't true or he'd vehemently insist if it was.

"Oh my God, I can't believe I fell for that," he said.

Lauren pursed her lips. "You deserve a lot more than that. How could you not tell me what you were really doing on the expedition? Does my father know about this?" she asked, thinking about all the times she'd been around her parents and neither one of them had hinted that Isaac was more than a doctor.

He shook his head. "No, they don't know. No one does. My family doesn't even know. I needed freedom to do what I had to."

They reached the shuttle and Burk looked as if he was speaking to them. Nance opened the hatch to the airlock and climbed inside. Lauren unmuted the team comlink.

"Let them come aboard but keep them in the passenger area. Do not let them roam around," Isaac said.

"Got it," Burk said.

Isaac and Lauren climbed through the hatch and into the airlock. The shuttle was still depressurized, so they were able to go right inside.

She heard Burk call out to the salvagers.

"Nance, help Burk with the salvagers," Isaac said. "Lauren, come with me to the cockpit."

Lauren followed Isaac through the shuttle to the cockpit. Isaac brought up the main holoscreen.

"What can I do to help?" Lauren asked.

"You can begin pre-flight checks for me."

Lauren accessed the shuttle's flight systems and initiated the standard protocols for bringing the engines back online.

"Shit," Isaac muttered. "The station's broadcasting an Alpha signal."

She looked at what he was doing. He had a signal analysis window up and compared it to the Vemus Alpha signal used during their war with the Vemus. It wasn't an exact match, but the probability was eighty-nine percent, which was close enough.

"Where is it broadcasting to?" she asked.

"I don't know. It seems to be going everywhere."

The shuttle's intercom became active. "We're all aboard. Get us out of here."

"Working on it. How good are you with point defense cannons?" Isaac asked.

"Are you serious? Point defense cannons are managed by the computer's AI systems," Burk replied.

"That's what I figured. Sit tight back there. Have everyone strap in. Stay on individual life support," Isaac said. He looked at

Lauren. "We need to take out the communications array. Can you fly the shuttle?"

Lauren's eyes widened. "The station is spinning. I can't line up a shot for you."

"Don't worry about that. I can get us there, but if I need to switch over control to you, can you fly us away?" he asked.

Lauren's gaze flicked toward the control console and then back at Isaac. "I can, as long as it's nothing fancy. I can fly us out of here."

Isaac nodded and brought the shuttle's engines online. "Open the point defense system."

Lauren navigated through the computer systems and performed the activation. "Ready."

Isaac detached the landing claws from the stations hull and used maneuvering thrusters to guide them a short distance away from it. Since they were already spinning with the station, they hadn't lost any velocity.

"You sure your dad didn't show you how to use the shuttle's weapons systems?"

"No, Isaac," she scowled. "He showed me how to use a rifle and some other personal weapons. He didn't show me how to use assault cannons."

"Sheesh, you don't have to get so touchy about it."

He thrust the shuttle forward and began circling around the station. Pieces of the station were detaching and flying off into space. Isaac maneuvered the shuttle to avoid them.

"Stand by to take control of the flight systems," Isaac said.

"What do you want me to do then?"

"Don't hit anything."

Lauren heaved a sigh.

"Who's being dramatic now? Hmm." He blew out a breath. "Just ease us away from the station. Then I'll take over."

"Got it."

The communications array was a series of small dishes and antennas. Lauren watched the holoscreen as they closed the distance to it. They were mostly covered with the Vemus exoskeleton except for the main antenna.

"Passing control to you. Just stay on course until I tell you otherwise," Isaac said.

Lauren grabbed the flight controls from the copilot's seat. Her HUD switched to green as control of the shuttle passed to her. She resisted the urge to slightly alter their course to test whether she was really in control of the shuttle.

"Firing," Isaac said.

The mag cannons on the shuttle's hull fired ahead of them, peppering the exoskeleton. Lauren glanced at the comms system, and it was still detecting the broadcast. Isaac tried to hit the antenna but kept missing. Lauren was sure mag cannons hadn't been designed for line-of-sight firing, but she wasn't going to tell Isaac that.

Their trajectory was bringing them closer to the hull.

"Steady," Isaac said.

Lauren swallowed hard and kept her hands still.

"A little to the left," he said.

Lauren moved the controls to the left and maneuvering thrusters brought them over.

The antenna blew apart and the signal went offline.

"Yeah!" Isaac said. "Ease us away."

Lauren engaged the maneuvering thrusters, and they began to move away from the station. Something large swung into view. Lauren inhaled sharply. A giant piece of the antenna swung wildly. She jerked the controls to the side and the shuttle banked hard. The breath caught in her throat as proximity alarms blared. She didn't have time to think. All she wanted to do was fly as far away from the station as quickly as she possibly could.

The shuttle lurched down, and her body pressed against the restraints that kept her in the seat.

Lauren cried out and pushed her hands forward, maximizing main engine output. A few moments passed. She clenched her teeth, waiting for something else to hit the shuttle.

"Ease up, Lauren. We're away from the station. Just ease up," he said gently.

Lauren blinked and pulled back on the thruster controls.

"That's it. Okay, pass control back over to me."

Lauren tapped the toggle switch that returned flight control back to Isaac. Several shuttle systems reported damage to them, but she couldn't read them.

Isaac scanned the data, and his head tilted to the side a little. "Damn. It hit our comms array. I can't get it back online. Hey, are you all right?"

Lauren turned toward him and eyed him for a moment. "No, I'm not all right. We almost died."

"But we didn't die. We're still here. You got us through it."

Lauren clenched her teeth and shook her head. She took several deep breaths and tried to calm down.

"We need to warn the CDF. The Alpha signal could be activating dormant systems," Lauren said.

"We will, but subspace comms is down. All comms are down right now. You banged up the shuttle pretty good."

Lauren's eyebrows pushed forward and she scowled. Then she hit him in the arm. "Me!"

"I was kidding. Come on. We have to fix our comms systems or we can't warn anyone," he said and stood.

Lauren stared at the holoscreen for a second. She wanted to argue with him. How could he just take these things in stride?

But what was the alternative other than sitting there feeling afraid? That wasn't going to help anyone. He was right. There was more for them to do. Lauren stood up and followed Isaac out of the cockpit.

He glanced over his shoulder at her.

She glared at him. "I'm fine!"

He held his hands up in a placating gesture and then headed toward the back of the shuttle.

28

CONNOR HEARD the chime of a comlink sound as he entered his ready room near the bridge. The lights brightened when he entered. He set down the hand towel he'd been carrying and accepted the comlink request.

Lenora smiled at him and took in his appearance.

He smiled. "I haven't been gone that long."

"Long enough to be missed."

"I'm sorry I missed our call yesterday. I finished up late and didn't want to wake you."

"I figured as much. I had a chat with Kate Burrows instead."

Connor scratched the top of his head. "I thought she preferred Katherine."

Major Katherine Burrows was the commanding officer of the CDF Destroyer *Python* and had to remain behind at Magnus Station while the rest of the expeditionary force was brought to Saturn.

Lenora shrugged. "She told me to call her Kate, so that's

what I'm going with. She updated me about the status of the mission."

Connor frowned a little. "Reports are filed for the envoy to review."

Lenora chuckled. "I know they are, but they are rather brief. Since I'm not there, Kate and I have had a little chat about how the mission is going. She's really quite good."

Lenora had good instincts when it came to assessing a person's capabilities, and over the years Connor had learned to trust his wife.

"She wouldn't be here with us if she wasn't, but thanks for that."

The CDF hadn't grown so large that it had to accommodate poor officer candidates who somehow failed upward, something he'd observed time and time again during his time with the NA Alliance. By the time it happened with the CDF, he'd be an old man and it would be someone else's problem.

"I've been seeing some new messaging in the common areas on the station now," Lenora said and smiled a little. "It's like they're sending multiple messages at the same time. Welcome people like us, but never forget the past and don't throw away everything they've built."

"Seems consistent with what we expected. They're worried that our arrival will upset the balance they've established."

Lenora nodded but also looked unconvinced.

"What is it?" he asked.

"My impression of Shao Fen is that we're something he has to tolerate for now. I've tried to be openminded, but he's still… reserved. Sometimes I feel like I can't get a good bead on him and what he's thinking."

"I know what you mean."

"We're here to help, but I also feel like we're stepping on his toes. Some of his senior officials are the same, but not all of them."

"This might be soon, but do you think it's time to leave?"

Lenora shook her head. "No, it's too soon for that. We're still working our way through the station. I don't think we're in danger or anything like that, but I will say that I don't think things on Magnus Station are as harmonious as it first appeared."

Connor sighed. "They've been through a lot, and we're still catching up, so I don't think we're too off the mark by taking our time with learning who we can trust." He frowned in thought for a moment. "Maybe 'trust' isn't the right word but learning who we can work with and whether or not they even want our help."

Lenora tilted her head to the side and her lips lifted into a small smile. "You always see right to the heart of things."

Connor chuckled. "I've learned a few things over the years. We had to be careful not to force ourselves—our way of thinking—onto the Ovarrow. It wasn't always a smooth interaction with them."

"You'd think it would be easier with our own species, but I understand what you're saying."

They eyed each other for a moment.

"I have to go. I need to get in the shower before going on the bridge," he said and Lenora nodded. He leaned toward the camera. "If you start to feel that things are going south on the station, don't hesitate to get our people out of there. No one likes to think like that, but if we're not prepared to act, we won't be able to when and if the time comes."

Lenora looked at him for a second. "I know. I just would rather it didn't come to that."

He smiled. "It won't. People like talking to you way more than they like talking to me."

"It's your stoic demeanor."

"If they only knew how you *really* are."

Lenora grinned.

He closed the comlink and stood in his office for a few seconds. Then he went and took a quick shower. He put on a clean uniform and checked his appearance in the mirror.

The two soldiers on post on the bridge saluted Connor as he entered and walked toward the command area where Colonel Oliver Martinez was speaking with his tactical officer. Connor looked at the main holoscreen where the planet Saturn figured prominently, along with icons for the eighty plus moons that orbited the gas giant. Saturn was one of the most beautiful planets in the solar system, but it had so many moons orbiting it that the planet could be considered a mini-solar system all by itself.

Over the past week he'd deployed the CDF ships to patrol the extensive infrastructure that had been built by a bygone age. Connor remembered there had been a vast network of space stations near Saturn when he'd taken his unscheduled trip aboard the *Ark*. However, there must have been advances made in the time between when he'd left and the rise of the Vemus on Earth because it was the only way to explain the massive structures that had been built so far from Earth. Some of them were interconnected, forming an extensive network of multiple space stations that were the size of small continents. It was no wonder Magnus Station had chosen to remain within the vicinity of Saturn. They needed to be near the abundant raw materials available here. Connor wished he could have seen it before the Vemus Wars. It must have been an impressive sight.

"Good afternoon, General Gates," Oliver Martinez said.

"How was the early morning watch?"

Martinez came to stand next to him and they both watched the main holoscreen. "Consistent with what we've been seeing.

There are quite a number of automated defenses still active even among the wreckage. General Quinn has been making good progress among the moons on the far side of the planet. The Talon V's A-Wings are able to penetrate deeply into some of the more dangerous areas and conduct surgical strikes to disable defensive turrets. It's a shame we didn't bring a larger force with us. Even spread out as we are, it's going to take time to really secure the area enough for the salvagers to begin picking away at the pieces."

The edges of Connor's lips lifted. "They're getting impatient, are they?"

"They call it insistent, and I honestly can't blame them. I've prepared a list of sections we've cleared out that I think they can start with but will need your approval."

"I'll review it."

"I still can't believe how much was built here. Was it like this everywhere?"

"Depends on the available resources. Mars supported an extensive infrastructure, and so did places within the asteroid belt and close to Jupiter, but there's a lot more here than when the *Ark* left the solar system."

Martinez nodded. "They just kept building and building. I wonder how many people lived out here. It makes what we've done at New Earth seem so much smaller in comparison."

Connor shrugged. "There were over ten billion people living in the solar system when the *Ark* left, and at least thirty percent of them were away from Earth, but I get what you're saying."

"Bernie thinks they must have had some significant breakthroughs with processing raw materials and massive printers. Sounds right to me. They would have to have been self-sufficient living way out here."

"We'll catch up one day," Connor said.

"Of course we will. We're colonials," Martinez replied with all the surety of a confident man who was old enough to have witnessed some of the harsh realities that life had to offer, as well as its rewards. "Scouting missions have uncovered vast sectors where the Vemus had a significant presence. Exoskeletal material covers much of those areas. The scouts have been keeping their distance by using reconnaissance probes."

"Understood," Connor replied.

The CDF had a lot of experience salvaging materials from the old Vemus fleet, but there was so much of it here that it was anyone's guess as to the best place to start. He didn't want to send soldiers, or salvagers for that matter, into an area where the Vemus might only be dormant. Many of those areas had received a once-over while they focused their attention on non-contaminated spaces to be secured.

At this rate, it didn't feel like they'd ever get to Earth, and Connor wondered if he would recognize it when he saw it. He couldn't help but think about how much it would have changed.

He spent the next few hours overseeing the deployment of CDF forces throughout the area. He'd spoken with Sean, who'd given him a similar update as Martinez's. One thing that was clear was that everyone they'd brought with them on this expedition was satisfied to actually be accomplishing something. The CDF was putting their extensive training to use, although taking out automated defenses wasn't like fighting an all-out battle or facing an enemy fleet. It was more akin to target practice. There had been a few injuries and several small attack fighters had been disabled. No one had died, but the threat was there, and Connor knew in his gut that it was only a matter of time.

He transmitted his approval of Martinez's proposed sectors, opening them up to salvagers from Magnus Station and the surrounding areas, and then broadcasted a general announcement from the *Douglass*. Thinking about Shao Fen and Magnus Station, he had to admit to himself that sometimes he couldn't resist stepping on a few toes. He wanted people to know that the newly secured sectors were available because of what the CDF had done. The salvagers would still need to trade with Magnus Station, but it was important for the survivors to realize that things in the solar system were changing. He was shaking things up, and as much as they tiptoed around, it was the honest truth of the situation. Shao Fen had surely realized that when they arrived.

"General? I have an emergency broadcast transmission from a transport shuttle," Specialist Gabe Marten said, and the tension on the *Douglass's* bridge increased.

Connor swiped away the holoscreen in front of him. "Where is it coming from?"

Martinez was right about the salvagers. They'd probably traveled into one of the unsecured sectors and expected the CDF to rescue them.

"I'm sorry, sir. It's from a colonial transport shuttle. It's one of ours, but it's only a partial message through subspace, General Gates."

Connor's eyebrows rose. "Send it to my station, Specialist."

A new holoscreen became active in front of Connor and his frown deepened when he saw Isaac Diaz's face. Lauren was seated next to him. They both wore EVA suits and were on individual life support.

"General Gates, a Vemus Alpha signal has been transmitted from an old research station. Coordinates of the message origins and detection signatures are attached. We don't know how long—"

The message was cut off.

A Vemus Alpha signal!

Connor glanced at the tactical plot on the main holoscreen. The fleet was spread among the vast network of aged space stations among Saturn's eighty moons. His mouth hung open, and every drop of blood drained from his face.

The screen blanked, and he stared at it, frozen in the command chair. This couldn't be happening. They'd scanned for Vemus Alpha signals and continued to monitor for them. His gaze sank to his own holoscreen, and he keyed in the coordinates from the message. Isaac and Lauren were twenty light-minutes from his location. They were halfway to Jupiter's orbit!

Twenty light-minutes…Isaac hadn't said when the Vemus Alpha signal started broadcasting before he was cut off. It should have already reached them, but they hadn't detected it.

Connor gritted his teeth. He'd taken every precaution, and yet here he was, caught with his pants down. Reminding himself that they were safe for the moment, he shoved thoughts of Isaac and Lauren from his mind. "Tactical, begin a scan for the Vemus Alpha signal. I'm transmitting a new signature to you now."

Silence enfolded the bridge crew as all eyes turned toward him.

"Yes…Yes, General Gates. I've received the new signature pattern," Lieutenant Jim Tucker replied. A few moments later he said. "General, we've included scanning of Vemus Alpha signals since our arrival and nothing has appeared on the scope, but I'm able to detect active broadcasts with the new signature!"

Connor's nostrils flared. The sound of his indrawn breath was harsh, and the heel of his hand scrubbed angrily on the arms of the command chair as he squared his shoulders.

"Put the detection sources on the main holoscreen, including the origin broadcast detected by the transport shuttle," he said in a deadly, hammered-iron voice.

Two marks immediately appeared on the main holoscreen. The first was the signal's origin, but the second signal was located near Saturn. Several more icons appeared as the Vemus Alpha signal was repeated, as if a restless dream had suddenly become a nightmare.

"General, I'm not sure…" Lieutenant Tucker's voice trailed off as if he was at a loss for words.

Connor took in the data on the main holoscreen, and something cold and deadly stirred inside him. "Ops, Action Stations. Set Condition One throughout the fleet. Vemus Alpha signal has been detected. Enemy forces may be coming online."

Klaxon alarms sounded throughout the *Douglass,* and within minutes, the rest of the fleet went to Condition One status.

"Tactical, we need to destroy all the broadcast centers of the Alpha signal as quickly as possible," Connor said.

"Assigning targeting priorities," Lieutenant Tucker replied.

The Vemus Alpha signal was transmitting using old communications technology and was limited by the speed of light. Subspace was a much faster mode of communication. Connor just hoped that the warning had come out in time. They needed to destroy those communication towers. More icons appeared on the tactical plot, and the CDF fleet was deployed right in the middle of them all.

29

SHAO FEN LISTENED to the colonial broadcast announcing the newly secured sectors open to salvages. They were free to retrieve the much-needed resources for Magnus Station and the surrounding outposts.

Le Shen's frowned deepened, and he sighed.

Shao Fen looked at the director of Magnus Security forces and raised his eyebrows.

"They go too far with this," Le Shen said.

Shao Fen closed the holoscreen, but it seemed as if the voice of the colonials could be heard everywhere.

"They haven't violated any agreement."

Le Shen shook his head and rolled his eyes. "Not directly, but this kind of communication should have come through us. Why aren't you angry about this, this…"

"Lack of decorum. Deference," Shao Fen said with raised eyebrows. "This is General Connor Gates's way of sending a clear message to us."

"The message is clear. They don't approve of how we do

things here. They come from a place of abundance, as if they're saviors. They could never have done what was accomplished here. They could never have sacrificed enough. Too much petty idealism. It spreads like a disease."

Le Shen was free to express himself while they were in private, but Shao Fen's patience was being stretched thin. "They are a necessary evil. Something to be endured and acknowledged."

"There have been stirrings in certain areas on the station and among the outposts. We should have rounded up the unclean while we had the chance. How do you think these colonials would react to that?"

"It is impossible for us to detect the tainted among us. It's been tried, and we all suffered for it without making any real gains. I won't repeat the mistakes of our leaders in the past. What is the status of the freighter?"

Le Shen heaved a long sigh and pursed his lips. "The ship is ready. The new batch of exiles are being flown there as we speak."

"What about the additional supplies?"

"They're onboard as you ordered. I hope we're not losing valuable supply caches for a bunch of exiles to squander."

"They only need to get through the orbital defenses and report the status of the planet. They also need enough supplies to survive for a short while in order to be convinced that they have a chance of survival. That's it," Shao Fen said.

"Won't the colonials detect the ship? What if they intercept it?"

Shao Fen looked out the window and clasped his hands behind his back. "Your concerns are well placed. We've never outfitted a freighter so well beyond the supplies and the people aboard. The ship can evade scanner detection. It's another object among an expanse of many others throughout the solar system. I think you're giving the colonials too much credit where their capabilities are concerned."

"That's just it. We can only guess at their capabilities. Specifically, their combat capabilities. They've been doing an efficient job at removing the automated defenses."

"You see, they're working for our benefit. Let them expend resources for us while we remain focused on our ultimate objective."

Le Shen came over and stood by his side. "Do you really believe Ivanov Yanovich has been successful?"

"Regardless of whether I believe it or not, we're going to learn the truth."

"There are plenty of places we can test the weapon here in a controlled environment," Le Shen said.

Shao Fen shook his head. "Unacceptable. The risk is avoidable. I'm going to test it and send a very clear message to not only the tainted but to everyone who's given them shelter all these years. I will have results, and I will use everything at my disposal to get them. However, that doesn't include ridding ourselves of the tainted living in secret among us here. First, they'll learn of our new capabilities, and then the message will be clear. They will leave the station or face the consequences."

"Shao Guo has also proposed target locations both on this station and several outposts that we should seriously consider."

Shao Fen considered it for a few moments and then turned toward Le Shen. "Show me the list. I'm still reluctant to proceed, but I will listen to what you have to say."

Le Shen smiled and folds of old, wrinkly skin lifted into a hungry smile. "I look forward to convincing you, President Shao."

Shao Fen listened while Le Shen went over the list of targets. Ivanov Yanovich had tested the weapon as much as he could. It wasn't supposed to affect humans, but Shao Fen was long past the ability to trust anything that came from a scientist. Too many times he'd experienced setbacks because of a scientist's unfulfilled promises. The people of Magnus Station had suffered as well. No, as brilliant as Ivanov Yanovich was, he was still very much fallible.

The colonials, including the diplomatic envoy, were quite sympathetic to them. He was winning their support, but it was taking time. He was a master of patience. He could wait, but events had been set in motion, and he could either get ahead of that change or merely be a witness to it.

30

CONNOR LOOKED at Sean on the holoscreen in front of him. "The analysts in CIC are working on the Alpha signal. It's different from the signals in our own records. Preliminary analysis indicates that it's a variant of the signal we're familiar with but different enough to evade detection by our sensors."

The *Odyssey* was on the other side of Saturn on the edge of the rings. Without subspace comms, they wouldn't have been able to communicate.

"The signal was used for command and control of Vemus forces. Our sensors haven't detected an attack force," Sean said and paused for a second. "About the only thing we've seen is the activation of other comms centers repeating the same broadcast."

"Not just any comms centers—the ones with the Vemus exoskeleton and presumably dormant Vemus inside."

Sean blew out a breath. "We can use heavy weapons until we pull out our destroyers, which are currently tasked with taking out the communications centers."

Connor nodded. "There's been an uptick in automated defenses coming online. That's not a coincidence."

"General Gates! The *Defiant* is under heavy attack," Lieutenant Jim Tucker said.

"Damage reported?"

"They've lost their port-side main engine. Looks like they were hit by something much heavier than auto-defense turrets, sir," Tucker said.

Connor looked at the tactical plot on the main holoscreen. The *Defiant* was deep within an industrial complex.

"Comms, tell Colonel Hoffman to withdraw from the sector. Ops, move the *Douglass* so we can provide covering fire to the *Defiant*," Connor said.

His commands were confirmed and followed.

He turned toward the comlink with Sean. "Things are starting to heat up over here."

Sean nodded. "Here, too. More powerful mag cannons are coming online from places we haven't detected from our initial sweep of the area. I'm tasking some of the attack wings to disable them."

Connor nodded. They had multiple squadrons of Talon V space fighters deployed. They could assist in taking out mag cannons, as well as the comms stations, but they'd be vulnerable to other kinds of attacks.

"Use the transport carriers. Get the rest of the squadrons deployed. We can extend their effective range with carriers," Connor said.

"Understood. I'll get to it, sir."

The comlink closed. Squadron leaders weren't going to like their orders at all. This tended to happen when they were deployed far enough away that they were reliant upon the carrier to return for a pickup or a refueling station was available to top them off. It was risky to deploy them that way, but Connor thought they could contain the situation if they silenced the comms stations. He had no way of knowing whether the additional defenses that were coming online would stop if the Alpha signal stopped broadcasting.

Connor looked at the tactical plot on the main holoscreen and wondered whether there could be a Vemus Alpha hidden away. The Alpha he'd help destroy over thirty years ago had been huge—over twenty kilometers across. It had been cobbled together from asteroids and space stations captured during the wars in the solar system. The Alpha signal was going to eventually reach Earth and the other human settlements between.

What had Isaac and Lauren been doing on a research station so far away from any outpost? Had they triggered the signal somehow? Connor hadn't been able to reach the shuttle, and no more transmissions had been received. Were they fleeing some remnant Vemus force? Transport shuttles only had minimal weapons capabilities.

He shook his head and cleared his thoughts. If there hadn't been so many CDF forces deployed, he would have order HADES VI missiles to be used with their most destructive yield. It would have made quick work of the defenses they'd seen, but it would have also vaporized all the available resources Magnus Station and the other outposts so desperately needed.

He might have to, but he could delay the order for a while longer. He had to give his fighting forces more time to put a stopper in the threat.

31

ETHAN CROSSED the flight deck of the armored transport carrier *Avalon*. Flashing amber lights pulsed along the walkway between the Talon V Stingers with their stub wings and elongated snouts. He spotted his ship and saw that a deck tech had one of the panels open underneath. It was never a good sign to see a ship being worked on by deckhands right before they were about to launch a mission.

He walked over and leaned down to look at what the tech was working on. "Don't tell me you broke it?"

The tech was a short young girl named Charlie. "Not a chance, sir. Just a last-minute update that the brass wanted us to push out before you boys left us."

"What's in the update?"

"Updated detection signatures for the Vemus Alpha. It'll help you locate the comms platforms," she replied and looked at him. "I thought you 7th jockeys were supposed to be the best."

Ethan chuckled. "We *are* the best."

"Oh yeah, then how come almost all of you locked out your

flight systems from updates? I could have pushed this out from the maintenance console, but jockeys like you made me come out here and get my hands dirty."

Ethan arched an eyebrow. "I thought you liked to get dirty?"

Charlie shook her head and laughed. "You're lucky you're cute," she said, and disconnected the cable that went from her tablet to his ship. She closed the panel.

"I'm sorry about that," Ethan said as Charlie came out from underneath his ship.

"I'm sure you are."

He shrugged. "We don't like last-minute updates being pushed to our perfectly running ships."

Massey howled in excitement from nearby and ran over to Ethan. "Yeah baby! We're finally gonna see some action," he said and looked at Charlie. "Did you finish with my ship yet?"

Charlie narrowed her gaze. "Don't even get me started about your ship, Lieutenant Massey." She jutted her chin toward Ethan. "At least he was only one update behind, but you were seven."

Massey's mouth hung open guiltily. "Oh…"

"Yeah, oh… I'm going to report this to my superiors—"

"No, no, don't do that. Can't we work something out? I'm sure there's something I can do for you. Come on. What do you say? Please be as sweet as you look. Please?"

Charlie looked at him for a few moments.

"Thanks for taking care of my ship. I won't let it lapse again," Ethan said.

Charlie's gaze slid toward Ethan and she smiled.

"Hey, would you mind telling me whose flight systems were up to date?" Ethan asked.

Charlie looked at her tablet computer. "Lieutenants Vijura, Kalas, and Trace."

He wasn't surprised to hear the two Ovarrows' names, but he hadn't expected to hear Eva's name on the list.

Eva walked by and overheard her name being mentioned. She smirked and twitched her eyebrows as she walked past them.

"Thanks again," Ethan said and used his implants to authenticate with the ship's computer systems. Two armored panels separated on the bottom of the space fighter and his chair lowered toward the ground.

Charlie walked away with Massey following her like some kind of eager puppy.

Ethan grinned as he put on his helmet and climbed into his seat, which then retracted into the ship. He brought up the ship's computer systems and they ran through their startup diagnostics that were part of the pre-flight checks. He saw an update window flash on the holoscreen, but it was gone in an instant.

He checked the status of the critical systems and then joined the strike team comlink. "Gates reporting in, Team Leader."

"Ah yes," Anton Stone replied. "Ladies and gentlemen, our own personal wild card has seen fit to join us."

Ethan heard several of the others laugh.

"Where's Massey?" Anton asked.

"Oh, he's trying to convince the tech specialist not to report him for failing to allow updates to his ship's computer systems," Ethan said.

"Oh yeah? They're really cracking down on that," Anton replied.

"So that's what was happening when I walked by. How outdated was his ship?" Eva asked.

"Seven," Ethan said with a grin.

"It's a wonder he hasn't had his flight status revoked," Anton said.

The comlink chimed as someone else joined. "Who had their flight status revoked?" Massey asked.

"You, you idiot. Seven iterations behind? Are you crazy? Are you trying to get yourself killed?" Anton said.

"I'm not going to die. Seven isn't that bad."

Silence over the comms channel.

"Hello," Massey said. "Is anyone there? Shit, maybe I got cut off."

Ethan shook his head. He tried to think of something clever to say but came up blank. He looked over at the space fighter next to his and saw Massey waving at him. Ethan frowned and shook his head.

Massey rolled his eyes and waved his hands vigorously. "I'm trying to talk to you!" he said.

"Hey, what happened to Massey?" Ethan asked.

"No idea. Can you see him?" Eva asked.

Massey looked as if he were punching the control panel in front of him.

"That's it, Logan. Hit it harder."

"Ethan, when I fix this damn comms system... It was probably that damn update that screwed it up."

"I'd say it was pilot error," Anton said.

Massey stopped speaking for a few seconds, finally catching on. "Screw you guys. You could hear me the whole time? I swear I'm going to get each and every one of you."

"Can someone mute his comlink, please?" Ethan asked.

"I sure can, Lieutenant Gates," Anton said. As the team leader, he could control the shared comlink, and Massey's comms became silent.

Ethan smiled and then waved at Massey, who shook his head and then flipped him the finger.

A priority comlink chimed into their session, and all of them became quiet.

"This is Colonel Walker. 7th, we've received updated mission priorities. Approximately thirty minutes ago, a Vemus Alpha signal was broadcast from a derelict research station. This caused a cascade of broadcasts to be taken up by comms platforms previously believed to be offline. Our mission priority is to destroy the comms platforms as quickly as possible in our sector."

"Colonel, has a Vemus Alpha been detected?" Ethan asked.

"Negative. No Alpha has been detected yet. However, additional weapons systems have come online, so if you see anything out of the ordinary, you're to report it to your team leaders."

The priority channel disconnected, and they were once again on their team channel. Anton hadn't rejoined them yet. He was on the strike-leader channel getting more detailed mission parameters. Ethan had lost his strike-leader status and hadn't had the opportunity to earn it back.

Anton rejoined their comms channel. "All right, listen up. We're going to deploy from the *Avalon* in waves so we can cover as much of the sector as possible and as quickly as we can. There's also a good chance that we'll receive updated targeting priorities once we're out there. Strike teams are as follows: Gates you're with me. Vijura and Kalas. Trace and Massey. This is as real as it gets. Let's get in there and see if we can stop the Vemus Alpha signal from broadcasting. Oh, and one more thing. Conserve your fuel as much as you can. We're going to be so far away from the fleet that we won't have the fuel supplies to make it back."

Ethan pressed his lips together and nodded.

Anton pushed out a list of priority targets to their ships while they waited for the *Avalon* to bring them to their deployment zone.

The armored carrier had two things going for it—the defenses in the form of armored plating and point defense systems, and the speed that its engines afforded. It was a fast-deployment ship designed to race into a hot zone and get out again.

They were the fifth group from the top and had to wait for their turn. Chitchat was kept to a minimum, and he watched as the other strike groups flew out of the hangar. Ethan familiarized himself with the target coordinates. There wasn't much more intelligence than that—no detailed scans or anything. This mission must have been so last minute that they hadn't been able to perform any type of scouting mission beforehand. They were to concentrate on the broadcast platforms and destroy them. He thought about his father, who was probably on the bridge of the *Douglass* on the far side of the planet. He wasn't prone to half measures. If his father believed there was a credible threat coming from these comms platforms, he would do his utmost to destroy as many of them as he could.

"Heads up. We're next," Anton said.

Ethan checked the power output of his ship's engines for what seemed like the umpteenth time. It hadn't changed. The ship was ready for action and so was he.

The mission status indicator on the HUD flashed green.

"Fly! Fly! Fly!" Anton said.

The edges of Ethan's lips lifted in anticipation, and he disengaged the ship from the flight deck and engaged the thrusters. Anton flew his fighter ahead and he followed. They were broken up into three teams of two. One person would lead the strike and the second would cover their six. They'd trade off just as they'd done in hundreds of training sessions before this.

Ethan flew the fighter in a tight formation with Anton's ship. This would reduce their chances of point defense scanners detecting the number of ships flying in their vicinity. He glanced at a sub window with the tactical plot, which had six icons representing their strike team. They quickly flew away from the *Avalon* even as it headed toward its next drop-off point.

The HUD in front him highlighted the coordinates of the nearest broadcast platform. Ethan peered ahead, trying to locate the broadcast comms station but couldn't see it. They were flying toward a vast network of interconnecting space stations forming a huge platform that dwarfed even the lunar shipyards back home.

Anton whistled softly. "I still can't believe the scale on which they built here."

Ethan didn't reply right away.

"Hey, you all right, Ethan?" Anton asked.

"Yeah," he replied somberly. "I just keep thinking about how many people died there."

Anton sighed heavily. "God, I almost can't imagine. I bet it was a lot."

They flew toward the massive habitat. He thought there were about forty decks from top to bottom.

"The broadcast must be on the high side," Ethan said.

"Let's go in high and tight."

They closed the distance to the habitat, and from far away it had appeared as if it were a single structure, uniform, but that wasn't the case as they got closer to it. Their angle of approach was from underneath, and Ethan saw massive holes in the structure that still had clusters of metallic debris near it. He wouldn't be surprised if they saw the frozen corpses of spacers who had died hundreds of years ago.

His mouth formed a grim line, and he increased the engine

output. He needed to focus on the mission, but part of him couldn't help thinking about the lives that had been lost here. He knew that the wars fought in the Sol System had been cataclysmic. He'd scoured every report he could find in preparing for missions just like this one, but he'd underestimated the stunning impact of the sheer loss of life that had taken place here. The massive scale of it was beyond anything he could have imagined, and this was only one sector of it.

The two Talon V Stingers flew over the top of the habitat. Vemus exoskeletal material engulfed huge portions of it like a wave of gooey mucus frozen forever in time.

"Broadcast tower located," Anton said.

Ethan glanced at his scope. "I see it, too."

"I'll get this one."

"I'm right behind you," Ethan said.

The two fighters sped forward over a graveyard of partially covered habitat. Towers poked through the exoskeletal mass. The habitat had been a veritable city, and parts of it still shone as it reflected the distant star.

They flew toward a cluster of towers and their scanners identified where the broadcasts were coming from. Anton edged ahead of Ethan's fighter, and Ethan glanced down at his scanner, looking for any point defense systems that were still active.

"My scope is clear," Ethan said.

"Right, I'm taking the shot."

Anton fired two of his forward-facing cannons and a stream of destructive force blasted through the comms tower. The broadcast stopped.

"Nice shot," Ethan said.

"Thank you very much. I couldn't have done it without you."

Ethan chuckled. A second later, another Alpha broadcast

began spewing from a nearby comms tower. "Redundant comms," he said.

"Let's go. We're just getting started," Anton said.

For the next few hours, they destroyed communications towers, and no sooner was one destroyed than another began squawking to take its place. The others were reporting similar events at their locations. Point defense cannons became active, which added to the challenge of the mission. Since the facilities were old and not maintained, they'd lost much of their effectiveness. The mag cannons were outright sluggish, and Ethan could take them out while conserving his ammunition stores.

"I know this is tedious, so I'm open to ideas and suggestions," Anton said.

"Why can't we just have one of the destroyers send a couple of missiles here and be done with it?" Massey said.

"I hate to say it," Eva said, "but Logan has a point. My ammo stores are fine, and fuel reserves aren't bad, but the rate this is taking, we'll need to refuel before we can complete the mission."

"They won't do it," Anton said.

"Why the hell not?" Massey asked.

"They're still trying to preserve these habitats so they can be repurposed."

Massey began to say something else, but Anton spoke over him. "This isn't going to devolve into a bitch-fest. So, if you don't have any real ideas to make this go faster, zip it."

The others became silent.

Anton cleared his throat. "Vijura? Kalas? Are you on comms?"

Both Ovarrow answered that they were.

"Good, I was just checking to see if you were still there."

"I don't have any suggestions. Our instructions are clear, but we haven't seen an alert about an attack force," Vijura said.

"The industrial complex has ship-busting defensive measures," Ethan said.

"Ship-busting?" Vijura asked.

"Large, heavy mag cannons designed to easily pierce the hull of an attacking vessel," Ethan replied.

"Where did you hear about that?" Massey asked.

"Yeah, I was just wondering the same thing," Anton added.

Ethan shrugged. "The *Avalon* still has a subspace data link to the *Odyssey*. I queried the fleet status."

"You don't have clearance for that. None of us do," Eva said.

Ethan shifted in his seat. "You just have to know where to look. Oh, I have an idea to make our jobs easier, if you want to hear it."

A round of affirmatives came over comms. Ethan glanced out the window of his fighter and saw Anton jut his chin up toward him.

"We need to destroy power stations. That will disable comms platforms and anything else that's coming online."

Massey grinned hungrily. "I like it. That's a fine idea. Good job, Gates."

"Agreed," Anton said.

"Wait a second," Eva said. "Aren't intact power stations on the list of places the salvagers want to recover precious resources?"

"Probably," Ethan replied. "But an Alpha signal should take a higher priority. We need to silence the broadcast as quickly as possible. This is how we can do it."

Vijura cleared his throat. "I agree with Ethan."

"Thanks for the support," he replied.

"Let's try that. Target power stations or relays near the comms platforms," Anton said.

The others jumped off Anton's comlink and it was just the two of them. "Nice work coming up with that."

"It still has to work."

"Oh, I think it will."

Ethan brought up the scanner interface and selected the appropriate filter to help them find active power sources. He then combined it with active comms broadcasts. His view of the outside dimmed as the HUD expanded into an overlay of the surrounding area, highlighting the targeting priorities he'd selected. Ethan shared the scan parameters with Anton and then offered it to the rest of the team.

His view of the habitat dimmed as if the view had been polarized against bright starlight. Shimmering amber targets began to flash as the powerful sensor array of the Talon V penetrated the metallic and exoskeletal hull of the space habitat.

"That's some view," Anton said.

"I'll take point," Ethan said and then added, "Try and keep up."

He maximized his thruster output and smirked as his fighter sped ahead. There were several alerts for new mag cannon batteries fired on them.

"I've got them," Anton said.

He followed a short distance behind, and Ethan saw a stream of fire from the ship's cannons.

Ethan flew toward the power station, which looked like a small mound that protruded from the Vemus exoskeleton covering the area. He fired all three of his mag cannons, blanketing that area around the mound. The high-density shots penetrated the exoskeleton, and after a few seconds, there was a burst of orange that lasted for half a second. The comms platform broadcasting the Vemus Alpha signal went offline, and no others in their immediate vicinity took up the call.

Ethan smiled. "I'd say that was a successful test."

"Agreed. Good shooting, Lieutenant Gates."

They flew onward and made quick work of the remaining habitat.

"That took a lot less time than I thought it would," Ethan said.

The habitat didn't have one all-encompassing power core but was comprised of multiple power stations that had been added as the massive habitat was expanded to its current size.

"Yeah, I just sent an update into COMCENT. They approved the tactic, by the way."

Ethan chuckled.

"And it looks like we're to regroup with the rest of the 7th," Anton said.

Ethan keyed in the coordinates, and they regrouped with the rest of the team before heading to the waypoint.

"I'm glad to be away from there," Massey said.

"What's the problem? Was the challenge not good enough for you?" Anton asked.

"It wasn't that. I kept wondering if there were Vemus alive back there," Massey said.

"We saw a lot of bodies on our run," Eva said.

Silence took over the group comlink like flames being doused by a bucket of ice-cold water.

"I hate this place," Massey said quietly. "It's not right that all those people were just left like that."

Ethan nodded and was reminded that as much as Massey got under his skin, there were times when they were in battle-steel agreement. "We'll set it right."

"How?"

"I don't know, but you're right. The people who died here shouldn't have been left like that."

"Your cremation and burial traditions seem inefficient for deaths on this scale," Vijura said.

"Geez, Vijura," Massey said. "No need to state the obvious."

"Have I offended you in some way?"

"No," Ethan interjected. "It's not going to be easy. This is probably something that your parents understand more than you do."

"You mean the great pain," Vijura said. "That is something I've only witnessed in the haunted retellings of our acclaimed archivists of the past. Now I understand. I will not be so insensitive from now on."

The Ovarrow had witnessed and participated in the destruction of almost their entire species. Vijura and Kalas were part of a new generation of Ovarrow born after the brink of such wanton destruction. Ethan looked at the habitats in the distance and thought that this is what it must have felt like for the Ovarrow to come out of stasis and see the remnants of their once proud civilization. They were spared the sight of the dead bodies, even from a distance, but it was still troubling to see. He'd tried to ignore the sight and focus on their objective. They all did. And they all failed to one degree or another.

They flew toward a distant industrial complex located on the outermost of Saturn's moons, a distance of three-point-five million kilometers from the planet and its majestic rings.

From a distance, the rings of Saturn had mesmerized people since they were first seen through the lenses of the earliest telescopes. Not much had changed. As they flew away from the rings, he switched his video display to the aft camera view. At this distance, Saturn looked peaceful.

"Ethan, have you managed to get anymore fleet status updates?" Massey asked.

"I've been a little busy to check."

"Yeah. Yeah, I get it. Could you check?" Massey asked but not in his usual bullish and demanding tone. He was more reserved and shaken up by what he'd seen.

A text message popped up from Eva.

Please do it. He's really upset.

"All right, I'll check, but it's going to take a little while to get a response. It's a low-level request that has the least priority."

"Thanks, I really appreciate it."

Ethan opened a data connection to the carrier ship *Avalon* and ran the same query he'd used before.

"Request sent. I'll let you guys know when the update comes back," Ethan said.

All the strike teams of the 7th A-Wing converged on a distant outpost of Saturn's farthest moon. The size of it could hardly warrant the classification of a moon, being on the smallest side of the spectrum. It barely had a spherical shape to it and looked more like a large chunk of some other celestial body that had either left a piece of itself behind or was orbiting the planet on some other plane.

Ethan spotted flashes of light in the distance but didn't know what they were. He increased the magnification of his HUD and the breath caught in his throat. Talon V strike teams sped across the outpost, and although he couldn't see it, he recognized the attack formation.

He checked his comms system, and it was fine.

"They're under attack. Dead ahead. Nothing on comms," Ethan said.

"Holy shit," Anton gasped. "Ethan, report this in to COMCENT. I'll try reaching the rest of the 7th."

Ethan opened a comlink to the *Avalon*. The comlink established a connection and then went offline. He blew out a breath and tried again. It didn't work. He checked the tactical plot, and the *Avalon* disappeared from the plot.

"Comms to the *Avalon* are offline," Ethan said.

"Offline!" Massey said. "That means it's been destroyed!"

The others began to speak at the same time, and Anton muted their comlinks. "Can it. Ethan, did you get an update out?"

"Negative, I wasn't able to get a connection. I bet no one knows about the attack."

"Understood. Broadcast our status over comms. It'll reach the fleet eventually."

"On it," Ethan replied and sent a data burst with a quick update. "Done."

It was going to take a while to get a response, let alone support.

"All right, we're going to rendezvous with the 7th as ordered. Let's get in there."

They maxed out their engines to emergency attack speed. Ethan was pressed back into his chair as the ships sped forth with such force that it stressed the inertia compensators.

Once they were within tight-beam transmission range, they received alerts from Colonel Walker, who assigned them to Captain Webster's attack force.

"Strike team delta," Captain Mike Webster said, "we're under attack. Our comms have been cut off by some kind of dampening field. The station appeared to be some kind of scrap shipyard, but it has heavy automated defenses, and there are enemy fighters similar to the Talon V Lancer class."

"Is it the Vemus?" Anton asked.

"Unknown, but I'd say it's a fair assumption that they are.

Regardless, they attacked us while taking out the comms platforms in the area," Webster replied.

"Understood," Anton replied. "What do you need us to do?"

"There are a few remaining comms platforms that might also be tied to the dampening field. Take them out and we get our comms back."

"Understood, Captain. We tried to reach the *Avalon*, but it went offline."

"They've just appeared on our scope. Take out the comms platforms and then contact me for further instructions. Webster out."

"You heard the man. We're to destroy the remaining comms platforms and then regroup with the others. Sending coordinates to all of you," Anton said.

"Who's attacking us?" Massey asked.

A new waypoint appeared on Ethan's HUD. It was located away from the fighting.

"They're not sure," Anton replied.

"Look at it over there. Looks like we're missing a hell of a fight," Massey said.

"The sooner we take out our targets, the sooner we can join up with the rest of the squadron. Eva, you and Massey fly ahead max speed to scout the area."

"Got it, sir," Eva replied.

The two Stingers raced ahead to the target coordinates.

"Data link is established. It'll be up to the rest of us to take out the targets," Anton said.

"Sir," Vijura said, "are we going to use Ethan's tactic with the power stations again?"

"It depends on what the scouts find."

They followed after Eva and Massey, maintaining a distance that kept them two to three minutes behind. Ethan watched the data feed that kept a comlink to the scouts. Scan data captured by Eva and Massey's ships would be beamed to them as well. Then they'd have to decide which comms array to destroy first.

"Watch out," Massey said.

"I saw them. Heavy defenses. Looks like a mix of grasers and mag cannons. The damn grasers started to penetrate the hull. This is a hardened facility. Someone wanted this place defended," Eva replied.

"There's no way we can penetrate those defenses and take out the comms platform. Look at how they're set up. It's almost complete coverage. We need to call in a missile strike," Massey said.

A few seconds later the scan data was received by Ethan and the rest of the team.

Anton cursed. "I hate to say it, but for once I'm inclined to agree with Logan."

"Don't sound so surprised," Massey replied.

Ethan studied the targeting data and the video captured by the scout ships. The problem was that the comms station was at the bottom of a crater that the facility was built on and had natural defenses. They'd have to fly past the ring of automated defenses, destroy the comms station, and then fly back out again.

"I can make that shot," Ethan said.

"No, you can't. The area is too hot," Eva said.

"Yeah, stop trying to show off," Massey said.

"Anton, I can make that shot. Taking out that comms station could end the dampening field and allow us to call in for reinforcements."

The others were quiet on the comms channel, waiting to hear Anton's response.

"I can do this. Our orders are clear. Take out the comms station. No one else is going to help us. It has to be done," Ethan said. He bit his lower lip for a second. "I'm the only one of us who can. Give me a window and I'll get that shot."

Eva and Massey launched into a tirade about how crazy he was.

"This isn't a training mission or a simulator," Massey said.

Ethan gritted his teeth. He couldn't snap at Massey as much as he wanted to. He glanced at the timer. They'd be at the target area in less than a minute.

"Ethan," Anton began.

He could hear it in his friend's voice. He shook his head. He was done with asking for permission. It was time for action.

Ethan shoved the throttle all the way up and his fighter sped ahead of the others.

"Ethan!" Anton shouted.

Ethan glanced at the tactical plot, and it showed Vijura and Kalas speeding behind him. Then Anton's ship increased velocity.

"We'll provide covering fire," Vijura said.

"Thanks," Ethan replied.

There was nowhere for him to take cover for his attack run. He was exposed, and the only advantage he had was the speed of his ship. Klaxon alarms blared in warning as the grasers locked onto his ship. Ethan nudged the maneuvering thrusters to alter his trajectory. If he went too hard in any direction, he'd tumble across the attack area, unable to destroy the target.

"We're on it," Vijura said.

The two Ovarrow-piloted fighters began firing their mag cannons, peppering the automated defenses. Targeting lock from the automated defenses chirped another warning. The nose of his ship began to register a heat warning. Ethan fired all three of his mag cannons. They were angled outward for the distant shot.

They closed in on the rim of the crater. Ethan angled his

approach to stay in line with it. If they flew higher or lower, more automated defenses could target them.

Kalas let out a strangled cry and his comms cut off. His ship disappeared from the tactical plot. He was dead.

"I'm going to draw their fire," Vijura said.

"No heroics. I just need to get past the initial line," Ethan said.

He'd have to fight to get out the other side of the crater, but he'd worry about that after he destroyed the comms station.

"Kalas is dead," Anton said. "Make this count, Ethan."

Ethan focused all this attention in front of him. Kalas's death wasn't real to him. He shoved away his memories of the quietly reserved Ovarrow he'd known for over a year.

The problem with flying so fast in one direction was that it made maneuvering costly to his fuel reserves, and he needed to alter course. He keyed his destination into the nav systems and the ship's AI would assist him with reaching his target.

Ethan squeezed the trigger for his mag cannons and the defense cannons returned fire. Several of them fired at Vijura and Anton as they attempted to draw their attention, which gave him the opening he needed on this suicide run.

He punched through the defenses, and his top board-thrusters fired. The fighter sank down into the crater. Point defense cannons fired at him, hitting one of the stub wings and disabling the mag cannon. His ship began to spin, and it took every bit of pilot instinct he had to regain control. He had seconds to lock in on the comms station. Ethan squeezed the trigger and his remaining two cannons fired on full auto. Thick, metallic slugs raced toward the target at near relativistic speeds. The crater wasn't overly large, but it was deep. He shot the area surrounding the comms station, including the arrays. There was a bright flash as it was destroyed.

Ethan shoved hard on the flight controls. The nose of his ship went straight up, and he engaged his main engines. The ship shot upward, but he was still closing the distance to the side of the crater. Automated defense cannons fired on, tracking him as he made his ascent. He gritted his teeth as his inertia dampeners were overwhelmed. The ship's AI fired maneuvering thrusters in precise increments, barely keeping Ethan from crashing into the side of the crater. He cleared the edge and swung the ship downward to avoid point defense cannons. He rolled to the side and shots from point defense cannons tracked his roll, narrowly missing his ship.

"Holy shit, he made it out of there!" Massey said.

"Ethan, are you okay?" Eva asked.

He blew out a long breath that he hadn't realized he'd been holding. "I got a few chunks taken out of me and I'm down one cannon, but I'm alive." He paused for a second, clearing his head.

They were far enough away from the point defense systems that it made their tiny spaceships almost impossible to target.

"Comms are back up! The *Avalon* is online. Patching us in," Anton said.

"Ethan, you're the craziest pilot I've ever seen," Massey said.

"Any chance that Kalas was able to eject from his ship?" Ethan asked.

"Negative," Anton replied. "I saw it happen. He never had a chance."

Ethan glanced behind him and sighed.

"His sacrifice was not in vain," Vijura said. "He shall be remembered."

"Damn right he will," Massey said.

"We're not finished yet," Anton said.

They were to join the main squadron. Communications were

still spotty, but they could at least use the *Avalon's* subspace comms system to contact COMCENT.

Ethan opened a private comlink to Vijura. "I'm sorry about Kalas."

"Sometimes sacrifice is required," Vijura said.

"I know, but still. I'm sorry," Ethan said.

There weren't as many Ovarrow as there were humans on New Earth, which was something that would take time to improve. They were all aware of the risks in joining the CDF, but being aware of the risks and living with them was like standing on two opposite sides of a barrier.

The 7th A-Wing squadron was flying away from the area, but they were still engaged with an unknown fighting force. Ethan tried to pull a fleet update through the *Avalon's* connection to the *Odyssey*, but communication was still intermittent.

The *Odyssey* was with the 7th. If they didn't want to be stranded out here, they'd have to regroup with the others.

They flew on an intercept course and the ship's computer managed their fuel reserve. Ethan glanced at it and knew they'd be cutting it close. They still needed to fight when they reached their destination.

The five Talon V Stingers raced to rejoin the rest of the squadron. The journey wasn't going to take long, and it gave them a breather.

The 7th was engaged in a fight with two freighter-sized ships. One of them was heaved to the side and looked to be in its final death throes.

"Where are all the other fighters?" Ethan asked.

"More than half are offline," Anton said. As team leader, he had access to the command channel.

"Oh my God. Why don't they withdraw?" Eva asked.

A nimbus of light flashed from the remaining ship, and

Ethan squinted his eyes. They flew toward the battle, but something didn't look right.

"Something's wrong," Ethan said.

An emergency broadcast came over comms. "This is Colonel Jon Walker. Our ships have been completely disabled. My ship's systems are down. I'm broadcasting from an escape pod. Don't approach the area. Repeat. Stay out of the area. Communicate our status back to COMCENT."

Ethan swallowed hard and scanned his HUD. This had to be a mistake. The ship status of the remaining squadron was offline except for the five of them.

"Anton, are you seeing this?" Ethan asked.

"Yeah," he replied quietly.

"There is an engine flare. Whatever that ship is, it's getting out of here," Eva said.

"What happened to the *Avalon*? Can anyone see it?" Massey asked.

Ethan checked his scanners. The armored carrier had been there when he'd checked only moments before.

"We can't leave them behind," Ethan said. "I won't leave them behind. I don't care what he said."

"He's right," Eva said.

"Something on that one ship disabled the power systems on our ships. That means the escape pods are running on emergency backup power. That won't last long enough for a rescue mission," Vijura said.

"We have to go after the escape pods," Ethan said.

"To do what? So we can watch them die face-to-face?" Anton snapped.

Ethan drew in a breath and held it for a few seconds. They were all on edge. He heard the strain in all their voices, including his own. He exhaled a slow even breath and said, "I'm going in.

The pods have a tether function that we can use to round them up. Maybe we can provide power from our ships. There have to be survivors."

"What if you're wrong?" Anton asked.

"Then at least we'll know. Would you really want to die alone?" The comlink was silent for a few long seconds. "I'm leaving. Is anyone else coming with me?" Ethan asked.

Another wave of silence seemed to build up on their comlink.

"I'll come," Eva said.

Vijura said the same.

"Come on, Anton," Massey said. "We can't let Gates capture all the glory."

"Damn it, Logan!" Ethan snapped. "It's not about glory. Our people are out there. Our friends. They'd do the same for us."

Anton sighed. "Ethan's right. We can't leave. I don't know what I was thinking."

Ethan led them toward where the squadron had last been located. There were docking platforms nearby where broken hulls of old ships remained in place, held by docking clamps. Vemus exoskeletons surrounded some of the hulls and parts of the docking station.

They flew by colonial fighters. They were completely dead, with no power remaining. Ethan didn't know what kind of weapon could do that. As they flew through the area, they were able to detect suit comms of the surviving pilots. They found escape pods that had been blown apart. They'd been targeted after their ships had been disabled or destroyed.

Ethan matched speeds with Captain Webster's escape pod. He hadn't responded to Ethan's comlink. He swung his ship around and saw that the canopy had been pierced and frozen droplets of blood hung around Webster's body.

Ethan grimaced and looked away. "Captain Webster is gone," he said, his voice sounding strained as sorrow threatened to close it up.

The others confirmed the status of the other pilots. Most were dead, but they found eight more that were alive, including Colonel Walker and Captain Kujura. Both had sustained injuries and were unconscious.

The escape pods were tethered to the remaining fighters. They were able to siphon power from the Stingers, so the immediate danger was past.

"There's another ship on the scanner," Ethan said.

"I see it. It's not moving very fast," Anton said.

"Looks like some kind of freighter. I think we can reach it. We could use it as a life raft," Ethan said.

"Hold on. We don't know if there's anyone on that ship," Massey said.

Ethan tried to hail the ship, but there was no reply. "It's got power. Our fuel reserves are low. If we don't find somewhere to regroup, we'll be too exposed."

"You don't get to make that decision. Anton does. He's the team leader. We could just as easily go back to the docking platform," Massey said.

Ethan scowled. "The docking platform! Are you serious? The one with exoskeletal material covering it? There could be Vemus waiting there for us. And what do you think the warships are going to do? There is no way they're going to allow any kind of salvage here."

"Fine, the shipyards are a bad idea. What about the *Avalon*?"

"It's been destroyed," Eva said. "I confirmed it. Something big pierced its armor."

Anton sighed heavily. "I'm so far out of my depth here. I agree with Ethan."

"But a ship is heading away from Saturn. It's following the same trajectory as that other ship," Eva said.

"It's our best option," Ethan replied. "We get aboard, turn it around, and contact the CDF. Plus, following that other ship isn't a bad thing. COMCENT is going to want to know about it."

"It's not your decision. Why do I need to keep saying this?" Massey said.

"Ethan's the team leader now. It's no use denying it. He's got a handle on it better than I do. It's logged now," Anton said.

No one argued against what Anton had said. The occupants in the escape pods couldn't really do much about it, and since their most senior officers were either dead or injured, it meant that Ethan was now in command.

"Thanks, Anton. Coordinates are in. Let's chase down that freighter," Ethan said.

Massey grinned a little.

"What are you grinning about?" Eva asked.

"When Kujura wakes up and finds Ethan in charge, he's gonna freak out."

Ethan snorted. "Yeah, well that'll be fun, too."

32

CONNOR'S MOUTH formed a grim line as he stared at the tactical plot on the main holoscreen. They were fighting a battle against old Alliance defenses that had been triggered by the Vemus Alpha signal.

"The *Wolf* and *Saber* have withdrawn from Sector 14, sir. The *Odyssey* reports that the *Python* and *Defiant* have reduced combat capacity," Lieutenant Tucker said.

"Acknowledged," Connor replied. "Ops, what's the status of the armor carriers? Have they cleared the area?"

"Six of nine carriers have reported in, sir. The Stinger squadrons have returned to the carriers and are on their way back. Three are overdue. All from the *Odyssey*, sir," Selina Wilson said.

Squadrons of Talon V Stingers had been the most effective at suppressing the Vemus Alpha signal being broadcast from communications platforms across all sectors, but it might not be enough. The broadcasts in the area had stopped, but they wouldn't know if those broadcasts had been processed elsewhere in the solar system.

"General Gates, I have Colonel Martinez requesting to speak with you," Specialist Gabe Marten said.

"Send it to my console."

Connor sat in the command chair and opened his personal holoscreen. Martinez's head and shoulders appeared amid the backdrop of CIC behind him.

"General, we're detecting new activity among areas covered with the Vemus exoskeleton," Martinez said.

Connor shook his head and swore. "That's it. We don't have a choice. I'm authorizing the use of heavy weapons on those areas."

Martinez nodded. "That's my recommendation, sir. I know we were trying to limit damage to the area, but there's simply too many things that can get lost in the shuffle. I'd rather not find that the Vemus have some kind of hidden fleet here."

"Agreed. They can hide a lot under that exoskeleton," Connor replied.

"I'm due to relieve you in an hour. I can come up sooner if you need, General."

Connor had stayed on watch through two standings. According to the regs that he helped write, he couldn't stay on for a third, not when there was an able-bodied executive officer available to come to the bridge and take over. But it was different during a battle.

"Just come on schedule. I'll make room for you in the command center," Connor replied and smiled with half his mouth.

"Understood, General. I'll be there in thirty then," Martinez replied and flicked his eyebrows.

"General Gates, a third request for an update has come in from the diplomatic envoy," Specialist Marten said.

"Status hasn't changed. I'll send them a formal update as soon as I can," Connor said.

He had no doubt that Fabian Dumont wanted a status update, but he was sure it was Lenora who was pushing for it this time. He'd put it off, but there were only so many times he'd be able to do that. He didn't have the time for it right now. He clenched his teeth and took a steadying breath before he spoke.

"Tactical, I need firing solutions using HADES VI missiles on the known Vemus exoskeleton areas. I want nothing left of those areas when we're done," Connor said.

He knew that destroying the vast majority of the space habitats around Saturn would deny Magnus Station precious resources, but the area was much too dangerous to salvage from. It had cost colonial lives, and he couldn't afford to allow an enemy to pursue them when they headed toward Earth. This was the only way.

"General Gates, I have a firing solution ready for the designated areas," Tucker said.

"Hold off on where our ships are making a tactical withdraw."

"Understood, General. Firing solution is ready."

Connor glanced at the list of missing carrier ships used for transporting fighter squadrons. His gaze slid toward a particular one, and its status seemed to glare back at him with a baleful red stare. Just because the armored transport was offline didn't mean the squadron was lost. They'd have to conduct rescue operations and investigate those areas. It was likely that Sean already had teams on the *Odyssey* doing that very thing.

"Fire," Connor said.

"Deploying missiles."

Connor watched the main holoscreen as a volley of HADES

VI missiles armed with fusion warheads flew toward their targets. He gritted his teeth and pressed his lips together, reminding himself that he'd chosen to come back to Earth. There was always going to be a price, and now it was time to pay the bill.

33

Fifteen hours had passed since the Vemus Alpha signal had first broadcasted from a derelict research station. Connor sat in his ready room near the bridge, reviewing an intelligence report that included a graphical model of how the signal had spread throughout the area. The broadcast had been repeated by compromised communication stations among the vast array of space stations, habitats, industrial processing stations, and everything in between. It was always looking back after the fact that yielded what he wished he'd known before. He should have known something like this was going to happen. He should have guessed. The risk of preserving the resources available at any of those derelict stations hadn't been worth the price the CDF had paid. There were even accounts of the demise of dozens of salvaging ships that were working in the areas Connor had authorized as secured and other places that they hadn't gotten to yet.

The Alpha signal had initiated a response from the areas where there was Vemus exoskeletal material, and what had been dormant was showing signs of activity. This was the justification he'd used to authorize the use of heavy weapons. He included it in his report to Dumont and the rest of the diplomatic envoy, who would then inform Shao Fen and the rest of Magnus Station.

A comlink chimed. Connor glanced at the sender and acknowledged it.

Sean Quinn regarded him with an expression almost devoid of emotion, but Connor saw it in his eyes. The news he had wasn't good, and Connor felt his stomach sink to the floor.

"The 7th A-Wing has been completely destroyed. Our search and rescue teams scoured the area. They were able to take a data dump from the *Avalon* and it confirms that there was a battle. We've parsed together fragments of logs, and there was another fighting force in the area," Sean said.

Connor narrowed his gaze. "The Vemus."

Sean frowned. "It's likely, but there is a lot of wreckage, and the battlefield was right on the doorsteps of exoskeletal material. My teams observed several wreckages being absorbed by the material. Targeting priority has been raised for that area."

Connor considered what Sean had said for a few moments. "Do you think there was a third party involved in the battle?"

Sean sighed. "I can't rule it out. We found evidence of Talon Vs without power. Something had disabled them and then destroyed the ships and the pilots inside them." He paused for a moment and looked away from the camera. "I couldn't find him, Connor. They searched for Ethan among the dead, but he's part of a group of about fifteen that are unaccounted for."

"He could be alive."

Sean stared at him for a long moment and then gave a slight shake of his head. "I'd love to give you something to hope for, believe me I would, but the evidence doesn't support that anyone from the 7th has survived. Ethan and the others will be classified as MIA but presumed dead. I'm sorry, Connor. I really am."

Blood thundered in Connor's ears as the pieces of him that was a father railed against the parts of him that was a soldier. The soldier knew the truth. That part of him was well-versed in the harsh realities of combat and the price that was paid, but the father in him refused to believe it. He couldn't allow himself to believe that Ethan was dead. His son was out there somewhere, clinging to life, but the soldier in him regarded the father with grim and absolute certainty that his son was dead. He exhaled forcefully and there might have been a harsh moan. Connor shot to his feet, shaking his head.

"He's dead," Connor said.

Sean's stoic facade began to break, but he steadfastly held it together. "Search and rescue has finished going through the entire area. There were no survivors. They searched within suit-comms range using reconnaissance drones and there is nothing."

Connor glared at the holoscreen, his eyes scanning the report that Sean had transmitted.

"What about the ship that attacked them? Was it among the wreckage?"

Sean shook his head. "No, and we haven't found any other ships in the area."

"I want that ship found. It managed to disable an entire squadron."

"Understood, sir."

Connor pressed his knuckles onto the desk. "I want the entire region sanitized. Nothing is to remain. Nothing!"

"Sir, the Vemus Alpha signal has been stopped. It makes sense for us to sanitize sectors with significant Vemus exoskeletal material, but we're not authorized to do any more than that."

"The entire region is compromised."

"Magnus Station and the rest of the survivors—"

"Can't stop us from doing this," Connor finished for him. "Do you have an issue with the orders I've given you?"

Sean eyed him for a moment. "Negative, sir."

"Then get to it."

"Yes, sir," Sean replied and closed the comlink.

Connor glared at the blank holoscreen and grabbed the edge of his desk. Growling, he heaved himself up, but the desk was bolted to the floor, and it wasn't going to give no matter how hard he pulled. Crying out in rage, he slammed his fists on the tabletop as images of the sons he'd lost flashed in his mind. Snarling, he came out from around his desk and stormed to the bridge.

The bridge crew stared at him, slack-jawed and rooted in place.

Martinez was sitting in the command chair. He turned toward Connor and stood up.

"Colonel Martinez," Connor began.

"General Gates," Specialist Marten said.

Connor swung his gaze toward the communications specialist and Marten flinched.

"I'm sorry, General, but I have a priority message—"

Connor exhaled explosively. "Tell the damn envoy that they can—"

"Sir!" Marten interrupted. "It's your daughter, sir. Priority message is from Lauren Gates. She's on a long-range shuttle. She says she needs to speak to you ASAP."

Connor's mouth hung opened. He was stuck somewhere between near-blind rage and the stark reminder that at least one of his children was still alive.

"Lauren?"

Marten nodded. "Yes, General."

Martinez stared at him for a second. "Send it to General Gates's ready room, Specialist."

Marten sagged in relief. "Yes, sir," he said and turned back toward his console.

Connor blinked a few times and looked at Martinez.

"She's waiting for you, sir," Martinez said.

Connor nodded and retreated off the bridge. The bridge crew hardly dared to move until he was gone.

34

CONNOR HASTENED BACK to his ready room and glanced at the mess he'd made when he cleared off his desk. He went behind the desk, righted the overturned chair, and sat down.

A prompt flashed on the holoscreen. A comlink was waiting for him. He rubbed his face vigorously for a few seconds and took a deep breath. Then he answered the comlink.

"Hi, Dad," Lauren said. She stared at him for barely a second. "What's wrong?"

Connor stared at the vidcom link with his daughter's beautiful face. "Lauren," he said and blew out a breath. He couldn't tell her about Ethan. Not yet. "I'm surprised to hear from you."

She smiled a little and then nodded. "Things are a little crazy. Isaac has us on an intercept course with the *Douglass*. Can you give us priority clearance to board? There's something we should really talk about in person."

A number of comlink requests ambushed the moment. Some

were from Magnus Station. Another was from Fabian Dumont, but it was the last one that made him wince. It was from Lenora.

"Dad, did you hear me?"

Connor shook his head and looked back at this daughter. "Yes, I heard you. Priority clearance to come aboard the *Douglass*. Yes, of course you'll have the clearance you need…" He frowned for a second. "Wait. Why don't you return to Magnus Station? It'll be safer there for you than here. The Vemus are coming out of hibernation."

Lauren nodded. "I know. That's what I need to talk to you about. It's much more complicated than that. We can't return to Magnus Station."

He stared at his daughter for a long moment, trying to figure out what she wasn't telling him.

"I'll authorize the shuttle to land, but you need to level with me."

"I'd route us to one of the secondary hangars and setup a quarantine section for us."

Connor leaned toward the camera. "Have you been exposed?"

She shook her head. "No, I'm fine, Dad. I promise you. It's a precaution. Please can you just be patient? Like I said, this is better discussed in person."

Connor nodded. He trusted Lauren. She'd proven time and time again that she was levelheaded, confident, and capable of making intelligent decisions.

"All right."

Lauren smiled. "Thank you. I'll see you in a little while."

The comlink ended and Connor sagged into his chair. He squeezed his eyes shut and just breathed, trying to think of the last time he'd spoken to his son and recall everything they'd said to each other. But he couldn't afford to do this now. He had to stay focused. If he went down this path, he would unravel. He opened his eyes and stared at the long list of messages that required his attention, and then his eyes sank toward Lenora's message. He keyed in a quick response, promising her that he would contact her as soon as he had a free moment. She'd know he was putting her off, and there was only so long he could do it. Connor had faced so much throughout his life. He'd been forged in combat. He'd lost friends and family over the years. He'd been afraid. Anyone who claimed otherwise had never fought in a real battle. But he'd rather revisit the darkest moments of his life a thousand times over than be the person who told Lenora that their son was dead.

He shook his head. Not yet. He couldn't do it.

He opened a comlink to Martinez.

"Sir?"

"There is a Horizon long-range shuttle inbound. Give it clearance to land in hangar bay seventeen. Inform the deck officer that quarantine measures are required."

Martinez nodded. "Understood, sir."

"Get a soldier detachment there as well."

Martinez frowned. "Sir, is there something I should be aware of?"

"Lauren requested this."

"I see that. Did you notice the clearance codes that came with the comlink?"

Connor frowned and shook his head. "No. What is it?"

"It's part of the priority. It's from the Colonial Intelligence Bureau."

"Does it indicate who from the CIB?"

"I was asking if you knew who it was, General."

Connor blew out a breath. "I have no idea. I think you should come down with me."

Martinez nodded. "I'll be right there."

A few minutes later Martinez was outside Connor's office, and they climbed aboard an elevator on their way to the secondary hangar bay.

"I know your daughter is a doctor, but I also have one of our medical teams meeting us there," Martinez said.

"Standard for the quarantine protocol."

They rode the elevator in silence. Martinez wasn't one to fill the time with idle conversation and remained quiet as if he sensed that Connor needed it more than he needed anything else at the moment.

A short while later they entered the hangar bay. The deck had been cleared of all non-essential personnel, and everyone who remained wore an envirosuit except for the platoon of soldiers. They were in combat suits with their kits ready for whatever happened to come their way. Connor and Martinez slipped into their own envirosuits and watched as the shuttle entered the hangar bay. He saw long gashes on the hull that looked like it had slammed against something rather than taking fire.

A squad of soldiers went to the side of the shuttle. The environmental systems in the hangar were isolated from the rest of the ship, and life-support systems were equipped to detect any contagions. They could have vented the atmosphere, but Connor didn't think it was necessary.

Lauren exited the shuttle first, followed by Isaac Diaz. Five other people wearing EVA suits disembarked, looking as if they couldn't protect a lifeless corpse, much less anything like the living person inside them. They were followed by two CDF soldiers who had been on protective detail.

Connor watched as Lauren and the others were guided toward the quarantine area where the medical team was ready to examine them. Connor and Martinez went into the observation area and watched.

Lauren spoke to the medical team and gestured toward the passengers. One of the medical team walked toward Connor, while the rest of the team continued to examine the others.

"General Gates," Dr. Petrov Kaminski said, "there's something I need to bring to your attention before we go any further. Dr. Gates claims that some of her passengers are some kind of Vemus Hybrid. There are trace mutations that are part of their DNA, but they aren't what we'd consider a Vemus."

Connor looked over at Lauren and the others.

"I can't authorize ship-wide access to them," Kaminski said.

"Was that the request?" Connor asked.

Kaminski blinked and glanced at Martinez.

"Answer General Gates's question, Captain," Martinez said.

Kaminski's gaze snapped back to Connor. "I'm sorry, General Gates. No, that wasn't the request."

Connor arched an eyebrow, having reached his limit for nonsense to last him the rest of his life. "Set aside the fact that Dr. Lauren Gates is my daughter. She's a specialist in infectious disease with intense study particular to the Vemus. Are you trying to tell me that your expertise is greater than hers?"

Kaminski shook his head. "That's not what I'm saying, sir. My concern is first and foremost for the CDF crew."

Connor held up his hand. "That's enough. Let me stop you right there before you snag enough rope to really hang yourself. What is it that Dr. Gates has requested?"

His voice echoed across the hangar bay.

"Sir, I was merely pointing out the apparent dangers that having anyone infected with the Vemus poses to the crew of the ship."

Connor stepped toward the man, and Kaminski flinched.

"The only thing apparent to me is the fact that you refuse to answer a fucking question. Get the hell off my deck, Captain. You're dismissed." Connor turned toward Martinez. "Get me someone else—*anyone else*—from medical down here who has a basic understanding of how to communicate." Connor looked at Kaminski, who stood in apparent shock. Connor raised his gaze to the nearest soldier. "You there, Sergeant. Escort Dr. Kaminski out of the hangar bay."

"Yes, General Gates!"

The CDF sergeant hastened over and ushered the mortified doctor away. Connor strode toward the barrier to the mobile quarantine center. Lauren looked over at him through the nearly translucent shield, registered the angry glint in his eyes, and ran over to him.

"Are you okay?" Connor asked.

Lauren smiled a little and nodded. "I'm fine."

He gave his daughter a once-over, parental instinct taking over. "You don't look fine."

Lauren drew herself up and met his gaze. "I could say the same thing about you," she replied with a tone to match his.

Connor held up his hand and sighed. "I'm sorry. That's not directed at you." He paused for a second, walling off his emotions. "I'm just really glad you're here. That you're safe."

Lauren's gaze softened. "That I can forgive. What happened to Dr. Kaminski?"

"I dismissed him because he wouldn't answer a question. Just tell me. Are we in danger from these people?"

"I don't think so."

"That's hardly ironclad, is it?"

"Isaac and I, along with Sergeant Burk and Corporal Nance, have been living among people who have trace amounts of DNA mutations associated with Vemus markers. We're fine. There's a lot we need to discuss, and I'd prefer to do it in person."

Connor stared at his daughter. She never liked going on EVAs. "Okay, we'll set up a clean room. I'll have food brought and some temporary living quarters until I'm assured that we aren't in danger."

Lauren nodded. "Thank you. I'll tell the others."

Connor's lips lifted a little as he watched his daughter return to her group. He then turned around. Martinez waited nearby.

"I figured you'd need a few moments alone."

Connor nodded. "Thanks. Let's get some food brought in and set up a clean environment for them. Then we'll debrief them."

It took less than a half hour to get the clean room set up and the salvagers cordoned off in their own area. Connor removed his EVA suit and walked through decom before entering the clean room where Lauren waited. He hugged his daughter.

Isaac Diaz stood nearby and wasn't quite fidgeting, but Connor could tell there was something on his mind. "Hello, sir."

Connor looked at him for a moment and snorted. "Agent Diaz, I presume."

Isaac's eyes widened for a fraction of a second, and he tipped his head to the side. "Communication protocols for the priority comlink. Yes, I'm a CIB agent. I'm here on orders from Director Natalia Vassar.

Connor shook his head, bemused. "I'm sorry, Isaac. I'm still trying to figure out how you became involved with the CIB," he said. Then it came to him. Isaac had been taken captive while at a colonial embassy. He stared at Isaac. "From back then, really? Almost 10 years ago?"

Isaac nodded. "They offered me the job after that. They

wanted me to continue to become a doctor, except now I do some additional things for the colonial government."

"He's understating it," Lauren said. "We wouldn't have made it if it weren't for Isaac."

Isaac shook his head. "That's funny, I was going to say the same thing about you."

There was something lingering in the way his daughter looked at Isaac, as if the two were sitting much closer together than they actually were. He suddenly felt as if he was intruding but dismissed the thought. He was tired and definitely distracted.

Over the next few hours, Lauren and Isaac gave him and Martinez a full debrief of what they'd been doing.

"I knew going to some of the distant outposts would give us a better insight into the people of Magnus Station," Isaac said.

Connor regarded him for a moment. "I understand your motives, Isaac. What I don't understand is why you'd choose to take…someone whose qualifications don't measure up to the apparent risks you encountered."

"Dad, there was no way Isaac or anyone could have known what was going to happen."

"That's no excuse for bringing you along."

"He didn't make me go."

"Then you should've known better."

"I'm not answerable to you."

"Yes, you are! Your brother—" Connor bit off his words.

Isaac stood up. "I took the actions I thought were necessary for the assignment I was given. I brought with me the most brilliant and qualified person I knew. Respectfully, I'm not going to apologize for it."

Connor stood up. "Respectfully," he said bitterly, "if you put my daughter's life in danger again, I'll personally see to it that you never work another assignment anywhere within the colonial government. Do we have an understanding?"

"That's enough. Both of you!" Lauren said and turned toward Isaac. "Give us a few minutes."

Isaac looked at Lauren for a second and nodded. Then he walked away. Martinez got up and followed Isaac. The two of them began talking.

"Dad, you're out of line. You shouldn't have said that to him."

Connor clenched his teeth, unable to control his temper. "He…" Connor bit his lower lip for a second.

Lauren stared at him, her radiant blue eyes a mirror image to her mothers.

He blew out a long breath. "Ethan is dead."

Lauren frowned in denial. Her mouth opened but the words hadn't come out yet.

"There was a battle, and some kind of ship disabled the ships of the 7th."

"Oh my God, Dad," she said and then whispered Ethan's name.

Connor crossed the distance and hugged his daughter. She sank into his arms, crying into his chest. They stayed like that for a while. The others gave them space, and Connor saw that the salvagers watched them from their designated quarantine area.

Lauren let him go and looked up at him with grief-stricken eyes. "Where's Mom?"

"She's on Magnus Station."

Lauren narrowed her gaze. "You haven't told her!"

Connor looked away and shook his head. "I can't."

"You have to."

"I can't do this to her."

"You're not doing anything to her. She has a right to know."

Connor winced and went blind for a moment. He hastily wiped the tears away.

"Dad, if you don't tell her, I will."

He inhaled a long breath and nodded. "All right. I'll tell her."

Lauren leveled her gaze at him. "Now."

She was right. He knew it and so did she. Connor walked out of the clean room feeling as if he were marching into a battle he couldn't survive, but it was worse. As he walked across the hangar, each step felt heavier than the last. He went to one of the workstations and initiated a comlink to Lenora. His wife answered almost immediately.

"Connor, it's about damn time..." she stopped speaking, and her mouth hung open as she braced herself.

Then Connor told her that their son was dead. He couldn't remember much after that as he finally gave in to his grief.

35

CONNOR DIDN'T KNOW how much time had passed. He'd lost count of how many times he apologized to Lenora, as if the more he did it, the more of a chance he might feel less responsible for Ethan's death. It didn't help. He couldn't escape the pain. It was like an old enemy that he couldn't defeat—an enemy that had dogged him for so long that he'd sometimes force out of his mind for a time, but it always returned to rear its ugly head again. He couldn't wait to end the vidcom with Lenora, as if the sight of her in pain hurt him as much as Ethan's death all over again in a vicious cycle of agony.

He would do it. He'd go through it as many times as it took.

"I need to be there with you. I'm going to be on the next shuttle off this damn station, and I'm coming back to the ship," Lenora said.

He wanted her there with him. He needed her there with him, but he couldn't allow it. "No, I can't let you do that."

Lenora glared at him, and she inhaled sharply, ready for battle.

"It's too dangerous. The Vemus Alpha signal started something, Lenora."

"I thought you commanded a fleet of ships. If there are Vemus in the area, then kill them. Do the thing that you do, Connor. Kill them."

Connor had rarely seen Lenora this furious, and she'd never demanded that he kill anything before. He wanted to do it. God help him, but he did.

"It takes time."

"No! Not this time!" She shrieked. Her voice cracked with emotion. She thrust her face toward the camera and snarled. "They killed my little boy. I don't care what you have to do, but you do it. You end them now. Do you hear me!"

Someone opened the door behind Lenora. She barely looked over her shoulder.

"Not now!"

Connor heard a muffled reply.

Lenora shook her head and she looked at Connor for a moment before her face crumpled and she wailed in grief. Connor stared, slack-jawed, and something inside him broke. It was like a snap inside him, as if someone had cut him open and pulled him inside out. All that was left was smoldering fury.

Lenora sank to the ground, and he watched as Samantha Orthon rushed into the room. She knelt on the floor and held Lenora, trying to soothe her. They rocked back and forth a little.

Samantha looked at the camera. "I've got her. I'll stay with her."

Unable to speak, Connor nodded and closed the comlink. He closed his eyes for a few moments. Random sounds from the hangar bay surrounded him—from the offhand clang of a maintenance crew performing their duties to the hushed conversations of the soldiers guarding the quarantine area.

Connor turned around and a wave of quiet spread throughout the people nearby. He just looked at them for a moment and then walked toward the quarantine area.

The soldiers looked everywhere but at him as he walked by.

Martinez stood just outside the entrance to the clean room. He was leaning toward his wrist computer. "How would you be..." He glanced toward Connor, and then closed the comlink.

Connor eyed Martinez for a few seconds.

"General Quinn was checking in on you, sir."

Connor nodded a little.

"Um, Lauren said she needed to speak to you. It's about... them," Martinez said, tilting his head toward the clean room.

Connor heaved a sigh and nodded. Without a word, he walked back into the clean room.

The hissing sound of the clean room doors opened, announcing his presence. Lauren turned toward him and then walked over. She seemed in better control than he felt. He squashed the thought and put it out of his mind.

"How is she?" Lauren asked.

He blinked, and in his mind, he watched Lenora sink to the ground. "Not good."

Lauren's bottom lip quivered, and she watched him as if she couldn't quite believe what she was seeing. "I should..."

"There isn't anything you can do for your mother right now."

Lauren flinched. "She'd want to be here."

"None of us should be here!" Connor snapped. "Not you. Not me. Not Ethan. And certainly not your mother."

Lauren swallowed hard and didn't blink. "No one made you come."

Connor stormed toward her. "No one made me come! The only reason I came on this expedition was because of you and your brother. Your mother volunteered after she'd learned that you two had decided to come."

He was shouting. He knew it was wrong, and he was certainly going to regret it later, but he couldn't stop. "So help me if something happens to your mother, I will never forgive you! This was all about you and Ethan trying to honor a ghost. A ghost you never even knew. Who didn't care about you, me, or anyone we know. A ghost who's been gone for two hundred and fifty years!"

Lauren stared up at him and snarled. She was never one to be intimidated by anyone. Her eyes blazed with fury. "How dare you!" she shrieked, and all regard for anyone around them sucked right out the proverbial airlock. "How dare you," she hissed. "Do you really think Ethan and I decided to volunteer for the expedition like we were deciding on what to have for dinner? Do you think we didn't seriously consider it? Do you think so little of us?" She glared at him with an angry sneer and with no less backbone than he'd ever had. For a fleeting moment he was immensely proud of her, but that was gone in an instant. "We talked about it for days. We know what you had to sacrifice. What you lost to come to New Earth."

"I didn't ask you to do any of this. I didn't want this for either of you."

"No, you'll never have to ask us to do the right thing. That's who we are. That's who Ethan is. That's who *you* are."

"I don't want this from you. Look at what it has cost. Look at what we've lost. He's gone, Lauren. He's gone!"

"I know he is, Dad. I know what death means."

"Do you! Do you really?"

"No! You don't get to do this to me. You're not the only person who knows death. I know what you're going to say. No one can compare with everything you've had to endure in your life. I know that, Dad. I know what the cost has been to you. I've seen it my entire life. We've all seen it."

Connor felt as if he'd been knocked back on his heels. He stepped back, and Lauren swooped toward him.

"He means something to me too, Dad. We knew you hated coming back here. But we also knew that you were strong enough to do it. No matter the cost."

Connor's gaze sank to the ground. He didn't look at her. "It's too much," he said softly.

Lauren drew in a shaky breath. "It's always too much," she whispered. "It's always too much. You need time."

Connor shook his head. "There isn't time."

"Yes, there is. There is too time."

Connor stared at her.

"Lean on the people you trust. It's what we're here for," she said and gathered her thoughts. She glanced over to the side where Martinez stood. He wasn't looking at them, but he was aware. "You can't lose control now. There are too many people depending on you."

Connor looked at Martinez and saw a worried frown in his eyes, as if he hoped he wasn't going to be called to do something he didn't want to do.

"Take a breath, Dad. That's what you always used to tell me when things got tough. You need to take a breath. Lean on Uncle Sean. He can take over for a little while until you've had some time to grieve. You know what will happen otherwise."

Connor winced. He knew what she was referring to. If he'd had someone under his command who was as emotionally compromised, he would have relieved them of duty. He looked at Martinez and saw it in his eyes. Martinez was keeping Sean informed of Connor's status.

"Don't make them force this on you," Lauren said softly.

Connor heaved a long sigh and nodded, sharing a look with his daughter. Then he turned toward Martinez. "I need you to contact General Quinn. He's to assume command of the expedition until such time as he sees fit that he is no longer required to lead."

Martinez looked visibly relieved. He stood up straight and gave Connor a crisp salute. "Understood, General Gates."

His executive officer left the clean room. Connor walked over to the nearby table, sat down and leaned back, allowing the chair to take all of his weight as he heaved another sigh. Lauren sat next to him. They stayed that way for a while, each of them quiet with their own thoughts but needing each other's company.

He'd thought that giving up command would be unbearable, but all he felt was numb and perhaps a little relieved. He'd been racing down a destructive path and taking the entire expedition with him. That wasn't fair to everyone else. He glanced at his daughter with renewed appreciation for her reserves of strength. She looked back at him.

"Thank you," he said.

She nodded a little. "You're welcome."

They shared a quiet meal. Isaac and the two CDF soldiers sat at a table on the other side of the clean room. The salvagers were cordoned off in another area. They were starting to get restless.

Isaac walked over to them. "Wakiya wants to speak with you. She's the leader of the salvager group we encountered."

"I'm off duty," Connor replied.

Isaac snorted. "Are we ever really off duty?"

Connor's eyebrow flitted toward the ceiling, and he glanced at Lauren.

"There's a lot more going on here than what we were led to believe," Lauren said.

"Okay."

"So you'll speak with them?"

Connor nodded. "I will."

"I don't think they need to be separated from us. We've been exposed to them for days and nothing has happened to us. They were pretty open about it once we got them to admit what they were," Lauren said.

"What exactly are they? Is that really what they look like?" Connor asked.

Lauren stood. "I think we should find out."

"You go on. I want to speak to Isaac for a second," Connor said.

Lauren glanced at Isaac and then back at Connor. Her look seemed to convey a stern warning that was reminiscent of her mother. Then she walked away from them.

Connor eyed Isaac for a second. "Agent Diaz."

"Yes, sir."

He chuckled. "Sir... I was there when you were born, Isaac."

Isaac smiled. "I didn't think it was appropriate for me to address you as Uncle Connor."

Connor was reminded of Juan Diaz's easygoing manner. He'd seen the same in his son. "Does your father know you're with the CIB?"

Isaac shook his head. "No." He pressed his lips together. "I think he suspects I'm more than a doctor."

These kids, Connor thought to himself, and shook his head.

"What?" Isaac asked.

"The way you said it. As if being a doctor wasn't enough." He eyed the young man for a moment. "I wouldn't put it past your father to figure it out, but he's wise enough not to put you in an awkward position."

Isaac considered that for a moment and then nodded.

Connor missed Juan. He could guess what Diaz would have

said to him if he were here.

Connor sighed and glanced at his daughter. She was speaking with Wakiya through the intercom. Isaac followed his gaze.

"She's a grown woman, capable of making her own decisions," Connor said. Isaac became still and met his gaze. "But she's still my little girl." He stood up and stared at Isaac, leaning toward him. And even though Isaac was a thirty-year-old man, he was still young enough to be intimidated by the secondary father figure in his life. "If you break her heart, no force in the world will keep me from extracting severe retribution from you."

Isaac swallowed hard and looked a little pale. "Yes, sir."

Connor held his gaze for a moment with a firm, fatherly glare. "All right then. Let's move on."

Isaac nodded.

Connor walked toward his daughter, hearing Isaac let out a deep breath. He'd always thought Isaac was a good kid and had grown into a good man, but the day he stopped looking out for his daughter would be the day he died, and probably not even then.

He walked toward the quarantine controls and entered his authentication, ending the quarantine protocol that kept the two sections separated. There was a pop-hiss sound as the mobile sections retracted to the side.

Wakiya stared at him, and the other salvagers came over.

"Lauren tells me you'd like to speak to me. We'll get to that, but first you'll answer a couple of questions of mine. If you answer them to my satisfaction, we'll sit down and have a conversation. If you don't, you'll be held here until I can arrange for you to return to your outpost."

The salvagers looked at him.

"You leave us with very little choice," Wakiya said.

Connor smiled. "But you do have a choice. According to

them," he said, tilting his head toward Lauren and Isaac, "you wouldn't have a choice if this were Magnus Station."

Wakiya looked up at her husband, Braun. He was easily as tall as Connor but thicker, as if he'd spent years laboring with heavy materials.

"Your treatment of us has been fair. We will answer any questions you have."

"Outstanding. Are you human?" Connor asked.

Lauren looked as if she were about to speak, but Connor held up his hand and she didn't.

"Yes, we're human," Wakiya replied.

The other salvagers nodded.

Connor regarded them. "But not completely."

"How do you measure your own humanity, General Gates? We look human. We act human. We think of ourselves as human. Then we are human."

Her answer was straight to the point, and he had no doubts that she believed what she told him.

"But you are different."

Wakiya was quiet for a few moments.

"Tell him," Braun said.

Wakiya nodded. "Some of us are more different than others. Our ancestors were exposed to the Vemus pathogen—a form of it—but they somehow resisted the change."

Lauren nodded. "Our researchers suspected, hoped really, that some kind of natural immunity had occurred, but we obviously couldn't confirm it until now."

"Are there Vemus left?"

"Yes, but you already knew that."

Connor nodded.

"Sometimes the mutations are slight. They appear in our children. Sometimes it's obvious from birth and other times it presents itself during puberty. Sometimes the mutations are so severe that the person dies from them," Wakiya said and looked at Lauren. Her gaze softened. "My daughter, Amelia, was such a case. We believed that she would not survive to become a woman."

Connor looked at Lauren.

"It's true. Her autoimmune system didn't function like ours. I used medical nanites to help teach her system to function properly. I checked our medical records, and the treatment can take months to work. Amelia showed improvement within hours. I suspect that her mutations made that possible," Lauren said.

"But they almost killed her, too."

Lauren shrugged. "It's nature, Dad. Sometimes it doesn't make sense initially. It's up to us to unravel its mystery. Evolution is often chaotic and not the same for everyone."

Connor gathered his thoughts for a few seconds. "So the mutations were a struggle. What else can you tell me about them?"

Wakiya gestured toward another salvager. He was a young man, lean with dark hair. "Torren can resist large exposures to radiation. His system is highly regenerative."

Connor looked at him. "Regenerative. You heal quickly?"

Torren nodded. "Yes, but I'm not invulnerable or anything like that. I just recover very quickly."

"Interesting. Did any of you react to the Vemus Alpha signal?"

Wakiya frowned and shook her head. "No, we're not compelled by the signal."

"Why not?"

"There is no way for us to confirm this, but we think that our ancestors' exposure was before the pathogen had been changed.

It went from spreading upon all mammals to targeting humans almost exclusively, but there was more to it. They preserved the DNA of previous mutations and somehow engineered it to force genes to express themselves. You've fought the Vemus. You must have seen this," Wakiya said.

The Vemus War had been almost thirty years ago, but he still remembered. A lot of colonists did. "Yes. The ones we encountered were more like a hive that served the Alpha. So, you're immune from the signal."

"As immune as you are, General Gates."

"Okay. The Vemus I encountered could morph themselves and change form. Almost completely. Is what I'm looking at when I see you—all there is to see? Does your appearance change?"

Wakiya's eyes widened a little and she looked at her husband. Braun gave her a small nod. He seemed to puff up as if he were bracing to defend his wife.

Wakiya blew out a breath and patted her husband's arm. "I must do this if we're to work with these people."

Connor watched as Wakiya's pale skin became darker and adopted a slightly purple color. Long streaks of darker skin appeared on her neck and formed an intricate pattern across her forehead. Her eyes became bigger and black, as if he were staring into an abyss.

Connors eyes widened and the breath caught in his throat. His eyes darted to the side and saw three of the salvagers' appearances change just as Wakiya's had. Years of training came to bear. He grabbed Lauren's arm and pulled her behind him, but the salvagers appeared to have expected his reaction.

"We learned to control the mutations. Limit them so we could blend in," Wakiya said.

Isaac gasped, and the two CDF soldiers rushed to Connor's

side. Connor felt as if he were staring into an echo of the past. The salvagers—

"We're hybrids, General Gates," she said. Even her voice had changed a little, becoming somewhat deeper.

They looked like distant cousins of the Vemus he'd fought, except they weren't eight feet tall. They looked more human than anything else. The Vemus he'd fought and killed were humanoid but could never be confused with being an actual human.

"This is our natural form," Wakiya said.

"No, it's not," Torren said.

Connor stared at him. "What do you mean it's not."

Torren's appearance changed back to what it had been before. "This is who I choose to be. The other is merely a part of who I am. There is a difference."

Connor saw a hardened glint in the eyes of the salvagers. All of them watched for his reaction. He glanced at Lauren, and she looked just as shocked as he was.

"Scan them," Connor said.

Lauren blinked a few times and then reached into her pocket for her medical scanner.

Connor turned back toward the salvagers. "Let her scan you."

"We will comply, General Gates," Wakiya replied. She smiled a little. Her teeth appeared a little larger than before but more or less human.

"I'll do it," Isaac said, striding forward with his own scanner. He went to Torren and held the scanner close to his skin. "Change back to the way you were before," he said.

Lauren walked to Wakiya and held up the medical scanner. She waved it in front of Wakiya's face and arms, watching the small holoscreen.

She returned to Connor and showed him the results.

"The DNA is still human. The genome is just like ours, but

they have additional genes activated."

Connor peered at the report. It was just a quick analysis.

"You still have doubts."

"I'd call it a healthy respect for things I don't understand," he replied.

"Would you be surprised to learn that we don't understand all of it ourselves, and we've had to live with it for a long time."

Connor watched her for a second. She seemed less agitated. "And if you were to show yourself on Magnus Station like this?"

"We would be killed."

"Not exiled?"

Wakiya shook her head. "No, not for us. They do exile others. Sometimes we can smuggle people off the station. I have answered your questions. Now may I ask some of my own?"

Isaac finished scanning the others and his results were similar to Lauren's.

"All right. Let's talk," Connor said and gestured toward the nearby table.

They could at least sit down and have a civilized conversation. The salvagers—Vemus Hybrids—were a little surprised but quickly sat down.

Connor smiled a little. "We've encountered other life forms before. They're aliens, but I wouldn't lump you into the same group as they are."

Wakiya glanced at Lauren for a few seconds. Connor guessed that Lauren must have told them about the Ovarrow. He anticipated that this conversation was going to be much longer than any of them would have expected. And as Wakiya spoke about the hybrids, Magnus Station, and all the smaller outposts, Connor had to accept that the status of the survivors of the Vemus War of Earth was more complicated than any of them could have imagined.

36

"We're not dead yet," Massey said.

Ethan nodded. "I like that you're finally looking on the bright side of things."

Massey shrugged. "Hey, I'm adaptable." He stretched his arms over his head. "I'm glad to finally be out of that cockpit."

It had taken them almost nine hours to chase down what appeared to be an abandoned freighter. They'd had to employ some creative fuel consumption tactics to reach the ship, but it had been their only option.

Massey looked at Ethan. "I'm man enough to admit when I was wrong. If we'd gone back to that dockyard, we wouldn't have made it."

Anton grinned.

Eva looked over at them. "What happened?"

"Massey is making heroic strides toward becoming a mature person. It's really something to see."

Eva looked at Massey. "Always knew you had it in you."

He rolled his eyes. "If I'm going to get nothing but grief for it, I'll just keep my mouth shut."

Ethan arched an eyebrow. "You know, that might not be a bad idea."

Massey wagged a finger toward him. "Only about that. You can't shut me up that easily."

"Don't we know it. However, you did want us to take shelter in a dockyard covered with Vemus exoskeletal material."

Massey's gaze went toward the ceiling for a second and then he nodded. "Yeah. Yeah. Then the entire area was obliterated."

Over ten hours into their journey, they'd seen bright flashes coming from the battlefield. His father or General Quinn must have used heavy weapons to destroy the Vemus remnants. If they had stayed there, they would have died.

Eva sighed. "It was a gamble either way. If we'd stayed, we might have been able to contact the CDF."

Their ships had taken some damage and their comms had been reduced to tight-beam transmissions, which was only a short-range option.

They'd managed to reach the freighter and land inside an open hangar bay. No one had responded to their communication attempts. The escape pods they'd been towing had a bumpy landing, but at least the occupants had survived.

Ethan stretched his back and rolled his shoulders. They were all stiff from spending so much time in a chair. The hangar bay doors were operational, and they'd used a control console to shut them. The ship was so old that it didn't have a working atmospheric shield, but the hangar bay doors sealed.

"Gates!" Kujura called out.

The Ovarrow was helping to get the survivors out of the escape pods. Ethan ran over to him, and the others followed.

Kujura had woken hours into their journey and was grumpier than normal.

"Sir," Ethan said.

Rice and Bentlix lifted Colonel Jon Walker from the escape pod and carried him over to the side.

"Has there been any contact from our hosts?" Kujura asked. He was pulling supplies out from the escape pod and hadn't looked at them.

"Negative, sir," Ethan replied.

Kujura set a survival container on the ground. He looked over at Rice and Bentlix. "Get something under his head. Rice, get a med kit and see if there is something in there that can help."

Kujura turned toward Ethan, then glanced at the others. "The rest of you help the others get our supplies organized. Except for you, Stone," he said, waving Anton over.

When it was just the three of them, he spoke more quietly. "Someone left the door open for us, which means they know we're here. Why haven't they tried to contact us?"

"The ship looked pretty old, sir. Maybe whoever's here doesn't know that we're aboard," Anton said.

Kujura considered it for a few seconds and then looked at Ethan. "Nothing to contribute, Lieutenant Gates?"

The way he asked made it sound like an accusation.

"I agree with Anton. I think we should send a team to explore the ship."

"This isn't the ship that attacked us," Kujura said.

"No, but it was heading on the same trajectory."

"Hardly coincidental. Okay, Gates, I want you, Stone, Massey, and Trace to explore the ship. Regular check-ins via comlink," Kujura said.

"Yes, sir," they both replied.

"Stone, stay here a moment," Kujura said.

Ethan went back to his ship and got his sidearm out. He rammed a charging pod into the stock and flipped it on, hearing the weapon hum. It was a sound that rose in pitch until it became an inaudibly high, ringing sound, indicating it was good to go. He holstered his weapon and told Eva and Massey that they had a field assignment.

Kujura spoke to Anton for a few minutes. Ethan wondered what they were saying. Kujura hadn't reacted too strongly when he learned that Ethan had taken over as team leader.

Anton saluted Kujura and hastened over to his ship. Ethan walked over to him.

"Everything all right?"

Anton loaded his sidearm and holster. "Yeah, he just wanted to know why I gave up the team leader position."

"What did he say?"

They began walking toward the interior doors across the hangar bay. Eva and Massey were waiting for them.

"Not much. I told him the truth. You were…you kept a level head out there and I didn't."

Ethan was quiet for a few moments. "Don't beat yourself up about it. The situation was intense and long."

Anton heaved a sigh and nodded. "We can do all the training, and it helps with the missions, but I still feel like I was unprepared. How do you do it?"

"Do what?"

"Keep calm. Stay focused. Work the problem and not get overwhelmed."

Ethan considered it for a few moments. He didn't want to tell his friend that it was something he could just do, even though it was true. "It's not like I wasn't scared, Anton."

"I know that, but…"

"It's just something I can do. We were flying by the seat of our pants, and I think the mission had just gone on so long that it was wearing on us all."

Anton stared straight ahead. "Some more than others."

Ethan shrugged. There really wasn't much he could say in response to that. "So does Kujura want you back in charge?"

Anton shook his head. "No."

"That's a surprise."

Anton gave him a sidelong glance. "You guys bump heads. He thinks you're too reckless, and... what is it you don't like about him?"

They'd reached the others.

Massey's eyebrows raised. "Don't like about who?"

"Kujura," Anton replied.

Massey's gaze flicked toward Ethan.

"He's had it out for me since I transferred and qualified for the 7th. I have no idea what his problem is."

Eva rolled her eyes and shook her head. "Seriously, you have no idea. Look, here comes Vijura. I bet he knows."

The Ovarrow pilot walked over to them. "Apologies for being late."

"You're not late," Eva said. "We were just talking about the lack of love between Ethan and Captain Kujura."

"Ah," Vijura replied.

Ethan shook his head. "It's time to go," he said and walked toward the doors. The others lagged behind. He rolled his eyes. "It's not a big mystery. He doesn't like me because I challenge the established protocols. I don't like him because he gives me way more grief than everyone else. Not everyone has to get along. Now drop it."

They exchanged looks.

Massey smiled. "Geez, you're really sensitive about it."

"Whatever," Ethan said and palmed the door controls.

The gray doors opened to a darkened corridor beyond.

Ethan pulled out his sidearm and turned on the flashlight underneath it. His neural implants helped compensate for the poor lighting.

"Yeah, this isn't too spooky or nothing," Massey grumbled.

Ethan walked out into the corridor, and once they were all through, the door shut behind them.

Ethan called out and waited, but there was no reply.

"Someone's got to be here. The ship has power," Eva said.

"Yeah, but there's no emergency lighting on," Massey said.

"I don't know. Let's make our way to the bridge and hopefully we'll find someone else here," Ethan said.

"Unless it's a ghost ship," Anton said quietly.

Massey blew out a breath. "You know I hate that stuff."

Anton grinned. "Yeah, I know. It's funny."

"It won't be funny if—"

"That's enough. Do I need to send you back? I'm sure Kujura can find something for you to do," Ethan said.

Massey actually remained quiet.

They walked down the corridors, following the signs heading to the bridge.

The freighter was long, designed for hauling big storage containers. They came to an intersection of corridors, and the section ahead of them was well lit.

"Thank God," Massey muttered.

Ethan heard faint sounds of people speaking. He didn't want to startle them, but he wanted to get closer before he called out to them. He gestured for the others to remain quiet as they approached.

They were within twenty meters of a well-lit open area.

Ethan heard the sound of a plasma rifle powering up behind

them. Ethan stopped moving and shook his head a little. "We just want to talk," he said.

There was a hearty chuckle behind them.

"Well, now I'm relieved. Do you hear that, Cyn. They just want to talk."

"I think we should hear them out, Clip," Cyn replied.

Ethan started to turn around.

"Not so fast. Drop your weapons," Clip said.

"That's a terrible idea," Ethan replied.

Clip grinned and made a deep, happy sound of someone who had effectively gotten the drop on them.

A group of people appeared in the room ahead. They were all armed.

"Ethan, will you stop screwing around?" Massey said.

"Let's just take it easy," Ethan said as he squatted down to the ground and placed his weapon on the floor. "I just meant that dropping my weapon was unsafe. It could go off and I wouldn't want to get accidentally shot."

"We got ourselves a joker," Clip said. "The rest of you…*lower* your weapons and place them on the ground."

Ethan smiled a little at the quip.

The others did as they were instructed.

"Okay, now walk forward to my friends up ahead. Slow and steady now. Don't want anyone to get accidentally shot," Clip said.

Ethan started to turn around, but a warning sound from Clip changed his mind. He walked to the end of the corridor and into the well-lit area. It was another cross-section that had several stacks of containers strategically placed, as if this were some kind of fortification. The people ahead of them all wore dark helmets, so he couldn't see their faces. They gestured with their rifles for Ethan and the others to stand to the side.

A tall man with broad shoulders walked into the area.

"Clip?" Ethan asked.

The man was older, looking as if he were in his…he did some quick math in his head since chances were that these people didn't have access to prolonging tech. Clip looked as if he were in his mid-forties. He had dark hair and a grizzled brown beard. He regarded Ethan with dark brown eyes.

A young woman came from the corridor. She had long, dark-blonde hair, pale skin, and honey-brown eyes that seemed to glisten in the light. She was tall, and her ship-suit accentuated the curves of her well-toned body. She looked at them with a guarded expression. She appeared impassive, but Ethan suspected that she was ready for action if the situation called for it.

"Eyes over here," Clip said. "What's your name?"

"Lieutenant Ethan Gates with the Colonial Defense Force —CDF."

"Never heard of it."

"That's not surprising."

Clip looked at the others. "Are all of you with this CDF?"

They nodded.

"How did you get on this ship?" Clip asked.

"There was an open hangar bay. We thought it might have been an invitation. We did try to hail the ship before we came aboard, but to be honest, we didn't have much choice."

Clip looked at Cyn. "I told you that dampening field was going to be a problem."

"It's part," Cyn began to say and then stopped for a second. "It's the strategy."

Clip rubbed his nose and looked at Ethan. "Are you alone?"

Ethan stared at him for a moment, deciding whether he should tell Clip about the others.

Clip gave him an icy stare. "Don't think. Just answer. Or I could just have Cyn vent the ship."

"No, we're not alone. There are more of us in the hangar bay. A couple of them are wounded. Don't vent the ship," Ethan said.

The edges of Clip's lips lifted. "You've got some balls, kid, but you know when it's time to just cooperate with the people who are holding all the cards."

"We didn't have a choice. We were in a battle at the dockyards, disabling the comms stations to stop the Vemus Alpha signal from broadcasting. Our squadron was engaged in a battle with another ship, and it used some kind of weapon to disable our ships. A lot of them died. We recovered the few escape pods and followed the ship," Ethan said.

Clip frowned thoughtfully and looked at Cyn. "They're definitely not with Magnus Station."

"That doesn't make them our allies either," Cyn replied.

"Hey, Cyn," Ethan said. She glared at him. "We don't want to be enemies here."

"Then you shouldn't have invited yourself on someone else's ship," she replied.

"Cynergy, I think we can hear them out," Clip said.

Cynergy walked a short distance away and leaned against one of the storage crates. She held her rifle loosely in her hands.

"No, we're not from Magnus Station, but we have met them. We have a diplomatic envoy there now," Ethan said.

Clip turned toward Vijura. "What are you supposed to be?"

"I am an Ovarrow."

"He's from the world we settled," Ethan said.

Clip arched a dark eyebrow. "Now this should be good."

"It's actually quite a story. I think you'd appreciate it," Ethan replied.

Clip gestured toward one of the others who wore a dark helmet. "Hash, I want you to listen to this. Go on, Ethan."

Anton gave Ethan a warning look. He wasn't sure what Anton expected. They were being held captive, and the longer they talked to these people, the more possibilities might come of it. Ethan told Clip and the others about the *Ark,* the colony on New Earth, and the Vemus invasion. He didn't bring up the Krake War or some of the other things because he didn't think it was relevant.

Clip looked at Vijura. "Ovarrow. You're part of the colony now. You're in their military."

Vijura stared at him for a moment. "We are part of the colony."

Clip frowned. "But they settled on your world. Didn't that upset your people?"

"We wouldn't have our world if it weren't for them. The Ovarrow are better for our alliance with the colony."

Clip pursed his lips and then looked at Ethan. "And the CDF is based off the NA Alliance military?"

"Yes, but the *Ark* had people from all the major alliances."

Clip waved away the comment. "Yeah, but it was predominantly the NA Alliance, right?"

Ethan glanced at the others, and they all waited for him to answer. "Yes."

Clip smiled. "I want to thank you for being honest with me."

Ethan frowned. "I am being honest with you, but how would you know if I was lying?"

Clip chuckled and gestured toward Hash. "He would know. Then he'd tell me, and I would have you shot."

"I guess that's lucky for me then."

"You didn't like that, did you?" Clip said. His voice took on an even tone.

Ethan didn't blink. "No, I wouldn't like being shot. But if you want to know if I'd put up a fight, there's one way to find out."

Clip considered this for a few moments and then nodded. "Not today, Lieutenant. I just wanted to get a feel for what kind of man you were. Now, if you look over here," he said, gesturing toward Massey. "He looks like he's about to explode."

Massey narrowed his gaze, but it was Ethan who spoke. "How would you feel in a room full of armed people who took your weapons?"

Clip shrugged. "You didn't have to give them up." He held up his hand. "Yes. Yes, I know. I'm glad you did. I really didn't want to have to shoot you." He paused for a few seconds, gathering his thoughts. "This expeditionary force. You brought powerful weapons with you?"

"Powerful enough," Ethan replied.

Clip smiled. "Vague enough. I wasn't sure how much you'd really say."

"Well, I'm not about to tell you our weapons capabilities if that's what you're asking. But I will say they're pretty good."

Clip nodded once. "They must be based on what I saw earlier."

"Okay, I told you about us, and I really don't think you're going to kill us. So why don't you tell us more about who you are," Ethan said.

Clip rested his hands on his hips. "You've been to Magnus Station... err, at least your envoy has."

Ethan nodded.

"Then you know that they're descendants of the Asiatic Alliance."

Ethan didn't know about that, but he nodded anyway.

"The Vemus Wars spread everywhere. It hit the NA Alliance

the hardest. It was the outposts and stations that were built way out here that managed to stay hidden. Mainly the Asiatic Alliance. Magnus Station has a stranglehold on trade and precious resources. The rest of us get by, but we don't have a choice but to deal with them. President Shao Fen has been in power for almost thirty years, and he's the worst of them."

"How so?"

Clip looked at him for a second. "It's time we showed them. Remove your helmets."

The others removed their helmets. They looked human, but at the same time they had traits of the humanoid form of the Vemus. Ethan's eyes widened. Their skins had dark purplish lines that formed intricate patterns on their necks, faces, and arms. Their eyes were darker and were somewhat larger than they should be.

Ethan looked at Cynergy. Her bright green eyes gleamed amid the dark skin. It was unsettling for him to look at, and he turned toward Clip and gasped. Clip was a few inches taller than him, but his skin had the same markings as the others. He smiled. Stark white teeth gleamed in the dim light.

"They're scared, all right," Hash said. "Especially that one." He gestured toward Massey.

"This is too much," Massey said. He backed away from the others.

"They're Vemus!" Eva hissed.

Two of their captors seized Massey.

"Get away from him!" Eva shrieked.

Cynergy darted toward her in the blink of an eye. She grabbed Eva's arm and twisted it behind her back.

Ethan started toward her, but someone held him back.

"Take it easy," Clip said. His voice sounded a little deeper and somewhat strained.

"Let them go!"

Ethan tried to push Clip's massive hand away, but he was too strong. Clip gave him a warning look.

"I thought you were smart. Now just calm down and give me a chance to explain who we are," Clip said calmly.

"Let them go first."

Clip sighed. "Cyn, let her go."

Eva spun around and punched Cyn in the face. The Vemus just smiled at her.

They let Massey go and he rushed to her side.

"We're not Vemus," Clip said. They looked at him. "Not the Vemus that your CDF fought."

"Then what are you?" Ethan asked.

He wished he had some of Lauren's expertise, or at the very least, a bioscanner.

"We're human," Clip said.

Ethan laughed. "What do you take us for? You are most certainly not human."

"We are. You said you have records of the Vemus War, right? Do any of us resemble the Vemus you fought?"

"So you're some kind of distant cousin. That doesn't make you human," Ethan replied.

Cynergy sneered. "They're just like the people on Magnus Station. They think they see a Vemus and nothing you say is going to change their minds."

"Well, if the shoe fits, honey," Ethan said.

Cynergy glared at him and started walking toward him.

Ethan backed up, seeing how fast she could move.

"Calm down, Cyn," Clip said. He looked at Ethan. "I listened to your explanation. Won't you extend me the same courtesy?"

Ethan glanced at the others for a second. "Give us some

space and we'll listen to you. Otherwise, forget it. And give it a rest with the rifles."

Clip studied him for a few moments and then looked at the others. "Give them some space. Lower your weapons."

Clip let Ethan go. He'd grabbed him pretty hard, but Ethan didn't rub his shoulder. He walked over to the others.

He looked at Eva. "You all right?" he asked quietly

She shook her head. "They're Vemus. They're either going to kill us or turn us into one of them."

"We're screwed. How are we going to get back to the others? Our ships are out of fuel. Why did I listen to you? I should've..." Massey's voice trailed off.

Anton looked at Ethan. "If you make a move, I'll back you up."

Ethan winced. "I appreciate it. But I also think they can hear us." Massey started to look over at them, but Ethan scowled. "Come on. Don't give it away. Look, we don't have much choice here. Let's hear what they have to say."

They didn't like it, but they really didn't have a choice. Ethan turned around and walked toward Clip.

"So, you were saying how you're not Vemus," Ethan said.

Clip told them how they were only part Vemus, that they'd been born this way because their ancestors had been exposed to some variant of the Vemus pathogen.

"But the Alpha signal doesn't have any effect on us," Clip said.

"How many others like you are there?" Ethan asked.

Clip smiled. "More than a few. Look I'm not going to share our population numbers. Just know that there are a lot of us. We're spread out."

"What are you doing here?" Eva asked.

"Our good friends of Magnus Station have this great little

program that the upper echelon calls the exile program. It's used to get criminals off the station. They're exiled and are never allowed back to Magnus Station. It's a nice big stick to keep the patrons of Magnus Station in line with whatever President Shao wants them to believe. But, it's also how he gets rid of people who spread certain ideas he'd rather didn't take root," Clip said.

"What kind of ideas?" Ethan asked.

"The same things your colonial government emphasized to the Ovarrow—individual rights, not having an overlord, free thinking. That sort of thing. Shao Fen and the rest of the Magnus Station rulers frown on that sort of thing. They emphasize a shared group-think where the individual has limited rights when it comes to balancing with what's best for everyone on the station."

"They have limited resources. Someone has to manage it," Massey said.

"Yeah, on the surface it sounds very fair, but it's never fair. It's never equal. You can't expect someone...anyone to treat you fairly when the other people have all the power."

"If that's the case, you'll return our weapons to us," Ethan said.

Clip chuckled. "Maybe later. What we do is we help the exiles. Give them a home. Learn what it is that Magnus Station security accused them of doing. The patterns are there. But there is also another use for the exiles. Shao Fen has plans to return to Earth."

"Isn't that the goal for you as well as them?" Ethan asked.

"For us, yes, but Shao Fen wants only what he calls pure humans to return to Earth."

"He'd fight a war over this?" Ethan asked.

"Wars have already been fought over this. We have some informants who live on the station."

Ethan frowned in thought for a few seconds. "How does he use the exiles to get to Earth?"

"Earth is protected by a blockade of defense platforms. It was part of the quarantine efforts to prevent the spread of the Vemus pathogen from leaving Earth."

Ethan blinked, and the edges of his lips lifted.

"Yeah, that didn't work so well, but the defense platforms are still there and quite operational. That's why no one can get to Earth."

"What does this have to do with the exiles?"

Clip smiled a little. "Every so often, they send a group of exiles on a ship bound for Earth. The ship is equipped with defensive measures that have a chance of breaking through the blockade. The exiles are then to determine whether it's safe for people to return to Earth. They're given a small biologicals lab and communication equipment that can only send a signal back to Magnus Station." He paused for a second and bit his lower lip, as if he was just remembering something. "No one has ever made it to the planet's surface. If they did, they didn't communicate anything back."

"Can you prove this?"

Clip tilted his head toward Cynergy. "She was one of the exiles we rescued." He frowned. "Was it eight years ago?"

"Nine," Cynergy replied.

Clip shrugged. "There you have it. It's not just her, but a lot of people we've rescued have the same story, the same type of equipment."

Ethan glanced at Cyn for a second. "You said they kill hybrids like you. Why would they exile you?"

"Because I hadn't changed yet. They thought I was just another human. And they don't only exile people. Very often they'll include families as well. It's a way to guarantee that they'll really try to reach Earth," Cyn replied.

Clip waggled his eyebrows once. "Isn't Magnus Station just the nicest place?"

Ethan considered it for a few moments. "The ship you're chasing." Clip nodded. "There are exiles on it?"

"Bingo, Lieutenant."

"But it disabled our squadron. They killed CDF soldiers."

Clip shook his head. "No, that's not possible." He held up his hand. "Just bear with me a second. The people onboard, the exiles? They have no control over that ship whatsoever. It's remote controlled in the beginning and then put on autopilot."

"There were other ships there. Space fighters."

"That would be part of Magnus Station's security."

Ethan glanced at the others in surprise.

Clip shrugged. "Like I said. Magnus Station is just great."

Ethan blew out a long breath.

"Yeah," Clip said softly. "If you're searching for an enemy to blame for the death of your soldiers, I've just given it to you. The question is: what are you going to do about it?"

"Our ships have almost no fuel left. We have wounded people waiting to hear back from us in the hangar," Ethan said.

Clip nodded slowly. "I propose we help each other out."

"What do you mean?"

"We're chasing down that ship. There are people onboard who really don't deserve to be there. You help us out with that. Then we'll take you to your superior officers and we can take it from there," Clip said. He stuck out his hand. "Do we have a deal?"

Ethan looked at Clip. "I'm not authorized to make that kind of deal. I can volunteer to help you in return for your help, but beyond that, I'd have to defer."

Clip shrugged and looked at his hand. "I can live with that."

Ethan snorted a little and shook Clip's hand.

Massey sighed heavily and Ethan looked at him. "Kujura is going to love this."

Ethan raised his eyebrows, then shrugged. "It's another thing to add to his list."

37

LENORA STARED AT HIM. "Did you hear me?"

There was no mistaking the determined look on her face as it appeared in startling clarity on the holoscreen.

Connor blinked a few times. "It's only been—"

"Two days, I know. I just don't think he's dead."

Connor blew out a breath. "I don't want to believe it either."

Lenora shook her head and squirmed in her chair, which she tended to do when she was annoyed. "You're not listening to me, Connor. I don't believe Ethan's dead. I don't feel it in here," she said, gesturing to her heart. "Now don't give me that look. I had the same feeling when everyone thought you were dead."

Connor smoothed his features. They'd been married a long time—long enough for him to at least consider her instincts, even when they flew in the face of logic. Despite all their efforts, there were still soldiers missing. Lenora likely wouldn't believe that Ethan had died until she saw his body. There was courage in daring to hope like that. Was it any less than struggling to accept that his son was dead?

"I want to believe, Lenora. More than anything."

"Then just believe. That's all. Just for a little while. You always told me that it's almost impossible to track everything in a battlefield, and the way you described the battlefield across the habitats near Saturn, it's a wonder we could track anything at all."

Then why hadn't they found Ethan? But he didn't voice the question because that would irritate her even more. It had only been two days, and the memory of her collapsing to the floor in grief was still too fresh in his mind.

"Try to believe, Connor."

He nodded once. "I will."

Lenora gazed at him for a few moments, then smiled a little.

"I have to go. I'm meeting with Sean and Martinez in the conference room."

"Will he return command over to you?"

The best thing Connor had done was to turn over command to Sean. It had given him some time to regroup.

"Only if he's convinced that I'm not a danger to myself and everyone else."

She smiled and arched an eyebrow. "Isn't that why they wanted you in the CDF in the first place?"

There were still lines of worry on the edges of her eyes, but it was an honest-to-goodness smile. She really did believe that Ethan was still alive.

He shrugged. "He's in a tough spot. If he wasn't capable of handling it, he wouldn't be in that position."

"One of your earliest protégés," she said and was quiet for a moment. "I know you think I'm being irrational."

"Not as much as you think I do."

"I just know."

They said their goodbyes, and Connor left his office and headed to the nearby conference room.

"Good morning, sir," Martinez said. "Do you want some coffee?"

It was just the two of them in the room.

Connor shook his head. "Thanks, but I'm fine."

"How you doing?"

"Better." He tipped his head to the side once. "It comes in waves."

Martinez nodded.

A comlink chimed, and they both sat at the conference room table. Martinez acknowledged the comlink and they were brought into a virtual meeting room. Sean was there, along with his XO Colonel Brad Sutton. Fabian Dumont was also attending.

Connor glanced at the ambassador with a thoughtful frown.

"General Quinn asked me to join the meeting," Dumont said.

"Normally, this would be handled internally, but since we're so far from COMCENT and there is some overlap with the diplomatic envoy, I wanted a representative to join us today," Sean said.

It made sense to Connor. His role in the expedition was both military and diplomatic. Even if he was relieved of duty for the CDF, he'd still have a diplomatic role as part of the envoy, at least until that was taken away from him if the governor saw fit.

"Understood," Connor said.

Sean nodded. "Let's get started. This meeting will be on the record. The purpose of it is to determine whether General Connor Gates is fit to resume command of the expeditionary force. I've spoken to Dr. Jake Forester and had him review the data. The results from the most recent psychological profiling indicates that…" He shook his head. "I was going to recount the medical terms used, but the death of a family member would shake anyone up, and it has. Connor, your actions speak to your integrity as a man and an officer who represents the finest tradition of the CDF. All of us look to you as our guide. There is no use hiding that fact, and I won't shy away from it here. Now, having said that I'm going to put the question to you, General Gates. Are you ready to resume command of the expeditionary force?"

Dumont waved his hand. "Excuse me. May I say something before General Gates answers that question?"

Sean glanced at Connor for a second, and then nodded.

"Thank you," Dumont said. "I realize I'm here as a courtesy. General Quinn, General Gates is your superior officer. How can you be biased about this? Shouldn't we have General Nathan Hayes in this meeting as he is the senior-most officer in the CDF?"

"I've spoken with General Hayes about this, and I have his full authority in this matter. He put it like this: 'You're there and I'm not. Make the decision.'"

Dumont blinked a few times. "Very well. Please continue."

Sean looked at Connor with raised eyebrows.

Despite whether he truly believed Ethan was alive, that wasn't an issue here. It came down to whether Connor felt he could resume command and that Sean believed him.

"My son is missing, presumably dead. This is going to affect me. The truth is that I don't know if I should resume command. As of this moment, I feel that I can. In this moment, I feel that I'm competent enough to resume my duties. But the question then becomes what happens if I can't? What if the waves of grief and anger become too much? I don't know if I can be the best judge of that. My instincts want me to get back in there and see this through to the end. I'm well aware of the price that being in command has on a person, but as to the issue of being emotionally compromised? I want retribution and justice for my son and the other soldiers who have died. I am capable of making intelligent decisions, so if that is the measure by which I'm to be judged, my answer to your question, General Quinn, is yes."

Sean looked at him for a few moments. "You've been my superior officer for my entire life. I wouldn't be the man that I am if it weren't for you. I would follow you anywhere, Connor. I speak for many when I say that you are not in this alone. We're here to support you. If you falter, then lean on us. You lean on me. It's what you trained me to do, and I'm damn proud for the opportunity to keep on doing it."

Connor's chest puffed with pride as he looked around at everyone in the room. "I won't let you down."

"Then as of this moment, General Connor Gates, you are cleared to resume command of this expedition, and we are waiting for your orders on how best to proceed with the rest of our mission."

Connor looked at them all for a few moments. "Thank you for putting your faith in me."

"I don't know what the appropriate response is to something like this. Congratulations doesn't feel right, so I'll simply wish you luck," Dumont said.

Connor nodded once.

"I should be going," Dumont said and started to rise.

"Actually, can you stick around for a few minutes?"

Dumont's eyebrows raised and he nodded.

"There have been some new developments that you're unaware of," Connor said.

Dumont was the only person at the meeting who was

unaware of the Venus Hybrids. Connor gave him a brief overview of what he'd learned from speaking with Wakiya and the rest of the salvagers who traveled with Lauren and Isaac.

Dumont's mouth hung open for a few seconds. "Of all the things I expected to encounter," he said and shook his head. "I guess I'm the only person here who didn't know."

Connor nodded. "I want to keep the people who know about this to a minimum for the time being."

Dumont nodded. "This is going to complicate our mission here on Magnus Station."

"It will, but you're also in a position to influence events. The CDF Destroyer *Acheron* is still nearby, and we have our protective details on the station with you. I want to avoid an incident until we've had a chance to investigate the claims made by Wakiya and the others."

"What is it you need me to do?" Dumont asked.

"Nothing for right now. Just keep doing what you've been doing. Do not give away that you're aware of the exile program or anything else that Shao Fen is involved in. It's not just him, but he's the leader," Connor said.

"We've made some contacts throughout the station. Perhaps it's prudent to find out what they know."

"You need to be careful. I don't want to back Shao Fen into a corner just yet."

"What are you going to do?"

"We're going on a recon mission to an outpost that is home to more of these exiles," Connor replied.

Dumont nodded and eyed Connor for a second. "When you say I'm the only one who knows, does that mean I'm the *only* one?"

"Lenora doesn't know, although she's had her suspicions of Shao Fen since we arrived."

"Understood. I won't take up any more of your time," Dumont said, and he closed his comlink session.

OVER THE PAST TWENTY-FOUR HOURS, reasonable responses pertaining to fleet deployments had been essentially thrown out the proverbial window. This was why Connor had moved the CDF fleet toward a distant outpost that was almost to Jupiter's orbit. The largest planet was nowhere near their current location. The official update was that they were investigating other facilities where the Vemus Alpha broadcast had been detected.

The deep-space outpost was small enough that it could have been missed by long-range scanners, even though it was home to over thirty thousand people. Connor stood on the bridge with Martinez at his side.

"The away team has just docked with the outpost," Connor said to Martinez. "Ops, open a data comlink to our guests."

Wakiya and the other salvagers had been given temporary space that granted them access to a small living area. CDF soldiers had been posted nearby.

A video comlink appeared on Connor's personal holoscreen. He gave Wakiya and the others a quick update, seeing that Lauren and Isaac were there as well.

"There hasn't been any response using any of the communication protocols you've provided," Connor said.

Wakiya glanced worriedly at the others. Connor didn't think she was pretending. Either way, they'd find out soon enough. Wakiya wanted to be on the away team going to the outpost, but with the lack of communications, Connor wasn't inclined to grant the request.

They watched the video feed of a reconnaissance drone as it

entered the outpost along with a squad of CDF soldiers. Once they were through the airlock, the drone flew ahead of the squad.

Captain Christoph Rahner led the platoon. "No response so far, sir."

"Proceed, Captain," Connor replied.

They watched as the platoon of soldiers walked down the docking tube and entered the outpost proper. One of the soldiers shouted in alarm. The combat suit cameras focused on a boy in the corridor. He stood there breathing heavily, his eyes wide in terror. There were blood stains on his shirt.

Rahner walked over to him. "Are you all right, son? Where is everyone?"

The boy blinked as if he'd just noticed the CDF soldier.

"This doesn't look like his blood. I don't see any wounds," Rahner said.

He squatted down so he was eye level with the boy, who looked to be about twelve or thirteen years of age.

"I'm here to help. Are you all right? Where is everyone?" Rahner asked.

The boy swallowed hard and looked at them. "They're dead."

"Who's dead?"

The boy licked his lips and said, "Everyone."

Rahner stared at him for a few seconds. "Torres, check him for injuries." Then he looked at the boy. "Can you tell me your name?"

"Will."

"Will, you're going to be all right. What do you mean everyone is dead? Where are they? Did someone hurt you?"

Another soldier came over and began running a biometric scanner on the boy.

"Hi Will, I'm Torrez. I'm just going to check you for injuries," she said.

Will nodded.

"Will, look at me," Rahner said. "Did someone hurt you?"

Will shook his head. "No, everyone just started falling down. They were coughing up blood. I ran away. I had to get away. Do you have a ship? Can I come on your ship?"

Will's lips trembled.

"We're going to take care of you, but we need to see if there is anyone else here. We need to find out what happened," Rahner said.

Connor watched as the CDF soldiers worked their way into the outpost. They found people slumped over tables or lying on the floor, with dark splotches of blood near their mouths.

Wakiya and the others cried out. They knew some of the people on the camera.

"Wakiya," Connor said, "you and the others don't need to see this."

"No, General Gates! I know these people. This place was supposed to be a secret from Magnus Station. We have to contact the other outposts. They must be warned."

"We need to figure out what happened here first. I promise you that we'll get to the bottom of this," Connor said.

"General Gates," Captain Rahner said, "I need to speak to you privately, sir."

Connor selected the option to isolate the comlink so the others couldn't hear or see them. Martinez gave him a nod.

"We're secure, Captain."

"Sir, Torres has detected our Vemus countermeasure in the atmosphere."

Connor's eyebrows knitted together. "What!"

Rahner nodded. "I can send you the results of her bioscans, but the analysis came back with the identified compounds that link it back to our Vemus countermeasure. Someone weaponized it and released it into the outpost's life-support system."

Connor glanced at Martinez for a second. This was an attack. "Okay, this is what I need you to do. Find a way to scrub the atmosphere of our countermeasure. Search for survivors. We were told that the population was a mix between humans and the hybrids, so there might be more people alive. I'll send over additional teams to help with the search, but you'll need to send a team to search for where they deployed the bioweapon."

"Understood, sir. We'll get started right away," Captain Rahner said.

Connor closed the comlink and looked at Martinez.

"There are thousands of people on that outpost, sir. You know what Wakiya and the rest of them are going to think—that this was an attack from Magnus Station."

Connor nodded grimly. "And we're going to help prove it. They couldn't have deployed a bioweapon into the life-support systems without leaving some kind of trace behind."

"But that will only give us the mechanism they used for the attack."

"It's a start. It's how we'll build a case," Connor said and sighed heavily. "We're going to need cleanup crews. It'll probably be safer to vent the atmosphere, remove the deployment method they installed, and then turn the life-support systems back on."

Martinez nodded. "We can do it in sections, but we'll need to find out if there are any survivors first."

"Agreed. We'll need to use the outpost's comms systems to broadcast a warning."

He glanced at the holoscreen where Wakiya and the others waited, then looked at Martinez. "Get started with the outpost. I'm going to speak to Wakiya about what happened."

"Yes, sir," Martinez said.

They needed evidence of the attack if they were going to accuse anyone of wrongdoing. If the evidence did lead back to Shao Fen and Magnus Station, he'd seriously underestimated what the man was capable of.

Connor activated the comlink to Wakiya and the others and told them what had happened.

38

ETHAN WATCHED Kujura speaking with Clip. They'd been at it for nearly an hour. He'd wanted to be part of the conversation, but Kujura told him in no uncertain terms that he'd done enough.

"They're still at it?" Anton asked.

Ethan nodded. "I thought about trying to listen in, but I figure I'm in enough trouble as it is. I don't need to give Kujura any more ammunition to use against me."

"Probably a good idea."

"It would be better if Colonel Walker was awake," Ethan said and glanced around to make sure no one else was listening to them. "Kujura is part of the CDF and the Ovarrow are part of the colony, but I wouldn't want any of them in charge when it comes to making decisions that could affect the rest of humanity."

Anton frowned while he gathered his thoughts. "I don't think he'd do anything foolish. He's a by-the-book kind of officer, and you're not. But I don't think I like where this conversation is heading."

"You heard what Clip said. This ship is on its last legs, and they were just using it to get them within the vicinity of the other ship. Then they were going to leave it to be retrieved later. Possibly never."

"All Kujura wants is to send a message to the CDF to let them know we're alive and then they can send someone to pick us up," Anton said.

"Yeah, I know. I tried asking some of the others about the comms systems, but while they were friendly enough, they weren't about to let me use them."

Anton arched an eyebrow toward him. "Did you ask everyone?"

Ethan frowned and shook his head.

They were in an open area near the bridge. The salvagers sat across the room speaking quietly among themselves while the CDF occupied the other side of the room. Eva leaned against the wall and watched them. Massey tried to talk to her, and she looked as if she was only giving him one-word answers. Massey shrugged and walked toward Ethan and Anton.

"I can think of someone else you could ask," Anton said and lifted his chin.

Cynergy walked into the room. She looked at them for a second, and then her gaze went to Eva. The two exchanged icy glares. Then she joined the other salvagers.

Ethan shook his head. "Not a chance. She looks like she'd rather be alone."

Anton chuckled. "Not up to the challenge."

Ethan rolled his eyes. "No, but there are easier targets. Seriously, I doubt she'd help us. She's loyal to Clip."

Anton shrugged. "I saw her look at you a few times."

Ethan shivered. "She almost shot me. Did you notice how fast she healed?"

"We all saw it. Anyway, if you're not willing to try, then wish me luck."

"Are you serious?"

Anton began walking away from him. "You know what they say. The tougher the nut is to crack, the better the inside is."

Ethan shook his head. "That's not how that saying goes."

Anton shrugged and walked across the room toward Cyn. She watched him come toward her. He waved and gestured toward her side. She pulled a combat knife from her belt and twirled it around for a second. Anton held up his hands in a placating gesture and backed away.

"What an idiot," Eva said casually.

Ethan hadn't heard her come over. "It's because Massey is always talking about the importance of taking chances, even when it doesn't make sense."

Eva grinned and shook her head. "Yeah, he does that to a fault."

Anton walked over and mimed a shiver. He eyed Ethan. "You were right."

"I'm glad you finally admitted it."

Eva blew out a breath. "What did you expect would happen?"

Anton shrugged. "I was just trying to get her to talk to me."

"Kujura is finished. Let's go find out what's going on," Ethan said.

Kujura walked away from Clip and gestured for them to follow. They walked toward him and rejoined the others.

"They're not going to allow us access to the comms systems until after they've captured that ship they're pursuing. He said it would trigger the ship's defenses and they'll only have a couple of chances to get on it," Kujura said.

"Sir," Ethan said, "they might only need one chance if we help them. There are passengers on that ship that were forced there against their will."

"I'm aware of that, but that is not our mission. We need to contact the CDF and rejoin the fleet. Colonel Walker hasn't regained consciousness and he needs medical attention."

"What if only some of us go? It'll give us a chance to figure out how that weapon was able to disable our ships," Ethan said.

Kujura considered this for a few moments, regarding Ethan. Then he glanced at the others. "Give us a few minutes alone."

Anton glanced at Ethan and made a take-it-easy gesture. Eva frowned and then followed the others.

Ethan crossed the distance to stand closer to Kujura. The Ovarrow peered at him for a few seconds.

"Lieutenant Gates, your instincts are what got us here in the first place. I understand the options were limited, but accompanying these...hybrids, in this rescue mission is reckless and I cannot authorize it."

"If there were Ovarrow on that ship, would your answer be different?"

Kujura narrowed his gaze. "You of all people know the history of the Ovarrow. You know we wouldn't hesitate to make tough decisions."

Ethan shook his head. "This isn't a tough decision. They're sending that ship to Earth. It's going to attempt to breach defense platforms to get there."

"Yes, and you want to try and stop the ship from reaching the planet. What if you can't? What if they can't?"

"Then I can help them make it past the defense platforms.

We have the best training of anyone here. We should be helping these people, sir."

"Our first priority is to contact the CDF."

"I agree with that, sir, but we can also help them."

Kujura regarded him.

Ethan knew he was way out on a limb here. He was questioning his commanding officer, but he noticed that Kujura hadn't given an order, at least not yet.

"Sir," Ethan said, "I'm going to help those people."

"And if I order you not to?"

They stared at each other for a few seconds. Whatever he said next would have implications for his future in the CDF.

"Don't," Ethan said.

Kujura shook his head and glanced toward where Colonel Walker was lying on a cot. He stared at the colonel for a few moments. Then he looked back at Ethan.

"I think Colonel Walker would authorize you to go with the hybrids. For some reason I cannot understand, he sees something in you. He called it 'out-of-the-box thinking.' So, I have a problem. I can't pass you up the chain of command, and if I order you not to go, you'll go anyway. Don't bother to deny it, Lieutenant, I can see it in your eyes. If I order you not to go and you disobey me, then your career in the CDF is finished, and the morale of what remains of the 7th would plummet because we can't see eye to eye."

Ethan looked at Kujura. He was right; Ethan was going to disobey orders, but he hadn't considered how it would affect the 7th moving forward.

Kujura glanced at the other soldiers watching them. "Your foolishness spreads like a disease. Not only would we lose you but at least four other good pilots as well. Soldiers with a real future in the CDF. Have you thought about that?"

Ethan swallowed hard. "Yes, I have, sir. When we joined the CDF, we understood that we would be risking our lives."

Kujura narrowed his gaze for a second and sighed, looking resigned. "You're the son of a war hero who managed to defy the odds. I doubt he would want you to emulate that. We had many heroes in our own history. They usually achieved an exalted status only after they died."

Kujura was part of a new generation of Ovarrow whose parents had gone into stasis pods to survive the Krake oppressors. Their history was filled with the sorrow and sacrifice that had honed their species. It was only after their dealings with the colonists that they'd returned to a more compassionate existence, and yet they still carried the brutal lessons of their past. Ethan found the hard certainty in Kujura's gaze a little unsettling.

"I just want to help those people, sir. I'm not trying to be a hero. I'm not a glory hound."

Kujura regarded him for a few moments. "Sometimes people believe that because we're a different species it impedes our ability to share burdens between us. Sometimes it's true, but not always." He glanced at the others for a second. "This is against my better judgement, but I'm going to authorize you to go. You can take five volunteers with you."

Ethan blinked in surprise. "Uh, thank you, sir."

"It's what Colonel Walker would have done. Of that I am convinced."

Ethan nodded. "Still, I know we've had our differences, but I appreciate you giving me some latitude on this, sir."

"Understood, Lieutenant. Get your volunteers and inform Clip that he'll have additional help on this rescue mission."

39

ETHAN LOOKED at the remaining pilots of the 7ᵗʰ. "So that's it. Captain Kujura has authorized me to help the hybrids rescue the exiles from the freighter. I'm looking for volunteers to come with me. I can take up to five."

The others were quiet while they considered what Ethan had told them. He'd had to emphasize that this was strictly a volunteer mission.

Massey raised his hand. "Question. That ship already disabled our fighters, so how are we going to sneak aboard it? Our fighters are extremely low on fuel anyway."

"We're not going to use our fighters. Clip assures me that they have a way to scramble the scanners used on the ship."

Eva tilted her head to the side. "How?"

"I didn't ask the specifics, but I doubt they'd launch a mission to storm a ship if they couldn't get to the ship in the first place."

Eva shook her head. "That's a heck of a leap, Ethan."

"They've done this before."

"They've seen the weapon that was used to disable our ships before?"

"A less powerful version of it. From previous rescue missions they've noticed that the scanner array is predominantly forward-facing. It makes sense if all they really care about is getting that ship past the orbital defense platforms. The ship has to make it past the defenses and land on the planet. It doesn't have to fly ever again, so its defenses don't give the ship the full coverage that we use on a warship."

Eva frowned in thought and didn't say anything else.

Massey shook his head. "What can we possibly do to help then? If we can't use our fighters, what's the point of us even going?"

Ethan had expected this question, but he hadn't expected to be drilled quite so much by Eva. "Our training and expertise enable us to help them take control of the nav system." He paused for a second because he was about to give the clincher. "If that fails, we can get that ship past the defense platforms."

There were several sighs from people and more than a few mutterings.

"The ship also has a powerful comms platform that we can use to contact the CDF. The whole point of the exiles was for them to reach Earth and contact Magnus Station. We've trained for missions like this," Ethan said, his gaze on Massey. "You don't have to go."

Massey stared at him.

"I'm going," Anton said.

"I will go as well," Vijura added.

The edges of Ethan's lips twitched. He'd suspected they'd come, and he gave them a nod. He stared at the others for a second. "Anyone else?"

Massey glanced across the room where several of the hybrids

were speaking to each other. They'd reverted to appearing like humans. "They look plenty capable enough to me. I think I'll pass."

Ethan nodded. "Probably for the best."

Massey's gaze narrowed. "What's that supposed to mean?"

Eva rolled her eyes. "He's baiting you."

Ethan smiled. "I am, but I'm not. Why bring someone along if all they're going to do is complain?" Massey started to reply, and Ethan held up his hand. "It's fine. You don't want to go. We don't have a lot of time here. We joined the CDF to protect the colony. The colony wouldn't be around if it wasn't for the ancestors of those people who fought and died to help protect the colonists on the *Ark*." He gestured toward the hybrids. He noticed Cynergy watching him. Could they hear him? He wasn't sure about that.

Eva shook her head and looked away. "Damn it." She sighed and looked at him. "I'll go."

Massey volunteered after that. Ethan thanked them and walked across the room toward where Clip was speaking to Hash. Clip jutted his chin up once.

"We're ready when you are," Ethan said.

Clip nodded. "Good."

Cynergy exhaled forcefully. "He had to all but bully them into coming."

Clip pressed his lips together. "They're putting a lot of trust in us, Cyn. You could be more accommodating."

Cyn narrowed her gaze and then rolled her eyes. "If they prove their worth, *then* I'll be accommodating," she said and looked at Ethan. "In the meantime, just stay out of our way."

Ethan was tired of her attitude. He grinned, and she frowned. "I think you've got that reversed."

Cyn glared at him. "What's that supposed to mean?"

"It means that while you might have a few tricks stashed away that could help, you haven't had the training we've had. Right now, all I see is a young girl who's full of attitude and fury toward anyone who speaks to her, with a few exceptions. Do yourself a favor and stay out of *our* way. You might learn something," Ethan said. He looked at Clip, who didn't look surprised. "We'll be right over for mission debrief."

He hardly glanced at Cynergy as he turned around, but he was sure there was a great big scowl on her face. Well, she could scowl as much as she liked. If she was only going to be hostile toward the people who were trying to help her, that's what she was going to get in return.

"Take it easy," Clip said to her.

"This is a mistake," she replied.

Clip sighed. "Maybe, but we'll know soon enough. Besides, he's not wrong. You could be nicer to the people trying to help us. It beats the alternative."

The edges of Ethan's lips lifted as he crossed the room. They went to the hangar to retrieve their field kits and survival gear. Ethan climbed into the cockpit of his ship and removed the comms module.

"What are you doing?" Eva asked.

He lifted the small module up for a second so she could see it, then put it away.

"Think it'll be as easy as plugging it in?" she asked.

Ethan shrugged. "We'll find out."

Clip returned their weapons to them. "Captain Kujura, thank you for loaning us some help. The comms system on this ship will be available in eight hours. You should be able to contact the CDF at that time."

He turned toward Ethan and the others. "Time to go."

Clip led them through the ship, and they reached a docking tube. "We're using a shuttle for the rest of the trip."

Massey gave Ethan an accusatory look, then followed the others into the docking tube. Hash keyed in his authentication and the airlock opened. On the other side was the entrance to the shuttle.

"It's a recon skiff. NA Alliance. Doesn't have much for weapons, but it can fly with the best of them," Clip said.

Ethan followed him into the ship. It wasn't dirty, but it definitely looked old. What had once been pristine white walls seemed to have a layer of smoke that had been baked into the hull. No amount of scrubbing would get it clean. The equipment was worn and looked to have been cobbled together from parts of other ships.

"How is this ship even space-worthy?" Massey said.

"Good point," Clip said. "I think you'd better go on your own individual life-support systems."

Ethan thought he was joking, but he wasn't. He put on his helmet and the others did the same. The hybrids followed suit.

Clip had the others strap themselves into the seats of the passenger area and invited Ethan to join him in the cockpit. His least favorite person was already there.

Cynergy did a double take when Ethan followed Clip into the shuttle's cockpit.

"Flight status?" Clip asked, sitting down in the middle seat. He gestured toward the seat beside him, and Ethan sat.

"They all check out. Hash managed to recharge the power core from the freighter. Should be enough to reach the target," Cynergy said.

"Understood," Clip said.

"Your power core loses integrity that fast?" Ethan asked.

"Sometimes. The emitters need alignment and replacement. You probably noticed how old the ship is."

Ethan nodded.

"We restore the ships as best we can."

Ethan knew that without fabricators, keeping ships or habitats safe was a monumental task.

"Release docking clamps," Clip said.

They detached from the freighter, and Ethan watched a video feed that showed them moving away.

Cynergy increased the engine output, and they increased velocity.

"The weapons systems on the freighter with the exiles—what happens if they target us?" Ethan asked.

"It'll disable our power systems just like it did to your ships," Clip replied.

"How does it work?"

"We're not sure. It functions like a focused EMP, but ship systems are hardened for that, so the weapons system has a way to get past standard defenses."

Ethan frowned. "I thought you'd captured these types of ships before?"

Clip nodded. "We have, but Magnus Station has a bunch of failsafes to prevent their tech from falling into the wrong hands. Believe me, we've tried to retrieve it before, and we've always failed."

"Does it just self-destruct if it detects someone tampering with it?"

Clip shook his head. "Not always. I think they have a subroutine that's designed to operate after a specific amount of time has lapsed. The code is embedded into all the components."

Ethan considered that for a few moments. He'd never come across anyone that paranoid about keeping their weapons systems out of enemy hands. The CDF had their own protocols, but he didn't think they were so sophisticated as to include individual component pieces.

The shuttle raced toward the distant freighter and was quickly closing in.

The freighter was small, with enough storage capacity for only two containers. The shape was that of a barbell, with the crew quarters located near the stern of the ship.

Clip increased the magnification of the ship on the holoscreen. "See those turrets located on the containers? There're probably a few on the bow of the ship as well. That's the automated defense system."

Ethan peered at the image. "Looks like a handful of mag cannons. I don't see any grasers. So those other turrets are the focused EMP systems?"

Clip nodded approvingly. He leaned toward Cynergy. "Looks like he knows his stuff, right, Cyn?"

"Maybe he should fly the ship in then," she replied.

"I can fly anything," Ethan said.

Clip laughed and wiped his eyes. "God, you remind me of myself when I was your age. What are you? Twenty years old?"

Ethan nodded.

"Thought so. Same age as Cyn here. Uh, don't answer that. Age is that unspoken topic. Is it the same with the colony you come from?"

Ethan shrugged. "Sometimes, but…we use prolonging treatments to extend our lifetimes."

"Must be nice," Cyn said.

Clip nodded. "Yeah, I imagine it would be. Tech like that is in the past for us. Most people don't even believe in it so much anymore."

Ethan shifted in his seat. "I'm sure we'll share the technology with you once all this is over."

Cyn made a noncommittal sound.

Clip pursed his lips in thought. "A lot of people would be happy to hear about that."

Something in his tone made Ethan think that the subject of prolonging might be more complicated than whether it was possible or not.

"There have been new developments. It's not limited to young people anymore."

Clip eyed him. "Really?" he asked, sounding unconvinced.

Ethan nodded. "My sister could tell you more about it. There's been a resurgence in researching it for the Ovarrow. As a result, discoveries have been made to improve the process."

Cyn looked at him thoughtfully. It was probably the first time she hadn't quite scowled in his direction.

"Sounds good," Clip said and opened a comlink to someone else. "Hash, bring up the scrambler."

There was silence for a few moments.

"Having an issue with it."

Clip's eyes widened. "Do we need to abort?"

Hash didn't reply.

Clip waited a few moments and then climbed out of this seat, saying he'd be right back.

Ethan considered going with him but decided to stay where he was. He glanced at Cynergy. "How does the scrambler work?"

"It projects a comms array that reflects scans back to the source, but it modifies the return so that it fools the scanner into believing it's scanning itself."

Ethan frowned. "That's it?"

She nodded.

"And you've used it before?"

She nodded again, looking at him expectantly.

"If I understand it right, that will make the scanner think it's not aligned right. So, won't the other scanners try to compensate for the blind spot?"

Her eyes widened. "Oh my God! You're right! How could we be so stupid? Thank you. No, seriously thank you for pointing this out to us. We never would've figured it out."

Ethan shook his head and glared at the main holoscreen.

She laughed, and it was so sudden that it surprised him. It sounded nice, even though it was at his expense. "I'm just teasing you."

"Yeah, well I'm just trying to understand how the scrambler works."

"Fine," she said and sighed. "It works exactly like you said it does, and we get a small window of time to reach the freighter and sneak aboard."

Ethan considered it for a second. "So, you're poking it in the eye and using the time it takes to regain its bearings to sneak past its blind spot."

She pursed her lips for a moment. "That's right."

Clip came back into the cockpit and sat down. "We're good to go."

They flew toward the freighter, and Ethan watched as the ship's systems detected the scans from the freighter. After the initial return, Cynergy increased their velocity and closed the distance to the shuttle. They flew at speeds that would make an AI uncomfortable, but Ethan was fine. Flying fast had never been a problem for him.

Clip identified the rear docking port, and Cynergy flew them toward it. She extended the docking clamps and a universal docking tube extended to the hatch. The whole thing went off without any issues.

"We'll lead the way," Clip said and then gestured toward Ethan. "You follow us in. The people aboard are frightened, but they're also armed, so don't take anything for granted."

Ethan glanced at the others to confirm that they'd heard him, and they nodded toward Clip.

They opened the hatch and stepped inside. Clip went to the interior doors and opened them to the access tunnel. Overhead lighting lit the tunnel just enough for them to see. Their helmets did the rest.

Clip took point, with Hash and Cynergy behind him. They were followed by the remaining hybrids and then Ethan and the others.

Ethan tried using his suit computer to connect to the ship's systems, but he was refused.

"It's gotta be locked down," Anton said.

Ethan nodded, and they followed the hybrids down the corridor.

"Heads up. We're almost to the hab sections," Clip called over his shoulder.

They made it to the door and Hash connected a device to the door controls. A few moments later, the door opened. The hybrids carried their weapons at the ready but tried to avoid pointing them at the people inside the room. Ethan heard people shouting.

"Easy now," Clip said. "We're here to get you off the ship."

A short man held his hands up over his head. Either none of them were armed or they'd hidden their weapons.

"We can't leave," he said.

"What's your name?" Clip asked.

"Trav Remington."

Clip smiled. "Trav, we know you're exiles. We know this ship is heading to Earth."

"Then you know why we have to go through with it."

"Why is that?" Ethan asked.

Trav glanced at him and took in Ethan's uniform. "Alliance military?" he asked, and then looked at Clip. "Did you find a supply depot or something?"

Clip shook his head. "Nope. They're the real deal, but not the Alliance you're thinking of."

Trav looked at Ethan and the other CDF soldiers for a second. "Look, if we tamper with the ship's systems, it'll send a signal back to Magnus Station and the people we left behind will suffer for it."

Clip nodded. "We know, okay? We know the threats, but we're not going to let you die because of it. We can disable the comms system if we have to."

"No! If you do that, they'll think it was us. There are worse things than exile!" Trav said.

Several of the other exiles nodded. They had a hardened glint in their eyes, as if they were resigned to accept their fate. Though they were unarmed, they looked ready to fight.

"What's going to happen to them?" Ethan asked.

"Magnus Security will take away their possessions and relocate them to the lower levels. Their living stipends will be slashed. Access to everything that comes through official channels will be restricted. They'll be treated like criminals."

The other people around him all nodded. They were more than afraid. It was as if they'd already accepted the fact that they were going to die but that they could save their friends and families they'd been forced to leave behind. It was a cruel twist to an unfair fate.

"Clip is right. We can help you," Ethan said.

Trav shook his head. "You can't. We tried taking control of the navigation system. They detected it. Magnus Station security sent us a recorded message of them putting our families into quarantine. They were being detained. There is nothing you can do to stop that."

"Yes, we can," Ethan said.

"I would listen to him," Clip said.

Trav blew out a breath. "Not another uprising. Not again."

"It's coming whether you want it to or not, but it's different this time. It's different because of them," Clip said, gesturing toward Ethan and the others.

Trav narrowed his gaze.

"We're colonists, and we have a diplomatic envoy at Magnus Station. We can negotiate to get your families removed from the station and relocated elsewhere. You don't need to endure this kind of treatment."

Trav looked away and shook his head.

"They have warships," Clip said. "We've seen them. Their weapons are powerful."

"Work with us," Ethan said. "Show us what you tried to do so we don't repeat the same thing. Then we can take it from there. Sitting here and hoping that this ship somehow will get you to Earth isn't enough. I promise that if we don't think we can get control of the computer system, we'll stop. We'll get off the ship and back onto the shuttle."

Trav's shoulders slumped. "We won't all fit on the shuttle."

Ethan frowned. "How many of you are here?"

"Forty of us."

Ethan blinked a few times. He looked at Clip, who seemed surprised.

"Forty! They've never sent that many before," Clip said.

"They told us this ship was special. That it contained the best chance of us reaching Earth."

"We'll need to take a look for ourselves," Ethan said.

Clip nodded. "Cyn, take them with you to the computing core. Hash, go with them and do a full diagnostic of the system. See if we can bypass whatever security measures Magnus Station put in our way."

They left the central area with Cynergy in the lead, following a map on her wrist computer. People lined the corridor but quickly got out of their way.

Massey walked next to Ethan and leaned over. "This just gets better and better."

"If it were easy, they wouldn't need us," Ethan said.

40

THERE WERE TOO many outposts for them to investigate to prevent the bioweapon from reaching them. Connor allowed Wakiya to work with his comms officers and send out encrypted messages to warn the outposts about the danger they were in. The bioweapon was created from what the CDF had developed to kill the Vemus during the colonial war. Shao Fen must have had someone capture the colonial probes before they'd been destroyed by the self-destruct mechanism and extract the Vemus countermeasure from it. They'd then created multiple delivery agents to spread the deadly countermeasure on populated stations. Humans without any Vemus adaptations within their DNA were spared, but everyone else died horribly.

Biological warfare was a nasty business. Connor hated it, and now that he'd met the survivors and learned about the victims, he was determined to remove Shao Fen and the rest of his administration from power at Magnus Station.

They'd begun receiving message confirmations of thwarted attacks on the outposts. One method of delivery was by using standard shipping freighters that ferried trade items among the different outposts. The ships' captains had been ignorant of what they were delivering. Connor was surprised by the simplicity of the plan. Some outposts were able to cut off the contagion by isolating the holding areas so the outposts' life-support systems didn't get contaminated.

Connor found that the small groups that lived together were actually quite resilient, and divides between the hybrids and humans were almost non-existent. They relied on each other to survive, and that was something Connor could relate to.

The door to his ready room chimed. One of the soldiers on guard duty stuck his head inside. "General Gates, you have a visitor."

Lauren walked in and he gestured toward the seat across from him.

"I'm requesting that the quarantine be lifted for Wakiya and the other hybrids. We're in no danger from them," Lauren said.

"The biometrics are still negative?"

She nodded. "Yes, and it was confirmed by your chief medical officer as well. He said he would send you his findings."

"Okay, we can find them better accommodations, but I thought they'd move onto one of the outposts."

"Some will, but Wakiya and Braun are going to stay here," she said and looked away for a moment. "I can't believe what's been done to them. We have to do something about this."

"We *are* doing something about this," Connor replied.

"Who would do such a thing?"

Connor stared at his daughter for a long moment. She was brilliant and strong but hadn't been alive long enough to realize that sometimes life could be far crueler than she'd ever expected. He didn't like that she had to see it now, but he couldn't shield her from it. Not anymore. "This is an ongoing struggle. We're doing everything we can."

"Why haven't we gone back to Magnus Station? Why haven't you removed Shao Fen and the rest of his administration from power?"

"We will, but it's also not that simple. We can't show up there and force a change on them. Facilitating change is a little more complicated. Right now, the people of Magnus Station are ignorant of what's been done. If we're to effect real change, we've got to do it from within."

"What if they don't believe all the evidence? They control the messaging their people receive."

Connor looked at her for a moment. "They won't control our messaging."

Lauren nodded. "There's more. Wakiya wanted to speak to you again."

Connor glanced at his holoscreen. He was due on the bridge soon, and he had to meet with his senior officers. "I'll get to her as soon as I can."

The edges of Lauren's lips twitched, and she arched an eyebrow.

Connor frowned. "What?"

She smiled. "You really need to speak to her again. She's just outside."

Connor's eyebrows raised and he glanced at the door. "Fine, bring her in."

Lauren went to the door and opened it. Wakiya walked in. There were several soldiers outside who must have escorted her here.

"He doesn't have a lot of time," Lauren said to her.

"I will be brief," Wakiya said and looked at Connor. "We believe that the bioweapon is being sent to Earth."

"How do you know?"

"Magnus Station sends exiles to Earth to try to breach the defense platforms. We've gotten reports of increased ship activity leaving the station, but we also have contacts within Magnus Station security who indicated the program had been resurrected. There had been a long hiatus."

Connor frowned in thought. "If there's a ship heading to Earth, the defense platforms should stop it."

Wakiya stepped toward his desk, her gaze hard as ice. "We can't allow this to happen."

He eyed her for a few seconds. "It's time for you to come clean and tell me what you know."

Wakiya inhaled deeply and nodded. "We've received partial transmissions from Earth in the past. There are survivors there who are using tight-beam transmissions, but they're sporadic and difficult for us to locate. We don't know who they are, but there's a strong possibility that there are people like us who survived on the planet."

Connor took a moment to gather his thoughts. "You mean hybrids like you."

"They're still people, General Gates. They don't deserve to die because of this bioweapon."

"No, they don't," Connor said and came around his desk.

"What will you do?" Wakiya asked.

"Well, I can't be in two places at once. If this bioweapon is heading to Earth, I'm going to stop it. It's about time we assessed the danger of returning to Earth for ourselves."

The Vemus countermeasure had been designed in such a way that it would spread throughout an environment. If the fauna left on Earth had found a way to adapt to the Vemus contagion, then the bioweapon would have a catastrophic effect. He wasn't about to let that happen. They'd come here to re-establish contact with Earth, not to enable mass genocide.

Connor stopped before the door. "You two go to the conference room just down the corridor. I'll join you in a few minutes."

He shut the office door and initiated a comlink to the *Acheron*, located near Magnus Station.

Major Ned Emery appeared on the holoscreen. "General Gates."

"I have a job for you."

Emery's eyebrows raised. "I'm at your disposal, sir."

"I'll bring you up to speed in a minute, but first I need you to know that this mission is going to have Dark Star status."

"Understood, sir. I confirm Dark Star status."

The operation was to be classified, and its classification conveyed to Major Emery that only the senior-most officers would know the exact mission parameters.

"It's time to enact Charlie Project contingencies. Our people on Magnus Station will need additional protection protocols."

"I'll inform the security lead at once, sir."

"It's also time to step up our reconnaissance efforts and infiltration of Magnus Station systems."

Emery's brow furrowed. "Sir, are we going to take over the station?"

"Only if necessary. We'll need to keep an eye on all senior leadership personnel, especially any and all contacts of President Shao Fen."

"Understood, sir. I've been reviewing the intelligence reports, and there is a significant majority of patrons who appear to be loyal to the president."

Connor nodded. "I understand. We're not about to round up civilians."

Emery blew out a breath. "I'm glad to hear you say that, sir. I'm not sure if we can capture the senior leaders. I'll need to work this through my team."

Connor knew all too well the complexities of an operation like this. "If we can't capture them when the time comes, then we can isolate them. An intelligence brief is going to be coming your way. Have you made any progress on infiltrating their comms systems?"

Emery nodded. "Yes, sir. But it's a fragmented system with a lot of control points."

"By design."

"Yes. I also have several operatives in the field doing local recon."

"Good. There will be a list of contacts for them to engage. They're part of a network of people who are sympathetic to the injustice that's been going on."

"Can they be trusted?"

"We can't do everything ourselves. Have your people take every precaution they believe is necessary when making contact."

"Yes, sir."

Connor spent the next ten minutes speaking with Major Emery, and when he finally closed the comlink he considered contacting Lenora. If Shao Fen was backed into a corner, he would lash out and attempt to use the diplomatic envoy as leverage. The envoy was being watched, and the best protection for them was that they continue on as if nothing had changed. Their protective details would change, and their schedules would be changed so they were within range of an egress point. Connor hoped it didn't come to that. Too many things could go wrong, but he needed time to stop the weapon heading to Earth.

41

THE COMPUTING CORE of the freighter was little more than a small room filled with computer towers. There were several small aisles that allowed them to access various parts of the core.

"They all have it," Hash said.

Ethan stared at the console where the navigation systems performed complex calculations to keep the ship on course. "I won't touch it."

Cynergy leaned around the corner and looked at him. "You can't manipulate the lockout devices."

"I know. I'm just using the system account that the diagnostic uses to explore some of the control systems," Ethan replied.

Anton glanced at him. "Where'd you learn this stuff?"

Ethan shrugged. "Some kids play with toys growing up, and I learned how to bypass secure systems."

Anton frowned.

"It was my dad's idea of constructive play."

"If you say so. Did he have you do seven-day survival treks, too?"

"Didn't yours?" Ethan countered.

Anton snorted.

Ethan brought up his wrist computer and downloaded the navigation data from the console. He eyed Cynergy, who was watching him, and he decided to play nice. "Want to see what I'm doing?"

She frowned for a second, considering, and then walked over. "How did you get that? You can't change anything, or it will be detected."

Ethan nodded. "I know. I haven't changed anything. The account used for diagnostics isn't able to change anything. It can just look at the data. I just recorded it with my wrist computer here."

He expanded the holoscreen so she could see it. "Now we can take a closer look without tripping off any alarms."

She snorted appreciatively.

He raised his hand to his ear. "I'm sorry, I couldn't hear that."

She shook her head. "I didn't say anything."

"You don't have to."

She rolled her eyes. "This doesn't get us control of the ship."

"No, but we can see how they're controlling it and what path the nav system has us taking to reach Earth."

Cynergy pursed her lips for a moment. Then she turned around and walked away from him.

"Where are you going? I thought you wanted to take a look at this?"

"I did," she replied over her shoulder.

Ethan glanced at Anton. "What's over there?"

Anton looked at this personal holoscreen. "The engine control systems."

Clip entered the computing core, his shoulders wide enough to brush both sides of the aisle. "Are you having any luck here?"

"I was able to pull the nav data from the system, but I can't figure out a way to register a change without the tamper protect alerting."

Clip nodded. "Rudimentary but effective. It simply flags all changes it detects."

Ethan frowned. "There has to be a way. They didn't expect the ship not to have to change course."

Clip looked at the data on Ethan's holoscreen.

"Clip," Cynergy called out, "we have another problem."

"Keep working on it," Clip said and walked away from them.

Ethan sighed.

"We keep banging up against the same wall. This isn't going to work," Anton said.

"We can't just give up," he said while looking at the nav data.

"I'm better at flying a space fighter. There isn't much I can do."

Eva contacted him on comlink. "Massey and I finished going over the main engines. The control system has the same lockout that's everywhere else. Also, the main engine power consumption is steadily increasing."

"Did that just start happening?" Ethan asked.

"I don't think so. It seems to be paired with course correction. They must be planned because they'd trip alarms." Eva paused. "I told you to leave it alone, Logan. Yeah, it's warning you to stop. Just listen to it."

Magnus Station used a controller AI to manage the ship's critical systems. It was the absolute authority, and upon registering any system access, it would send a broadcast back to Magnus Station, or a relay would get the data to where it needed to go.

"Okay, wrap up over there and meet me on the bridge," Ethan said.

The comlink closed and they walked to where Clip and Cynergy were speaking.

Clip looked at them and raised his eyebrows.

"The ship is increasing its velocity," Ethan said.

"I told you," Cynergy said.

"There are too many of them to fit aboard the shuttle," Clip said.

"Wait a minute. You want to abort?" Ethan asked.

Clip shook his head. "No, I don't want to, but I'm not going to ride it out with them."

A klaxon alarm sounded, followed by a shimmer that went along the walls of the corridor. Ethan braced himself on the wall and the others did the same.

Ethan looked around, and Clip opened a comlink to someone.

Ethan checked on the others and they were fine. No one knew what had caused the alarm.

"What do you mean it's gone!" Clip scowled. He stormed down the corridor, and they followed him.

Ethan glanced at Cynergy. "What happened?"

She shook her head. "I don't know."

The klaxon alarms stopped bellowing, but there were orange flashing lights toward the stern. One of the hybrids stood outside the airlock doors to the docking tube. He was leaning against the wall, gasping for breath.

"Zarmer, what happened?" Clip asked.

Zarmer shook his head. "It's gone. Maintenance bots cut away the damn docking tube. The shuttle is gone!"

Clip peered through the airlock windows and cursed.

Ethan looked through the window and saw the shuttle falling

behind with about five meters of docking tube held in place by the shuttle's clamps.

He looked at Clip. "Can you remote-operate the shuttle?"

Clip shook his head.

"Do any of your EVA suits have thrusters?"

Cynergy blew out a breath. "No. We're using equipment that's hundreds of years old. All those types of redundant systems don't work. The shuttle flew manually. That's it. We can't reach it!"

"Fine, we can't reach it. Then we have to get onto the bridge and fly this ship ourselves," Ethan said.

A shout came from nearby. Remington pointed a finger toward them as he stormed down the corridor. "You can't do that! I told you not to go poking around the ship's computer system. Now you're stuck like us."

"We'll see about that," Ethan said.

Remington shoved him back.

Ethan brought up his hands, ready to fight, but the exile didn't attack. "I don't want to hurt you."

"I'm not going to let you hurt our people."

Remington stared at him.

"I'm going to the bridge, and we don't have a lot of time. The ship is speeding up. The timer you've been watching is incorrect."

Remington pressed his lips together and then shook his head.

Ethan saw Cynergy start to lift her plasma rifle, and he stepped toward the exile, putting his body between them.

"Please let me through. You can't stop them. I promise that I'll do whatever I can to avoid tripping any of the fail-safes that alert Magnus Station."

Remington blew out a long breath, his gaze darting toward the others like some kind of cornered animal that was about to attack. Ethan had to say something, or the man was going to be shot.

He heard Cynergy step closer. "Back off a second," Ethan growled. He turned back toward the exile. "Look at me. Watch me. Don't look at them."

Several more exiles gathered in the corridor.

"If I can get control of the ship's systems, including the comms systems, I can contact the CDF. They can locate all of your friends and families, but you've got to trust me."

Remington blinked and stepped back.

"Come on. Just let us do this and you stand that much closer to being reunited with the people you love," Ethan said.

Remington swallowed hard, and then his shoulders slumped as if his strength had been taken from him.

Ethan walked toward him and put his hand on the man's shoulder. "Thank you."

The exile nodded and moved out of their way. Ethan hastened down the corridor. He followed the guides posted on the walls and found his way to a shaft with a ladder inside. He climbed up to the top and found that the door to the bridge was locked.

Cynergy glanced at him and then at the door.

"I forgot my key," Ethan said.

The edges of her lips lifted into a small smile as she handed him her rifle. She pulled out several explosive charges and set them on the hinges.

Ethan saw the others climbing the ladder and told them to wait. She finished placing the charges and crossed the area to stand next to him.

"You better take cover," she said.

Ethan squatted down and faced away from the door. She did the same, then activated the charges.

There was a loud pop and smoke rose from the hinges, which were now only scorch marks. Ethan reached out with a gloved hand and pulled the door down. The hatch opened and clanged onto the floor.

"Clear," Cynergy said to the others.

The bridge of the freighter had a few workstations where a crew would serve a standing watch. He walked down the small center aisle and glanced at the astrogation workstation. The main holoscreen showed a distant view of Earth. It was bright blue with bands of white. He stared at it for a few seconds. He'd seen models of Earth before, but this time he wasn't seeing a recording of the humanity's home. He was seeing the real thing, and the moment wasn't lost on him.

"Good job before," Cynergy said.

Ethan frowned and glanced toward her.

"With that exile," she said.

He nodded. "I didn't want you to shoot him."

"I didn't want to shoot him either."

They stared at each other for a long moment, and then the others entered.

The bridge had been designed in a half-moon shape with several small workstations evenly spaced. Ethan went to the command center and brought up the workstation there. An amber-colored holoscreen appeared and he could see the ship's status.

Eva came to stand behind him, glancing toward Cynergy for a second and then back at Ethan. "There are no weapons systems that I can find."

He nodded. "It's a freighter, so it wouldn't have anything like a tactical console here."

"I was hoping we could control it from here," she replied and brought up another holoscreen.

Ethan stared at the control menu and frowned. "This interface is based on restricted access. If I can bypass it, maybe we'll have more options."

Clip came over. "Hash is unable to get access to the computing core. It's up to us here."

"I have a command module from one of our ships. I think I can take control of the ship's systems, but it'll probably be detected by the AI," Ethan said.

Clip considered it for a second. "What does the module do?"

"It contains the nav system and combat AI that our ships use. I think it can override the controlling AI, but I wanted to warn you first."

Clip nodded. "Well, that's better than my idea."

"What was that?"

"A hard reset of the computing core."

Ethan glanced at the nav monitor on the main holoscreen. Their distance from Earth was decreasing as the ship continued to accelerate.

"It might not come back up in time. Or worse, you still wouldn't have control when it did," Ethan said.

He pulled out the module and set it on the floor, connecting it to the data cable underneath the workstation.

"This can't be a good idea," Cynergy said.

Clip frowned. "Why not?"

"Because it could overtax the computing core. The controlling AI will try to resist the takeover and expunge the rival system. That's going to take away resources used to defend the ship," she replied.

Ethan grinned. "You think that old bucket in the computing core is going to keep up with this? I don't think so."

"I thought you were just a pilot," she said.

He glanced at Clip. The hybrid gave him a single nod.

Ethan connected the module to the command console and a second holoscreen came online. It had a familiar layout to anyone who'd used colonial operating systems found anywhere back home.

The command module attempted to establish a connection to the computing core. They waited while a few data windows flashed onto the holoscreen. A few minutes passed and then the holoscreens across the bridge went dark. Seconds later they came back online.

"The options are different," Eva said.

Ethan peered at his holoscreen. "I think that worked. It wasn't a full reset of the system."

"Good. Can you turn us around?" Clip asked.

Ethan brought up the navigation interface. They were still flying the route set by Magnus Station security.

Several bright blue beams flashed across the main holoscreen, and he spotted an explosion off to the side.

"They look like Maser mines. It's a damn minefield!"

They were flying straight into a minefield. He brought up the flight control systems.

"Wait!" Eva said. "There's a tactical interface available now. Scans are showing…" she swore. "We can't turn around. Look!"

Eva put the tactical feed on the main holoscreen. They were surrounded by mines. Maser mines were fusion-powered weapons that expended their energy in a powerful beam before exploding. The beams were powerful enough to penetrate even the battle-steel hulls of CDF warships. Their freighter didn't stand a chance.

"Turn the ship around. Get us out of here," Clip said.

Ethan shook his head. "I can't. We're already in too deep, and we've tripped the mines. They'll continue to fire until this region of space is flooded with high-powered beams. The only thing we can do is outrun it."

Clip leaned toward him. "The defense platforms are ahead. They'll be targeting this ship any second now."

The mines performed double duty in that they were scattered to damage or destroy unsuspecting ships, but they also forced them toward the defense platforms' weapons systems.

Ethan brought up the flight control system from his module and keyed in updated targeting parameters. The freighter's engines increased their power draw.

"How are those weapons systems coming?" he asked.

Eva's hands flashed through the interface. "They're offline. I can't access any of the options."

Ethan looked at Clip. "Warn the others to get strapped in and go to their own life support if they can."

Clip sighed explosively and stormed off.

Massey and Anton sat at the neighboring workstation, and Cynergy came to stand behind Ethan.

Eva scowled at her. "Don't you have somewhere else to be?"

The hybrid ignored her. "Can you fly the ship or not?"

"I have flight control," Ethan replied.

"Good, because the defense platforms are firing on us."

Ethan peered at the main holoscreen and could only make out a subtle flash of mag cannons firing their weapons on them.

He shoved his hands onto the control interface and initiated evasive maneuvers. The freighter dove down fifteen degrees, and then banked hard to the side. Bright blue beams crossed in front of them as they triggered more proximity mines in the area. A nearby explosion shoved the old freighter's stern section to the side. Ethan used the maneuvering thrusters to alter course and absorb the blast's energy.

Damage alarms blared as sections of the ship lost life support. Atmospheric readings flatlined.

"I got it!" Eva shouted. "Weapons systems are online."

Ethan looked at the status on the main holoscreen and his stomach sank. "Why aren't they firing?"

Eva's mouth hung open and she blinked several times.

"I know what it is. Here, take over flight controls," Ethan said.

Eva brought up a secondary flight control interface and he gave her control. He accessed the command module and isolated the freighter's weapons systems. Then he enabled the freighter's computer system AI to control them.

The weapons system switched to green and the focused EMP weapons began firing. He peered at the holoscreen, but there was nothing for him to see. The only evidence that the weapons were working was the destruction of the Maser mines, which were going offline without exploding, and the increased power consumption of the ship's power core.

"It's working," he said.

"Good, I can swing us around and get us out of here," Eva said.

"Stay on course," Ethan said.

Eva hesitated and looked at him.

"Get us out of here," Cynergy said.

He shook his head. "No, the only way we survive this is if we breech the blockade. Otherwise, those weapons will take out the ship and we've got no chance."

Eva exhaled explosively. "Damn it! You'd better be right about this!"

Thousands of defense platforms circled the entire planet, and hundreds of them began firing their weapons. Mag cannons and grasers filled the space in front of them. He was sure that if there were any missile systems still available, they would be targeting them as well.

His stomach leaped up to the top of his throat as Eva avoided the onslaught of weapons fire. An alert appeared on the holoscreen. They were losing power. The freighter's power core wasn't designed for the sustained heavy use that the additional weapons systems required.

Ethan isolated life-support systems to the central habitation deck and then initiated a lockdown of the other decks. A few seconds later, he rerouted power, assigning priority to the weapons systems.

A channel of clear space appeared on an angle in front of them. The defense platform covering the sector went offline.

"Eva!"

"I got it."

The freighter climbed twenty degrees on an approach vector, heading straight toward the defense platform.

The main engines cut off as the ship's AI devoted all available power to the weapons system.

"I've only got maneuvering thrusters left," Eva said.

Ethan watched as the aged defense platform filled the holoscreen. Maneuvering thrusters nudged the ship over to avoid a collision. They sped past the platform and were en route toward Earth.

A navigation sub-window appeared, and a new waypoint flashed onscreen.

"That's our heading," Ethan said.

He didn't want Eva to waste time trying to alter course. They only had partial control of the ship's systems.

Something big hit the ship, sending vibrations through the floor. They lost the main engines, and the rear half of the ship was cut off by mag cannon fire. Ethan watched through the video feed as the canon began to track toward them again, and then it simply stopped firing.

The ship continued toward the planet, and Ethan watched as Eva tried to keep them on course. If they pierced the atmosphere on too steep an approach, they'd break apart.

The ship lurched to the side. Cynergy lost her footing and fell. Ethan reached toward her. She grabbed his hand, and he hoisted her up. She staggered to a nearby chair and strapped herself in.

The freighter broke through the atmosphere, piercing the thick cloud cover of the North American continent.

"Maneuvering thrusters aren't giving me much to work with!" Eva shouted.

Ethan's eyes widened. "Hold on!"

The ship sped downward, and their remaining thrusters fired a full burst in an effort to slow their descent.

He wasn't sure it was going to be enough.

42

THE FREIGHTER'S weapons systems drained all but emergency power. Ethan watched as Eva tried to get the nose of the ship up so their crash landing wouldn't end up with them all dying. He gritted his teeth and watched the blank video feed on the main holoscreen. The cameras were the first to go offline as they plummeted through the upper atmosphere.

They were flying blind. Ethan brought up the ship's sensor feed and the computer system used the data to create a three-dimensional grid layout of their trajectory as they streaked across the sky. They were well off course from the waypoint that had been programmed in by Magnus Station security. It had them going to the other side of the planet.

The ship's sensors built an image of the landscape that showed massive craters along the eastern seaboard of North America. Emergency sails deployed from the cargo container and their speed decreased. The remaining thrusters increased their flight path beyond the Atlantic Ocean, heading to an area just beyond an old mountain range in the lower middle of the continent.

The lower cargo container skidded along the ground and the ship turned on its side, slamming onto the ground. Everything around the bridge shook so violently that Ethan expected it to break apart. He clenched his teeth and squeezed his eyes shut, hoping it would all be over soon.

The ship hit something big, causing it to swing around and roll across the landscape. Loose items flew around the bridge as they tumbled, but eventually they slowed to a halt.

Ethan opened his eyes. Warning messages flashed on the holoscreen. Part of the hull had sheared off, and a thin sliver of sunlight streamed right through the holoscreen, distorting the barrage of damage reports.

He blinked his eyes several times and turned to look at the others. Eva was slumped over the workstation. Ethan unbuckled himself and pulled Eva back into the chair. He called out her name.

She slowly opened her eyes and winced. "I think I bruised my ribs," she groaned.

Ethan looked down. "Doesn't look like anything punctured your suit. Sit tight, I'm going to check on the others."

She gave him a thumbs up.

"Sound off!" Ethan said.

Massey and Anton called out to him. Ethan turned around and saw Cynergy standing up.

"Are you all right?"

"I'm fine." She frowned at her wrist computer. "I'm trying to reach the others."

Ethan looked at his own wrist computer. His suit only had thirty percent of life support left. He glanced at the crack in the hull, then at the atmospheric readings detected by his suit computer. He retracted his helmet and inhaled. The air was cool and humid. He thought he smelled smoke.

"We've got to get out of here. Let's try to reach the others."

Massey pointed at him. "You sure that's a good idea?"

"The air is breathable, so yeah, we should be fine."

"But what if the Vemus contagion is still around?"

"We're all right. It wasn't airborne."

Massey frowned and shook his head. "Damn, that's right. I completely forgot."

Massey, Anton, and Eva retracted their helmets into a small compartment on their EVA suits just below the backs of their necks.

Cynergy removed her helmet and wedged it under her arm. She peered at the sliver of sunlight for a few seconds and then followed them.

They went to the ladder and climbed down to the corridor below. The ship was pitched at an angle, as if it were leaning against something. They called out to the others as they walked down the corridor.

They reached the central hab unit and opened the door. He heard shouting coming from inside. Twelve of the exiles had sustained injuries, and two people had died.

Ethan found Clip lying on the ground. His eyes were closed, and he had a metallic shaft stuck into his side. Dark blood seeped through his suit.

Cynergy rushed to his side. "Get his helmet off of him!"

Ethan quickly removed Clip's helmet. His skin was pale, and he was barely breathing.

"Damn it, Clip! Don't you dare die on me!" She peered at his wound. The blood was dark.

Ethan looked around. "Is there a first aid kit!"

Someone shouted that they had one.

Cynergy grabbed the shaft and yanked it out of Clip's body. He didn't even wince or cry out. Dark blood squirted onto the ground, and Cynergy slammed her hand onto the wound.

"Come on. Come on," she said, watching him as if waiting for him to respond.

Ethan searched for more injuries but couldn't find anything. One of the exiles handed him a first aid kit. He pulled out a trauma pack and handed it to Cynergy. She shoved it onto the wound.

"We're here, Clip. This is what you've always talked about. You have to see it. Open your eyes. You have to see it."

Blood soaked through the trauma pack and Ethan didn't think Clip was going to survive. He came to her side and placed his hand on her back. She snarled and shook him off.

"I don't think he's going to make it," Ethan said.

She glared at him. "You don't know what you're talking about."

Ethan watched, expecting Clip to stop breathing altogether, but he didn't. His breathing quickened, as if he were regaining consciousness. Then his eyes popped open and he gasped.

Cynergy cried out. "That's it. That's it. You've been injured. There is a deep puncture on your left side. Focus on that."

Clip squeezed his eyes shut and his face contorted with effort. Cynergy pulled her hands back to check on the wound. The bleeding slowed down to a trickle and then stopped.

Ethan watched as new skin grew over the wound, forming a pale scar. The wound continued to heal, and Clip's breath became long and steady.

"Is he asleep?"

Cynergy nodded. "Yes, it's part of the healing process. He's focused on repairing his body."

"I've seen quick healing before with medical nanites, but this looked more like regeneration."

She looked at him for a second. "You really don't know much about the Vemus."

He frowned. "What do you mean?"

"Do you know where it came from?"

"Somewhere in the Pacific Ocean."

"And it infected mammalian life, some of which were capable of skin and tissue regeneration. Complete regeneration if they didn't bleed out."

Ethan shook his head. "How could anything control bleeding in the ocean?"

She arched an eyebrow. "I guess your extensive training didn't cover this."

"Hey, we're alive, aren't we. I'd call that a win in my book."

She rolled her eyes.

"Stop being difficult for five seconds and just tell me."

"They swam deeper and used the additional pressure from the ocean to stop the bleeding while the regeneration occurred."

Ethan glanced down at Clip's wound. The skin had become a pale shade of pink.

"He won't even have a scar from it."

Massey walked over and looked at them. "What did I miss?"

"They don't scar."

He pursed his lips appreciatively, then shrugged. "Anton and Hash found a way out. We're unloading the equipment, and we need help moving the people with injuries."

Cynergy stood up.

"Shouldn't we carry him outside?" Ethan asked.

She shook her head. "It'll disrupt the process. He's better off resting here for as long as he can."

They went to help the others offload the supplies that had

been stored on the ship. It wasn't much—maybe a week's worth of rations, along with some water. At least they'd given them a small water reclaimer. Most of what they had was a couple of power generators and communication equipment.

The exiles and hybrids paused outside the ship and looked at their surroundings with wide-eyed amazement. They looked warily up at the sky with a mixture of awe and a little bit of fear.

"What's wrong with them?" Massey asked.

"They've never stood on a planet without protection before," Ethan replied.

Massey frowned thoughtfully.

Eva came to his side. "Just give them a few minutes to take it in."

Vijura looked around and nodded to himself. "I can see why you adapted so well to Bhaneteran. Very similar, but also alien."

Anton grinned. "The only alien here, my friend, is you."

Vijura laughed and the others joined in.

"I miss New Earth," Eva said.

Ethan nodded and they were all quiet for a moment.

"I'll be right back."

Ethan went back to the bridge and retrieved the command module. They carried the equipment away from the wreckage. The crash had cut a swath right through the trees, and there were several small fires along the path. He didn't think they'd burn for long, not with the area so damp.

Ethan and the others split up to walk around the ship, doing a damage assessment as they went. It would never fly again. Looking at the damage inflicted by the defense platforms and the fact that a large portion of the stern had taken out the main engines, he realized they were lucky to have survived.

Ethan sent a text message to the others, and they met a short distance from the ship. All of them were feeling out of their depth, and since Ethan had been responsible for them being there, he felt that he needed to regroup with them.

"The ship's power core is completely drained. We're lucky it lasted as long as it did. That weapons system was a huge drain," Eva said.

"How do you know so much about it?" Massey asked.

"I was on an engineering track before I decided to become a pilot."

He smiled. "As if I wasn't already impressed, you had to go and raise it up a notch."

She lifted her eyebrows once.

"We need to send a signal to the fleet," Anton said.

Massey gestured toward the camp. "Look at them working on the portable comms equipment. They won't let anyone else near it."

The exiles gathered around the equipment they'd offloaded from the ship. A group of them formed a perimeter while the others worked.

Ethan looked at the exiles and then back at the others. "I thought we could try using the ship's comms systems, but that's not going to work. We need to get access to that comms station."

Massey shrugged. "You talked Remington down once. Maybe he'll listen to you again."

Ethan nodded. "I've got to try." He started to walk away and paused for a moment. "There are thousands of platforms surrounding the planet. We have no idea how many of them are active."

"Don't forget the minefield just outside the moon's orbit. I don't know if our sensors would detect them until it's too late," Eva said.

"We've got to warn them."

"Assuming that we can send a signal past the defense platforms," Anton said.

Ethan frowned. "Comms blackout for the entire planet? Is that even possible?"

He shrugged. "I don't know. Did you see the scans when we came in? They dropped a lot of bombs on this planet. I'm surprised it's so warm."

"Why wouldn't it be warm?" Massey asked.

"Because they used WMDs during the Vemus Wars to prevent the spread off Earth."

"Anton's right," Eva said. "I'm surprised there's anything left alive here."

Ethan shook his head. "Not necessarily. It's been a couple of hundred years. The atmosphere could have recycled in that time. There's no guarantee that it would have been stuck in an ice age for thousands of years."

Eva smiled at him. "All that extra study time didn't go to waste."

"But it's not going to help us reach the CDF."

"Come on. Do you really think the scanner arrays on our warships aren't capable of detecting a minefield?" Massey asked

Ethan shook his head. "I'm not so sure. With so much detritus around the planet anyway, sensors might just determine it to be space junk left over from all the battles fought here. The mines are likely shielded against scans until they become active."

Massey jutted his chin toward the exiles. "Let's stop standing around and go see if that comms station is working."

They walked over to where the exiles were setting up the portable communications station. Several of the exiles eyed them warily.

"Is it going to work?" Ethan asked.

Remington looked at him. "We're short a generator. We lost two of them during the crash, including the backup."

Several people had connected a satellite dish atop a long metallic pole. Two portable power generators had cables connected to a storage container that had been part of the commutations station.

"Do you have enough power to reach Magnus Station?" Ethan asked.

"I don't know. It'll take eighty minutes for a signal to get there, and another eighty minutes to get a response."

Ethan brought up his wrist computer and scanned the generators. They'd retained seventy percent of their charge. The comms station had to pierce the atmosphere and then travel billions of kilometers to reach Magnus Station. They only had a few hours to try before they'd have to wait.

"There's an alternative," Ethan said.

Remington turned away from the console screen with a raised eyebrows.

"We can contact the CDF. They're bound to be closer than Magnus Station."

Remington shook his head. "No, we're following the protocol that was given to us."

He turned back to the console and powered it on. It began to hum, and Remington brought up the control interface. It was a simple prompt, with a predefined set of coordinates. He pressed the button, and the hum from the station increased to a high-pitched whine.

A warning barked from the console. Ethan read it and then looked at the others and shook his head.

Remington frowned. "Signal error..."

Ethan began to walk away.

"Hey, did you do something to this? Did you cause it to fail?"

Ethan turned back. "I didn't touch it. It doesn't have enough power to establish a link. We either have to find more power or find some kind of satellite relay to strengthen the signal."

Remington looked up and sighed. "How are we supposed to do that?"

"We can scout the area. Maybe we'll find something that will help. In the meantime, see if there are any options to scan for a relay station."

Remington turned back toward the machine and began checking the options on the menu.

Cynergy, Hash, and Clip walked toward them. Clip still looked a little pale, but he'd almost died less than an hour ago. He kept his hand on his side.

"Did it work?" he asked.

"You need to sit down," Cynergy said.

Clip started to shake his head and winced. The two hybrids helped him to the ground.

"It didn't work," Ethan said. "Either they don't have enough power to establish a connection, or the defense platforms are blocking the signal."

Clip nodded and winced again. "What about the CDF? Could you reach them using that equipment?"

"I don't think so. We could try using it to broadcast a signal, but we couldn't establish a comlink unless we knew exactly where the fleet is located," Ethan said.

"If we'd gotten a better look at things on our approach, we could have looked for a communications satellite still in orbit," Anton said.

Ethan doubted there were any comms satellites left. "We

need to take a look around. Get to high ground and get the lay of the land."

Massey sighed. "Can we just take a moment to catch our breath. What is it, late afternoon here? Won't it be dark soon?"

"What? Are you afraid?"

"No, I just don't want to get lost out here. We don't know what's out there."

"The creatures of New Earth are much more dangerous than anything we're going to find here," Ethan said.

"Oh yeah, how do you know?"

Ethan frowned. He didn't know. "Regardless, we need to take a look around. Stay here if you want. I'm going over there to climb one of those trees."

Massey shook his head and sighed. "I am going to stay here," he said and stormed off, muttering to himself.

Ethan looked at the others. He felt a pang in his gut. "I'm sorry."

Anton shook his head. "He's just blowing off steam. We volunteered. You didn't make us come."

Eva nodded. "I'll check to the south."

They split up, and Ethan hiked away from camp. He checked his wrist computer, but there wasn't much that it could do. He was cut off from any colonial signal. About the only thing he could do with it was short-range communications. He kept thinking about what his father would do. He'd been cut off from support many times. The first thing he'd focus on was getting a high-level view of their surroundings.

Ethan glanced up at the sky, feeling completely exposed. Their field kits were only equipped for basic survival. He could have used a couple of recon drones right about now.

He picked out a tree that he thought he could climb and

started his ascent. It only took him a few minutes to reach the top, and he looked around.

"See anything?" Cynergy called up from the ground.

Ethan sighed. "More trees." He turned. "There might be an old city or something in that direction."

She climbed up and was soon on a tree limb adjacent to his. "I see it."

"We're going to have to scout the area."

She frowned and then looked around, uncertain. She saw him watching her and smoothed her features. Then she climbed back down.

Ethan followed. "Want to take a walk?"

Birds chirped from nearby, and Cynergy spun toward them. She had her rifle raised.

"Take it easy, they're only birds."

She looked at him.

The edges of his lips lifted. "I didn't even realize."

She lowered her rifle and frowned. "Realize what?"

"You need time to get used to it. Planet-side, I mean."

She looked away from him.

"It's all right to be afraid."

"I'm not afraid!"

He held up his hands. "Alarmed then. Understandably cautious, maybe?" He smiled. "Come on. It's nothing to be ashamed of. Anything could be out there. It's better if we stick together."

She looked back toward the camp.

Ethan opened a comlink to the others. "I'm going to scout farther away. I did see what might be an old city in the distance. I'll check back in an hour."

He started walking away from camp, and after a few moments, Cynergy followed him. They walked through an open field of tall grass. Several deer lifted their heads to peer in their direction.

Cynergy stopped, eyes wide. "I've only seen them in archives preserved on one of the outposts."

"I've never seen one either."

The deer stared at them until they'd moved away.

They hiked for another thirty minutes without encountering any other animals. There was so much they didn't know about what had happened here. What kind of animals had survived? He glanced at Cynergy. If there were Vemus here, would she know? Would she be vulnerable to them like he would?

"Why do you keep doing that?" she asked.

"Doing what?"

"Looking up at the sky?"

"Oh, New Earth has a brilliant set of rings that you can see day or night. The sky looks strange without them."

Cynergy considered it for a moment. "New Earth? That's what the colony called your planet?"

He nodded.

"The Ovarrow have another name for it."

He frowned and cocked his head to the side, listening.

"I hear it. Something's happening at the camp. Come on," she said.

They ran back toward the camp, quickly retracing the path they'd taken. They closed in on the camp and Ethan stopped. Cynergy came to his side. They peered through the trees. The camp was surrounded by brown rovers with mag cannons on top of them.

Something landed behind them, and Ethan spun toward it. It was a man in some kind of combat suit made from a patchwork of greens that would make it hard to spot.

Ethan pulled out his sidearm, and five more soldiers ran toward them. They pointed their rifles at them.

The man cleared his throat. Ethan turned toward him and tried to peer through the helmet to get a look at his face but couldn't.

"I think you ought to put that away," he said. The helmeted head turned toward Cynergy. "Did you really come all this way just to start a fight?"

Ethan smiled a little. "That depends. Are you looking for a fight?"

The man chuckled, and the other soldiers joined in. "Are you? There aren't many of us left. Let's go back to your camp and have some introductions. Then we can take it from there."

Ethan didn't know whether he could trust the man or not, but it was a reasonable request. If those combat suits were anywhere near as capable as those that the CDF wore, they didn't have a chance of escaping anyway.

43

THEY WERE ESCORTED BACK to the camp. The soldiers didn't speak that much, but Ethan had been around soldiers his entire life. They moved and covered the area with a practiced efficiency that was familiar to him. Cynergy watched them with more uncertainty than he'd expected she would. He made a take-it-easy gesture toward her.

The soldier that spoke to them led them toward the center of camp. Vijura stood apart from the others, and one of the soldiers spoke to him.

"What are you?"

Vijura replied, and the soldier shook his head.

"You're not going to understand him without a translator," Ethan said.

The soldier turned around and stared at him.

"I found a couple of stragglers returning to camp, Colonel."

"I see," he said and looked at Ethan. "I'm Colonel Elias Cooper."

His helmet retracted. The man was older, with silver hair

and piercing blue eyes. He had an outdoorsman's tan and a long scar from his cheek to beneath the neckline of his combat suit.

"I'm Lieutenant Ethan Gates, Colonial Defense Force."

Colonel Cooper pursed his lips thoughtfully. "Never heard of that one."

Ethan smiled. "No, I imagine you haven't." He lifted his chin toward Vijura. "His name is Vijura. He's an Ovarrow, and he's also in the CDF."

Colonel Cooper glanced at Vijura, then gestured toward Eva, Massey, and Anton. "Five of you," he said, and looked at Cynergy with raised eyebrows.

"I'm not with them," she said.

Colonel Cooper grinned. "Looks like you're all in this together, regardless."

Cynergy looked where Clip and other hybrids were gathered.

"You're a hybrid?" the colonel asked.

Cynergy's eyebrows raised, and she blinked.

"It's all right. You can tell me," Colonel Cooper said.

She eyed him coolly.

"Captain Taylor, would you mind showing yourself to our skittish guest here," Colonel Cooper said.

"Yes, sir."

The soldier who had escorted them in removed his helmet. His dark skin had a purplish coloring to it, and his dark eyes had some yellow around the edges. Ethan thought he heard a very faint sound coming from him. Cynergy shifted on her feet and exhaled softly.

Dark purplish lines formed intricate patterns on her pale face and neck, and then the rest of her skin darkened. Her bright green eyes gleamed as she stared at the soldier.

Ethan leaned toward her, trying to hear the sound.

"It's difficult for us to hear," Colonel Cooper said. He looked at Taylor. "Thanks, Captain."

Taylor nodded once and smiled toward Cynergy.

Ethan glanced at her and saw that the intricate pattern of dark lines on her face seemed to glisten a little bit.

Colonel Cooper grinned. "I'd call that a friendly response. You can go wait with the other hybrids."

Cynergy changed her appearance back to normal. "I'll stay here."

"I see," Colonel Cooper replied and looked at Ethan. "You were saying about a translator?"

Ethan nodded. "Yeah, we've got them in our implants so we can understand him. He can understand you as well."

Colonel Cooper turned toward Vijura. "Is that right."

Vijura nodded once.

"It appears we have a lot to discuss, Lieutenant Gates." He looked at the crashed ship behind them. "You've managed to break through the defense platforms."

"We didn't have a choice."

Colonel Cooper nodded. "Indeed. Why don't you tell me how you came to be here. I'm sure you have questions as well, which I will answer to the best of my ability. Then we can take it from there."

Ethan looked at him for a second. "Just so I'm clear on one thing, sir. Are we prisoners?"

The others watched intently, and Colonel Cooper regarded him for a moment. "No, you're not prisoners. Think of us as curious neighbors who happened to have seen your ship crash in the area."

Ethan didn't think Cooper was lying to him. He glanced at the others, and they relaxed a little bit. He hadn't been sure what to expect would happen if they'd found people on Earth.

Speculation by colonial scientists presented more than a few
different scenarios. People could have become territorial and
primitive from the lack of technology in a world so different than
what it had become. Alternatively, people could choose to pool
their resources and rebuild a better world than the one they'd
lost. He thought it was somewhere in the middle, but there was
only one way to find out.

Over the next few hours, Ethan spoke with Colonel Elias
Cooper—Coop—and the other Earthers who had survived the
Vemus Wars. The wars had changed the entire planet, and the
people who survived were those who'd managed to find a place in
underground bunkers. Coop and the other soldiers were part of a
network of settlements whose ancestors had lived in mountain
bunkers. They'd lived over fifty years in those bunkers until the
atmosphere recycled itself to more livable conditions. When
they'd first emerged above ground, scientists estimated that
nearly seventy percent of life hadn't survived. They'd lost a lot of
knowledge and technology that had been so readily available
prior to the Vemus Wars. Over time, more people emerged from
bunkers and other shelters, and they encountered the existence of
Vemus Hybrids—people who hadn't succumbed to being fully
infected with the contagion. Somehow, they'd adapted. They
weren't sure how. There were so few people that it was better if
they worked together rather than continuing with struggles that
predated life before the bunkers.

"Have you been able to contact other people around the
planet?" Ethan asked.

Colonel Cooper nodded. "We've sent expeditions, and we've
had contact with other groups. Communication is still a
challenge." He raised his chin toward the sky.

The Earthers had to resurrect old technology to use for
communication since they didn't have access to satellites, nor

could they leave the planet. Ethan had hoped there would be some way to signal the CDF, but it wasn't possible.

"It's disappointing to find out that people are still struggling out in the solar system," Cooper said.

Colonel Cooper told them that their military was small, and its function was more akin to Colonial Field Operations than the CDF.

"Resources are limited. They need to come back here to carve out a future for themselves," Ethan said.

Coop nodded. "God knows there's plenty of room. Our best estimate of human population puts us in the millions."

Taylor joined them. "You're a pilot?"

Ethan nodded. He gestured toward the others. "All of us are."

"That's amazing. We don't have many pilots, or ships for that matter."

"How come?"

"There used to be efforts to go back into space, but the defense platforms put a stop to that. We still use some ships designed for atmospheric flight, but we don't use them as much as we used to. There really isn't a need."

Ethan frowned in thought. "I don't understand."

Colonel Cooper heaved a sigh. "It's a reminder of what we lost. All the destruction. Plus, we haven't been able to build any more. We've focused on using rovers and hab units. It's a simpler life, but it's a peaceful one. We've also reintroduced animals that have gone extinct."

"Yeah, but you can't leave."

Colonel Cooper pressed his lips together and considered Ethan for a moment. "The human race is getting a much-needed breather. Maybe one day we'll figure out a way to disable the defense platforms."

Ethan glanced at his companions. They shifted

uncomfortably. "Um, we need to contact our fleet. They can disable the defense platforms, but we need to warn them first."

"I'm sorry, but it's just not possible. We've tried to send signals into space and have never gotten a reply."

Ethan powered on his holoscreen and brought up images of CDF warships. "These are the ships in our fleet. What we don't have in numbers, we make up with firepower. And this is the Talon V space fighter Stinger configuration that we fly."

"Best fighter of them all," Massey said.

Taylor's eyes widened and he looked at Colonel Cooper. "Sir!"

"Captain, it's not going to help them."

Ethan looked at them. "You've seen this type of ship before?"

Colonel Cooper bit his lower lip for a second. "Similar. Not exact."

"Where?"

"They're in a factory a few hundred kilometers south of here."

"Are they intact? Could they be flown?"

Cooper shook his head. "They've been sitting there for decades...probably since the Vemus War. I doubt they'd be operational."

"Can you take us there?"

"I just said they're not operational."

"With all due respect, Colonel, there is no way you can know that for sure. This is our area of expertise. Depending on how they were stored, their power cores could still be intact."

"Where would you fly to? There's nowhere for you to go."

"Yes, there is. We can take that portable comms unit into space and broadcast a signal to the fleet."

"You're overlooking the fact that there are defense platforms that will shoot you down. Assuming you can get any of those ships to even fly."

"They're a hard target to hit. The weapons on the freighter disabled hundreds of platforms. We have a chance to make this work."

Cooper sighed. "There are repair drones that work all the time repairing and maintaining the defense platforms. So even if what you say is true, they're likely being worked on right now. Going up there is a death sentence."

Ethan stood. "Can you at least tell me where the factory is?"

The others stood up, and they were joined by Clip and the others.

Captain Taylor looked at Cooper. "It's worth a shot, Colonel. They deserve a chance to try, at the very least. Think about what this could mean."

"Taylor, you've been looking for any excuse to go back there."

Taylor laughed and gestured toward Ethan and the others. "And look what just fell out of the sky right into our laps. I'd call that a sign. If we leave now, we can be there in about four hours."

Cooper looked at him for a few seconds and then sighed. "I'm going to make you contact Rosier and tell her why we're not coming back home tonight."

Taylor grinned. "She loves me, sir."

Cooper nodded and then looked at Ethan. "All right, Lieutenant Gates. We'll give you a ride tonight."

Ethan smiled. "Thank you."

"Go get whatever you need. We leave in ten minutes."

Ethan turned toward the others.

"This is a long shot," Eva said.

He nodded. "It's the only shot we have. Kujura might have already contacted the CDF by now. They'll be heading here, and we've got to warn them."

"What about them?" Eva asked and nodded toward Clip and the other hybrids.

Clip smiled and walked over to them. "Yes, what about us?"

"You heard that?" Massey asked.

Clip waved away the question. "If those ships are space-worthy, you'll need help getting them ready."

"I appreciate the offer, but don't you want to go back to their city? Meet others like you?" Ethan asked.

Clip arched an eyebrow. "We're not that different. Besides, we wouldn't want to miss all the fun. Also, getting the ships ready to fly is only one step. You've got to get up there, and you'll need time to contact the CDF. It's going to take more than just the five of you to do that."

Massey nodded. "He's got a point."

"All right. Let's get moving," Ethan said.

They gathered supplies. Remington and the other exiles were staying behind. Cooper assured them that more people would come and bring them back to their city. They'd be welcome to live with them. Given what Ethan and the other colonists had observed from the other survivors out in the Sol system, it was reassuring to see that human decency wasn't completely gone.

44

"WHO MADE ALL THESE?" Massey asked.

They stood in a massive warehouse facility that was hundreds of meters across.

"Robotic construction bots," Taylor replied.

Massey glanced at Ethan and then looked around. "Where are they now?"

Taylor shrugged. "Probably in storage somewhere. We haven't explored the entire area. But these are replicas of your ship, right?"

Ethan peered down the long assembly lines. Spotlights from the rovers lit the entire area. Some of the components looked similar, but everything was in pieces. If they had to assemble the ships they intended to fly, they'd never warn the CDF in time.

"I think so," Ethan replied. He walked past another aisle. "Are there any that are assembled?"

Taylor nodded. "But first look at this." He walked over to one of the assembly lines, leaned down, and dusted off one of the consoles. A partial holoscreen came on, and he gestured toward it.

Ethan leaned toward the flickering image of a space fighter. "Looks really similar."

Eva nodded. "We need to find one intact."

They drove the rovers farther into the warehouse. Ethan wondered how many ships could be produced when it had been operational. What else did they build here? How had it survived all these years virtually untouched? He looked at Taylor and Coop. The latter had insisted on being addressed by his nickname. He had a bearing that came from a purposeful life. He wasn't haunted by his past but chose to focus his attention on things he could influence rather than on everything beyond his control.

Cynergy watched him. "What is it?"

Ethan shrugged. "The main part of our efforts to help Magnus Station and the salvagers was so they could reclaim precious resources. Look at everything here. Sure, it's been exposed to the elements for a while, but there's a lot of useable material left. And how many other places are just like this elsewhere on the planet?"

She nodded. "I see what you mean."

"Plenty to share and rebuild with," Eva said.

Cynergy glanced at her, and the edges of her lips tightened.

They didn't speak much, and Ethan doubted they'd ever be friends. Cynergy seemed to have become less standoffish with him since they made it to the planet. The hybrids had lived a hard life. They'd endured exile from Magnus Station and waged a type of rebellion against those in power. It was ongoing, but it had been a long time since an actual battle had been fought. Clip had told him that destroying what little everyone had left to change the heart and minds of the people you had to coexist with was a huge disservice to all people. They only had a short time to create their own legacy, and it should be something to be proud of rather than endured.

The struggles of the descendants of the people who had somehow survived the Vemus Wars were as complex as the issues that the colony had faced during their short history. Ethan didn't think there were easy solutions for the people here, but if he could help them gain access to Earth, the sacrifice by the colonists who came on the expedition would have been worth it. This was something he would be proud to have as part of his own legacy.

They came to the final assembly area of the space fighters. Some were only partially assembled, but others looked more intact.

"Two-person fighters," Massey said. "Side by side, too. Looks strange."

The cockpit had two seats with a center console between them. Beyond the cockpit, the design was similar to the Talon V. There were small wings and ports for mag cannon assemblies that hadn't been installed.

Ethan went closer to some of the other ships, but they all had missing components. They looked intact, but they'd never fly in their current conditions.

"These aren't going to work," Eva said.

They split up to check other fighters along the assembly line. Ethan climbed inside one of the fighters and looked at the layout of the controls. Eva climbed in and sat in the seat next to his.

She smiled. "Well, isn't this cozy. Could you imagine being stuck in here with someone you didn't like?"

Ethan chuckled. "It's strange. It's almost like the Lancer class Talons, but those are essentially gun ships with three to five occupants, none of which has side-by-side seating like this. I wonder if these were designed for something else besides combat."

Eva nodded. "Probably reconnaissance. Primary pilot controls are there and over here could be sensor controls."

"With the right company, it wouldn't be a bad way to spend a mission."

Eva looked at him. "Maybe."

Cynergy called out to him, saying that she'd found something.

"You're being summoned," Eva said.

Ethan climbed out of the seat. "She's not so bad, you know."

"Something about her rubs me the wrong way. I don't know what it is. Go on. I'm going to take a closer look at the control panel."

Ethan jumped to the ground and Anton joined him.

Cynergy stood near a tall dark wall thirty meters away from the end of the aisle. The ceiling was wide open to the night sky and dirt crunched under their boots as they walked over.

"Help me open this," she said.

There was a small gap on the side that went all the way to the ceiling. They shared a glance and then pulled on it.

After a few seconds, Cynergy said. "Are you guys even pulling? Come on, you can do better than that."

Ethan and Anton groaned with effort, but the wall wouldn't budge. He looked to the side, and Cynergy's shoulders were shaking in silent laughter.

Ethan stood up and saw that some of the others had started laughing at them. Massey clapped.

Anton frowned as if he didn't understand. "What are they laughing at? Do they think we can't get this open?"

Ethan arched an eyebrow. "I'd say that's exactly what they think."

She called out to Taylor. "Bring the rover over here."

Anton looked at Cynergy. "Aren't you super strong or something?"

"Why would I strain myself when there's a perfectly good vehicle that can do it for me?" She looked at Ethan and smirked. "Clip didn't think I could get you to try it."

Ethan looked for Clip and saw him about forty meters away. He waved.

Ethan turned back toward Cynergy. "What is this thing?"

"I think it's a shipping container. It's still sealed, even with the gap," she replied.

Taylor drove the rover to them and opened the winch near the front. He pulled out a long cable with a metallic ball attachment. Then he placed it near the center of the door. He powered it on, and six legs opened from the top and anchored themselves in the door. He climbed back in the vehicle and engaged the winch while reversing the rover.

A loud screech echoed from metal that hadn't been moved in hundreds of years, but it finally gave way. After the breaking point, the giant door swung open the rest of the way. The bright lights from the rover lit up the massive storage container. Packed inside were dozens of space fighters, and they looked to be in pristine condition.

Anton whistled appreciatively. "Look at that. Prepped and ready for transport. This container must have been sealed since before the Vemus War."

Ethan walked to a console on the interior wall. It still had power. He waved his hand near the console and a holoscreen appeared. "Looks like a shipment heading to an Admiral Jace, NA Alliance Navy." He kept reading the manifest and then his eyes widened. "Holy crap! They're in standby with long-term storage configuration."

Massey, Vijura, and Eva ran over to them.

"Is that what I think it is?" Massey asked.

Ethan smiled. "I think so."

Cynergy looked at him. "What's so special about long-term storage configuration?"

"It means they were kept in a standby state on minimal power. This massive storage container was meant for a lengthy voyage. According to the data on the console, the battery backup keeping power to these ships is still working."

She frowned. "How, though? They shouldn't have been able to last this long."

Ethan brought up the power status. "They're running at twenty percent charge, but they're drawing power from a generator somewhere. I think we can actually get these ships to fly!"

The shipping container had counter-grav emitters underneath. They got enough of them to work so they could move the container away from the warehouse. Then they offloaded the ships and began checking them. The container was broken up into sections that included ammunition for the ships.

Anton sighed and looked at Ethan. "We've got more ships than we do pilots."

He shrugged. "Better than the other way around."

"We're going to need to test their flight capabilities before we even think about taking them up there."

Eva stuck her head out of a cockpit. "Still got that control module handy?"

"I do," Ethan replied.

"Good, because I think we're going to need it."

45

ETHAN FLEW the two-hundred-year-old space fighter across the continent. Even having been sealed in a storage container for all that time, the ship flew well. He checked the systems status on his HUD.

"Flight systems check out. All diagnostics are green."

"Tactical systems check out as well," Cynergy said.

He glanced at her in the seat next to him. The jade-colored holoscreen reflected from her helmet.

"How's the copilot's seat?"

"It's fine," she replied.

"Good," he said and opened a comlink to the others. "Final check-in."

Each of them had been paired off with a member of Clip's team. Taylor had been disappointed, but Colonel Cooper reminded him that Ethan and the others had years of extensive training. That same experience couldn't be taught in a few hours.

The others checked in.

"For a two-hundred-year-old ship, it doesn't fly too bad. It's not like ours, but still," Massey said.

"We'll see how you fly when you're the same age," Eva replied.

"Better than I am today. I aim to improve with age, sweetheart."

Cynergy glanced at Ethan. "Is he always like this?"

He nodded.

"Our primary objective is to contact the CDF. Thanks to our friends on the ground, we know we can fly into Earth's lower orbit and the defense platforms will ignore us. Beyond that and it's anyone's guess. We contact the CDF and warn them about the minefield and the defense platforms. We each have our assignments. Good luck."

Ethan watched the four other space fighters fly away from them. They'd divided the sky into sectors that would give them the best chance of getting a signal out to the CDF.

He increased power to the engines and the ship increased its velocity. He felt a slight pressure on his chest.

"Do you feel it?"

"Yes."

"Let me know if you get uncomfortable."

The ship's inertia dampeners didn't perform nearly as well as that of the Talon Vs, and it was a bit of an adjustment to get used to it.

"Copy that," she replied.

They flew upward, climbing out of the atmosphere and into low orbit. He felt a slight sensation of weightlessness until the artificial gravity emitter came online. He changed the ship's engine configuration to zero-atmosphere mode for space travel.

Over the next hour, they flew to the target coordinates.

"Okay, broadcasting comms signal," he said.

"How long will it take for them to respond?"

"Assuming that they're on their way here, it could be anywhere from twenty minutes, or more if they're farther away."

She looked at him with a thoughtful frown. "You sound impatient."

He snorted. "Well, yeah. We have subspace comms, which allows for instantaneous communications across vast distances. We haven't had to contend with latency-types of comms in a while."

"But your fighters don't have it."

"No, they don't. Not yet, anyway. We use an intermediary ship to remain in contact with the fleet."

Ethan looked at the tactical plot. The defense platforms had an extensive coverage area, but the freighter had put a significant hole in them. He hoped that the gap in them also extended to the comms dampening they'd observed.

He angled the ship on a trajectory that would take them toward the gap. He glanced at the mission clock. The others should reach their coordinates soon.

"I don't know another way to ask this, but will your people come back to Earth?"

"Many of them will, assuming that your fleet can destroy the defense platforms."

"Oh, they can. It's the minefield I'm worried about. They can do a lot of damage."

"I understand. What about you and the other colonists? Will you return to Earth?"

Ethan pursed his lips in thought. "I don't know. Maybe. The colony is something to see. New Earth is an amazing planet. Maybe you'll see it one day."

She didn't reply and he looked at her.

"No reply to that?"

She stared at him for a second. "Will we be allowed to visit your colony?"

"Why wouldn't you be?"

"We're hybrids. Part Vemus, and that's not going to change."

"What if there was a cure?"

Her gaze narrowed for a second and then she turned away.

Ethan frowned, feeling like he'd said something wrong. "Wouldn't you want to be cured?"

She blew out a breath. "Just drop it, okay."

"Look, if I offended you, then I'm sorry. I didn't mean to."

She turned back toward him and looked as if she were about to speak when a message appeared on comms.

Ethan looked at it. "Yeah, baby!" He looked at her, smiling. "That's the CDF."

It was just a data reply, but it contained the coordinates for them to use to open a comlink. He entered the coordinates and initiated.

"This is Lieutenant Ethan Gates of the 7th A-Wing..." He recorded the message and sent it along with a data package containing crucial intel.

They had to wait twenty-five minutes for a response. He tried to contact Anton and the others but couldn't reach them.

They were both quiet as they waited to hear back from the CDF. He had no idea who had replied to them, but he was just happy to get a response.

A new message chimed, and Ethan opened it.

The head and shoulders of a woman appeared. She had dark blonde hair and brown eyes.

"Lieutenant Gates, I'm Major Jane Russo, commanding officer of the CDF Destroyer *Wolf*. A lot of people are going to be relieved when they hear about you and the other survivors of the 7th. We've received the tactical data of Earth's defenses. I'm afraid your work isn't finished. At this moment there are an unknown number of ships en route to Earth that are carrying a biological weapon of mass destruction. We estimate that there are at least two ships. They must be kept from reaching Earth. The bioweapon is a weaponized version of the colonial Vemus countermeasure. If it reaches Earth, it will spread throughout the biosphere and could have catastrophic consequences for anyone or anything left alive there. The fleet is en route, but you'll need to delay or stop those ships. Major Russo, out."

Ethan stared at the HUD for a moment. The jubilation of finally reaching the CDF fled in the wake of the message they'd just received. He looked at Cynergy and saw that she was just as shocked as he was.

"Magnus Station," she hissed. "They did this, but how did they get this bioweapon?"

"It's ours. It was developed to stop the Vemus from invading New Earth, and it was used to kill the Vemus Alpha. It was included in the interstellar probes sent to Earth."

"Why include a bioweapon? Why would anyone do that?"

"It was to help the survivors in the event that the Vemus still had a significant presence here. We never anticipated...we never even thought that there would be anyone like you and Clip or any of the others. All the data we'd received indicated total domination from the contagion. There was never any mention of people adapting to it."

Cynergy clenched her teeth and shook her head. "And you sent it to Magnus Station?"

Ethan shook his head. "No. No, of course not. They must have retrieved one of our probes before they'd self-destructed. They must have been working on this for months."

She looked away from him, her eyes darting back and forth while she collected her thoughts.

"We need to contact the others," Ethan said.

She nodded. "Right."

Ethan had to fly back toward Earth to be able to open a comlink to the others. He gave them the update from Major Russo, and they were stunned.

"Another ship," Massey said. "I don't get why everyone is so quiet about this. The defense platforms should make short work of it."

Ethan shared a look with Cynergy, then said. "No, it won't."

"Why the hell not? It did a great job before."

"Yeah, but now there's a major hole in the defense platforms and the minefield. We have to be the last line of defense for Earth."

The others all began speaking at once and then stopped. Ethan entered a set of coordinates into the nav and showed it to Cynergy. She peered at it for a moment and then nodded.

"Hold on a second, Massey," Anton said. "We don't have to engage in close quarters. If we keep our distance, we should be able to stop the ships from reaching the atmosphere."

"It's a good tactic to start with, but we have to stop the bioweapon no matter the cost," Ethan said.

The others were quiet for a few moments.

"He's right," Eva said. "We have to stop this. Now that we know there are people who survived, we can't let this happen."

"Ethan, I see your ship on my scanner. Where are you going?" Anton asked.

"I'm going to see if I can plug a hole," he replied.

"Where's he going?" Eva asked.

"He's going back to the defense platforms that were disabled on our way in. Ethan, that's suicide. You don't know if you'll even make it."

"The other platforms are farther away. We're still a hard

target. It's worth the risk. If we can bring it back online, then we have a much better chance at stopping that ship."

"Or ships. There could be more than one of them," Cynergy said.

"Ethan, wait for one of us to reach you," Eva said. "You need someone to cover your six."

"There's no time. The *Wolf* is scouting ahead of the fleet. Comms took fourteen minutes to reach them. The enemy ship is much closer than that."

Eva blew out a breath and cursed.

"Go on. We'll get there as soon as we can," Anton said.

"Good luck. Drinks are on me after we get this done," Ethan said.

The others echoed the same.

Ethan closed the comlink and watched the area in front of them. They didn't have a visual of the defense platform, but that didn't mean it couldn't detect them. He wouldn't risk a scan until they were closer. Hopefully, they could remain undetected long enough to reach the platform.

"If I can get us there, can you restore power to the platform?" he asked.

Cynergy grinned a little and shook her head. "Now you ask?"

He shrugged. "I figured between the two us we should be able to figure it out. If not, we'll get back on the ship and take our chances."

"It's as good a plan as any."

He glanced at her. "I think it's a better plan than that. We can raise the bar a little bit."

She turned toward him. "Is everything a competition?"

He nodded. "Absolutely."

46

"GENERAL GATES, I have a priority comlink from the *Wolf*," Specialist Gabe Marten said.

Connor strode back to the command chair and sat. "Send it to my station."

A small holoscreen appeared.

"General Gates, we've established contact with survivors of the 7th A-Wing. You're not going to believe this, but they've made it to Earth!" Major Jane Russo said and proceeded to give him the rest of the update.

Ethan was alive!

His son was alive!

Connor looked away from the holoscreen and tried to get his emotions under control. More than a few of the bridge crew glanced in his direction. He blew out a long breath.

"Major Russo, on behalf of my entire family, I thank you for giving me this news."

"My pleasure, sir. I'm happy to be able to give good news for a change. He also sent the last known coordinates of the rest of the 7th that remained aboard a freighter. Some of them were injured, including Colonel Walker."

Connor nodded. "Good, we'll send a team to retrieve them ASAP. Have you detected our priority target?"

"Negative, sir."

"Understood. Stay on course," Connor replied.

Colonel Martinez hastened over to him. "Did I hear that right? There are survivors from the 7th?"

Connor nodded. "They're alive."

Martinez whistled softly. "That's one debrief I don't want to miss."

Connor blew out a breath and chuckled. Then he told Martinez the rest of the update.

"Some kind of focused EMP weapon. Explains why the 7th sustained such heavy losses."

"Yeah, and there's at least one other ship with the same weapons on the way to Earth."

Martinez frowned in thought. "Would they send only one ship?"

Connor's brow furrowed and he cursed. "If one ship made it past the defense platforms, there's a gap in the line."

"Ethan and the others would notice that."

Connor clenched his teeth. "They're only five ships, flying two-hundred-year-old fighters. Not exactly combat-worthy..."

Martinez stared at him. "We're already moving at best speed."

"And it's not fast enough. Damn it."

"There's something we can try. If we use the I-Drive, we can get there faster. Much faster. Maybe even in time to stop those ships from reaching Earth."

Connor glanced at the tactical plot. "Ops, bring up the I-Drive. Helm, stand by for a course update. Comms, open a comlink to General Quinn."

LENORA WALKED onto one of Magnus Station's many elevators. Her protective detail had grown to six soldiers. Four of them were disguised, but she doubted that it fooled anyone.

She opened a comlink to the *Acheron*.

"Dr. Bishop," Major Ned Emery said. "I have a spec ops team en route to station administration."

"He'll lock it down as soon as he suspects we're coming for him. He can still do a lot of damage. I can buy the teams time to get into position," Lenora said.

Major Emery inhaled sharply. "Fabian Dumont is on his way to President Shao as we speak."

"I'm closer to him. This operation needs careful timing. That's what you told me, and that's what we coordinated with the others. Anyone who's crazy enough to use bioweapons anywhere will not hesitate to use them here."

Major Emery pressed his lips together and gave her a grudging nod.

"As soon as you have control of the station's comms systems, broadcast the truth to everyone."

"But you'll be his hostage. We can't guarantee your safety."

"It's worth the risk. I'm the only one here close enough that he can't ignore. Sergeant Bashir is with me if it comes to a standoff."

Major Emery sighed. "Very well, Dr. Bishop."

Lenora smiled. She knew the CDF was particular in their efforts to protect Connor and their entire family. "Don't be so hard on yourself, Major Emery. My husband usually can't talk me out of anything either. This has to be done."

Major Emery snorted and looked resigned to the fact that he wasn't going to get her to an egress point.

She closed the comlink.

Sergeant Bashir stared at the elevator floor indicator.

"Are you ready?" she asked.

"We wouldn't have been assigned to protect you if we weren't, ma'am," Bashir replied.

The other soldiers gave a nod.

"Good, let's hope we can keep this from spiraling out of control."

"We're with you, ma'am," Bashir said.

The elevator reached the administration level where President Shao's offices were. Amandara Kumar met her a short distance from the elevator. The dark-haired, olive-skinned woman didn't appear surprised to see Lenora.

"Dr. Bishop, I didn't expect you to return so quickly."

"I had to cut my visit short I'm afraid. I'm on my way to see President Shao."

Lenora walked and Amandara kept pace with her. She leaned over and whispered. "He's not alone. He's got station security in there with him, along with…"

"I just want to speak with him," Lenora said.

Amandara nodded.

Lenora walked toward President Shao's offices and told one of the clerks why she was there. The young woman's eyes widened, and she glanced at the CDF soldiers for a second.

"He's not available at the moment."

"He'll make time to see me," Lenora said.

The young woman swallowed hard and checked her holoscreen.

"You know, I don't think I'll wait. I know the way," Lenora said.

She walked past the desk, and the young woman called after her. Lenora ignored her. A squad of station security officers were just outside President Shao's office. They watched them approach and noticed the clerk calling after them.

One of the officers walked toward them while holding his hand up. "President Shao isn't seeing anyone today."

Lenora read his name. "Captain Qiu. He's going to want to see me."

The captain stuck out his hand to block Lenora. Sergeant Bashir grabbed him and shoved the station security captain back.

Captain Qiu glared at him while shaking his hand. The other officers pulled out their stun batons, but Bashir pulled out his sidearm and pointed it at Captain Qiu's head.

"Stop!" Bashir bellowed.

The door to Shao Fen's office opened and a man walked toward them. He regarded the entire standoff with passive interest. Station Security officers seemed to defer to the man.

He walked toward Lenora and bowed his head a little. "Dr. Bishop. I'm Cheng Zhi, personal assistant to President Shao. There's been a misunderstanding. President Shao will see you at once. And you as well, Director Kumar."

Cheng Zhi gestured toward the door.

Lenora started to walk, and the CDF soldiers followed her.

"I'm afraid your soldiers will need to wait outside."

Sergeant Bashir looked at him. "That's not going to happen."

"Then I'm afraid you will not be meeting with President Shao today," Cheng Zhi said. He gestured toward the station security officer. "Captain Qiu, escort the colonial ambassador back to the offices provided to the envoy."

Sergeant Bashir looked at Lenora expectantly.

"Cheng Zhi," Lenora said. "By our agreement with President Shao, any colonial delegation is afforded the right to bring their own security with them. Are you saying that President Shao is not going to honor this agreement?"

The Asian man regarded her for a second. "We are at a heightened state of security. This exception was included in the agreement."

"It's because of the current state of Magnus Station that I'm here. Now why don't you pass this along to President Shao. If he refuses to see me, I will have no choice but to pass this along to the rest of the envoy. It will be viewed as a lack of cooperation between our two governments. If it's President Shao's goal to sever ties with us, then so be it. Will you convey that message to him?"

Cheng Zhi stared at her for a long moment and looked away. He seemed to be looking at something on his own personal HUD that she couldn't see.

"Very well, Dr. Bishop. President Shao will see you and allow you to bring one representative from your protection detail. The rest will remain out here."

"Understood," she replied.

Sergeant Bashir spoke quietly to one of the soldiers and then told her he was ready.

Shao Fen's office was a wide-open space that had a large seating area. Broad windows showed a stunning view of Saturn.

Lenora followed Cheng Zhi toward Shao Fen's desk. The leader of Magnus Station was speaking to someone on comlink and Lenora waited for him to finish.

"Dr. Bishop, you were rather insistent on seeing me without delay," Shao Fen said. He looked at Amandara. "Director Kumar, you were scheduled with the colonial delegation at our medical center near the market district."

"Our meeting had to be pushed back, President Shao," Amandara said.

"I see."

"President Shao," Lenora said. "We have evidence of a

bioweapon being used on two remote outposts and an attempt for it to be used on thirty others."

Shao Fen looked at her. "It's a tragedy. I've just learned of this. We will offer aid to the survivors, of course."

"Is it a tragedy? We've traced the origins back to this station, and we've also found a research station. There's a scientist there that I believe you're familiar with. Ivanov Yanovich."

Shao Fen's eyes became cold, and his gaze flicked toward Cheng Zhi. "What is it you think you know?"

"That you attempted to murder thousands of people on remote outposts across the Sol System. That you're responsible for exiling people from Magnus Station for random offenses, but the commonality that I found interesting was the history of the exiles stowed aboard ships bound for Earth—a suicide run with the promise of severe consequences for the victims' close families and friends left on the station. It's fascinating what we've learned by speaking to various residents here on the station, as well as remote outposts in the region."

"And now you presume to judge me."

"Your actions are deplorable, President Shao. The fact that you murdered thousands of people and attempted to murder tens of thousands more puts you on a level of tyrant that I've never seen before. I'm sure a more thorough investigation will reveal more crimes committed by your administration."

"No crimes were committed because they're not people."

Lenora frowned. "What!"

"I haven't committed murder. Only a person can be murdered. The ones that died are Vemus. They're the enemy."

"They're people whose only crime was that their ancestors somehow resisted becoming consumed by the Vemus pathogen."

Shao Fen narrowed his gaze and stepped toward her. "How dare you judge me. Your colony survived because of the sacrifice of my ancestors. We had to pick up the pieces. We had to make the tough choices so we could survive. We had to scrounge out a meager existence to build what we have today. It required sacrifice and came with a price to be paid. And you, so self-righteous. You would protect the Vemus! They're to be eradicated in any form until they're wiped out of existence!" He glared at her with pure vehemence and not an ounce of regret for what he'd done.

"That may have been true at one time. When the Vemus Alpha bludgeoned its way through the entire solar system, they were a hive, but this is different."

Shao Fen slammed his fists on his desk. "It's not different!" He jabbed a finger toward her. "Did the hybrids tell you that they can spread the contagion? They can force people to become like them. Children born from a union with a hybrid have the greatest chance of dying before they reach their third year. A smaller fraction never make it beyond adolescence. You stare at me as if I'm some kind of monster. They're the monster."

"They can't help the way they were born. We should be helping them, not murdering them."

Shao Fen shook his head. "No, the only way this ends is with their eradication. You may have stopped the purge on those remote stations, but Earth will be forever denied them. Earth will only be the dominion of humanity and not some evolutionary freak show."

Lenora studied him for a few seconds. "Then why operate in the shadows? Why hide your actions from the people of this station? Is it because they'd never go along with this? Would they start to doubt your perfect system where everyone has a place until you decide they don't? Then they get exiled."

Shao Fen drew himself up. "This conversation is going nowhere."

"Your reign is over, President Shao. You're finished."

Shao Fen glanced at Cheng Zhi, and the edges of his lips lifted into a sneer.

"I've indulged you long enough, Dr. Bishop."

"I'm not going anywhere. You can't hide this anymore, not when we've just told everyone on the station what you've been doing."

Shao Fen frowned. Alerts began chiming from the holoscreens above his desk and he walked around to see them. "Secure the prisoner."

Cheng Zhi turned toward them.

Sergeant Bashir moved between them, and Lenora saw several station security officers walking in through a small door across the room.

"Wait, Sergeant," Lenora said.

Cheng Zhi walked toward them with a predatory grace.

Lenora had seen her share of dangerous men. She was married to one. Cheng Zhi was a killer and was trying to intimidate them.

"I'm not going anywhere."

Cheng Zhi smiled. "I was hoping you'd resist." His gaze slid to Sergeant Bashir.

"Call off your dogs, Shao Fen," Lenora said.

Sergeant Bashir was moments from attacking.

Shao Fen had multiple holoscreens up and all were playing variations of what was being broadcast across Magnus Station. He glared at her. "This is you! Tell them to stop the broadcast immediately."

Lenora smiled. "Never. There is nothing you can do to stop it."

Cheng Zhi raised his hand to his ear and frowned. "President

Shao, station security is reporting civilian unrest throughout the station. There are unlawful gatherings."

"This is the end for you, President Shao. There is nowhere for you to escape to."

Amandara spoke to someone on her wrist computer. Then she looked at Shao Fen. "A quorum has been called, President Shao."

"Preposterous. Only Nagini Shree can call a quorum, and she won't do it."

"She *has* done it. See the broadcast for yourself," Amandara said.

A new holoscreen opened that showed Nagini Shree broadcasting in real time to the station.

Lenora smirked. "You can't sweep us all under the rug. As I've said before. You're finished. It's time for you to admit it to yourself and surrender."

Shao Fen inhaled explosively and sneered.

"Sir, we have contingencies in place. This is a coup. We have to get you to safety," Cheng Zhi said.

Shao Fen looked at the holoscreen in utter disgust. Veins popped out on his forehead, and he screamed.

47

THE OLD EARTH defense platform loomed in front of the space fighter. As they flew closer, Ethan saw the large rear accelerators for the twin mag cannons. The entire platform was just another lifeless husk. It was cube-shaped and had tilted to the side, slowly losing its position because of the lack of power to its maneuvering thrusters. Smaller flak cannons would have prevented his unauthorized approach to the platform, but they were dead. Not even battery backups were online.

"Those look like scorch marks along the hull," Cynergy said.

He squinted at the HUD. She had sharper eyesight than he did, even with neural implants. Long, diagonal scorch marks ran along two sides of the cube.

"I see them. They look recent."

"Doesn't match up with a focused EMP weapon."

"It had to be more than that. Our ships are protected against EMPs, but they somehow managed to figure out how to beat those defenses."

Cynergy exhaled through her nose. "More like someone from

Magnus Station discovered a weapons system capable of doing it. They don't make anything...none of us do."

It wasn't the first time he'd heard the bitterness in her tone. She had no love for Magnus Station, and at the same time she resented the ongoing struggle to survive. He supposed meeting the colonists was like a slap in the face. They showed up from a home where they'd been able to thrive.

"We can change that," Ethan said.

"Should be safe to approach. We can't dock with it, but there has to be a maintenance hatch somewhere."

Ethan glanced at her. She was focused on her HUD, searching for a hatch to use.

"You have to believe in something," he said.

She sighed. "I believe that Shao Fen wants to kill all hybrids everywhere, and now he has the means to do it."

She wasn't wrong, and yet he knew that there had to be more to her life than what her experience had been. He couldn't figure out what she wanted, but maybe she didn't know either.

She looked at him. Her large, honey-brown eyes seemed to lure him in. "I know what you're trying to do. I appreciate it, but we need to focus on the mission."

Ethan pressed his lips together and nodded. "Right. Focus on the mission. Inspiring the hearts and minds to something greater comes later."

She chuckled and rolled her eyes a little.

He sighed. "I know. I'm right on target."

She smiled, and for a rare moment she let her guard down. "All right. Enough touchy-feely stuff. Let's get this done already."

He flew the ship toward the platform, and they found a maintenance hatch near the middle section. When he deployed the landing skids and magnetized them, the ship locked into place on the hull.

"As long as our ship has power, it should stay right here," Ethan said.

They went on individual life support and he vented the atmosphere inside the ship. After opening the canopy and climbing down to the hull, they magnetized their boots and walked toward the hatch.

The defense platform didn't have any artificial gravity emitters because it hadn't been designed to be crewed over the long term. He saw a maintenance bot near one of the scorch marks. It was dead and stuck in place as if part of it had been melted onto the hull.

They opened the hatch using the manual override and stepped inside.

"Doesn't look like anyone's home," Ethan said, walking to the airlock doors.

He pushed the heavy door open to a long, dark corridor beyond and walked inside.

"How do you know where you're going?" Cynergy asked.

"The design is similar to our defense platforms. There should be a computing core near the middle. That's where we need to go."

The core of the defense platform was where the main power was located, along with the computing core. They were side by side like two halves of a brain, working from the place where they had the most protection.

Ethan glanced into the power core. It was completely dark except for the lights on their helmets. "There's more scorching inside here. It's got to be a multistage weapons system."

Cynergy frowned. "What do you mean?"

"The first stage penetrates the target and then a secondary or even tertiary stage delivers the focused EMP. The weapon has to be powerful enough to penetrate the armored hull and then wreak havoc on power systems."

Cynergy looked at the power core and nodded. "We're not going to be able to restore power, so we can't bring the defense platform back online. We should head back to the ship."

Ethan shook his head and started to follow her back down the corridor. He stopped outside the computing core and frowned.

Cynergy looked over her shoulder. "What are you doing? That freighter could be here any minute."

"Go back to the ship. I just want to check the computer core," he said and walked into the room.

The computing core was only twelve meters across with a single aisle along the middle. He hastened toward the console, hearing Cynergy coming back toward him.

"We should stick together," she said.

Ethan nodded.

He squatted down, opened an access panel underneath the console, and pulled out a data line, connecting it to his suit's computer.

"You can't power the entire computer core from your suit."

"No, I can't, but I might be able to access the communication systems and broadcast a signal. Then I can send targeting priorities from our ship's scanners."

Cynergy frowned and then her eyebrows raised. "It'll be a trusted broadcast because it's coming from the defense platform."

Ethan smiled. "That's right."

He brought up two holoscreens from his suit computer, then remote-accessed the ship's systems and brought up the scanner interface. After a quick check of the scanner filters, he initiated a scan.

He tried to access the platform's communications systems on

the second holoscreen. The defense platforms were networked to each other, but the option to initiate a broadcast weren't available. He stared at the holoscreen for a few seconds, trying to think of a workaround.

"See if you can reset it. That should start a new network session," Cynergy said.

Ethan tried that while the connection was reestablished. The options to do anything else were locked out.

An alert appeared on the scanner interface from the space fighter. There were two ships en route. He swore and shook his head. "This isn't going to work. I can't override communications."

He detached the data line from his suit, and they ran back to the ship. They didn't waste time with closing the defense platform's airlock doors and hatches. They were soon on the hull of their fighter, and Ethan saw a bar of blue light in the distance. The freighters were traveling through the minefield. There must have been some left over from when they'd made the trip.

They climbed into the cockpit and closed the canopy.

"We have to stop those ships," Cynergy said.

"I know."

"We'll fly out there and get them. We've got weapons. We can do this. Engage them from a distance."

Ethan thought about what had happened to the 7th and knew they couldn't make a frontal assault on the freighters. He brought up the scanner interface and increased the signal strength. More powerful scanner pulses came from the ship.

Cynergy saw what he'd done and then checked the tactical plot. "That's working. The nearest platforms are targeting the area."

The defense platform spun around, and Ethan saw a debris trail from a mag cannon ordnance hitting the defense platform.

He stopped the scanner. He needed the other platforms to detect the incoming freighters.

The defense platform continued to spin, and they watched as Maser-mines and mag cannons from the other defense platforms attempted to destroy the two inbound freighters.

Ethan opened a comlink to the others. "Targets incoming. I'll broadcast scan data as it becomes available."

"We're making our way to you," Anton said.

"Negative. Maintain low orbit. I'll see if we can slow them down, and then you can finish them off."

"That's not going to happen," Anton said, and the others repeated the same.

Ethan checked the tactical plot. Anton and the rest of his teammates were still too far away. They'd close the distance eventually, but he couldn't wait for them to arrive.

The defense platform spun faster as they took fire from other defense platforms. Ethan was pressed to the side. Mag canon fire burst through the platform right in front of them in a cascade of eruptions. Ethan's eyes widened as he slammed the controls to disengage the landing skids. They demagnetized and the centrifugal forces shoved them from the hull. He engaged the ship's engines. Proximity alarms blared as they flew through metallic debris. A barrage of damage alerts came to prominence on the holoscreen. Ethan engaged the thrusters and flew back toward the defense platform to seek cover.

"We've been hit! Comms are offline. We're cut off from the others!" Cynergy said.

Ethan scanned the alerts and then a dark shadow momentarily blotted out the sun as a freighter flew by. It was heavily damaged from the Maser-mines, but it was still flying. Ethan engaged the engines and brought the ship around, and Cynergy fired the ship's weapons.

Mag cannons fired into the freighter's engines.

"Target the front of the stern," Ethan said.

He flew up twelve degrees and then leveled off, giving Cynergy a clear shot. Mag cannon fire pierced the freighter's hull, triggering smaller explosions from inside the ship.

"Nice shooting!"

A turret swung toward them, and Ethan tried to keep ahead of it. The nose of the space fighter darkened as if suddenly under intense heat. He swung the ship to the side, and the freighter's weapons clipped the edge of their ship as the freighter rolled away in the throes of death. The panels to Ethan's left burst into flame, and an arc of electricity spiked out from them. He jerked back and felt something hot burn through the side of his flight suit. Ethan howled in pain and squeezed his eyes shut.

He heard Cynergy shouting at him, but he couldn't understand her. His breath came in gasps as he tried to open his eyes. His body contorted to the side, and his suit computer spoke.

"Burn trauma detected. Releasing pain medication. Emergency medical nanites released."

He opened his eyes, and his vision swam. Cynergy spoke to him, but it sounded like she was so far away.

"Stay awake, Ethan!"

Ethan tried to keep his eyes open but couldn't. He knew he should, but everything in his mind slowed down as pain medication flooded his system.

48

THE CDF FLEET transitioned back into n-space near Earth.

"Ops, start scanning the area," Connor said. He glanced at the fleet status on the main holoscreen. The *Odyssey* returned to green and was followed by their remaining destroyers.

"Sir, scanners detecting a field of Maser-mines. Defense platforms are engaging two targets. Seems to be isolated. Hostile scans detected," Lieutenant Selina Wilson said.

"Tactical, are the attack drones ready?" Connor asked.

"Synchronizing targeting across the fleet. Stand by," Lieutenant Tucker said.

Connor gritted his teeth and squeezed the armrests of the command chair.

"General, I have a comlink request from Lieutenant Anton Stone of the 7th A-Wing. Voice only," Specialist Marten said.

"Send it here." The comlink became active. "Lieutenant Stone, this is General Gates."

"General, there are two freighters trying to make it past the defense platforms. Ethan took out one of them, but we've lost contact with his ship."

"Understood," Connor said, his voice like stone. "And the second freighter?"

"Unknown. The defense platforms might have destroyed it, sir, but we haven't been able to confirm. We're en route to the freighter's last known location."

"Stand by, Lieutenant," Connor said and muted the comlink. "Tactical?"

"We're ready, sir. All ships report in. Attack drones are ready to deploy across the fleet."

"Fire!"

Hatches opened across the fleet and attack drones burst forth, vaulting into active combat state. Each drone burned with the heat of a main sequence star, and they sped like a wave of destruction toward the field of Maser-mines.

Connor opened the comlink to Lieutenant Stone. "Clear the area. Attack drones are en route."

"But sir, Ethan is still out there!"

Connor swallowed hard and steadied his voice. "I know, Lieutenant. I know he is, but we can't let that bioweapon reach the Earth. You and the others need to fall back. You've done enough, son. It's time to fall back."

A few moments of silence passed.

"Yes, sir."

The comlink went dark, and Connor inhaled deeply.

"Tactical. Nothing gets through. We don't know how many ships came from Magnus Station."

"Yes, General."

Connor stood up and walked toward the tactical plot. His fists were at his sides, and he stood very still. He glared at the main holoscreen and whispered a prayer for his son to survive.

Martinez came to stand next to Connor. He didn't say anything but just stood there in a show of silent support for Connor as thousands of attack drones raced through the old defenses that had closed Earth off to the survivors for far too long. He wanted to scream, but he clenched his teeth instead. He watched, waited, and hoped for a miracle.

49

"ETHAN, WAKE UP!" Cynergy's voice jolted through his brain. He blinked a few times and felt something rub his arm. "I need you to wake up. Come on!"

Ethan opened his eyes and saw her staring at him. Her helmet was off, and a lock of dark blonde hair hung near her cheek.

He smelled the sulfurous odor of charcoal and burnt meat. She'd removed his helmet. He turned his head and glanced at the left side of his body, gasping. His flight suit had burned away on his arm, leg, and part of his torso. It looked like pieces of his flight suit had become part of his skin in a blistering, bloody mess. He tried to lift his arm.

Cynergy reached across and pushed his shoulder back. "No, don't move your arm."

"What happened?"

"You're hurt is what happened."

"No, the freighter."

"It was destroyed."

"What about the second one?"

She blinked for a second. "I don't know. The ship systems are going through a repair cycle because of the damage. There's a list of isolated systems. Comms are down, but we've got engines and weapons capability."

Ethan looked at the holoscreen in front of him and saw the tactical display. Cynergy pulled away from him and craned her neck to look behind them.

"What's back there?"

She frowned as she peered out the canopy. "I'm not sure. It's like a wave of bright lights are heading towards us."

Ethan frowned thoughtfully, and then his eyes widened. He reached out with his right hand and swung the ship around. "Those are attack drones."

"Drones? But they're bright like the sun."

Ethan nodded. "They're hot like it, too. The CDF is here."

"There are thousands of them. Look at how fast they're moving," she said with awe in her voice.

The drones were flying through the Maser-mines and hitting them so fast that they didn't have a chance to arm themselves. They could burn through the battle-steel armor of any warship, and the only thing that could stop them was a combination of heavy weapons and a massive artificial gravity shield.

"We have to get out of here."

A chime came from the ship's systems as scanners came back online. Ethan peered at the tactical plot and his mouth hung open.

"That's a freighter. That's the second freighter. It's past the defense platforms!" Cynergy said.

"And we can't warn the others. You're going to have to fly the ship. Passing control over to you. Give me the weapons systems." His voice went higher as a spasm of pain coursed through him.

"Ethan…"

"Don't argue with me, damn it! Take flight controls and give me the weapons!"

The holo-interface in front of him switched to weapons controls.

"I have flight controls."

"Now follow that ship. Line us up."

"All right."

The ship lurched forward, and he winced as he was jostled to the side for a second. He gritted his teeth and kept his hand on the weapons control interface.

Scanners showed turrets swinging toward them. Cynergy banked to the side.

Ethan engaged the mag cannons at full auto.

"Don't stop! Keep going! We have to stop that ship!"

Cynergy pushed the throttle all the way up, and the space fighter flew toward the damaged freighter.

Ethan growled as he fired the ship's weapons. Turrets blew apart on the freighter, but not before their fighter took fire from the focused EMP weapon.

The ship's power went offline. Cynergy tried to get it back, but it was hopeless.

"Hold onto something!" Ethan shouted as the ship slammed into the freighter.

The fighter tumbled toward the Earth in slow rotations that gave them partial gravity, which made his wounds hurt like hell. He searched for the freighter.

"Do you see it? Did we get it?"

A few moments of silence passed while they searched.

"I see it. You got it! It's going to come apart when it hits the atmosphere."

Ethan blew out a breath and groaned.

"Aren't the medical nanites helping?"

Ethan looked at the alerts from his biochip on his internal HUD and shook his head. "They're not going to be enough. I need an actual doctor." He winced. "Too bad we can't call for help."

Cynergy exhaled explosively. "No." She yanked the cover off the panel in front of her and jerked her hands back. The overload had burned out the console. If they still had power, there would have been a fire.

"You need to go onto your own life support. I'm not sure how long we can last without emergency power. I guess there are limits to that weapon, or maybe we didn't get the full blast."

She shook her head and glared at him. "What's the matter with you! The ship doesn't have power. We can't call for help. And we're tumbling toward Earth!"

"At least you didn't get burned."

Her mouth opened and she simply stared at him. "How can you make a joke at a time like this?"

"It helps distract me from the pain." He swallowed hard. "Because goddamn it… it hurts."

Cynergy's expression softened, and her eyebrows drew together in concern.

"Don't look at me like that. You have to be nice to me. I'm hurt."

She closed her eyes and shook her head. He didn't like what he saw in her eyes. It was the look someone gave to a person who was about to die.

"Hey, don't be like that."

She glared at him, and if it had been any other time, he thought she might have hit him.

"Can I call you Cyn? The first time we met I tried, and I

thought you were going to shoot me, but it should be okay now, right? We're friends, right?"

Her shoulders slumped and she sighed heavily. Then she smiled a little. "You can call me Cyn."

"Oh good. You know, because Cynergy is kind of a mouthful. I like Cyn. It's straight to the point and because it sounds a little wicked and…" His voice trailed off as another wave of pain overwhelmed him.

"You've given this so much consideration."

"Thanks for noticing. I did, but only just now. I don't know why."

She swallowed hard and looked at him. "Why do you do it?"

Ethan blinked. "Do what?"

"You try so hard. When you first learned about the exiles, you'd just gotten in your ship before you started planning a rescue. Then, when you learned about the bioweapon, you focused on doing everything you possibly could to stop it. Why do you want to help so much?"

Ethan turned toward her as best he could. "You really have to ask me? Don't people help each other here? It's what we do. It's what I was taught to do."

"By whom?"

Ethan swallowed hard. "My parents. My father risked his life many times to save the colony. How could I do any less?"

Cyn stared at him for a long moment.

"The colony had to find a way to coexist with the Ovarrow— not just the ones we got along with but others as well. Why can't people like us do the same? The weapon was created for another enemy, not you. It wasn't meant for hybrids."

A warning flashed on his wrist computer, and Cyn's eyes darted toward it, widening. "Terminal threat. You're going to die!"

"Help me put on my helmet. Then you're going to have to jettison the escape pod, otherwise, we won't survive re-entry."

He felt cold and numb in different places.

She looked at him for a few moments. "What if there was another way?"

"What? What do you mean?" he asked and glanced out the window. "You have to hurry. We must have picked up speed because we don't have much time."

She looked away for a second as if she were working up the courage to speak.

He reached toward her. "No matter what happens to me, it was worth it. The future *is* worth fighting for."

Tears welled up in her eyes as she unbuckled her straps and crawled over to him.

Ethan's eyes widened as her face came close to his. Then he smiled a little. "A kiss goodbye?"

He winced again and his body shook. He felt her hands reach behind his head and massage his neck. He opened his eyes. Her skin darkened and her eyes became a luminous green. The dark purple lines seemed to pulse along her skin.

She leaned toward him. "No, it's a kiss to save you."

She pressed her lips to his and he felt a warmth pierce his neck as something squeezed inside him. He didn't know what it was. He couldn't open his eyes but could still feel Cynergy on top of him. Pain seemed to be pushed to the back of his mind, and a chilling tingling sensation swept across his skin.

"Don't fight it. Embrace it, Ethan."

He couldn't move or speak. He felt like he was both present and detached at the same time.

He heard a klaxon alarm. Cynergy must have jettisoned the escape pod. Somewhere among his scattered thoughts, he could feel Cynergy near him, as if she were holding him, embracing him. It was like being enfolded by the softest blanket, and he couldn't escape the feeling of being surrounded by sunlight. It was warm and peaceful, lulling him into oblivion. He decided to let go and simply breathe as his thoughts became nothing more than vague urges that he didn't have the strength to think about.

50

Something roused Ethan from a deep, dreamless sleep. He opened his eyes and saw Lauren smiling at him.

"There you are, little brother."

Ethan blinked. A breeze blew in through an open window and the air smelled fresh, carrying scents of distant wildflowers.

"Where am I?"

Lauren glanced at a nearby holoscreen and then looked at him. "Earth. We recovered the escape pod four days ago. You've been asleep since then."

"Asleep?"

"More than that. It was like a brief hibernation. Not quite a coma, because your vitals were fine, but we couldn't wake you up either."

"The ship? Did we stop it?"

Lauren nodded and sat on a nearby stool. "What do you remember?"

He cleared his throat and sat up. "Our ship was disabled.

Cynergy tried to repair it, but everything was completely fried. Is she okay? Did she make it?"

"She's fine. She hasn't gone far away from you since we arrived."

Ethan took a deep breath and exhaled long and steady. His mind cleared and he became more aware. "We were falling to Earth. I told her she needed to jettison the escape pod. Then she…" he blinked a few times. "She did something." He looked down at his body and frowned. "My burns. They're gone."

"Regeneration without the recurrent use of medical nanites and new skin."

He peered at his forearms and saw faint dark lines beneath his skin. They became more prominent as he stared at them. He looked at his sister, eyes wide. "What's happening?"

"Take it easy," she said, moving closer to him. "Cynergy changed you."

Ethan's brow wrinkled. "Changed me…Do you mean she infected me? Am I a Vemus?"

Lauren shook her head. "You're a hybrid now, Ethan. It's different than what Dad fought back home. There were other strains of the contagion. People adapted. We're still learning all we can about it."

He sat up and examined his arms, then pulled off the sheet to look at his bare legs. "What's going to happen to me?"

"Everything is stable. You've always been in excellent shape, but even your baseline vitals have improved. You'll need to be monitored—"

"I want *you* to monitor me."

The edges of her lips lifted, and her eyebrows drew together. "Of course, I'll monitor you."

"I don't want to become some kind of lab animal."

She looked him in the eye. "That's not going to happen."

"Are you sure? Remember what happened to Dad after the Vemus Wars? They kept him in isolation."

"This is different, Ethan. You're different. And by all available data, your body hasn't rejected the changes at all. Quite the contrary, actually. I've seen others who weren't so lucky."

"Others? Who else has this happened to?"

"It's a long story. There are hybrids born who really struggle with it. I'll tell you more about it later."

Ethan looked away for a few seconds. "They're going to kick me out of the CDF."

She shook her head. "You have to calm down. And no, they're not going to kick you out. You're still you. Do you feel different?"

Ethan simply stared at her. "Of course, I feel different."

She leaned toward him. "How so?"

"I... I don't know. It's different. Look at my arms. It's like there's something underneath my skin."

"It's on your face and neck, too. It's actually on your back. They're markings of some sort."

Ethan looked at the ceiling and sighed. "Great, everyone is going to stare at me like I'm some kind of..."

"You almost died, Ethan. I saw your injuries. I accessed your biochip. It's a miracle you survived. You should be thankful."

"I am, but things are going to change."

Lauren glanced out the window and Ethan heard the dopplered wail of a shuttle flying overhead. "Everything is going to change. It has to. That's life. You just need some time to get used it."

"Has Dad seen me? Where's Mom?"

"Dad saw you when we first arrived. Mom is on her way here from Magnus Station. A lot has happened since the attack."

Another shuttle flew overhead.

Ethan glanced at the window and frowned. "What's going on?"

She smiled. "People are being brought back to Earth."

Ethan stood and walked to the window. He almost expected that his legs were going to wobble, but they didn't. He felt strong, as if he'd gotten a good night's sleep.

"How do you feel?"

"I feel fine. A little thirsty, but no murderous thoughts, so that's good I guess, all things considering."

Lauren grinned. "There's water over there. I'll need to run more tests, but they can wait."

Ethan poured himself a glass of water and drank it. "What kind of tests?"

"The kind that measure your abilities, both cognitive and physical. We'll compare them to what's on file for the CDF. I'll also need to monitor your biochip readings. Unless you'd like someone else to?"

Ethan shook his head. "I trust you, but I guess this isn't something I can keep between us, is it?"

"No. There will be other doctors involved. Isaac will be involved, too."

Ethan nodded. "Is he here?"

"He's not far. He'll meet up with you later."

"Can I get some clothes? I'd rather not walk around in this patient gown."

"I don't know, I think it really suits you. Are you sure?" She winked at him, and he threw her a fake scowl. "Fine, there are some clothes over there."

Ethan started to get dressed. "So can I leave, or do I need someone to keep an eye on me?"

Lauren had turned around while he dressed. She shook her

head. "Yes, you can leave, and no, you don't need an escort. Do you want me to stick around?"

Ethan finished dressing himself and walked over to her. "No, I'll be all right. I should probably check in with the CDF."

"They're fine. Anton and the rest of them have been by to see you. They rescued the others, too. They're still on the *Douglass*, but your team stayed here. You all earned some off-duty time."

They walked outside and Lauren left him. When he activated his wrist computer, he was inundated with messages. He sent a quick message to Anton and the others. Then he put it on "do not disturb" and ignored it.

"He lives!" Clip called out, walking toward him with a wide grin.

Ethan waved.

"How does it feel? You're a hero."

"It wasn't just me," he said, realizing that was exactly how his father always responded to that kind of comment.

Clip put a companionable hand on his shoulder and squeezed. "You saved a lot of people. Not just all the people on the planet, but the outposts as well. Earth is open to them now."

Ethan's mouth became dry.

"Thirsty?"

"I could use a drink."

Clip chuckled. "So could I, but you should stick with water for now," he said, handing him a large bottle of water.

Ethan drank it all. "I don't know why I'm so thirsty."

"It's part of the change," Clip said.

Ethan glanced around, wondering if anyone was listening to them.

"It's nothing to be ashamed of. I wanted to talk to you about it. Hold onto that bottle. You'll probably need to refill it before long."

Ethan held the water bottle at his side.

Clip became serious. "I wanted to talk to you. Needed to, actually. I bet you have a lot of questions."

"Cynergy did what she thought she had to in order to save my life."

Clip looked at him for a second. "She did a lot more than that, but we'll get to that in a minute."

"I didn't know you could make me into a hybrid."

"Not all of us can. But the change occurs for the rest of us as we get older."

Ethan's eyebrows raised.

"I'm serious. It's the truth. I don't know why. Mostly we go around without flaunting what we are. People look at us differently. You'll find out."

"Even on the outposts?"

Clip shrugged. "Sometimes. It just depends. The fact of the matter is that you're alive because of the change. It increases your adaptability. As it matures, you'll learn ways to utilize it."

"To do what?"

"Regeneration, for one. Quick healing. Longer endurance without the use of implants or stims. Resistance to infections. Things like that."

"Doesn't sound so bad."

"There are some drawbacks, but that depends on how your body reacts to it."

"My sister said I wasn't rejecting it at all."

"That's a good sign. Sometimes it can be debilitating. It's like your body doesn't know what to do with itself."

"I feel like something is crawling under my skin, but it comes and goes."

"That'll pass."

Ethan looked around, and Clip smiled.

"You're looking for Cyn?"

"Yeah, I need to talk to her. Is she all right? I mean, was she hurt?"

Clip arched a gray eyebrow. "Don't you know?"

Ethan frowned. "How should I know?"

Clip stared at him.

"Is that what this feeling is? It's like, I don't know, something extra."

Clip nodded a little. "You're joined to her. The connection between the two of you is intimate."

"Intimate. What do you mean?"

"It's just that you can sense each other's moods. It's like when people live together for a long time and get to know all the nuances and mannerisms of their partner. It's similar to that. Another way to explain it is that it's as if you were twins. Sometimes there's a connection there."

"How does it work?"

"I was born this way and I can't change anyone, so I'm not exactly sure. When we show ourselves, our senses increase. Others can sense it as well."

"I don't know what to think about all this. I don't know whether to be concerned, angry, excited, or all the above."

Clip pursed his lips. "Fair enough. Don't avoid Cyn. You should go to her. What she did wasn't easy. She did it at great risk to herself."

"What do you mean?"

"She could have died."

Another large transport shuttle flew overhead.

"Refill that water bottle, and I'll check back on you later, but right now I have to go meet that shuttle," Clip said.

Ethan walked back into the building he'd woken in and filled the bottle with water. Outside, temporary hab units were being set up, leaving him to wonder just how big this camp was going to become.

He'd walked a short distance when he felt someone watching him. He looked around and saw Cynergy walking toward him. She wore dark clothing, and her golden blonde hair hung past her shoulders. Their eyes locked, and Ethan felt his chest tighten. He smiled and hastened toward her. She smiled back at him.

"I hear you saved my life."

Her head tilted to the side. "What can I say? I got used to having you around."

Ethan arched an eyebrow. "You kissed me."

"It was the only way I could think of to get you to calm down."

Ethan chuckled and shook his head. Then he became serious. "Thank you."

She gazed at him for a moment. "You're welcome."

"So, what happens now?"

She pursed her lips and raised her eyebrows. "What do you mean?"

"I don't know about you, but this is all new to me. Have you done this to anyone else?"

She laughed. "You want to know if I have a harem of men I've changed into hybrids?"

Ethan's mouth hung open for a second and then he grinned. "You're backing me into a corner here, because yeah, I am wondering something like that. I wouldn't put it in terms of a harem, though. So, have you done this before?"

She shook her head. "No. I've never done it before."

"But you must have known that you could?"

She nodded slowly, looking oddly vulnerable.

Ethan stepped closer to her. He felt a tingling sensation in his hand and noticed that she glanced down at hers as well.

"Do you feel that?" he asked.

She looked up at him. "Yes."

He held out his hand and she placed hers into his. Warmth spread up his forearm and he sucked in a breath. Then, he pulled her closer and kissed her. Their lips pressed together in gentle surges, and he felt his whole body respond. They held each other for a few moments and then pulled apart. They stared at each other, and Ethan wished they could find someplace to be alone.

"Please tell me you felt that too," he said.

She smiled and nodded. "I did."

"I'm glad it's not just me."

She snorted. "I was there, too."

He chuckled. "This isn't…is this real? I mean, is this some kind of byproduct of getting turned into a hybrid?"

"I don't know. It could be because there was some attraction before."

"I guess we'll just have to see where it goes then."

She smiled. "I guess we will."

51

Connor looked at Lenora. "No, I just got the message from Lauren that he's awake."

Lenora nodded. "We'll be there soon."

"Do you want me to wait for you?"

She shook her head. "Don't be silly. Go see him." She paused for a moment and her eyes drew down in concern. "What if he's different? What's to stop him from...What if he's not the same? What if something's wrong with him?"

"Lauren said he was fine. She's been watching over him ever since we retrieved the escape pod."

She nodded. "I know. I'm just worried."

Ethan had almost died. They went from believing he'd died to learning that he'd survived, only to be confronted with the fact that he'd almost died again. Connor was ready to get off this emotional rollercoaster for good.

"I am, too. Brings back some memories, doesn't it?"

Lenora looked at him for a second and nodded. "Yeah, it does."

"I'm going to see him now. You can catch up when you arrive." He paused for a second. "I trust Lauren's judgement."

"Me, too."

"Then everything is going to be all right."

She waved. "Go on. I'll see you when I get there."

The comlink went dark and Connor left the command center walking outside to look up at the clear blue skies. He kept expecting to see New Earth's rings in the sky, and it was throwing him off that they weren't there. He missed home and longed for a meal at the Salty Soldier.

He walked through the camp and found Ethan in the mess tent, finishing off a meal. A pretty young blonde woman sat next to him. They both looked up at the same time.

Ethan stood up and walked toward him. Connor pulled his son in for a hug.

"It's good to see you," he said. "Damn, boy." His throat became tight. Right then, he wasn't a general in the CDF. He was a father reuniting with a son he'd almost lost.

Ethan stepped back and smiled. Connor drank in the sight of him, and he laughed.

"This is Cynergy," Ethan said and gestured toward the young woman.

She walked over to them.

Connor hugged her, too. Normally, he wasn't one to show public displays of affection, but this wasn't one of those days.

He let her go. "I'm so glad to meet you."

She smiled. "Thank you, General Gates."

Connor shook his head. "Not for you. You can call me Connor. Always."

"What's this about a medal ceremony?" Ethan asked.

Connor looked at his son for a second. "You, Cynergy, and

the rest of the 7th stopped a bioweapon from reaching Earth. This is how we honor extraordinary deeds."

Ethan looked as if he was about to say something more but was quiet instead.

"I know that's not why you did it, but you earned it. Both of you have."

Ethan shared a smile with Cynergy. "Maybe I'll catch up to you one day."

Connor chuckled. "God, I hope not. I hope there aren't reasons that require such desperate acts of heroism. We're too often left to pick up the pieces."

Medal ceremonies were good for morale, but Connor and many other veterans knew they were another way to show that sometimes people just got lucky that their tickets hadn't gotten punched. When he thought back on his own life, he knew he didn't want to tempt fate again because there were no guarantees that he'd keep beating the odds.

"You've got that look again," Ethan said.

Connor smiled a little. "I know. We thought you were dead."

Ethan looked away for a second. "I'm sorry. We…"

"It's all right. I know how events can happen so fast that we just get swept along with them."

"Did you find anything about that weapons system they were using?"

Connor nodded. "It was a prototype system developed during the Vemus War. They'd reversed-engineered it before our probes arrived."

Sean called out to them and laughed. "Well, look who decided to kick his own ass all night long. Lieutenant Gates, you're out of uniform."

Ethan laughed. "I'm off duty, sir."

Sean waved the comment away and looked at Ethan with a

bemused expression. "If I didn't know any better, I'd say you were trying to catch up to us."

"I think I've had enough for a good long while," Ethan replied.

Sean nodded and looked at Connor. "I need to borrow you for a few minutes."

Connor nodded. "I'll be right back. Don't go anywhere."

"I won't," Ethan replied.

Connor walked with Sean a short distance away near the edge of camp.

"Is that her?" Sean asked.

Connor nodded.

"She's pretty. Those scars on his skin, is that from becoming a hybrid?"

"I don't think they're scars, but yeah."

Sean sighed. "I saw Lauren's report."

"Me too. She wants to continue monitoring him. In fact, she's got a bunch of tests scheduled for Ethan to participate in."

"I bet he's going to love that."

"He'll do it."

"I know he will. I'm surprised he hasn't asked about his status in the 7th."

"Maybe he's afraid of what the answer will be."

Sean chuckled softly. "Neither one of your kids are so afraid of something that they'll run away from it."

Connor smiled and regarded Sean for a few seconds. "This could've gone badly."

"But it didn't. That's a victory in my book."

Isaac Diaz walked toward them. He came from around one of the hab units and walked over like he'd known exactly where they were.

Sean leaned toward Connor. "Now that's one we need to keep an eye on."

Connor nodded. Isaac was an agent for the Colonial Intelligence Bureau. He must have been on quite a few missions to be assigned to the expedition. The director of the CIB would never have sent him otherwise.

Isaac smiled. "Now, don't get quiet on my account."

"That depends. Is this conversation being recorded?" Connor asked.

Isaac shook his head. "Of course not. I thought you'd like to hear the news from Magnus Station."

Shao Fen and quite a few senior officials were to stand trial. General outrage had grown among the people of Magnus Station when they'd learned what their leadership had been doing. There were a number of divisions in the station, and the latest news seemed to radicalize all of them. But the promise of returning to Earth had prevented widespread destruction.

"And you heard about it before we did?" Sean asked.

Isaac shrugged.

Sean looked at Connor. "If you want, I can stun him. Knock him out for a while."

Connor arched an eyebrow toward Isaac. "It's tempting. He's gotten pretty bold lately, but," Connor said with a sigh, "I promised Lauren I wouldn't give him too hard a time."

Sean glanced at Isaac. "Lauren?" he said in a tone that implied quite a bit.

Isaac didn't quite wince, but it was close enough. Then he shrugged, as if to say that things were as they were, and Connor was going to have to accept it.

"What have you got, Isaac?"

Connor did like Juan's son.

"Guilty verdicts for Shao Fen and a bunch of the others. They also sentenced them to exile."

Connor considered that for a few moments.

"There's more. There'll be a ship on a one-way trip to Sirius. It'll have enough supplies for them to live out the duration of their lives. They should get there in a few hundred years or so. No comms, just a basic nav setup and a means to feed themselves. I'd hate to be on that ship."

Shao Fen had been responsible for thousands of deaths. If it were up to Connor, he'd send him on a one-way trip to the sun.

"Too bad Magnus Station couldn't make an exception to their 'no death penalty' law," Sean said.

"Either way, Shao Fen is gone, and no one is going to be coming to their rescue," Connor replied.

"There isn't much we can do about it, though," Isaac said.

Sean shrugged. "I don't know. Accidents happen all the time on older space crafts."

Isaac looked at Connor for a moment and then back at Sean. "Sometimes you're a little bit scary, General Quinn."

Connor grinned. "All right. We need to broker peace for everyone here. Earth needs to be a safe haven for all. The people on Magnus Station and remote outposts need to have the option to return to Earth and rebuild, not to continue with old hostilities."

"How do you propose we do that?" Isaac asked.

Sean watched him with raised eyebrows. "Give them time to rebuild and forge a future for themselves, along with a promise that they'll have the option to leave and explore other star systems one day. The future is impossible to predict, but it can be built one step at a time."

Isaac nodded. "I hope they can live up to it. A lot of people died because of Shao Fen."

Connor nodded. "He's as good as dead. However, not worrying about whether your old outpost or space station is going to hold up goes a long way toward making people more civilized."

Sean cleared his throat. "There are still stations with Vemus exoskeletal material on them. Presumably, there are Vemus there. I spoke with several people, including a hybrid named Clip. They're aware of these locations and offered to work with us to find them."

"Good, they'll need to be sanitized."

Isaac frowned. "Sanitized?"

"Destroyed," Sean said.

"Oh, I see." He paused for a second. "What about the aliens who brought our probes here?"

"As far as we've been able to tell, they didn't leave a way for us to contact them," Connor replied.

"So that's it then? They deposited the probes throughout the star system. It's like they wanted us to know the layout or something," Isaac said.

"Maybe they just wanted to lend us a hand. They could be observing us even now, and we don't know it. Maybe one day we'll find out what they want."

Isaac blinked several times and then sighed.

Sean shrugged. "It's a big galaxy out there." He looked at Connor. "Does this mean retirement is off the table?"

Connor smiled. "Adapt or die, right? I think there's something for me to do other than ensuring the CDF is ready to protect the colony."

Sean nodded slowly and grinned. "Well, would you look at that."

Isaac frowned. "What? What does that mean?"

Sean smiled with half his mouth. "It means that Connor is going to be getting a new job."

Connor grinned. "Like you said. There's a big galaxy out there, and I certainly can't wait to see more of it."

AUTHOR NOTE

Thank you so much for reading. *Expedition Earth* is the 14th book in the First Colony series. This series has been home to my imagination for a long time. Helping me to stay motivated to write these stories has been the enthusiasm of the readers who've reached out to me and the people who took the time to review my books. I sincerely hope you enjoyed this latest book in the First Colony series. Almost inevitably, I get the question about whether this will be the last book in the First Colony series. No, it won't. I think there are a lot more stories to tell in this series and more characters to explore.

Writing *Expedition Earth* allowed me to explore and answer one of the most enduring questions since the series began. What happened to Earth? Did anyone survive? How did they survive? Who are they, and what are their struggles?

One of the things I've enjoyed about writing this series is that it builds on itself. The colonists develop new tools and methods to meet the challenges they face. One of the questions I often get asked is whether I'd planned out the entire series, which at this time is 14 books long. No, I didn't. This series was developed in chunks, based on ideas that I've had and reader reactions to the story. It's been a great ride, and I look forward to writing more in this series.

I hope you enjoyed getting to know Ethan and Lauren, and the continued appearance of the enduring characters in the series. I couldn't wait for Connor's children to grow up and take their place among the cast of characters, making their contribution to this series.

I continue to write stories in the First Colony series because I enjoy it and because people keep reading the books. The best way for me to gauge whether people want more First Colony stories is by people reading the books and perhaps leaving a review, or recommending it to a friend or a group. Word of mouth is crucial. I take a lot of pride in my work because I think the quality of the story matters, as well as your experience reading it.

Thanks again for reading my books. Please consider leaving a review for *Expedition Earth*.

If you're looking for another series to read consider reading the Federation Chronicles. Learn more by visiting:

https://kenlozito.com/federation-chronicles/

I do have a Facebook group called **Ken Lozito's SF readers**. If you're on Facebook and you'd like to stop by, please search for it on Facebook.

Not everyone is on Facebook. I get it, but I also have a blog if you'd like to stop by there. My blog is more of a monthly check-in as to the status of what I'm working on. Please stop by and say hello, I'd love to hear from you.

Visit www.kenlozito.com

THANK YOU FOR READING EXPEDITION EARTH - FIRST COLONY - BOOK 14.

If you loved this book, please consider leaving a review. Comments and reviews allow readers to discover authors, so if you want others to enjoy *Expedition Earth* as you have, please leave a short note.

If you're looking for something else to read, consider checking out the following series by visiting:

https://kenlozito.com/federation-chronicles/

https://kenlozito.com/ascension-series/

If you would like to be notified when my next book is released please visit kenlozito.com and sign up to get a heads up.

I've created a special **Facebook Group** specifically for readers to come together and share their interests, especially regarding my books. Check it out and join the discussion by searching for **Ken Lozito's SF Worlds**.

To join the group, login to Facebook and search for **Ken Lozito's SF Worlds**. Answer two easy questions and you're in.

ABOUT THE AUTHOR

I've written multiple science fiction and fantasy series. Books have been my way to escape everyday life since I was a teenager to my current ripe old(?) age. What started out as a love of stories has turned into a full-blown passion for writing them.

Overall, I'm just a fan of really good stories regardless of genre. I love the heroic tales, redemption stories, the last stand, or just a good old fashion adventure. Those are the types of stories I like to write. Stories with rich and interesting characters and then I put them into dangerous and sometimes morally gray situations.

My ultimate intent for writing stories is to provide fun escapism for readers. I write stories that I would like to read, and I hope you enjoy them as well.

If you have questions or comments about any of my works I would love to hear from you, even if it's only to drop by to say hello at KenLozito.com

Thanks again for reading *First Colony - Expedition Earth*

Don't be shy about emails, I love getting them, and try to respond to everyone.

f

ALSO BY KEN LOZITO

First Colony Series

GENESIS

NEMESIS

LEGACY

SANCTUARY

DISCOVERY

EMERGENCE

VIGILANCE

FRACTURE

HARBINGER

INSURGENT

INVASION

IMPULSE

INFINITY

EXPEDITION EARTH

Federation Chronicles

ACHERON INHERITANCE

ACHERON SALVATION

ACHERON REDEMPTION

ACHERON RISING (PREQUEL NOVELLA)

Ascension Series

STAR SHROUD

STAR DIVIDE

STAR ALLIANCE

INFINITY'S EDGE

RISING FORCE

ASCENSION

SAFANARION ORDER SERIES

ROAD TO SHANDARA

ECHOES OF A GLORIED PAST

AMIDST THE RISING SHADOWS

HEIR OF SHANDARA

BROKEN CROWN SERIES

Haven of Shadows

IF YOU WOULD LIKE TO BE NOTIFIED WHEN MY NEXT BOOK IS RELEASED VISIT KENLOZITO.COM

Made in the USA
Coppell, TX
01 September 2022

82398942R00288